MW00412865

6

THE PAPER *Swan*

LEYLAH ATTAR

PITCH73 PUBLISHING

SOUTH ST. PAUL PUBLIC LIBRARY
106 3rd Ave No.
South St. Paul, MN 55075

This book is a work of fiction. References to real people, events, establishments, organizations, or locales are intended only to provide a sense of authenticity, and are used fictitiously. All other characters, incidents and dialogue, are drawn from the author's imagination and are not to be construed as real. The author acknowledges the trademarked status and trademark owners of various products and locales referenced in this work of fiction, which have been used without permission. The use of these trademarks is not authorized, associated with, or sponsored by the trademark owners.

Copyright ©2015 by Leylah Attar
Editing by Lea Burn
Proofreading by Shh Mom's Reading
Cover Design © Hang Le
Formatting and Interior Design by Perfectly Publishable
'This Too Shall Pass' Illustration © Tasha B.

10 9 8 7 6 5 4 3 2 1
ISBN: 978–0-9937527–7-3

Printed in the United States of America

All Rights Reserved. No part of this book may be used or reproduced in any manner whatsoever without written permission from the publisher, except in the case of brief quotations embodied in critical articles and reviews.

PITCH73 PUBLISHING

This Too Shall Pass

For my father

SKYE

IT WAS A GOOD DAY for Louboutins. I hadn't planned on wearing statement heels on the runway to death, but if this was it, if I was going to be killed by some random psycho with a thirst for blood, what better way to go down than with red-soled 'fuck yous' to my murderer?

Because fuck you, *asshole, for turning me into the victim of a senseless crime.*

Fuck you *for the indignity of not letting me see your face before you blow my brains out.*

Fuck you *for the cable ties that are so tight, they're cutting deep, red slashes across my wrists.*

But most of all, fuck you *because no one wants to die a day short of their twenty-fourth birthday—blond hair shiny from a fresh cut, nails gelled to perfection—on the way back from a date with a man who just might be* "the one".

My life was set to be a series of standing ovations: graduation, wedding, a house worthy of being showcased in a slick magazine, two perfect kids. Yet here I was, on my knees, a sack over my head, the cold barrel of a gun against the base of my skull. And the worst part? Not knowing why this was happening, not knowing why I was going to die. Then again, since when did these things make sense? Random or meticulously planned? Murder, rape, torture, abuse. Are we ever able to truly understand the 'why' or do we simply yearn for labels and boxes to organize the chaos we can't control?

Financial Gain.

Mental Disorder.

Extremism.

Hated Bitches with Acrylic Nails.

Which of these motives would my homicide be filed under?

Stop it, Skye. You're not dead yet. Keep breathing. And think.

Think.

The rough, coarse smell of burlap invaded my nostrils as the boat swayed in the water.

What do you do, Skye? Esteban's words rang loud and clear in my mind.

I fight.

I fight back and I fight hard.

A laugh-sob escaped me.

I had shut Esteban out for so long, but there he was, climbing into my head, unexpected and unannounced as always, sitting on the ledge of my consciousness as if it were my bedroom window.

I remembered taking an on-line quiz that morning:

Who is the last person you think of before you fall asleep?

Click.

That's the person you love the most.

I thought of Marc Jacobs and Jimmy Choo and Tom Ford and Michael Kors. Not Esteban. Never Esteban. Because unlike childhood friends, they stayed on. I could let myself fall for their seduction, bring home their glittery creations, and go to sleep, knowing they would still be there in the morning. Like the Louboutins I'd debated over earlier—the flirty, fuchsia ones with satin straps around the ankle or the towering half d'orsay golden pumps? I'm glad I chose the latter. They had spiked heels. I tried to see them in my head, picturing tomorrow's headline:

'KILLER SHOES'.

The image would feature a deadly, lacquered heel sticking out of my abductor's body.

Yes, that's exactly how this is going down, I told myself.

Breathe, Skye. Breathe.

But the air was dark and musty inside my hood, and my lungs were collapsing under the weight of doom and dread. It was just starting to sink in. This was happening. This was *real.* When you've led a charmed life, something kicks in to insulate you from the shock—a sense of entitlement, as if this too, would be looked after. Holding on to that gave me a sense of bravado, of flippancy. I was loved, valued, important. Surely, someone was going to swoop in and save the day. Right? *Right?*

I heard the rack slide back on the gun, the kiss of the barrel now steady against the back of my head.

"Wait." My throat hurt, my voice raw from screaming

like a banshee when I'd come around and found myself trussed up like a wild hog in the trunk of my car. I knew because it still smelled of tuberose and sandalwood, from the perfume I'd spilled a few weeks before.

He'd grabbed me in the parking lot as I was getting into my sky blue convertible—pulled me out and slammed me, facedown, against the hood. I thought he'd take my bag, my wallet, my keys, my car. Maybe it's a protective instinct; maybe you just focus on what you *want* to happen next.

Just take it and go.

But that's not what happened. He didn't want my bag or my wallet or my keys or my car. He wanted *me*.

They tell you it's better to yell 'Fire' than 'Help', but I couldn't get either word out because I was choking on the chloroform-soaked rag he had over my nose and mouth. The thing with chloroform is that it doesn't knock you out right away—not the way you see in movies. I kicked and struggled for what seemed like an eternity before my arms and legs went numb, before darkness overtook me.

I shouldn't have screamed when I came around. I should have looked for the trunk release, or pushed the brake lights out, or done something that journalists want to interview you about later. But you can't shut Panic up, you know? She's a screaming, thrashing bitch, and she wanted out.

It made him mad. I could tell when he pulled over and opened the trunk. I was blinded by the cold, blue glare of the streetlight over his shoulder, but I could tell. And just to be clear, he dragged me out by my hair and stuffed my mouth with the same chloroform-soaked rag he'd used to overwhelm me.

I gagged on it as he forced me out towards the quay,

my wrists still tied behind my back. The sweet, pungent smell was not as powerful, but it made me queasy. I almost choked on my vomit before he pulled the rag out of my mouth and slipped a sack over my head. I stopped screaming then. He could have let me choke to death, but he wanted me alive, at least until he was done with whatever it was he'd abducted me for. Rape? Captivity? Ransom? My mind ran wild with a kaleidoscope of gruesome clips from news reports and magazine articles. Sure, I had always felt a pang of compassion, but all I had to do was change the channel or flip the page and I could turn the ugliness off.

But there was no turning *this* off. I could have convinced myself that it was a vivid nightmare, except the raw tingles on my scalp, where he'd ripped my hair out, stung like hell. But pain was good. Pain told me I was alive. And as long as I was alive, there was still hope.

"Wait," I said, when he forced me to my knees. "Whatever you want. Please . . . just. Don't kill me."

I was wrong. He *didn't* want me alive. He wasn't locking me up or demanding a ransom. He wasn't ripping my clothes off or taking pleasure in making me suffer. He'd just wanted to bring me *here,* wherever *here* was. This is where he was going to kill me, and he wasn't wasting any time over it.

"Please," I begged. "Let me look at the sky one last time."

I needed to buy some time, to see if there was any way out. And if this really was the end, I didn't want to die in the dark, suffocating on the fumes of fear and desperation. I wanted my last breath to be free, filled with the ocean and surf and sea spray. I wanted to close my eyes and pretend it was Sunday afternoon, and I was a gap-toothed little girl, collecting seashells with MaMaLu.

There was a moment of stillness. I didn't know my captor's voice or his face; there was no picture in my head, just a dark presence that loomed like a giant cobra behind me, ready to strike. I held my breath.

He lifted the bag and I felt the night breeze on my face. It took a moment for my eyes to adjust, to find the moon. And there it was—a perfect, crescent shaped slice of silver, the same moon I used to watch when I fell asleep as a child, listening to MaMaLu's stories.

"You were born on a day when the clouds were big and swollen with rain," my nanny would say as she stroked my hair. "We were ready for a storm, but the sun filtered through the sky. Your mother held you by the window and noticed the gold flecks in your little gray eyes. Your eyes were the color of the heavens that day. That is why she named you Skye, *amorcito*."

I hadn't thought of my mother in years. I had no memories because she'd died when I was young. I didn't know why I was thinking of her now. Perhaps it was because in a few minutes, I would be dead too.

My insides rattled at the thought. I wondered if I'd see my mother on the other side. I wondered if she'd greet me like the people on talk shows attested to—the ones who claimed to have been there and back. I wondered if there *was* another side.

I could see the twinkling lights of high-rise condos on the harbor, the traffic trailing its way like a red snake through the downtown core. We were docked in a deserted marina across from San Diego Bay. I thought of my father, who I'd conditioned not to worry, to just let me be and breathe and live. I was an only child, and he'd already lost my mother.

I wondered if he was having dinner out in the courtyard, perched on a bluff overlooking a quiet cove in La Jolla. He had mastered the art of drinking red wine without soaking his mustache. He used his bottom lip and tilted his head just so. I was going to miss his bushy, gray whiskers even though I protested every time he kissed me. Three times on my cheeks. Left, right, left. Always. It didn't matter if I had just come down for breakfast or was leaving for a trip around the world. I had closets full of designer shoes and bags and baubles, but that's what I would miss the most. Warren Sedgewick's three kisses.

"My father will pay you whatever you want," I said. "No questions asked." Pleading. Bargaining. It comes easy when you're about to lose your life.

My declaration earned no response, except for a firm nudge, forcing my head down.

My killer had come prepared. I was kneeling in the center of a large tarp that covered most of the deck. The corners were chained to chunks of concrete. I could picture my dead body being rolled up in it and dumped somewhere in the middle of the ocean.

My mind rebelled against the image, but my heart . . . my heart knew.

"Dear Lord, bless my soul. And watch over Dad. And MaMaLu and Esteban." It was a prayer from the past, one I hadn't uttered in years, but the words formed automatically, falling from my mouth like little beads of comfort.

In that moment, I realized that in the end, all the hurts and grudges and excuses are nothing more than floaty apparitions that scatter like pale ghosts in the face of all the people you loved, and all the people who loved you. Because in the end, my life boiled down to three kisses and three faces: my father, my nanny and her son—two of whom I hadn't seen since we took the dry, dusty road out of Casa Paloma.

Who are the last people you think of before you die?

I squeezed my eyes shut, anticipating the *click,* the cold, lead-weighted inevitability of death.

Those are the ones you loved the most.

Two

IT WAS DARK. PITCH DARK. The kind of darkness that's surreal—deep and still and vast. I was suspended in its emptiness, a speck of awareness with no hands or feet or hair or lips. It was almost peaceful, except for the dull throbbing that kept flowing in and out of me. It rolled over me in waves, louder, stronger, until it was crashing and pounding inside of me.

Pain.

I blinked and realized my eyes were already open, but there was nothing around me—nothing above me, nothing below—just the pain, hammering away in my head. I blinked again. Once. Twice. Three times. Nothing. Not a shape or a shadow or murky vagueness. Just absolute, engulfing darkness.

I bolted upright.

In my head.

In reality, nothing happened. It was as if my brain had been severed from the rest of me. I couldn't feel my arms or legs, or my tongue or my toes. But I could hear. Sweet Jesus, I could hear, even if it was only the sound of my heart racing like it was about to burst right out of me. Each frantic beat amplified the pain in my head, as if all of my nerve endings ended there, in a thumping pool of blood.

You can hear.

You can breathe.

Maybe you've lost your sight, but you're alive.

No.

No!!!!!

I'd rather be dead than at his mercy.

What the fuck has he done to me?

Where the fuck am I?

I HAD BRACED MYSELF FOR his bullet, but there was a moment of silence after I'd said my prayer. He picked up a strand of my hair and stroked it gently, almost reverently. Then he whipped me with the butt of his gun, a sharp whack that felt like he had split my skull. The San Diego skyline tilted and started disappearing in big, black blotches.

"I didn't give you permission to speak," he said, as I keeled over from the blow. My face hit the deck, hard and fast, but it seemed like everything was happening in excruciatingly slow motion.

I caught a glimpse of his shoes before my eyes closed. Soft, hand-tooled Italian leather.

I knew shoes, and there weren't too many of those

around.

Why didn't he pull the trigger? *I thought, as I blacked out.*

I DIDN'T KNOW HOW LONG I was unconscious, only that the question still sat with me, like a dragon at the mouth of a cave, refusing to budge, ready to unleash the fire of all the monstrous possibilities that were worse than death.

Why didn't he pull the trigger?

Maybe he planned to keep me blind and drugged and tethered to his side.

Maybe he wanted to cut out parts of me and sell them.

Maybe he'd already scooped up my insides and it was just a matter of time before the anesthesia wore off.

Maybe he thought he'd killed me and had buried me alive.

With each passing thought, pain transformed into Terror, and let me tell you, Terror is a bigger bitch than Panic. Terror swallows you whole.

I felt myself sliding deep inside her belly.

I smelled Terror.

I breathed Terror.

Terror was eating me up raw.

I knew my captor had given me something, but I didn't know if the paralysis was temporary or permanent.

I didn't know if I'd been raped or beaten or hideously mutilated.

I didn't know if I wanted to find out.

I didn't know if he was coming back.

And if he did, I didn't know if *this,* whatever hellish state I was in, was better, safer, easier.

Terror continued stalking me through the labyrinth of my mind, but there was one place she could never get me, one place I knew I'd always be safe. I turned into that corner in my head and shut myself off to everything but MaMaLu's lullaby.

It wasn't really a lullaby, but the way MaMaLu sang it—soft and dreamy—always soothed me. She sang it in Spanish, and I didn't remember all the words so I put my own spin on the meaning, conjuring up images of armed bandits and danger, although I had a feeling it was really a song about love.

Down from the Sierra Morena mountains,
Cielito lindo, they come
A pair of black eyes,
Cielito lindo, they're contraband . . .

I saw myself in a hammock, blue sky above me, Esteban giving me an occasional absentminded push, while MaMaLu sang as she hung clothes up to dry. Those afternoon naps in the gardens of Casa Paloma, with my nanny and her son, were my earliest memories. Hummingbirds buzzed over red and yellow hibiscus, and bougainvillea spilled from fat, unkempt hedges.

Ay, yai, yai, yai,
Sing and do not cry,
Because singing cheers us up,
Cielito lindo, our hearts . . .

MaMaLu sang when Esteban or I got hurt. She sang when we couldn't sleep. She sang when she was happy, and she sang when she was sad.

Canta y no llores
Sing and do not cry . . .

But the tears came. I cried because I couldn't sing. I cried because my tongue could not form the words. I cried because MaMaLu and blue skies and hummingbirds defied the darkness. I cried as I held on to them, and slowly, one step at a time, Terror retreated.

I opened my eyes and took a deep breath. I was still engulfed in darkness, but I was aware of a constant rocking motion. Maybe my senses were starting to kick in. I tried to flex my fingers.

Please.

Be there.

Work.

Nothing.

My head was still pounding, from where he'd knocked me out, but beyond its *boom-boom-boom* there were voices, and they were getting closer.

"You pass through Ensenada often?" A woman's voice.

I couldn't make out the whole reply, but it was deeper, definitely male.

" . . . I've never got the red light before," he was saying.

My abductor's voice, etched in my brain, along with his shoes.

"No big deal. Just a random check before . . . crossing the border." The woman's voice was fading in and out. "I need to make sure . . . vessel's serial number matches the engine's."

The border.

Ensenada.

Shit.

The rocking motion suddenly made sense. I was on a boat, probably the same one he'd taken me out to. We were at Ensenada, the port of entry into Mexico, about 70 miles south of San Diego, and the lady was most likely a customs officer.

My heart picked up.

This is it. Your chance to escape, Skye.

Get her attention. You have to get her attention!

I screamed and screamed, but I couldn't make a sound. Whatever he'd given me had paralyzed my vocal cords.

I heard footsteps above, which made me think I was probably in some kind of storage space below the deck.

"Just to verify, you're Damian Caballero?" the woman asked.

"Damian," he corrected. Dah-me-yahn. Not Day-me-yun.

"Well, everything looks like it's in order. I'll take a pic of your hull identification number and then you can be on your way."

No! I was losing my window of opportunity.

I couldn't kick or scream, but I found I could roll, so that's what I did. Left to right, side to side. I rocked, harder, faster, not knowing if I was knocking up against anything, not knowing if it was making any difference. The sixth or seventh time I did it, I heard something grate above me, like wood scraping against wood.

Oh please.

Please, please, please, please.

I put everything into it, even though it was making me dizzy.

Something crashed. A loud thud. And suddenly it wasn't so dark anymore.

"What was that?" the woman asked.

"I didn't hear anything."

"It sounded like it came from below. Mind if I take a look?"

Yes!

"What do you have in here?" Her voice was clearer now.

She was close.

Really close.

"Ropes, chains, fishing equipment . . ."

I was starting to make out faint lines running vertically above me, inches from my face.

Yes. I can see! My eyes are okay!

I heard a lock turn and then the room flooded with glorious, blinding light that made me want to weep.

I tried to align my eyes with the gaps above me, the ones that allowed the light through. It looked like I was on the floor, trapped under planks of wood.

A man's silhouette appeared on the stairs, with another figure behind him.

I'm here.

I started to rock furiously.

"Looks like one of your crates fell over," said the customs officer.

I pushed it over. Find me. Please find me.

"Yep." He walked towards me. "I just need to secure them." He jammed his leg against my crate, preventing it from moving.

I could see the lady clearly now, through the slits of the lid—not all of her, but her hands and torso. She was holding some paperwork, and there was a walkie-talkie hanging from her belt.

I'm here.

Look up from your clipboard. You'll see the light shining on my eye.

One step forward and you can't miss me.

One. Lousy. Step.

"Need some help?" she asked, as the man picked up the crate that I'd managed to dislodge and put it back on top of me.

Yes! HELP. Help me, you dumb twat!

"I got it," he replied. "A bit of rope, some hooks and . . . we're good to go. There. All secured."

"Those are some good-sized crates. Expecting a big catch?" I heard the thud of her steps on the stairs.

No! Come back.

I'm sorry I called you a dumb twat.

Don't leave me.

PLEASE.

DON'T. LEAVE!

"Sometimes I manage to reel in a good one," he replied.

The smugness in his voice sent a chill down my spine.

Then he shut the door, and I was plunged back into complete, utter darkness.

I WAS CRAWLING THROUGH A tunnel of sandpaper. Every time I moved forward, my skin caught on the rough, dry surface.

Scrape, scrape, scrape.

The sound of my cells sloughing off, layer by layer. My knees were raw, my back was raw, my shoulders were raw, but I could *feel* the warmth of the sun. I knew that if I just kept reaching for it, I'd make it out. I kept going and going, and soon I had room enough to stand. There was gravel all around me.

My heels sank into small stones and pebbles.

Crunch, crunch, crunch.

I kept walking. Everything hurt, but I trudged towards the light. And suddenly it was on me, all around me, making me squint from the sheer brilliance. I blinked and woke up, letting out a deep breath.

Whoa. Talk about a freakish nightmare. I was safely tucked away in bed, and the sun was streaming through the window. I sighed and snuggled back under the covers. A few more minutes and then I'd skip downstairs to collect my three kisses before my father left for work. I wasn't going to take them for granted anymore.

Crunch, crunch, crunch.

I frowned.

It wasn't supposed to follow me into reality.

I kept my eyes closed.

The covers felt funny, rough and coarse, not at all like my soft, silk duvet.

The window, the one I'd caught sight of momentarily, it was *small* and *round*. The kind that belonged on a *boat*.

And I hurt. I could feel it now. I hurt everywhere. My head was thick and heavy, and my tongue was stuck to the roof of my mouth.

Crunch, crunch, crunch.

I knew it was bad, whatever that sound was. It was coming from behind me and I knew it was bad and evil, and it was going to pull me right back into hell.

"About time," it said.

Fuck, fuck, fuck!

Dah-me-yahn.

Damian Hair-ripping, Skull-bashing, Coma-Inducing, Caballero.

He was here and he was real.

I squeezed my eyes tight. I'm pretty sure a wobbly tear would have escaped, but my eyes were so dry, my lids felt like sandpaper. *All* of me felt like that—raw and scraped, inside and out. No wonder I had been dreaming about tunnels of sandpaper. I was probably dehydrated. Who knew how long I'd been out or what the side effects were of whatever he'd used on me?

"Did you . . . what did you do to me?" My voice sounded weird, but I had never been more grateful for it. The same went for my arms and my legs and the rest of me. My head hurt, my bones ached, but I was still in one piece and I was never, *ever* going to hate my belly or my ass or the dimples on my thighs again.

Damian didn't reply. He was still behind me, out of my line of sight, and he kept doing whatever the hell it was he was doing.

Crunch, crunch, crunch.

I started to tremble, but stifled the whimper that threatened to escape.

It was a slow, psychological game—him, being in total control, and me not knowing what was going to happen next, or when, or where, or why.

I startled when he slid a stool next to me. It had a bowl filled with some kind of stew, a hunk of bread that looked like it had been ripped off—no knife, no niceties—and a bottle of water. My stomach jumped at the sight of it. I felt like I hadn't eaten in days, and although I wanted to throw it all back in his face, I was ravenously hungry. I lifted my head and sank back down—the motion, combined with the rocking of the boat, making me woozy and disoriented. I attempted it again, more slowly this time, coming up on my elbows before sitting up.

Crunch, crunch, crunch.

What the hell *was* that?

"I wouldn't turn around if I were you," he said.

Interesting. He didn't want me to see his face. If he planned to kill me, why would he care? It would only matter if he didn't want me to be able to identify him.

I spun around. The world went all dizzy and blurry, but I spun around. Maybe I was a crazy-ass bitch, but I wanted to see his face. I wanted to memorize every last detail so I could nail the bastard if it ever came down to it. And if he killed me, so be it. At least we would be more even.

I saw your face: *Bang Bang*.

Rather than I-Have-No-Clue-What-I-Did-To-Deserve This: *Bang Bang*.

He didn't react to my defiance, not the slightest hint of a response. He just sat there, dipped his fingers in the paper cone he was holding and tossed something in his mouth.

Crunch, crunch, crunch.

His eyes were shielded by a baseball cap, but I knew he was watching me. I shuddered when I realized he was taking his time, weighing my punishment like he weighed whatever he was eating, before chomping it down with his teeth.

I didn't know what I was expecting. I already knew I hated him, but now I hated him even more. In my mind, I had pictured someone completely different, someone as mean and ugly on the outside as he was on the inside. That made sense to me. Not this. Not someone so *ordinary*, you could walk right by him on the street and never realize you'd just brushed past pure evil.

Damian was younger than I'd anticipated—older than me, but not the grizzly, hardened thug I'd assumed he'd be. He might have had an average build and height, but he was strong as hell. I knew because I had kicked and punched and fought him like a wildcat in that parking lot. Every inch of him was cold, hard steel. I wondered if it was a requirement in his line of work: abduction, mock executions, smuggling girls across the border.

He hooked his foot around the stool and pulled it towards him. The glossy, custom shoes were gone. He was wearing ugly, generic boat shoes with ugly, generic sweat pants and an ugly, generic t-shirt. His lips curled mockingly, as if he was fully aware of my disdainful appraisal and was enjoying it. The asshole was *enjoying* it.

He tore the bread in half, dipped it in the stew, letting it soak up the thick, brown gravy, and bit into it. Then he sank back, chewing it slowly, while I watched. It was sourdough bread. I could smell it. I could almost taste the crispy crust, followed by the soft tang of the dough melting in my mouth. The steam rising from the stew filled my stomach with the promise of carrots and onions and pieces of soft, tender meat—a promise that Damian had no intention of keeping. I knew that now. I knew this was my punishment for turning around when he told me not to. I knew he was going to make me watch as he finished every last bit of the food that was meant for me.

The kicker was that he didn't even want it. He looked like he was so full, he had to force every delicious fucking bite into his mouth while my stomach clamored, and I went dizzy with raw, gnawing hunger. My mouth puckered each time he swirled the bread in the stew, picking up chunks of slowly simmered vegetables and gravy. I watched him finish the bowl, unable to look away, like a starving dog ready to pounce on a stray morsel, but there was nothing left. Damian wiped every drool-inducing bit of it clean with the last piece of bread. Then he stood and uncapped the bottle of water, holding it over me.

Oh God. Yes. Yes.

I held out my hands as he started pouring, my dry, cracked lips anticipating that first thirst-quenching drop of water.

The water came. It did. But Damian held his dirty hand over me, the one he'd used to eat with, so that the water passed through his soiled fingers before it got to me. I had a choice. Accept his degradation or go thirsty.

I closed my eyes and drank. I drank because I couldn't have stopped myself even if I wanted to. I drank because I was a ravenous, rattle-boned animal. But most of all I drank because some stupid, irrational part of me that sang stupid, irrational lullabies, still held hope. I drank till the water slowed down to a trickle. And when Damian flung the empty, plastic bottle across the room, I watched it roll around on the floor, hoping he would leave so I could stick my tongue inside and lick the last few drops out of it.

I thought back to the Swarovski studded bottle of Bling H2O that Nick and I had barely touched on our last date. He had just made assistant to the district attorney and his first official case was the next morning. It was a celebration that called for something harmless, but with the fizz and pop of a freshly opened bottle of champagne. I should have finished that beautiful, frosted bottle of sparkling water, and gone home with Nick. I should never have headed into the parking lot alone.

I looked up at my captor. He was wiping his hands on his sweatpants. I used the opportunity to take stock of my surroundings. It was a small stateroom with a queen-sized berth. The walls were dark wood cabinets. I guessed they doubled as storage space. There was one window (*not big enough to crawl out of*), an overhead latch that let through plenty of light (*but was bolted down with a chain*), and a door. Even if I got out, we were on a damn boat, in the middle of the ocean. There was no place to run and hide.

My eyes came back to Damian. He was watching me from under his baseball cap. It was navy blue with the initials 'SD' embroidered in white, the official insignia for the San Diego Padres. Apparently, he was into baseball. Or maybe he wore it because it summed him up perfectly:

Sadistic Douchebag

Also, if he really was a Padres fan, then *Stupid Dreamer,* because because the team had yet to make it to the World Series, though my father remained hopeful at the start of every season:

Good luck, San Diego Padres. Break a leg!

"Try anything stupid and I'll break your legs." Damian picked up the empty bowl he'd just finished and headed for the door.

I should've bashed him over the head with the stool.

I should've tackled him so the bowl would slip and break, and then stabbed him with the broken glass.

"Please," I said instead, "I need to use the bathroom."

I couldn't think beyond emptying my bladder. I was reduced to nothing but hunger and thirst and bodily functions. And I was totally dependent on him. 'Please' and 'thank you' come automatically when you are at someone's mercy. Even if you hate their guts.

He motioned for me to get up. My legs were wobbly and I had to hold on to him. I was wearing the same clothes—a cream, silk-georgette top and cropped cigarette pants, but they were barely recognizable. Isabel Marant's Parisian chic looked like it had spent the night rolling around with Rob Zombie.

Damian led me through a narrow hallway. On the right was a small bathroom, with a compact shower stall, a vanity, and a toilet. I turned to shut the door, but Damian stuck his foot out.

"I can't pee if you're watching."

"No?" He started pulling me back into the room.

"Wait." God, I hated him. I hated him more than I thought I could ever hate another human being.

He waited by the door, not bothering to turn away. He wanted to make sure I understood the situation—that I didn't count, that I didn't have a say, that I wasn't going to be afforded any privacy or mercy or grace or consideration. I was his prisoner, subject to his every whim.

I scooted over to the toilet seat, thankful that I was somewhat shielded from Damian's view by the vanity. I unzipped my pants, noticing the scratches for the first time. My skin must have scraped against the sides of the crate he'd locked me up in. I touched the back of my head and felt an egg-sized lump that hadn't stopped throbbing since I'd come around. My legs protested as I sat down, and there were deep, purple bruises on my knees from rattling around in that wooden crate for who knows how long. Worse, my pee would not come, and when it did, it burned like hot acid. There wasn't much, probably because I was so dehydrated, but I kept sitting, taking a few deep breaths before standing to wipe myself. I pulled my pants back on and was about to wash my hands when I caught my reflection.

"What the hell?" I turned to him. "What the hell did you do to me?"

He continued staring at me impassively, like he didn't hear me, like I wasn't worth answering.

My eyes swung back to the mirror. He'd hacked off my long blond hair and dyed it jet black: butchered it with a blunt pair of scissors and poured some caustic store-bought color over it. Bits of blond hair still stuck out under the dark pieces, making it look like I was wearing a cheap, goth wig. My gray eyes, that had always called attention to my face, faded against the harsh dye job. Combined with my pale eyelashes and brows, I looked like a living ghost.

My nose was scratched, my cheeks were scratched. Dried up rivulets of blood were caked over my ears from where he'd ripped my hair out. Deep, blue hollows ringed my eye sockets and my lips looked as painful and cracked as they felt.

My eyes stung with unshed tears. I couldn't reconcile this person with the girl I was a few days ago, the girl who was going to turn heads on her twenty-fourth birthday. My father had to know by now that I was missing. I would never have skipped out on the birthday bash he was throwing me. He must have talked to Nick, the last person I'd been with. I didn't know how many days had passed, but I knew my father had to be looking for me. He would hire the best and he wouldn't stop until he found me. If he'd tracked my car down to the quay, he would already have considered the possibility that I was on a boat. The thought comforted me. Maybe he was close. Maybe all I needed to do was buy some time so he could catch up.

I felt under my blouse and sighed with relief. It was still there—the necklace my father had given my mother when I was born. It had been passed on to me after her death and I'd worn it ever since. It was a simple gold chain with a round locket. The locket had a transparent glass window that opened like a book. Inside were two rare gemstones—alexandrites—and a pink conch pearl.

"Here," I unclasped it and dangled it before Damian.

It wasn't like I could trade it in for my freedom, since he could easily just take it from me, but if I could lure him with the promise of more, if I could whet his appetite with monetary compensation, maybe I could buy some time and stall whatever he had planned for me.

"This is worth a lot of money," I said.

He didn't seem to care. Then the indifference left him. His whole body stiffened and he took his cap off. It was an odd gesture, the kind of thing a man does when he's informed of someone's death. Or maybe he did it out of reverence, like when you're standing in front of something big and beautiful and holy. Either way, he reached for it, very slowly, until it was swinging from his hand.

He held it up to the light and for the first time, I saw his eyes. They were dark. Black. But the kind of black that I'd never seen before. Black was One. There were no shades to black. Black was absolute, impenetrable. Black absorbed all the colors. If you fell into black, it swallowed you whole. Yet here was a different kind of black. It was black ice and burning coal. It was well-water and desert night. It was dark tempest and glassy calm. It was Black battling Black, opposite and polar, and yet still . . . all black.

I could see my mother's necklace suspended in Damian's eyes. It reminded me of what it's like to stand between two mirrors, staring at the seemingly endless line of images fading into the distance. There was something in his eyes, in his face that I couldn't place. He seemed mesmerized by the locket, like he'd fallen into some kind of a daze.

He had a chink in his armor after all.

"There's more where that came from," I said.

He tore his eyes away from the necklace and looked at me. Then he grabbed me by the arm, dragged me through the galley, up a short set of stairs, and onto the deck. I stumbled after him, my legs still wobbly and weak.

"You see this?" He gestured around us.

We were in the middle of nowhere, surrounded by miles and miles of dark, rolling water.

"*This*," he continued, pointing at the ocean, "doesn't give a fuck about *this*." He shook the necklace in front of my face. *Your gems are nothing but washed up grit to me*. "Pity," he said more softly, holding the locket up to the sun. "Such a pretty little thing."

My father couldn't decide what color of stone to get my mother. He told me he had chosen alexandrites because they were like the rainbow. They went through dramatic shifts in color depending on the light. Indoors, they looked reddish purple, but here in the sun, they sparkled with a bright, greenish hue. Their light glinted off Damian's face.

"Such a pretty little thing," he repeated quietly, almost sadly.

"The stones are very rare. The pearl too. You'd never want for anything. You could go anywhere. Disappear. Do whatever you like. And if you want more—"

"How much do you think your life is worth, Skye Sedgewick?"

He knew my name. Of course he knew my name. He'd probably ransacked my handbag. That, or he'd been stalking me, in which case this was a deliberate act, not some random abduction.

"How much do think *my* life is worth?" he asked, holding up the locket again. "The length of this chain? The pearl? These two *rare* stones?" He looked at me, but I had no answer.

"Have you ever held a life in your hands?" He dropped the locket in my hand and closed my fingers around it. "Here, feel it."

He was nuts. Stark-raving nuts.

"Do you know how easy it is to destroy a life?" He took

the necklace from me and slowly, deliberately, dropped it.

It fell by his feet. He played with it for a while, sliding it back and forth over the smooth deck, with the toe of his shoe.

"It's really, ridiculously easy." He stepped on the necklace and ground down with his heel, all the while looking at me.

The glass started cracking under his weight.

"Don't," I said. "It's the only thing that's left of my mother."

"It *was*," he replied, not letting up until the locket shattered.

The way he said '*was*' creeped me out.

It *was*.

I *was*.

Things that came on board.

Things that never left intact.

He picked up the broken keepsake and examined it.

I felt a rush of triumph because the stones and pearl remained unscathed. Of course they did. It must have shown on my face because he grabbed my neck and squeezed so hard, I was gasping for air.

"Did you love your mother?" he asked, finally letting go.

I bent over, trying to catch my breath. "I never got to know her."

Damian walked to the railing and held the necklace over the water. I watched, still on my knees, as it floated in the wind. I knew what he was going to do, but I couldn't look away.

"Ashes to ashes . . . ," he said, as he dropped it into the ocean.

I felt like he'd thrown a piece of me overboard, like

he'd dishonored the love my parents had shared, the memories they'd made—the two rainbow alexandrites, and me, their pink pearl. Damian Caballero had destroyed what was left of our pretty, glass world.

I couldn't cry. I was too exhausted. My spirit was crawling through tunnels of sandpaper, being skinned alive. Scrape off my freedom. Scrape off my hair. Scrape off my dignity and my self-worth and everything I possess, and cherish, and hold dear. I lay there looking up at the sky, looking up at the sun that I'd been yearning for, and I didn't care.

I didn't care when Damian forced me to get up and shoved me back downstairs. I didn't care about counting windows or marking the exits. I didn't care when he locked me up or when the engine picked up, taking us farther away from my home, my father, my life.

All I knew as I lay in bed, watching fluffy white clouds morph into strange, hideous forms through the overhead latch, was that if I ever got the chance, I wouldn't hesitate a single second before killing Damian Caballero.

Four

IT WAS DARK WHEN DAMIAN came in again.

I was dreaming of pink-frosted cake and piñatas and Esteban.

Touch her again and I'll see you in hell, he said, as they dragged him away.

He'd been my self-appointed protector, but there was no protecting me from the man who stood in the doorway now.

The light from the hallway outlined his form, casting a sinister shadow over my bed. I wanted to hide somewhere it couldn't reach me.

Damian placed a tray on the bed and pulled up a chair. He left the lights off, but I smelled food. He'd brought me food.

I approached the tray cautiously, keeping my eyes

averted. I remembered what had happened the last time I'd defied him, and I was going to be a good girl. I was going to be a good, conditioned girl. I could barely contain the hunger pangs that were rolling through my stomach in short, tight contractions, but I forced myself to slow down, to behave, to be *civil* and not bury my face in the plate like I wanted to.

It was some kind of fish, simply grilled, with rice on the side. God, it smelled good. There was no cutlery, which was fine, because all I wanted to do was rip into it, but I knew he was watching, so I pinched off a piece with my fingers, and the oil and cooking juices mingled with the rice.

"Not so fast," he said.

Oh God, not again. Please just let me eat.

I wondered what he'd do if I licked my fingers.

I could taste the fish *so bad.*

"Stand up," he instructed.

I swallowed the dry lump in my throat, the one that wanted to scream and cry and whimper and beg. I swallowed the tasteless, fishless lump and stood.

"Take your clothes off," he said from the shadows.

I had been expecting it. Sooner or later, one way or another, it always came down to their dick. Suck it, lick it, stroke it, fuck it.

Because my mother didn't love me.

Because my father hit me.

Because my teacher fondled me.

Because I was bullied.

Because my wife left me.

Because my kids don't talk to me.

That's why I drink.

I gamble.

I can't stop eating.

I'm addicted to sex.

I cut myself.

I pull out my eyelashes.

I do drugs.

But it's not always enough, you know? And sometimes, it spills over because you can't control it, because you need to make others feel your pain, your hurt, your rage, because it's tough to walk around all scarred up, in a world full of slick billboards and bright, smiley toothpaste ads and shiny, happy people. Life's not always fair. So suck it, lick it, stroke it, fuck it.

I didn't care what category of dysfunction Damian fell in to. Sometimes it's because *I'm just pure evil,* you know? I kept my mind on the prize as I unbuttoned my top. It might have looked like I was staring at the floor, but I was eating rice and fish with my eyes. It's amazing—the things you can do in survival mode. I stepped out of my pants and stood before him in my bra and panties. Agent Provocateur. Midnight Captive Collection.

"Take them *all* off," he said, emphasizing the word as if I was incapable of comprehending a simple command.

I unclasped my 34C black fishnet lace bra, shimmied out of the matching panties and stood before Damian. Naked.

He shifted in his chair. "Turn on the light."

Fish. Think fish, I told myself as I felt around for the switch.

"Higher, to the right," he said.

My fingers shook as I flipped it on.

"Good girl. Now walk towards me."

Like he was directing a fucking porn movie.

I kept my eyes down until I got to his chair, until I was

looking at his ugly boat shoes. God, I hated those shoes. I hated the laces and the leather and the sole and every single stitch that held them together. I hated them because he had taken away my beautiful golden pumps and now I was barefoot and weak and naked and hungry and hurting and it was fish vs fuck. So fuck him and his shoes and his dirty, psycho games and—

"Turn around," he said.

I looked at him then, expecting lechery and lust, but he was inspecting my body with a detachment that infuriated me. I was used to men staring at me, wanting me. My body wasn't runway perfect, but I owned every inch of it. It was my power, my weapon, my ticket to exclusive clubs, front lines at fashion shows, red carpet treatment. Guys did things for me, girls did things for me, and it mattered because it was for *me*, not my name, or fame or fortune, or the string of hotels that my father owned. I had a good body and I wasn't ashamed to flaunt it. I didn't sleep around, but I wasn't averse to using it.

And now Damian was taking that away from me too. He was stripping me down to body parts. *Inspecting* me—my arms, my legs, my back, my feet—not me the *woman*, but me his *prisoner*, a collection of separate, movable parts. There was nothing sexual about Damian's perusal and I hated that because it left me even more powerless. I stood with my back turned to him, feeling his eyes on my skin, wondering if any trace of food remained if I were to lick my fingers now.

I felt the air shift around me. He was standing behind me now, his breath fanning against my shoulder.

"You stink," he said. "Get in the shower."

A shower. Soap and water. And a reprieve from Damian.

I'd done well.

Wait for me, Fish. I looked longingly at the plate before heading for the bathroom.

The stall was tiny, with barely enough room to move, but the warm water felt like heaven, even though it stung where my skin was raw and bruised. I started to wash my hair and held back a sob because for a while, I'd forgotten that my long, luxurious locks were gone. I had barely finished rinsing it when the door swung open and Damian turned the faucet off.

"This isn't a fucking spa. It's a boat with a water tank. You'll do well to remember that."

He held out a towel. It was threadbare, but clean. I caught sight of my reflection as he escorted me back to the room. The girl with the weird hair startled me yet again.

Modesty had fled out the window. I dried myself in front of Damian and looked around for my clothes. He opened one of the cabinets and started throwing shopping bags on the bed. They were all mine. Kate Spade. Macy's. All Saints. Sephora. Zara. It wasn't as if I had to work for a living, but I'd graduated with a degree in fine arts and was embarking on a career as a fashion consultant. I told myself it was research. I went on shopping sprees and left everything lying around in my car for days, sometimes weeks.

Shit.

He could only have gotten these if he'd gone back to the car. And if he'd gone back, there was a good possibility he'd either disposed of it, or moved it. Either way I was screwed. The trail of breadcrumbs I was hoping my father would follow was starting to disappear. My only hope now was that the parking lot I'd been abducted from had caught something on the surveillance camera. His height, his weight, his face—anything that would help with the investigation. No matter what, I knew my father would not give up. And right now, that's exactly what I needed to do.

Not. Give. Up.

I started emptying the bags. Stupid sequin mini skirt. Stupid gauzy, halter dress. Stupid giant bling ring. God. How could I fill so many bags with so much crap? I would have to wash and wear the same underwear. Agent Rinse and ReProvocateur.

I was still sorting through the bags when Damian started stuffing everything back into the cabinet. There was a pair of black yoga pants (*yes!*) and a flimsy white thong (*no!*) on the bed. He pulled out an ugly, generic t-shirt and threw it at me. Judging by the size, it was his.

"Drop the towel," Damian instructed.

Like I said, it always came back to the dick. Now that I didn't stink.

I closed my eyes, expecting the rustle of his pants as they hit the floor.

It never came. Instead, I felt him rub something into my hairline. It smelled medicinal and stung like hell, especially where the follicles had been ripped off. He did the same around my ears. Then he applied salve on my back, on all the nicks and cuts and bruises he'd noted when he'd inspected me.

I got what he was doing—rewarding my good behavior with kindness, soothing the wounds he'd inflicted upon me. I was supposed to feel grateful, dependent, to bond with him over small mercies, but that whole Stockholm syndrome thing? Yeah, I really wasn't feeling it. If I ever found where he'd stashed my spiked heels, I was going to nail his black heart to the mast of his fucking boat.

Die, Dah-me-yahn. DIE.

"You can manage the rest yourself," he said, flinging the tube onto the bed.

He left, leaving the door open, and I could hear him brushing his teeth.

Screw the salve. I jumped on the now-cold plate of fish and rice.

Fish did not let me down. Fish was the juiciest, most delicious thing I had ever tasted. I wept as I ate Fish.

I picked up the rice with my fingers and closed my eyes, savoring its thick, starchy goodness. My taste buds were exploding over white fucking rice.

Yes. Yes. Yes. More!

I licked the plate clean. No, really. I *licked* the plate clean and then went over it once more, for good measure. I had no idea when my next meal would be, or what I would have to do for it. I changed into the clothes Damian had left for me, smelling him on the t-shirt. I nearly brought Fish back up. Not that it smelled bad. It was just downright animalistic—sun and sea and sweat—the kind of odor no amount of detergent could erase.

I peeked through the doorway. Damian was still in the bathroom. I started rifling through the cabinets: linens, towels, rain gear, scuba stuff. I was almost through when I stepped on something round and hard. Lifting my foot, I found a roasted peanut stuck to my sole. There were more peanuts on the floor, and it looked like they had rolled out of a discarded paper cone, the one Damian had been munching out of.

I sat on the chair he'd been sitting on and popped one in my mouth.

Crunch, crunch, cru—I stopped as he walked through the door.

He looked like he had just showered. His hair was slicked back and he'd changed into gray sweatpants and a white t-shirt. His eyes narrowed when he saw me.

"I have a life-threatening allergy to peanuts and I just ate a whole bunch," I said. "If I don't get immediate medical attention, I'll die."

He looked at me for a beat, before opening one of the cabinets I hadn't gotten around to.

Yes! Maybe he had a satellite phone or a walkie-talkie or whatever boats used to communicate.

He pulled out a jar and sat on the bed. He uncapped it and proceeded to moisturize his feet.

He fucking moisturized his feet.

"Did you hear me?" I squealed. "I'm going to die." I started taking deep breaths.

He took his time, first one foot, then the other, like it was the single most important task in the world. Then he pulled on his socks and closed the jar. "So die."

I fucking hated him. He didn't want money. He didn't want sex. He didn't care if I lived or died. He wouldn't tell me where we were going. He wouldn't tell me why. And now he was calling my bluff.

"What do you *want*?" I screamed.

I was sorry the minute I said it. He moved fast. Lightning fast. Before I could apologize, he had me gagged, bound, and secured to the bedpost.

Then he turned off the light and got into bed.

The bastard wasn't even out of breath.

I didn't know which was worse—my arms stretched painfully over my head, the sides of my cracked lips bleeding on the gag, or knowing that this was how it was going to be. One room, one bed, my captor sleeping next to me, night after night.

Five

I WOKE UP STIFF AND sore. Damian was gone, and I was still tied to the bed. He took his time getting back to me. I felt a surge of relief when I saw him standing there with the now familiar tray.

I had once attended a spirituality workshop that taught me to be witness to the moment, to not analyze or reason or think about the when or the why or the how. It was really an excuse to hang out with a bunch of girls, get Ayurvedic massages and bitch over green juice. My friends had long since drifted, but that's the way it goes when you bond over the latest trends and hippest places. Things shift and change. And after MaMaLu and Esteban, I'd pretty much closed myself off. It had been just me and my father for the longest time. Nick was a possibility, and the fact that he got along with my dad was one of the reasons he'd lasted longer than most of the guys I dated. I liked my men to get along. I pictured the two of them beating Damian up and it made me happy. I liked witnessing the happy much more than I liked acknowledging my reaction to Damian. I was starting to associate him with food and bathroom breaks and relief from the pain of being bound up.

Breakfast was some kind of sloppy goo. I had a feeling it started off as oatmeal, but got beefed up with protein powder or egg white or something equally distasteful. He could have thrown in liver and onions and I'd still have finished. My arms felt like they were going to drop out of their sockets from being tied up all night, but I'd earned a metal spoon. And there was an apple. And water.

I looked up to find Damian watching me. There was an odd shadow in his eyes, but he blinked it away. When I was done, he let me use the bathroom. He'd put out a toothbrush for me, and a comb. Things were starting to look up.

I didn't bother with my hair. I tried to avoid looking at it altogether. Damian watched me the whole time. I followed him back to the room like a good girl, and let him lock me up. I even smiled as he shut the door on me.

Then I fell back on the bed and let out a deep breath. The uncertainty was killing me. I'd braced myself for another painful encounter, another round of humiliation and degradation before I earned my privileges. I'd held the possibility, all tight and tense, in my shoulders and neck. But Damian had done the unpredictable, and that was far worse than a patterned system of abuse, because now I was in a state of constant alert, fearing what would come and fearing when it didn't.

How do we kill him, Esteban? I closed my eyes and

remembered the two of us, plotting in my room. I'd been an earnest eight year old, four years younger than him, but an equal instigator in all our adventures.

HE GAVE MY QUESTION CONSIDERABLE thought before responding. I liked the way he twirled his hair when he was deep in thought. His hair was long and dark, and when he let it go, it left a little curl. MaMaLu was always after him to cut it and the times she succeeded, he came home with nowhere to hide his face.

"I don't think we have to kill him," he said. "Just teach him a good lesson."

Gideon Benedict St. John (pronounced Sin Gin), formally nicknamed Gidiot by Esteban and me, was the bane of my existence. He was ten, but bigger than the two of us combined, and when he pinched me, he left big, blue bruises on my thighs.

"Esteban?" I fake-smiled in the mirror. "Would you make a tooth for me?"

He was stretched out on my bed, folding and unfolding a sheet of paper, trying to figure out how to turn it into a giraffe.

"You want a paper tooth to hide the gap between your teeth?" he asked.

I nodded and went back to examining it in the mirror.

"He's just going to find another way to tease you, güerita.*" Esteban called me* güerita. *Blondie. "And how are you going to make it stick?"*

"Make it out of cardboard and I'll tape it in the back." I opened my mouth and pointed to the spot I'd picked out.

We both jumped when the door opened and MaMaLu walked in.

"Esteban! You're supposed to be in school."

"Going!" he yelped, when she smacked him.

MaMaLu hit Esteban a lot, but she hit him like she was swatting a fly, out of irritation and frustration. Esteban got swatted a lot because Esteban misbehaved a lot. He propped a half-finished giraffe up on the sill, scrambled out the window, and shimmied down the tree. MaMaLu slid the glass pane down and watched as he high-tailed it across the garden.

"How many times have I told you not to let him in? If Señor Sedgewick finds out—"

"He won't," I said.

"That's not the point, cielito lindo.*" She picked up the brush and started combing my hair. "You and Esteban . . ." She shook her head. "The two of you are going to get me in trouble one day."*

"Can you do my hair like yours?" I asked.

MaMaLu had thick, dark hair, which she braided and folded into a bun. I wanted to crawl into the 'U' it made on her nape because it looked like a little hammock.

"That's old lady hair," she replied, but she sectioned off two side braids and combined them in the back, leaving the rest of my pale, blond hair loose.

"So beautiful," she said. She removed a small, red flower from her hair and tucked it into mine.

"Gidiot says I'm a witch because witches have gaps between their teeth."

"It's Gideon," she chided. "And when God made you, he left that space so your true love could slip his heart through it when he finds you."

MaMaLu was full of stories; there was a tale behind everything.

"Then how did Esteban's dad give you his heart? You

don't have a gap between your teeth."

Esteban's father had been a great fisherman. He died at sea when MaMaLu was pregnant, but she told us all about his adventures—about magic and monsters and mermaids in the sea.

"Well then, I probably never had his heart." She smiled and poked me in the nose. "Run along now. Miss Edmonds is already here."

"Is Gidiot there yet?"

MaMaLu refused to dignify that with a response.

I grabbed my school bag and went downstairs. Everyone was already gathered around the dining table. The only space left was next to Gidiot, because no one wanted to sit next to him.

"Good. We're all here. Ready to begin?" asked Miss Edmonds.

Gidiot stomped on my foot under the table. I winced as I opened my textbook.

"Everything all right, Skye?" asked Miss Edmonds.

I nodded and gave her a small smile. I wasn't a tattletale, but I knew I was in for another long afternoon.

Three times a week, Miss Edmonds came in from the city to Casa Paloma. My mother had inherited Casa Paloma as a wedding gift from her father. It was a lavish, Spanish-inspired estate on the outskirts of a fishing village called Paza del Mar. There was a small school in Paza del Mar where the locals sent their kids, but the expatriates and wealthier families preferred private tutoring for their children, and so we met in our house, which was the largest by far.

We were learning about soil erosion and landslides and earthquakes when Gidiot pulled my braid so hard, the little red flower MaMaLu had adorned it with fell to the floor. I blinked a few times, refusing to cry, and focused on the diagrams in my book. I wished Gidiot would fall down one of the fault lines, and into the molten core of the earth.

"Ow!" Gidiot howled, rubbing his leg.

"What's the matter?" Miss Edmonds asked.

"I think something bit me."

Miss Edmonds nodded and we continued. Bugs were common. No big deal.

"Ow!" Gideon jumped. "Swear there's something under the table."

Miss Edmonds took a quick look. "Anyone else feel something?"

We shook our heads.

My eyes darted to the big, antique hutch behind Miss Edmonds. On the bottom were two paneled doors with lattice inserts. The crisscross pattern was purely decorative, but as Esteban and I had discovered one afternoon, they made perfect peep holes if you were hiding in there.

I smiled, knowing Esteban had backtracked in from the garden. He hated school so he hid in the hutch on the days Miss Edmonds was there. That way, he had something to tell MaMaLu when she asked him what he was learning in class.

Esteban poked his fingers through the wood and mini-waved at me. He held out a straw, or maybe it was one of his paper creations. The next minute, Gidiot was hopping around the table on one foot, massaging his calf.

"Ow, ow, ow, ow!"

"Gideon!" Miss Edmonds was not amused. "You're distracting everyone. Wait outside until the rest of us are done with today's session."

I picked up an orange seed from the floor as Gidiot left. There were a few more under the table. Esteban had been shooting orange seeds at him through the straw. I could see little red marks on Gidiot's legs as he left the room. Esteban gave me the thumbs up from his hiding place.

I LAUGHED AT THE THOUGHT of his crooked thumb sticking out of that old wooden cabinet. I was still laughing when I heard the lock turn on the door.

Damian was back. And this time there was no tray.

"It's time you earned your keep," he said.

I nodded and followed him out.

I'd spent all my time in the room, but now we were standing in the U-shaped space that functioned as the kitchen. It was done in mahogany and teak, and part of the countertop was cantilevered to accommodate a pair of barstools. There was a sink, a refrigerator, a two-burner cook-top stove and a microwave oven. All the drawers were locked down, but there was a chopping board, some potatoes and a big-ass butcher knife on the counter.

"I need those peeled and cubed," said Damian.

And he was going to let me use the knife? He had balls.

"Sure." I was already thinking of which way to slice them.

I started rinsing the potatoes, but had to grip the sink for a second. My head still hurt and my legs felt weak. My eyes were still closed when Damian grabbed my left hand, forced it palm-down on the cutting board and *WHAM*!

He severed the tip of my pinky finger off, sliced the top third—nail, bone and all—clean off, as if it were a carrot he was chopping for a salad. The pain set in a few seconds later, after the blood started spewing all over the counter.

I *screamed* from the agony of it, from the horror of seeing the top of my finger sitting there, dull and lifeless, like some plastic Halloween prop. I closed my eyes and screamed louder when Damian applied pressure to stop the bleeding. I backed into something—something solid and firm—and slid down until I was on the floor.

I tried to pull my finger away, but Damian held on to it. He was keeping it elevated, wrapping it up, doing God knows what, and all I could do was scream and scream and scream, because everything he did made it ten times worse. I screamed until the sobs set in, until I was rolled up in a tight ball, until the tears stopped and all I could manage were soft, soundless whimpers.

When I opened my eyes, Damian was holding a phone over me.

"Did you get that?" he said to the person on the other side. "Good." He walked to the other side of the counter. "Send the recording to Warren Sedgewick. Tell him that's what she sounded like when I hacked her body to pieces."

He picked up my dead finger, put it in a zip-lock bag and threw it into the freezer. "And tell him to expect a souvenir in the mail. It's the only part of her he'll have because the rest is scattered all over the place."

I could hear the faint sound of the other person on the line.

"I know I've done it before." Damian sounded agitated. "This was different. I froze, damn it! She started praying right before I pulled the trigger. She fucking *prayed*." He slammed his fist down. The knife clanged loudly on the counter.

"I messed up, Rafael," he continued. "I wanted him in

the morgue, identifying his daughter's dead body on her birthday. I know. I'll figure something out." He paused and raked his fingers through his hair. "I don't give a fuck about that. He can hire every Goddamned bounty hunter in the world. I just want him to *feel* it. I want him to *suffer*. As far as Warren Sedgewick is concerned, his daughter is *dead*." He turned and fixed his eyes on me. "And who knows? In twenty-one days, she just might be."

He hung up and wiped the blood off the blade. Then he poured a glass of orange juice, propped me up, and held it to my lips.

I sipped it slowly, because my teeth were chattering. I was hot and cold and sweaty and dizzy, and there was still blood dripping off the counter and splattering onto the floor.

"Why don't you just kill me?" I asked when I finished the juice. This was not some random kidnapping. This was a murder-turned-into-abduction. This was a screwed-up moment of weakness. This was a personal, targeted attack against my father. "What happens in twenty-one days?"

Damian didn't respond. He finished cleaning up the bloody mess in the kitchen before examining my finger. Some pink was showing through the bandage and it throbbed like hell, but he seemed satisfied.

He left me on the floor, propped up against the cabinet and started cutting the potatoes. "Cold cuts and potato salad for lunch?"

Six

DAMIAN SENSED SOMETHING HAD BROKEN inside of me, or maybe he felt a vague sense of remorse over what he had done. Whatever the reason, he no longer tied me up at night, although he still locked the door and kept the key on him while we slept. When I woke up, the door was always open. He left me something to eat on the same counter where he'd chopped off my finger, and although the knife was nowhere in sight, the threat of it was lodged deep in my brain.

I was free to go about the boat as I pleased, but I spent my time curled up on the settee across from the kitchen. Damian stayed up top, at the helm station, for the most part. Two people, forced into close proximity, day in and day out, can communicate volumes without uttering a single word. He reminded me of pain and darkness and a double-gauzed finger. I must have reminded him of botched-up vengeance and the monster within, because we both steered clear of each other, except for the times when we had to eat or sleep.

I didn't ask him what my father had done. Whatever wrongdoing Damian was holding him accountable for had to be a lie or a misconception. Warren Sedgewick was the kindest, most generous soul in the world. He used his hotel connections to build dams and wells and water pumps for people in the most remote regions of the world, places that no one gave a damn about. He financed micro-loans and schools and food banks and medical aid. He rallied against injustices, treated his employees with respect and dignity, and he always, always made his daughter pancakes on Sunday.

When my father and I had first arrived in San Diego, they were Mickey Mouse pancakes with powdered sugar and loads of syrup. Then they turned into hearts and princess stuff. And even though I was all grown up, he refused to let me move out and held on to those traditions. Recently, he'd started making caricatures of my shoes and purses, big shapeless blobs of batter that he insisted I had to look at from different angles to appreciate. The condiments changed with my tastes—bananas with Nutella, fresh berries with brown sugar and cinnamon, shaved dark chocolate with orange zest. My father had the uncanny ability of tapping into my brain, pulling out all of the things I craved, and turning them into reality. I thought of lemon curd, swirled in mascarpone cheese, not because I wanted pancakes, but just so he could feel it—my topping of choice for the day—so he'd know I was alive.

Most of my bruises were healing, but my finger was

still a red, raw reminder that a part of me was sealed in a plastic bag, iced over in the freezer. I peeled off my acrylic nails, biting and picking until I'd ripped into the nail bed—nine nail beds instead of ten—all cracked and ridged and covered with ugly, white flakiness. I thought it was an appropriate send-off for a fallen comrade. A nine-finger salute.

I missed the weight of my mother's necklace on my skin. I missed my pinky nail. I missed my hair. I felt like all the bits that held me together were slowly coming unglued, falling off, piece by piece. I was disappearing, disintegrating like the rocks that get eaten by the sea.

I made my way up to the deck for the first time since Damian had dragged me there, the day he threw my locket into the water. We were on a mid-sized yacht, powerful enough for deep sea sailing, but inconspicuous enough to avoid attention. Damian had it on autopilot and was sitting on a deck chair, with a line in the water. Whatever he caught would be dinner tonight.

I could feel his eyes on me as I made my way to the railing. The water parted into two foamy trails as we cut through it. I wondered how deep it went and how hard I'd fight when my lungs started filling up with it. I thought of sinking to the bottom, in one glorious piece, instead of breaking apart tortuously, one tiny piece at a time.

Forgive me, Dad.

I stole a quick look at Damian. He had gone still—deathly still—like he knew exactly what was going through my head. I knew his body stance now. He'd been the same way, all his muscles pulled in, alert and tight and tense, right before he'd had his slice of vengeance. I'd felt it then, and I could feel it now.

The bastard. He wasn't going to let me do it. He'd be

on me before I could step a foot off the boat. He owned me. He owned my fate—my life, my death. He didn't need to say a word; it was there in his eyes. He compelled me off the edge. And I obeyed. I couldn't stop the sobs so I cried and I cried.

I cried the same way I'd cried when Gideon Benedict St. John had broken the clasp on my necklace and left chain marks on my neck.

ESTEBAN HAD FOUND ME AND was ready to go kick Gidiot's ass.

"Don't you dare." I made him promise. "You know what happens if you get in trouble one more time."

"I don't care." He swiped the hair off his forehead. He meant business when he did that.

"Please, Esteban. MaMaLu will send you away and I'll never see you again."

"MaMaLu's just bluffing."

Esteban called his mother MaMaLu. He'd always called her MaMaLu. She was his mama, but her name was Maria Luisa, so somewhere along the way, he'd started babbling MaMaLu, and it had stuck. Now everyone called her MaMaLu, except for Victor Madera, who worked for my father. He called her by her full name and MaMaLu didn't seem to like it. Or him.

"MaMaLu said next time you misbehave, she'll send you to your uncle."

"Ha!" Esteban laughed. "She can't even go a day without me."

It was true. MaMaLu and Esteban were inseparable, a hard-loving, quick-fighting part of my life. I couldn't imagine one without the other. They slept in a separate part of the estate, removed from the big house, a small wing that accommodated the help, but I could still hear them some nights—like the time Esteban was gone all day and didn't get back until past midnight.

That was the first year the cinema had opened in the village. They showed The Good, the Bad and the Ugly, *and Esteban stayed for all four screenings. MaMaLu had a right fit.*

"Estebandido!" She'd gone after him with a broom when he finally showed up.

Esteban knew he was in big trouble when she called him that. I heard his howl all the way up in my room. The next day he showed up for his chores, looking like Blondie, Clint Eastwood's character from the movie, wearing MaMaLu's shawl—all squinty-eyed and chewing on a whittled down tree stub.

The following year Esteban watched Enter The Dragon *and thought he was Bruce Lee.*

"What do you do, Skye?" he asked.

"I fight back and I fight hard." I repeated the line he had coached me to use, over and over again, because that was a line from one of the movies he'd seen.

"Ready?" he said. "On five."

5, 4, 3, 2, 1 . . .

I attempted to free myself from his chokehold. I grabbed his arm using both my hands and followed through with the move he'd taught me, trapping his leg with mine and making a sharp 180-degree turn before pulling him across and away from my body.

We ended up on the grass, a pile of limbs and sharp elbows. I laughed. Esteban did not think I made a good martial arts apprentice.

"You need practice. And discipline. How do you

expect to take on Gidiot if you can't even handle me?"

And so we practiced. Every day, Esteban turned into Estebandido, although he never liked playing the bad guy.

"Just for practice," he said. "Just for you, güerita. *Do it like this. Whoee-ahhhhh! Ready? On five."*

5, 4, 3, 2, 1 . . .

"No, no, no." He shook his head. "You have to make the sound."

"Whooo-ah!"

"No, Skye. Like a cat. Whoee-ahhh!"

The couple of times I managed to land Esteban on his back, his eyes shone with adoration.

"You're not so bad for a girl," he said.

We were lying in the shade of a tree, looking up at the sky. The branches were covered with clusters of delicate flowers, like yellow lace dripping down from brown limbs.

"I'll bring you cake tomorrow," I said.

He nodded and blew the hair out of his face. "Kick his butt if he tries anything, okay?"

I clasped his fingers and smiled.

Esteban wasn't invited to my birthday party, but Gidiot was. And all of the other kids who private-tutored with Miss Edmonds. There was a magician and a clown and an ice cream truck and piñatas. Silver and pink balloons bobbed all around the garden. I blew out nine candles while my father went nuts with the camera.

"Wait. I didn't get that. MaMaLu can you light the candles again? Skye, slowly this time," he said.

Esteban was perched on a ladder, cleaning the windows. Every so often, I looked over and he'd grin. He could see the big slice of cake I had hidden under the table. It had three juicy strawberries on it. Strawberries were Esteban's favorite, but he rarely got to eat them. The cake was our little secret and it made me feel like he was part of the festivities.

By the time we were done with the games and loot bags, the pink frosting was melting off Esteban's cake, so I decided to sneak off and give it to him.

"Where are you going, Skye?"

Gidiot had tailed me.

We were standing by the side of the house. I had Esteban's cake in one hand and a glass of lemonade in the other.

"Let me pass," I said when he blocked my way.

"Are you going to eat all that?" he asked.

"What's it to you?"

"Skye has a hole in her teeth and a hole in her tummy. She's a witch with a piggy tummy and no mummy!" He yanked me back as I pushed past him and the cake went splat on the ground.

I threw the lemonade in his face. That made him good and angry. He grabbed me by the waist and lifted me off the ground, shaking me like a rag doll.

"Skye!" Esteban stood before us. Sweat was pouring off his face from being in the sun. "On five."

We counted down together in our heads: 5, 4, 3, 2, 1 . . .

I kicked Gidiot in the knee. He doubled over. It was enough for Esteban to catch him unawares.

"Whoeee-ahhhh!" Esteban's fist connected with his face.

Gidiot let me go and staggered back. He put his hand to his mouth and spit out a tooth. Gideon Benedict St. John looked like a pink-gummed, gap-toothed old lady.

Then he let out a scream that was heard clear across Casa Paloma.

"If you can't take, don't give," said Esteban.

I'm pretty sure it was some lost-in-translation line from a martial arts movie. It didn't matter. Esteban didn't have time to elaborate. Victor Madera found us. He took one look at the situation and grabbed Esteban by the collar.

"You little punk!"

Esteban twisted and turned in Victor's grasp as the man dragged him away. "Touch her again and I'll see you in hell," he said to Gideon.

He was going all out with the movie dialogues. If I wasn't so terrified for him, I would have laughed.

The adults started to gather and everyone was fussing over Gidiot. They were trampling all over Esteban's strawberries.

It wasn't fair!

I chased after Victor and Esteban, but they were nowhere in sight. I gave up and trudged back up to my room.

Esteban had been there, probably before the party started. He'd left me a present on the bed. A perfect paper giraffe.

I picked it up and marveled at his dexterity. When Esteban was little, he didn't have many toys, so MaMaLu taught him origami. He couldn't afford to buy me fancy gifts, so he created whole worlds out of paper—magical, wondrous animals we'd only seen in books, or heard about in the stories that MaMaLu made up: dragons and lions and camels, and something that looked like a kangaroo, but had a horn sticking out of its nose. A kangaroceros?

"Skye?" My father knocked on my door. "Want to tell me what happened with Gideon?"

"Not really." I picked up the gangly giraffe and propped its neck up.

"Is that from Esteban?"

I didn't reply.

"Let me see." He took it from me and examined the gold leafed calligraphy on the paper.

"It's beautiful, isn't it?" I asked.

"It is. It's also from a rare book that's missing from my collection. I know you're friends with him, but he just knocked Gideon's tooth out, and now he's taken a book from my library? That's theft, Skye."

"He didn't take anything! I gave it to him."

"Really?" My father put the giraffe back down. "Then you'll know what color the cover is." He looked at me expectantly.

"Dad . . ." I was on the verge of tears, torn between my father and my friend. "Esteban probably thought it was just a dusty old book that no one would miss. I know he would never take it. He just borrowed it because he likes making me things out of pretty paper."

My father was quiet for a long time. "You're so much like your mother." He ran his thumb over the locket I was wearing. "She had me wrapped around her finger too."

"Tell me the story of how you met."

"Again?"

"Again."

He laughed. "Well, I had just graduated from college, not a penny to my name, but I wanted to see the world and found myself in Caboras with a few of my buddies. On our last night, we crashed a wedding and there she was: Adriana Nina Torres, the most beautiful girl in the world. I told her I was a successful entrepreneur, a friend of the groom's. She called security on me and had me thrown in the lock up for impersonating a guest at her brother's wedding. I knew it was love at first sight when she came to bail me out the next day."

"I wish I knew her." I never got tired of hearing their story, of how he had to prove himself to win her family over.

"You were the most precious thing in her life, Skye. I couldn't protect her, but I promise it will be different for you. I'm almost there. Just a little longer and we'll be free."

I didn't know what he meant, but I knew he missed my mother, and he loved me even though he was always away.

"Señor Sedgewick," Victor Madera interrupted from the door. "Gideon St. John's parents are downstairs. They are demanding something be done about Esteban."

"Dad." I tugged my father's hand. "Please don't tell MaMaLu about . . ." I gestured towards the paper giraffe. I didn't want to give Victor any more ammunition than he had. He seemed to enjoy tormenting Esteban. "She said she'll send him away."

"I want the book returned right away." My father shot me a warning look. "And no more 'borrowing'." He took my hand and we went downstairs to face Gidiot and his parents. They were seated stiffly on the sofa while MaMaLu and Esteban stood behind them.

For all of MaMaLu's threats, she protected Esteban fiercely when it came down to it, but she also knew her place and she knew her limits. "I will agree to whatever punishment Señor Sedgewick sees fit for my son." She held her head high.

Mr. and Mrs. St. John turned to my father while Gidiot smirked at Esteban and me.

"I'm sorry," said my father as his phone rang. "I have to take this." He talked for a few moments and hung up. "I'm afraid something urgent has come up, but I can assure you the matter will be dealt with properly." He left the St. John's little room to protest as he saw them out. "Look after it, Victor." He motioned to Esteban after they'd gone.

Victor smiled at MaMaLu, but she didn't smile back. I don't think she liked Victor picking Esteban's punishment.

"And one more thing." My father returned before she could say anything. "Tell Miss Edmonds she can expect a new student starting next week. I want Esteban to join the class."

MaMaLu's jaw dropped. "Thank you, Señor Sedgewick. Thank you so much."

"I believe you have a book to return, young man," my father said to Esteban. "I expect you to be in class and to stay out of trouble." I knew he was doing it to keep MaMaLu from sending him away.

"Yes, sir. I will." Esteban was smiling so big, I thought his face would crack.

"Happy Birthday, Skye." My father winked at me before he headed back out. In that moment, my world was complete. I was so happy, I didn't even care when Victor told Esteban to follow him out for his punishment.

MaMaLu stayed with me. We opened the rest of the presents and she ooh'd and aah'd over the extravagant gifts. We put Esteban's giraffe away last, with all of his other creations, because she knew I liked it best.

It was almost dark when MaMaLu opened the window and gasped. I flew to her side and saw Esteban on his hands and knees in the garden, cutting the grass . . . with a pair of scissors. It was the garden in the back, with prickly poppies and spiny weeds. Esteban winced with every step. His palms and knees were raw and his t-shirt clung to him from sweat and exertion.

I knew MaMaLu wanted to cuss Victor out, but she bit her tongue. She brushed my hair and tucked me into bed.

"Are you going to tell me a story tonight, MaMaLu?" I asked.

She got into bed with me and put her arm around me.

When Esteban finished, he climbed through the window and listened. It was a tale we hadn't heard before, about a magic swan that graced the grounds of Casa Paloma. If you caught a glimpse of it, you would be blessed with a rare treasure. MaMaLu told us that the swan hid in the garden, but once in a while, on a new moon, it liked to swim in the lily pond, by the tree with the yellow flowers.

Esteban smiled at me. He flexed his fingers because they were numb from holding the scissors for so long. I smiled back. Casa Paloma meant House of Doves. *Trust MaMaLu to throw in a swan. We both knew there were no magic swans, but we liked the sound of MaMaLu's voice.*

"Sing us the lullaby," I said, when she finished the story.

Esteban scooted over and knelt by the bed. MaMaLu turned her face away from him. She was still mad at him for punching Gidiot, but she let him put his head in her lap.

De la Sierra Morena,

Cielito lindo, vienen bajando . . .

It was Esteban's lullaby, from when he was a baby, but I was their cielito lindo*—their little piece of sky. I snuggled closer as she sang about birds that leave nests, and arrows, and wounds. Esteban and I lay with MaMaLu between us. We didn't move when it was done because it was soft and quiet, and we wanted to stay there forever.*

"Come, Esteban," said MaMaLu. "It's time we said goodnight."

"Wait." I wasn't ready to go to sleep yet. It had been the best birthday ever, in spite of Esteban's punishment. Tomorrow, he would go to class with me and not have to hide in the hutch anymore. "I haven't said my prayer."

We closed our eyes and held hands in a circle.

"Dear Lord, bless my soul. And watch over Dad. And MaMaLu and Esteban." My voice quivered with laughter because Esteban peeked and caught me peeking, and MaMaLu opened her eyes and rapped her knuckles on our heads.

IT WAS THE PRAYER THAT had saved me. Or doomed me. I couldn't decide which.

Damian had gone back to watching his line, supremely confident that I wouldn't do something as stupid as try to drown myself. His gaze was focused on some invisible spot on the horizon.

I looked through the railing and followed the flight of sea gulls as they caught an air current and rode it to the shore.

The shore.

I blinked.

For the first time in days, I could see land. We weren't heading towards it, we were running parallel to it, but I could make out trees and small structures and the glint of glass.

What do you do, Skye?

My eyes searched the deck.

I grab the fire extinguisher and bash his brains out.

I stood up slowly and made my way towards the shiny red cylinder.

Damian had his back to me so he didn't see it coming. I swung at him and felt an odd thrill at the sound of metal colliding against bone as it slammed into his jaw. *KLUNK.* His head flopped to one side and the fishing rod clattered to the floor. I hit him again, attacking the other side, and knocked him clean off the chair. He toppled over, back curled, limbs drawn to his chest, nursing his head between his hands.

That's right, asshole. How does it feel to be on the other side?

I was ready to whack him again when he went limp. His hands fell away and his face turned expressionless. I kicked him a few times, disappointed when he didn't respond. My hands were shaking and there was a wild beast within, a beast that wanted to pound and pound and pound the fire extinguisher into his face until his eyes and nose and lips turned into a bloody, scrambled mess. I didn't want him to go so easily. I wanted him to *suffer*.

I stopped, realizing that's exactly what he'd said about my father:

I just want him to feel *it. I want him to* suffer.

I was caught up in the same cycle, feeding the same monster. I was turning into Damian, thinking like him, acting like him, becoming a slave to the same dark, powerful emotions. It scared the hell out of me because even knowing that, I still held the fire extinguisher high over my head, wanting nothing more than to bring it down on Damian, again and again.

Vengeance only begets more vengeance, more chaos, more darkness. Vengeance abducts us and imprisons us and mutilates us, and we suffer and suffer until we unravel its probing parasitic suckers from around us.

I took a deep, steadying breath and let go of the fire extinguisher. When I could think clearly, I searched Damian. I knew he had a phone, but it wasn't on him. I ran to the deckhouse and started rifling through it. There was a steering station with panels for electronics and engine instrumentation, a chart table, seating area, and a mahogany entertainment center. I pulled all the drawers open. Roasted peanuts rolled around. Snacks, papers, maps, life jackets, a flashlight. No phone. I stared at the one drawer that was locked. It had to be there. It *had* to.

"Looking for this?" Damian staggered in, dangling the key before me.

Fuck.

He wasn't dead. He'd passed out and I'd been too busy to notice when he'd come around. He was like a ten-headed hydra. You cut off one head and he just keeps coming. I should have flattened his face into a bloody pancake.

I fled out the other door. I was still faster than he was. He plodded after me, clutching his head. I climbed the ladder to the roof of the deckhouse. If I could launch the rubber dinghy off it, I could get to shore. It was secured to some kind of pole and bolted down with ropes and hooks. I started tugging on one of hooks. It was halfway unlatched when I saw Damian's fingers grasp the top rung of the ladder. I tugged harder.

His head cleared the top.

I was almost there. But even if I managed to free the dinghy before Damian caught up to me, the cover was stretched tight across, and I had no idea how to start the engine.

Damian hoisted himself over the ladder.

I was out of time. I ran to the edge of the roof. We were closer to the piece of land jutting out in the horizon.

I was a strong swimmer.

I could make it.

I heard the thud of Damian's foot as he climbed on the roof.

I took a deep breath and dived into the water.

The salt water set my severed finger on fire. I came up, gasping for air. Damian was looking down at me from the boat, an ominous shadow against the backdrop of white clouds—an *unsteady* ominous shadow. He was struggling to stay on his feet.

Good. I got him good.

I oriented myself with the horizon and started swimming towards land. The water was much colder than I anticipated, but it was calm and the adrenaline was pumping through my veins with each breath I took. I had gone a good distance before I looked back.

The boat was in the same spot and Damian was nowhere in sight. Maybe he'd figured it best to let me go. Maybe it was enough that my father had really experienced my death, *felt it, suffered*. Whatever his reason, Damian chose not to follow me.

I resumed my strokes. *1, 2, 3, breathe. 1, 2, 3, breathe.* I paused after what felt like an eternity, and looked up. I didn't seem to be any closer to the shoreline. Distances are tricky in the water—what seems like a short distance can take hours. I kicked off my pants, and kept swimming and breathing and swimming and breathing. When the pain in my finger started to subside, I realized my extremities were going numb. I stopped to catch my breath.

The boat was still visible and Damian had now resumed fishing.

Un-fucking-believable. Shouldn't he be bleeding out from a concussion or fleeing for safety? My father was going to unleash the hounds of hell on him.

I had gone a few more paces when I froze. There was something in the water, a few feet away. It broke through the surface and I caught sight of a black fin. It disappeared, but I could feel its dark form circling around me.

Fuck.

No wonder Damian hadn't bothered coming after me. We were in shark-infested waters, and I had jumped in with a bandage soaked with blood.

I had single-handedly solved his dilemma of what to do with me.

An hour ago, I'd wanted to drown myself, but I really, *really* didn't want to go this way, ripped to pieces by a sea monster with conveyor-belt rows of sharp, pointy teeth.

"Damian!" I started waving my arms. "Damian!"

I didn't know why I was calling for him. Maybe it's just basic human instinct to turn to the only person around. Maybe a part of me sensed that somewhere, deep inside, he still held a shred of humanity.

I felt something brush against my feet, something cold and hard. I probably shouldn't be moving or making so much noise, but I didn't know how else to get his attention. I removed my waterlogged, bloody bandage and tossed it as far away from me as possible.

"Damian. Help!" I screamed.

I saw him get up and peer into the water. Then he went to the deckhouse and brought out binoculars. I waved frantically while he looked through the lens. The damn thing was circling me openly now, preparing for the kill.

Damian looked a little longer. Then he dropped the binoculars and sat back down. I could see him reach into his tackle box and pull out something.

Yes. A gun. A sniper rifle. A mother-fucking harpoon.

He retrieved something I couldn't make out, put his feet up and popped something in his mouth.

I choked on a lungful of seawater.

He was eating *peanuts* while he watched, as if it was time for popcorn and a matinee.

I coughed and flailed around. How could I have even entertained the notion that he would jump to my aid? So he hadn't killed me. And he'd stopped me from killing myself. But he wasn't opposed to letting me go this way. The hot blond in shark movies always gets ripped to shreds.

I could feel the water churn around me as the shark got closer. A dark face broke through the surface and I screamed. It disappeared and came forward again. I braced myself, expecting the sharp slice of teeth, but what I got was a beak. I was nose to nose with a smiley-faced dolphin. My heart was still racing a mile a minute when it nudged me, as if to say, "Hey, lighten up."

I let my breath out in a big splutter that must have startled it, because it drew away. It had a prominent back fin and its flippers were long and slender with pointed tips.

Not a shark, Skye. A dolphin.

And judging by the size of it, a curious baby.

It zoomed around me, showing off its pink underbelly, before turning sharply and swimming away. I made out another form—this one bigger, most likely the mother. The two dolphins exchanged high-pitched squeaks before the little one came back to me. It swam beside me for a while, mimicking my motions, floating when I floated, flipping when I flipped. Then it whistled three times—little dolphin chirps—before taking off.

I watched the mother and calf disappear. I could see the flash of binoculars from the boat. Damian was watching too. He knew the sea, he knew the difference between a shark's fin and a dolphin's, and he'd chosen to let me be.

I floated on my back, exhausted, elated, horrified, glorified. I thought I was going to die and yet I'd never felt more alive. I heard the engine rev up and I knew Damian was coming for me. He cut the engine a few feet away from me. I looked longingly at the outline of the land mass on the horizon, but I knew I'd been foolish to think I'd get there. Damian had known that too. He'd just hung back, waiting for me to wear myself out. And it had worked. I couldn't go any further, float any longer.

I would have to plan things more carefully next time.

I climbed up the ladder at the back of the boat and flopped, belly down, on the deck.

Damian continued fishing.

Seven

WHEN I WOKE UP, I was still facedown on the deck. The stars were out and Damian had covered me with a blanket. It was late May or early June. I had lost track of the days, but I knew we were heading south, somewhere along the Pacific coast of Baja Mexico.

I was born in Mexico, birthed by a midwife at Casa Paloma. Mexico had been home for nine years, but I had never been back. I wondered how far we were from Paza del Mar, and if MaMaLu had retired there, and bought a white house with a red tile roof—the kind she'd always stopped to admire on our way to the market. I wondered if Esteban put in a wrought iron fence and helped her plant flowers in the yard. It would be small, of course, because MaMaLu never dared to dream big, and she was always afraid when Esteban did. Even then, he had been larger than life, and no one, and nothing was going to stand in his way. And if he knew someone had abducted me, he would find me and rescue me, and God help Damian.

Maybe he already knew. Maybe he'd heard the news. Maybe he believed I was dead, just like my father. Either way, Esteban would not rest until he had Damian. He was my hero, my champion, my lean, mean, Gidiot-punching machine. I could picture him in pirate garb and a fake eye-patch, commanding a ship from Paza del Mar, scouring the seas for me.

I smiled, because the brain can conjure up the most ridiculous, improbable scenarios that are so far off center, you have to wonder at the power of imagination. Even in his absence, Esteban was keeping the bad guys and bad thoughts at bay.

I heard the scrape of something on the deck.

Damian was unfolding a deck chair. He propped it up beside his, with a small table separating the two.

"Eat." He motioned to the plate on the table, before digging into his own. One hand held a bag of ice over his jaw, where I'd hit him.

I got up warily, not knowing what to expect. Food? Punishment? Retaliation? But he said nothing as I took the seat next to him. Maybe he was just as tired and wrung out as me. I was suddenly aware of being pant-less, and wrapped the blanket tighter around myself.

Dinner was the same as always. Fish and rice. Maybe a different kind of fish, but always the same rice. I guess it was convenient—it didn't spoil and it did the job. Simple, uncomplicated rice.

We ate in silence, watching the half-moon that rose in the sky. It was bright and warm, like a slice of powdered lemon candy. Without any lights to obscure them, the stars were dazzling and diamond clear. Big bands of light glowed in the water as swirls of fish streaked phosphorescent trails below the surface. Larger, darker forms chased after them and they danced like whirling dervishes around the boat.

It was better than any fashion show—the shine and sparkle and music of the night. The water was miles and miles of midnight velvet, and we were bobbing up and down on it like a piece of lint, small and insignificant in the face of its majesty.

I thought of all the nights I'd spent in temperature controlled clubs and restaurants, under artificial lights, drinking artificial cocktails with artificial friends. Artificial problems. Artificial drama. How many *real*, glorious nights had I missed? Nights like this, when the universe dances for you, and you become a tiny but beautiful note of the magical song it sings.

"Skye," said Damian, but I couldn't stop the tears.

It was like a great, big cleansing. All the good and bad and sad and glad broke loose.

I hated being weak in front of him. I hated when he picked me up and I clung to him. I hated when he carried me downstairs and put me in the shower. I hated when he wiped me dry and helped me dress. I hated when he put medicine and a fresh bandage on my finger. I hated when he tucked me in and turned off the lights. I hated that I wanted him to stay and hold me and stroke my hair, because that Stockholm syndrome shit? I *hated* that it was happening to me.

I AWOKE THE NEXT MORNING to what sounded like dozens of cannons being hurled into the sea. We were under attack—someone had caught up to us. I ran up the stairs, expecting to be surrounded by a fleet of boats, with my father holding a loudspeaker:

Come out with your hands in the air.

He'd see me and I was alive! And three kisses would turn into six, and nine, and twelve.

Thank God you got here, Dad, because it was just me and Damian, and he cut my finger, and I was surrounded by sharks, and he left me, but it was just dolphins, you see, and then I saw a real *night, and something was starting to happen, and my head wasn't right and—*

There were no boats. No loudspeaker. No Dad.

We were anchored in the shadow of a steep cliff.

Dozens of pelicans were diving into the water, and coming up with sardines for breakfast. Sometimes they hit the water at the same time and the resulting splashes sounded like shells exploding in a war zone.

Damian was swimming on the other side of the boat. His strokes were long and lean, and he was oblivious to the chaos around us. He had the perfect swimmer's body—powerful legs, broad shoulders, narrow hips. He rotated his body left and then right, one shoulder out, as he breathed through each stroke. He was quiet and efficient, barely lifting his chin above the surface, but I was so focused on each inhalation that everything else faded—all the noise, all the birds—until there was only him, his breath, and the wet rasp of his lips. It was rhythmic and steady and forceful and mesmerizing and . . . overwhelmingly male.

Something clicked inside me at that moment. I stood outside of myself, realizing how easy it was to judge someone, to vilify and condemn the things we don't understand, because:

OMG. How can she even THINK that way about the guy who kidnapped her? HE CUT HER FINGER OFF!

Or

That person should have known better than to get into the car with a stranger.

Or

How could she stay with him that long when he abused her day in and day out?

Or

Monster. He shot and killed his own family.

Because those are all things we're not supposed to do, and yet inside of me was a kernel of the inexplicable from which dark things bloom, something I couldn't understand or justify. I knew better than to *romanticize* my captor, but there it was—sick and twisted and disgusting as it was. And it scared me. It scared me because I saw a glimmer of all the terrifying things we're capable of, because the human psyche is such a fragile thing, a yolk contained within a brittle shell—one crack and out it spills: a neighbor goes on a suicide mission, tribes massacre tribes, countries turn their faces away from injustices. And it all starts within, because within is where all things begin.

I ran to the bedroom and shut the door. I needed to barricade myself against . . . myself. I needed to think about foosball and Pacman and pizza with Nick—a triathlon of nice, normal things with a nice, normal guy—someone worth romanticizing.

"Breakfast." There was no knocking or privacy or nice, normal courtesies with Damian. He just walked in.

We faced each other for the first time since my stupid, clingy breakdown the night before. I didn't know where he'd slept, but he hadn't come down after he put me to bed. He looked at me like he always did—intense and impenetrable. He must have showered because he smelled like absinthe and mint. And I really, really wanted him to smell like pelicans and sardines.

"We'll be anchoring in Bahia Tortugas tonight," he said as we ate. "We need to refuel and fill up the water tank."

I had no idea where Bahia Tortugas was, but fuel and water meant some kind of port or marina, and that meant we'd be around people.

Damian was warning me. *Don't do anything stupid.*

I nodded and finished my food. *We'll see about that.*

I was even more desperate to escape now.

IT WAS DARK WHEN THE rugged hills of Bahia Tortugas came into view. I had a feeling it was more out of design than coincidence. Damian had planned it so we came in when it attracted the least amount of attention. My heart started to race as we approached the harbor. I had to grab whatever opportunity presented itself in the next few hours.

I stood in front of the mirror and took a deep breath. My hair was dirty and knotted, and I was floating in one of Damian's t-shirts. I jumped in the shower and washed my hair. People were less likely to help a greasy haired androgynous runaway, so I rifled through my shopping bags and put on a slinky top and frayed denim shorts. Boobs and legs always get noticed. I found a make-up palette and applied some eyeliner and lip gloss.

By the time I was done, Damian had dropped anchor. We weren't as close to the pier as I'd hoped to be, and looking out from the porthole I could see only two other boats. It was the perfect lonely outpost for a pit stop.

My spirits lifted when a couple of pangas came out to greet us. If it weren't for the yellow glow from the kerosene lanterns on their masts, I would have missed the small dugout canoes. I remembered enough Spanish to figure out that the men were offering their services and negotiating rates for diesel and water. I thought of running topside, screaming for help, but it was dark and Damian could easily overpower me before I attracted much attention.

I was still peering out of the stateroom window when Damian came in. He stopped in his tracks when he saw me. For one full, glorious second, he wasn't in control. His gaze swept the length of my legs, over the hip-hugging shorts, and lingered on the swell of my breasts under the scandalous top. Ha! He wasn't immune after all. He caught the smug look on my face before I could wipe it off, and his eyes narrowed.

Shit.

I took one step back for each one he took forward, until I was jammed up between him and the wall.

God, he was intense. And deliberate. And he could say things with his eyes that made my knees tremble. One side of his face was bruised and distorted from where I'd hit him. He grasped both my wrists in one hand and pinned them above me. Every part of me felt flush with the heat emanating from his body, even though that was the only point of contact. He hooked a finger in the 'V' of my blouse, tracing the dangerously low cleavage. His touch was so soft, it was barely discernible.

"Skye?" He seemed hypnotized by the rapid rise and fall of my chest.

I swallowed.

"Don't play with scorpions unless you intend to get stung." He yanked the neckline apart.

Round, glass buttons popped onto the floor and rolled around like eyeballs, astounded by the sight of my bare flesh.

"We're harsh and predatory and full of venom." He gnashed his teeth at me and ripped my blouse in two.

He tore off a strip and bound my wrists. Then he used the hanging trail like a leash and led me to bed.

"You've been trying to get a rise out of me for days. Now that you have my attention, what are you going to do?" He leaned forward, so close that I fell back onto the mattress, trying to get away from him. "Or is it that you want *me* to do all the work so your pampered pussy gets a taste of the other side, but you can tell yourself you didn't have a choice?" He crawled up over me, slowly, until we were nose to nose.

I felt like hell was about to consume me. I could hear the men outside, gearing up to fill the tanks. Would they hear the sound of my screams?

"Would you like me to invite them in?" Damian secured my wrists to the bed post. "Do you really think you'd be safer with them instead of me?" He tore off another strip, giving me the chance to scream or yell or shout for help. When I didn't, he tied it around my mouth.

He sank back on his heels, kneeling between my legs, and ran a finger from my neck to the front clasp of my bra. I stopped breathing. He moved on, trailing over my stomach, until he got to the band of my shorts. He toyed with the tab, enjoying the start-stop effect it had on my heart.

"Such a frightened little bird," he said. Then he yanked my legs around his hips so I was flush with his rock hard arousal. "You should know better than to provoke me."

He rocked against me like that, fully clothed, imprinting his full weight and length on me. Then he got off the bed and spread my legs, tying them to opposite corners. I squeezed my eyes shut as he walked around, checking the knots, ensuring they would hold. Everything inside me was quaking and quivering. I was completely, *completely* at his mercy.

"Maybe now you'll behave," he said.

My heart was beating triple time.

I expected his hands on me, but he put on his baseball cap, turned off the lights and left, locking the door behind him. I heard him conversing with the men, and then the sound of a small engine, as one of the pangas took off for the shore.

I wondered if he'd taken my severed finger to mail to my father:

Warren Sedgewick: Special Delivery.

I should have felt relief for whatever task had called him away, but I felt only apprehension—not knowing when he'd return, or what awaited me. My mind spun infinite, terrifying wormholes in the dark, the worst of which was the shameful possibility that I wouldn't fight him when he came back.

THE FUEL LINES WERE STILL running when Damian got back. He wasn't alone. I knew the tap-tap-tap of high-heeled shoes; he had brought a companion.

My muscles tensed as I heard footsteps outside the door. I was soaked in a pool of sweat, and my finger was starting to throb. I jumped at the loud thud on the door, expecting it to burst open, but it remained locked. There was a muffled gasp and then more thudding.

For a moment I thought he had dragged in another victim, that she was struggling to get away, but the thudding turned rhythmic and the sounds coming out of her alternated between pleasure and pain.

Damian was fucking her against the door. Hard. Fast. The sick bastard wanted to make sure I knew exactly what he was doing—he was choosing her over me, working out the sexual frustration I'd stirred up in him. He'd rather pay a local hooker than acknowledge lust, desire, or weakness for any part of me. I was a non-entity, an empty vessel for vengeance. All the time that I'd spent imagining him forcing himself on me had been cruel, deliberate punishment. He'd set it loose in my head—passed on the baton and I'd run with it. I had let him defile me and violate me in the most unspeakable ways and I had done it all by myself, in my head.

I didn't like the emotions surging through me. I should've been grateful it was her and not me, but I felt humiliated. Dejected. Rejected. I should've been disgusted by the sounds of their sex, steadfast in my hatred of Damian, but I was wobbly and confused.

The woman cried out when she climaxed—a sharp, shuddering sigh. Everything went still, except for the sound of heavy breathing. It didn't last long though. The pounding resumed. I could hear her begging, pleading, but I didn't know whether it was for him to stop or *not* stop.

They moved away from the door. There was a crash. Something cluttered to the floor. I closed my eyes, hoping to shut out the guttural sounds coming from the galley. It's a silly thing we do—shutting our eyes to stop ourselves from hearing something. And it made it worse. I could picture them in the room now, her bent over the chair as he took her like an animal, because that's what sex with Damian sounded like—wild and primal and ferocious.

It went on forever. The man was a beast. When he let go, it was in a series of short, breathless grunts. I unclenched my teeth, realizing I'd been coiled up through the whole thing, as if I'd been there with him.

The woman said something, but it was too soft for me to catch. I thought I heard Damian laugh, but I couldn't picture him doing that—*ever*—so I must have imagined it. They conversed in low tones for a while. Then I heard their footsteps up on deck.

Damian was paying the men, or the woman, or both. Fuel and water for the boat, a good fuck for its owner. We were all set. I didn't stand a chance—there would be no opportunity to escape. I listened to the drone of the pangas fading into the distance.

Damian entered the room when they were gone. He was still wearing his baseball cap. I doubted he'd let the woman see his full face, or if he'd even completely disrobed. Probably just dropped his pants and taken her against the door.

He surveyed me as I lay on the bed, my legs splayed, with nothing on but my shorts and my bra. "Dinner," he said, as he removed the gag from my mouth.

"I'm not hungry."

He took his time undoing the straps around my legs and wrists.

"I think you're forgetting how this works," he said quietly, deliberately examining my bandaged finger.

He didn't have to say anything else. I loathed him, loathed *myself* for letting him break me. I followed him out to the galley, rubbing my sore wrists. He unfolded a greasy paper bag and placed some hot dogs on a plate. I should have been all over them after days of fish and rice, but all I could smell was Scent of Whore. The dish rack was on the floor and things looked liked they'd been swept right off the counter.

"Eat." Damian wolfed down his share, and started putting away the supplies he'd picked up.

When the fridge was stocked up, he got a can-opener and opened a can of evaporated milk. I watched him pour it into a clear, lidded jar. I guessed it stored better than fresh milk. He turned to the coffee maker and started measuring out the coffee.

My eyes fell on the jagged, metal top of the can he'd just opened. It was lying in the garbage, by my feet. I reached down and grabbed it. Damian still had his back to me.

I closed my palm over the circular piece of tin and felt the sharp, barbed edge. That's what I needed to sink into his jugular.

On five, Skye. On five.

I took a deep breath and counted down.

5, 4, 3, 2, 1 . . .

I caught him as he turned. It was a perfect cut, except he intercepted my wrist before I could go deeper. His eyes widened at the sharp, piercing pain before the hard *thwack* of his slap hit me. He flung me clear across the kitchen, my cheek turning red from the imprint of his palm.

He plucked the metal out of his neck and clamped his hand to the wound. I wanted his blood to spurt out onto the counter, where he'd spilled mine. I wanted him to fall to his knees and die in a pool of red vengeance. I wanted to see me in his eyes when he took his last breath.

None of that happened. Damian swore and removed his hand to inspect the damage. It was a nice sized gash, but I had just scratched the surface—a couple of Band-Aids and he'd be good to go. He started walking towards me, an unrelenting, indestructible force that I just *couldn't* get away from, and I broke down. I nursed my throbbing cheek and sobbed. And sobbed.

"If you can't take, don't give," he growled.

If you can't take, don't give.

If you can't take don't give.

A boy I once adored had said that. Right after he'd knocked Gideon Benedict St. John's tooth out.

My thoughts flip-flopped like livewires on an overloaded circuit.

No.

Every atom in me rebelled at the idea.

I looked up at the figure looming over me. The boy had changed into a man—his body had changed, his voice had changed, his face had changed. But people's eyes should never be so different that you no longer recognized their souls; they should never turn so hard that they shut all the doors to the past.

"Esteban?" I whispered.

No. Please say no.

"There is no Esteban. Esteban died a long time ago." He pulled me up and trapped me against the counter. "There is only Damian. And you don't defy or escape or seduce Damian. And you sure as hell don't *fantasize* about him," he spit out.

I blinked, trying to come to terms with the fact that the boy I'd worshiped and the man I abhorred were one and the same, but I couldn't bridge the bleak, black chasm in-between. It started stretching, opening, swallowing me up. The ground was disappearing from under my feet.

"Skye." Damian shook me, but it only made the crack inside me worse. I felt myself falling into it, welcoming the nothingness that enveloped me.

Nine

WHEN I CAME AROUND, DAMIAN was sleeping next to me.

Yes, Dah-me-yahn.

Because that's who he was now. I tried to look for the boy I'd known, but there was no place for him to hide in the harsh planes of Damian's face. He had been twelve years old the last time I'd seen him. Fifteen years had changed him into the man before me now, taken away the softness, the expressions, deepened his voice, hardened his heart. The moon turned his skin a silvery-blue and accentuated the shadow of his brows and nose. He was sleeping shirtless for the first time, as if he was done with all the masks and layers and pretenses. For all I knew, he wasn't wearing a stitch under the covers.

I inched away from him, towards the edge of the bed.

Something wet and lumpy shifted under me. A thawed out bag of frozen veggies for my cheek.

That's right, Damian. Slap me and ice me better.

Can't kill me, but can't let me go either.

I finally understood what I had seen in his eyes. Black battling Black. Damian keeping Esteban at bay. Cruelty with glimpses of mercy. Friendship holding vengeance back by a thread.

I couldn't understand his actions, but there was obviously bad blood between my father and Damian, and I needed to figure it out. As far as I knew, the last time the two had been together was the day of my ninth birthday, when my father had asked Victor to enroll him in Miss Edmond's class.

Esteban had never showed. I had woken up and waited for MaMaLu, but she never came—not that day, or the next, or the day after that. When one of the maids came in and started packing my clothes in a large trunk, I threw a tantrum.

"Why is Abella putting my things away?" I asked when my father arrived. "Where is MaMaLu?"

"We're going to San Diego, Skye." My father folded the papers he was holding and rubbed his temples. "We'll be away for a while. MaMaLu took another job."

"You never said anything about going away! When? MaMaLu and Esteban would never leave without saying goodbye."

"Skye, I know you've always thought of them as family, but they go where MaMaLu's work takes her. I'm sure they just wanted to make this easy for you."

"I don't believe you." I pushed him away. "I'm not going anywhere until I see them."

"Those can stay," my father said to Abella, who was

tucking away the paper creations that Esteban had made for me.

"I'm not leaving those behind!" I grabbed the box from her.

"We only have room for important stuff, Skye, and we have to be quick about it. We leave for the airport soon. I need you to help Abella, and get ready. Can you do that, Skye?"

"No! I won't! I'm not going anywhere. I'm not packing anything. You *go."*

"Skye—"

"You're always gone anyways. I'm staying here, and when MaMaLu finds out, she'll come back and we'll—"

"Skye!"

I don't know which of us was more surprised when he slapped me. It was hard and sharp, and it stung. The box fell out of my hands and we both stared at the paper animals lying at our feet.

"When are you going to understand that they're just the help?" said my father. "They're not blood, they're not family. The only person you can count on is me. And the only person I can count on is you. Everything else and everyone else will come and go. If MaMaLu and Esteban want to see you, they will find a way. And you can write to them. As often as you like. But we have to leave now, Skye. We don't have a choice."

And so I'd gone, even though I kept turning back as we left Casa Paloma. I thought I heard Esteban calling my name, but all I saw through the rear window were plumes of dust as we drove down the dirt road. I turned back when we left Mexico. I turned back when we landed in the States. I turned back every time I saw a boy with skin like Esteban, and I turned back every time I caught a glimpse of long, dark hair adorned with flowers.

After a while, I stopped turning back because MaMaLu and Esteban never replied to the strawberry scented letters I sent, or the carefully glued photo collages I made: *This is my new school. This is my new room. This is my new address. This is my new hair cut because my hair grew too long and there's no one to brush it for me, now. I miss you, MaMaLu. Write back, Esteban. On five, okay?*

Eventually, I buried the memories, along with the hurt. Our trip to San Diego turned out to be a permanent stay. When my father slapped me that day, he'd slammed the door shut—my world had turned wary and guarded. Family is family. Friends aren't forever. Everything will break. People say goodbye. Get too close and you get hurt.

When Damian slapped me, he'd blown the same world apart, bringing down tiny little pieces that I was still trying to put together. There was more to the story than my father had told me. MaMaLu and Esteban *hadn't* just left without saying goodbye. Something had happened. Something that had turned Esteban into Damian.

I thought he'd chopped and dyed my hair black to keep people from recognizing me, but he'd done it for himself, so I bore no resemblance to the girl he used to know. Damian was set on revenge for whatever horrible, terrible thing he thought my father had done, and whatever associations he had of me were buried so deep in his psyche that he was able to do horrible, terrible things to me. He treated me like a *thing* rather than a *person* to safeguard himself. He hurt me, humiliated me, shut out my voice, my face, my tears. But once in a while, those memories came back, and they still meant something because they shook him out of the red haze of anger and hatred. The Esteban I knew was in there somewhere, and he'd heard me praying for him.

He was the only reason I was still alive.

I didn't know how long I had, but I knew there was no point asking Damian to explain *why* he was doing this. He would never have come this far if he didn't feel justified. There was only one person who could get through to him.

I had to find a way to get to MaMaLu before it was too late.

Ten

BREAKFAST WAS TIGHT-LIPPED AS DAMIAN and I stared into our plates. I wanted to look at him so badly in the daylight, to really, *really* look at him. It hurt to chew. My lip was swollen so I pushed the food around. Damian had covered the cut on his neck with a piece of gauze. The longer we stayed together, the longer our list of cuts and bruises grew—both inside and out.

"How is MaMaLu?" I asked, holding on to my coffee.

The sea was rough and things were sliding back and forth on the counter.

"I'd like to see her," I said, when he didn't reply.

He dumped his plate into the sink and turned to me. "That's where we're headed. If you can make it through the next fourteen days, you'll get to see her."

Damian had mentioned twenty-one days earlier.

We had been on the boat for about a week, which meant that he had been counting down the days until he saw MaMaLu.

"Does she know . . . ?" *That you planned to kill me?* "Does she know to expect me?"

I caught a pained expression cross his eyes before he turned away. Of course she didn't know. She would never stand for it. If I could just make it to her in one piece, MaMaLu would fix everything. MaMaLu knew how to fix things—lost things, hurt things, cracked things, cut and bruised things.

I watched through the porthole as we left Bahia Tortugas. A colony of sea lions surfed behind us, playing in our wake.

Ay, yai, yai, yai,
Sing and do not cry. . .

The thought of seeing MaMaLu comforted me and for the first time, I felt a glimmer of hope.

We sailed past rocky cliffs obscured by swirling clouds of haze. As the day progressed, the waves got choppier and the sky turned dark and ominous. I could hear the crackle of the radio from upstairs, but Damian's voice was drowned out as the bar stools toppled over. Everything went crashing and rolling as the boat lurched and heaved.

I held on to the walls as I made my way upstairs. Sharp, cold needles of rain pelted down on me. The sky was a scene of high drama. Black clouds roiled towards us, dragging deep shadows across white-capped water. The wind whistled in the rigging and came at me in shrieking gusts. I couldn't make out the horizon. Then I peered into the eerie darkness and realized why. Up ahead was a wall of water so high, that I had to tilt my head back.

HOLY FUCK.

"Get back down!" Damian shouted over the chaos as I struggled to stay on my feet.

The boat began flying off the crests and crashing into the troughs, bringing us to an abrupt, heart-stopping halt through each terrifying wave. I held on to the railing, but the metal was wet and I kept losing my grip. Buckets of water were being tossed in my face and my feet slipped on the deck.

Damian barked something into the radio and hung up. He made his way towards me, fighting against the wind, and slipped a life vest over me. I couldn't hear what he was saying. We were falling into each wave with a resounding crash. He pointed towards the stairs and started inching his way back to the cockpit.

I was almost there when I heard something whip past me—a high-pitched, metallic *whoosh*. I looked up and realized that one of the lines securing the dinghy had come loose and was whipping around in the wind—probably the one I had unlatched partially when I was on the roof. The heavy, steel fastener at the end had just missed me and was swinging back, heading straight for me. I stood paralyzed, unable to move, unable to breath, as the wrecking ball of death came for me.

"Skye!" Damian pushed me out of the way a millisecond before it hit.

I rolled on the deck, knocked off my feet. I heard a crash, the sound of glass shattering, and opened my eyes. The line had slammed into one of the windows and the hook was lodged in its frame. The dinghy was barely contained by the two remaining latches, and looked like it was about to come loose.

"Damian." I turned to him.

He was lying by my side, but didn't respond. There was big, wide gash on the side of his head. Blood was oozing out and mixing with the rain.

"Damian!" I knelt beside him.

Oh God. Please wake up.

But his body was limp and his head rolled from side to side as the boat lurched like a bucking bronco.

"Damian, please," I cried. *I can't do this alone.*

The ocean swelled around us in wild, terrifying chaos. I needed him. I needed his fierce brutality to conquer the waves and take us to MaMaLu. I needed his frost and his bite and his unrelenting fury to power us through the storm.

"What do you do, Skye?" I thought I heard him say as I held his bleeding head in my lap.

I glanced at the cockpit. Damian hadn't locked the radio up. It was still crackling with static. This was my chance—to escape, to get away, to make a run for it. So why was I still holding on to Damian?

Because he saved you.

Because he pushed you out of the way.

Because if you call the authorities, you know they'll put him away.

Don't be a fucking idiot, Skye. Make the call!

I stumbled to the radio, my stomach dropping every time the boat fell into a wave. I fiddled with the controls until I figured out which one I pressed to talk. I had no idea who was out there, in Mexican waters, or what the proper procedure was for a distress call.

"This is Skye Sedgewick. Hello? Can anyone hear me?"

Nothing.

"This is Skye Sedgewick. I am the missing daughter of Warren Sedgewick. I've been kidnapped, and am somewhere off the Pacific Coast of Mexico. Our boat is caught in a storm. We need urgent help. Please respond."

I closed my eyes and held my breath. The contents of the cabin were spilling everywhere—books, charts, cushions, pens.

A garbled message came from the other end.

"Hello?" I prompted. "Are you there?"

More static, and then a man's voice. He said something about not being able to receive the message clearly, and then I heard the word 'phone'.

"Hold on," I said.

A key was sticking out of the drawer that Damian kept locked. There were three things inside: a rusted metal box, a revolver, and a satellite phone.

"I have it!" I grabbed the phone. "What's your number?"

I jotted down what the man told me and called him. My hands were shaking as I explained the situation.

"Where is the man who kidnapped you?" he asked.

"He's hurt. He passed out."

"Can you give me your co-ordinates?"

"I don't know how to read the panels."

I listened as he guided me through it, and then I read the numbers back to him.

"Is the boat on autopilot?" he asked.

"How do I tell?"

He talked me through it and had me set the course so we could meet his boat faster.

"We're not too far. Hold tight. Don't panic. Help is on the way."

"Thank you." I let out a deep, shuddering breath.

It was happening. I was getting rescued. I was going to make it through this dark tunnel of hell and high water; I was going to make it back to three kisses; I was going to have more Pancake Sundays with all the toppings I could dream of. Suddenly, I was filled with a deep longing to hear my father's voice again, to let him know I was alive.

I dialed his number and waited.

"Hello." He sounded groggy and tired. It must have been late where he was.

"Dad?" I wanted to weep, but I didn't want to alarm him, so I clenched my throat to choke back the sobs.

It was so quiet at the other end—stillness—when everything around me was rolling and churning.

"Skye?" He fumbled. I knew he was looking for his glasses, as if putting them on would make my voice more real.

"Skye? Is that you?" He was completely alert now, completely awake.

"Dad." I couldn't keep my voice from cracking.

"Skye." This time it wasn't a question. He grabbed on to my name like he'd been flailing around for a lifeline and now he'd found it.

"I'm okay, Dad." I sobbed.

Neither of us could find the words to say anything else. I'd never heard my father cry before.

"Tell me where you are," he said.

"I'm on a boat. I don't know exactly where, but I'm being rescued. I'll be in touch whe—" The call got cut off before I could finish.

"Hello." I paused. "Hello?"

The battery was dead. I hugged the phone to my chest, knowing my father was still at the other end.

Stay with me.

Stay with me just a little longer.

The wind had died by the time I put the phone away. The storm was starting to pass. The dinghy had held, but the waves remained strong. Damian was still out, his body rocking with the motion of the boat.

I grabbed the first aid kit from the deckhouse. Then I went back and got Damian's gun. I cleaned and dressed his wound, with the gun tucked firmly in my pants. I wasn't taking any chances. The cut was deep. Damian needed stitches, but all I knew was the basics, so I covered it up with thick gauze. It didn't take long before the blood had seeped through. I held a towel to his head, hoping the pressure would slow it down.

We were drifting on autopilot when the radar started beeping.

My rescue was almost here.

I pushed Damian's hair away from his forehead. It was caked with blood.

Why, Estebandido?

I wanted to weep because someone I loved had died in that face, and I didn't know when or how, and I never got to mourn him. And now they were going to take him away, the boy inside the man.

Lightning split the sky and for a second, I saw him. Esteban. His fingers were stained, his smile was wide, and he had just tasted strawberries for the first time.

What happened to you?

What happened?

I cradled his head and rocked back and forth.

And then the other boat was upon us, and a man was climbing aboard.

"It's okay. Everything is going to be all right," he said.

"You can let go of the gun."

I didn't realize I'd been holding it until he pried it away.

He took the towel from my hand and inspected Damian's wound. It was soaked in bright red.

Damian's eyes flickered open. "Rafael," he whispered, when he saw the man.

The blood chilled in my veins. I knew that name. I'd heard Damian talking to him on the phone.

Did you get that? Damian had said to Rafael, the man on the other end, who had been recording my screams.

"I'm here, Damian," said the man I thought had come to rescue me. "I'm here."

Eleven

WE SAILED PAST COVE AFTER cove along the coastline, with Rafael manning Damian's boat, and his friend, Manuel, following behind on the other one. I sat with Damian's head on my lap, as he bled out in the night. A couple of times, he opened his eyes, but they were glazed over. Each time, a raw, primitive grief overwhelmed me because there were flashes of Esteban in those eyes. Whatever he was feeling, whatever he was thinking, Damian was lying bare before me now. I could *feel* his pain. Not the kind that was slowly seeping out of him, but the torment that was bottled up inside. It was rattling up against the iron cage of his heart, with no way out. Damian tossed and turned as I tried to contain him.

"*Shhh. Shhh.*" I don't know when I started humming MaMaLu's lullaby. I don't know if it was for him or for me, but it seemed to comfort him and he stopped thrashing around.

The water was calm now, but it was cold, and we were both soaking wet. Damian was shaking. I held him closer and he shifted in my lap, burying his face in my stomach.

He thinks he's a little boy. He thinks I'm MaMaLu.

I wanted to hold him tighter. I wanted to push him away. How could I even think of comforting Damian? How could I not?

I sang to him until the sun began to rise, until we anchored at a small island with forested hills that sloped seaward to meet sandy white beaches. As far as I could make out, there were no buildings on the island, no roads, or cars, or telephone lines.

The men carried Damian from the boat to a small villa hidden among the palm trees. Damian groaned as they lay him on the flamingo colored couch. I was amazed he'd lasted through the night. No one could lose that much blood and survive. Rafael seemed to think otherwise.

"You're going to pull through, Damian. You hear me?" he said, even though Damian had turned pale and unresponsive. He sent Manuel off on the boat to obtain medical supplies, while he rifled through the first aid kit.

He had the same dark complexion as Damian, but that's where the similarities ended. Rafael was a few inches taller with light hair and green eyes. He didn't wear ugly, generic clothes. His t-shirt was made of fine, pure cotton and the seams were zigzagged to lie flat and straight. His watch cost more than Damian's boat, and his shoes . . . his shoes reminded me of the ones I'd seen on Damian when he'd abducted me. Soft, hand-tooled, Italian leather.

I tried to make sense of what had happened. It occurred to me that Damian had been talking to Rafael when the storm hit. It was possible that the two of them had already planned this meeting point. Rafael had been close enough to intercept us, and this location was too remote to just be chanced upon. When I'd called on the radio, it was set to the channel they'd been using to communicate, but anyone could have tuned in, so Rafael had asked me to switch to the phone.

"He should have finished you off." Rafael looked at me pointedly as he stitched up the gash on Damian's head.

"He was taking me to see MaMaLu." If Damian died, I knew I was in bigger trouble with Rafael. I didn't know who he was or how they were connected, but I needed to find a way to keep afloat. The one thing I had going for me was the call I'd made to my father. He knew I was alive, and satellite phones use GPS. It wouldn't take long to trace the number and narrow down the search area.

"Damian was taking you to Paza del Mar?" Rafael's brows shot up. "He never takes anyone to see her."

"You know MaMaLu?" I asked. At least I knew where she was now.

"I've known Damian since he was twelve. We grew up together. There's nothing I wouldn't do for him."

"So if something happens to him . . . if he dies . . . you'll keep his promise? You'll take me to MaMaLu?"

Rafael finished stitching Damian up before replying. "Do I look like your chauffeur?" He took a step towards me. "Your butler?" Another step. "Your fucking concierge?" He spat down at me. "You don't give a shit about Damian or MaMaLu. So don't pretend you want to see MaMaLu when all you're trying to do is save your own ass. You live in your high and mighty castle with your high and mighty head in the clouds. The only person you look out for is *you,* because you're nothing but a spoiled brat. Well, guess what?" He pulled out his gun and held it to my temple. "I'm not going to let Damian take the fall. He might have gone soft on you, but your luck just ran out, Ms. Skye and Mighty Sedgewick. We're going to end this. Right now." He nudged me towards the door.

"But, I—" My eyes drifted to Damian. He was lost in uneasy sleep.

"He can't save you now, princess," said Rafael. "March. Out back."

We walked through the wraparound verandah, past the coconut palms and into the jungle.

"Stop. Right here," said Rafael, when we came to a small clearing.

I was facing away from him, looking down at my shadow on the sandy mound. It was long and thin in the setting sun. Rafael stepped behind me. Together we looked like long-limbed aliens, with one ready to zap the other into another galaxy.

It was almost a relief, to let go, to resign, to accept. Hope is a hollow backbone. It can't always carry the weight of reality. And I was tired of propping it up. I was tired of mending it each time it snapped. You can only cheat death so many times; you can only fight so long, so hard.

"Just one thing before you shoot, Rafael." I turned around and looked him in the eye. "I need to know. Tell me what happened to Esteban. Tell me how he ended up as Damian."

ESTEBAN

Twelve

THE FIRST TIME ESTEBAN SAW Skye, it was through a set of wooden bars. He didn't know whether they were there to keep her in, like the dangerous animals at the zoo, or to keep him out, like the display windows he pressed his nose against when he went to the big city with MaMaLu.

"Why is she in a cage?" he asked.

"It's not a cage." MaMaLu laughed.

"It's a crib," said Adriana Sedgwick. She was the baby's mother, and she looked like she had stepped out of the glossy magazines she read.

Esteban was four years old. He had never seen a crib. He slept with MaMaLu, in a small room in the staff wing. He liked it much better than when they'd stayed with MaMaLu's brother, Fernando. Some days Fernando came home drunk to find MaMaLu had locked him out. Those nights, he yelled and cursed and banged on the door. Other times, he bought them *elote*, boiled corn on the cob, and rowed them out to sea in his panga. Esteban could never tell what kind of day it was going to be, so he'd constantly walked on eggshells around his uncle.

One evening, Fernando brought home a friend.

"Come, Esteban." He waved the boy over. "Say hello to my buddy, Victor Madera."

Just then, MaMaLu came in and Victor Madera's gaze was quickly averted. "And this is . . . ?" he asked.

"My sister, Maria Luisa," replied Fernando.

Victor couldn't keep his eyes off her. He had heard about Maria Luisa. It was his business to keep track of everyone and everything. Fernando had told him things about her that he should probably have kept to himself, but when a man has a weakness, be it gambling or alcohol or women, you can always get him to talk.

"Fernando tells me you're looking for a job," said Victor.

"I am," she replied. Her dress was stretched tight across her bosom

"I might have something for you." Victor wanted nothing more than to see her naked.

That night, he went to Adriana Sedgewick, and told her that he had found her a nanny.

"Tell her to come see me tomorrow for an interview," she said.

Victor had worked as a bodyguard for her father, a wealthy businessman who dealt with the Mexican underworld. His family's safety was of prime concern. Victor had been employed by her father for many years, but he made Adriana uneasy. She wished her father had not insisted that Victor accompany her when she married Warren, but that had been one of his conditions. The other being that Warren entered into the family business.

"What was that about?" asked Warren. He circled his wife's pregnant belly and nuzzled her neck.

She didn't answer, choosing instead to entwine her fingers with his and lead him to where the baby was kicking. "Do you ever regret it?" she asked.

"Regret what?"

"Marrying me. Leaving San Diego for Paza del Mar. Getting involved with my family."

"Adriana, we've been over this before. Besides, they're not directly involved and neither am I."

"Laundering money for the cartel *is* direct involvement, no matter how many people separate us from them. I know you did it for me. My father—"

"Your father saw a young American punk in love with his daughter and offered me a choice. He saw someone who could get money out of Mexico and I saw an opportunity to give you the things you're used to. We collect our cut and in a few years, we get out. That's the plan, baby. Short and sweet." He kissed her. "So what did Victor want?"

"He says he knows someone who would make a good nanny."

"Victor is recommending nannies now?"

Adriana laughed. "If she's anything like him, I don't think I'm going to like her."

But Adriana was pleasantly surprised. She had been expecting someone older, colder, but MaMaLu was sharp and vibrant and intelligent. She was bilingual and switched easily from Spanish to English. What Adriana liked best was that she came in with her son on her hip.

"This is Esteban," she said, as if he was her proudest accomplishment.

Adriana asked questions, but more than that, she watched the two of them interact. By the end of the interview, she knew. If anyone was going to help raise her child, it was MaMaLu. She was a nurturer, but she wasn't afraid to discipline. She knew when to yield and when to give. She was full of stories about everything, and real or made up, there was something enthralling and magical about them, about *her*.

"The baby isn't due for another week, but I'd like you to get oriented. Can you start tomorrow?" Adriana asked.

And so began a deep and abiding friendship between two unlikely women.

Adriana died when Skye was three years old. She was in the city, visiting her father, when it happened. Everyone knew the bullet was meant for him, over a dispute he'd had with the cartel. After he buried his daughter, he gave up all his dealings with them, but he couldn't get his son-in-law out. The cartel wanted someone with a U.S. passport, and they wanted him enough to threaten Skye. It took Warren six years to get out and in that time, MaMaLu made sure that Adriana's daughter never felt the loss of her mother. She loved her like her own. When Skye woke up, MaMaLu was the first person she saw, and when Skye went to sleep, it was to the sound of MaMaLu's voice.

Esteban resented the little girl who had stolen his mother. He wanted all of MaMaLu's smiles and all of her lullabies. At night, he waited for her to come home, and when she didn't, he climbed the tree to Skye's window and sat there and sulked. Skye had outgrown the crib and MaMaLu sat beside her in bed, putting her to sleep. Sometimes MaMaLu called Esteban over, but he always shook his head. He was pretty sure the little girl wasn't real. Her hair was the color of the halos he'd seen on paintings in church, and the light from the bedside lamp made it look like soft, golden feathers. Esteban wasn't fooled. He knew that one day she was going to fly away, but until then, she was pretending to be real so MaMaLu would stay and look after her.

Esteban came to Skye's room every day to catch bits and pieces of MaMaLu's stories. Pretty soon, he was climbing inside and sitting on the floor so he could hear what she was saying. He inched forward, bit by bit, until he could lean against MaMaLu's leg. One night, she sang him the lullaby she used to sing when he was little. Esteban knew it was for him because Skye was sleeping, but as soon as MaMaLu stopped singing, Skye rolled over.

"Again, MaMaLu," she said.

"No!" Esteban got up and wrenched MaMaLu away from her. "That's *my* lullaby!"

"Ban?" She rubbed her sleep drenched eyes and looked at him.

"It's Esteban, not Ban!"

"Ban." She got out of bed, dragging her comforter along, and deposited it at his feet.

"What does she want?" Esteban eyed her warily.

"She wants you to stay," said MaMaLu.

The little girl curled her hand around his before he could climb out the window. Her chubby little fingers felt pretty real as she tugged him down. She stretched out on the comforter and put her head on his lap. Esteban was confounded. He looked at MaMaLu, but she just covered the little girl up with a blanket and resumed the lullaby. Esteban didn't move a muscle until Skye fell asleep. When he was sure she wouldn't wake up, he touched her angel hair. Huh. That felt pretty real too.

Every day after that, the little girl looked out for Esteban. She refused to fall asleep until he'd climbed through her window.

Ban turned to Eban.

And Eban turned to Teban.

And Teban turned to Esteban.

Esteban had started coming for MaMaLu, but now he came for Skye. As the years passed, their friendship grew. He taught her how to make kites out of newspaper and broomsticks, and she introduced him to the CDs her father got for her when he went to the States. When they listened to "Drops of Jupiter", the sun was shining in Skye's hair and Esteban thought Jupiter must be made of the palest gold. Sometimes he imagined whole galaxies fitting inside the necklace she wore.

When Esteban watched Warren Sedgewick with Skye, he wondered what it would be like to have a father. He hoped MaMaLu did not marry Victor Madera, who sneaked in when they thought he had gone to sleep. Those nights, MaMaLu pulled the makeshift partition in their room. He couldn't see through the heavy fabric, but he could hear them, and he hated the greedy, heavy sounds that Victor made. Esteban always knew when Victor was going to visit, because MaMaLu did not sing that whole day.

One night, MaMaLu and Victor had a fight, and MaMaLu threw him out. He showed up the next night with white lilies in a terracotta pot.

"Marry me, Maria Luisa," he said. He insisted on calling her Maria Luisa because he couldn't stand the thought of her being Esteban's *MaMa*Lu, or of another man touching her.

MaMaLu didn't reply. She started closing the door on his face.

"So this is what it's come to?" He jammed his foot in the door. "Have you forgotten who rescued you from Fernando, who got you this job and a place for you and your son?"

"That was years ago, Victor. I've been paying my dues ever since. I'm done. I want nothing more to do with you."

Victor forced the door open and flung the flowers away. MaMaLu stumbled back, stepping on mud and fallen lilies.

"You think you're too good for me, don't you?" Victor sneered. "Have you told your son that he's a bastard?"

MaMaLu gasped.

"You think I didn't know? Oh yes. Fernando told me. Esteban's father didn't die in a fishing accident. He took off while you were planning your little wedding. He wanted nothing to do with you or your bastard baby. I'm giving you a chance to reclaim your honor. You should be grateful I'm willing to give the boy my name."

"He doesn't need your name. And neither do I. I'd rather live with no honor than take the name of a man who trades lives for money."

"I'm a bodyguard. I *defend* people."

"Then where were you when Adriana Sedgewick was shot? You were supposed to be with her. It seems rather convenient that you got called away when you did. In fact, I would bet—"

"Shut up!" Victor grabbed MaMaLu by the neck and shook her until she was gasping.

Esteban shot out of bed and launched at him. He rammed his head into Victor's stomach and knocked the wind out of him. "Let her go!"

But Victor was much stronger. He let go of MaMaLu as he held Esteban at bay. Esteban kicked and punched in the air before Victor tossed him to the floor.

"You're going to regret this." Victor pointed his finger at MaMaLu. His voice was cold and hard.

"Get out," said MaMaLu. "Get out before I call Señor Sedgewick."

Victor spat at her feet and turned on his heel. MaMaLu stood tall and straight until he was gone. Then she rushed to Esteban's side. "Are you all right, *cariño*?"

Esteban swallowed the lump in his throat. "Is it true what he said? My father didn't die? He just . . . left? He never wanted me."

"It wasn't your fault, Esteban. It was mine. I was young and foolish. I thought he loved me."

For as long as Esteban could remember, MaMaLu had been a fighter. She was proud and strong, and she never cried. But now big, fat tears quivered on the brink of her lashes. She held them back as long as she could, but when she blinked, they left wet trails down her cheeks.

And then MaMaLu wept—odd, stilted sobs that tore Esteban to pieces. He hadn't been able to defend her. He didn't know how to comfort her. So Esteban did the only thing that comforted him. He put her head on his lap and he sang to her.

Ay, yai, yai, yai,
Sing and do not cry . . .

Thirteen

ESTEBAN GOT INTO A LOT of trouble after that. He stayed late at the village, watching good guys fight bad guys in the first of the many western movies that he grew to love. He was Blondie, the professional gunslinger in *The Good, The Bad and The Ugly*, except he wasn't out to earn a few dollars. He was the hard-ass who would come to MaMaLu's defense. There was just one problem. When he got home, he was the one that needed defending. From MaMaLu.

"Estebandido!" She only called him that when she was pissed. And when MaMaLu was pissed, she came after him with a broom.

Every time Esteban felt the stiff fibers scratching up against the back of his legs, he ran faster, until MaMaLu gave up. She would head back in, but leave the broom by the door. Esteban would wait a while before returning.

"MaMaLu, it's me." He would shuffle his feet at the entrance. "Your Estebandido is home."

MaMaLu would open the door and stare him down. When he was sufficiently shriveled up under her death glare, she'd turn away and get back into bed. She always left him a plate of *tostadas* and a glass of *horchata*. He would eat in the dark and smile, dreaming of the day he would kick Victor's ass.

When Esteban saw his first martial arts movie, he painted Victor's face on a fence and kicked it in. That earned him a year's worth of chores. MaMaLu did not believe in going easy. Of course, it didn't help that Victor was always picking on him. It was a sure-fire way to get to MaMaLu, and Victor took great pleasure in tormenting her for having rejected him. When Esteban punched one of the kids at Skye's birthday party, Victor could barely conceal his glee. He dragged Esteban out by the collar, hoping MaMaLu would follow, pleading for him to go easy, but she was too proud for that.

Ultimately, it didn't turn out as satisfying as Victor had thought it would. Cutting the rough, weed-infested grass with a pair of scissors should have broken Esteban, but the boy didn't complain. The satisfaction of knocking Gideon Benedict St. John's tooth out made it worthwhile. That, plus the fact that Warren had invited him to attend classes with Skye had Esteban smiling, even though his knees and elbows were red and raw by the time he was done.

Victor wanted nothing more than to wipe the infuriating grin off Esteban's face, but he had things to do. Big things. Warren was meeting with El Charro, the quasi-legendary drug lord who ran a profitable subsidiary of the

Sinaloa cartel. This was Warren's first face-to-face with the *capo,* and it was up to Victor to arrange for security.

El Charro traveled with his own bodyguards, but Victor had to ensure the grounds were swept clean that day, and that the staff steered clear of the main house. So far, no-one could attest to Warren's connection with the cartel, and it was important to ensure there were no witnesses to the meeting.

On the day of the meeting, Victor had extra men stationed at the gate and around the perimeter. When it was almost time, he went inside and waited at the bottom of the stairs for Warren.

Warren took a deep breath as he peered at his reflection in the mirror. He'd waited six years for this day. He *had* to convince El Charro to release him from the organization, but it wasn't going to be easy. No one got out squeaky clean, if at all. Warren picked up the photo of him and Adriana on their wedding day and traced his wife's smile.

I miss you so much, babe.

He heard laughter from Skye's room, and put the frame down.

I'll get her out, Adriana. Whatever it takes. I promise.

"MaMaLu." He knocked on Skye's door. "I'm expecting an important guest," he said when she opened the door. "Make sure you and Skye stay here until my meeting is done. We are not to be disturbed. Under any circumstances."

"Yes, Señor Sedgewick." MaMaLu watched as he made his way downstairs. He left with Victor to receive the car that had just pulled up.

She was about to shut the door when Esteban came in through the back door, carrying a notebook and pencil.

She'd forgotten to tell him that his first class with Miss Edmonds had been canceled.

"Esteban!" She waved from upstairs. "Go home. There's no class today. And make sure Señor Sedgewick does not see you. No one's supposed to be here. You hear me?"

"Okay." Esteban had no idea what all the fuss was about, but when MaMaLu used that tone, you listened.

MaMaLu went back into Skye's room and shut the door. For a moment, Esteban debated if he should sneak upstairs, but the front door swung open and Warren entered with a group of men. Esteban didn't want to get into any more trouble so he darted into the dining room. He crawled into his hiding space in the hutch, waiting for them to pass, but they entered the room and sat at the table. Victor shut the door and stood behind Warren. Esteban could not make out the other men. All he saw as he peeked through the crisscross lattice was their legs.

"This is a great honor," said Warren. "I wasn't expecting all of you."

"We have been doing business for a long time. It was time we met," said the man sitting next to Warren.

"Of course. May I offer you gentleman a drink?" Warren got up and walked over to the hutch. Esteban heard the tinkle of ice.

Just then, the door swung open and Skye ran in. "Esteban! I forgot to tell him—"

"Skye!" MaMaLu stumbled in after her, trying to restrain her. "I'm so sorry, Señor Sedgewick."

There was a moment of complete silence. Warren turned around slowly to face her. MaMaLu looked around the table and quickly looked away. "Sorry to have disturbed you. Come on, Skye." She started leading Skye out.

"But—" Skye turned around, trying to see past her father to the place Esteban usually hid.

"Get back upstairs, Skye." Warren's voice was dull and flat. "Gentleman, I apologize for the interruption," he said, after MaMaLu and Skye had left.

It seemed to Esteban that the room was quiet for a long, long time.

"We've been compromised," said the man who had spoken earlier.

"That was my daughter's nanny. She's been with us for many years. She can be trusted, Charro. I give you my word," Warren replied.

"El Charro and the rest of us need more assurance than that, especially if you plan on leaving." One of the other men at the table spoke up.

"We have your terms of release, but we can't afford any loose ends," said El Charro. "It's not just us we're worried about, you understand? You have a young daughter. I'm sure you wouldn't want her to be caught up in all this."

Warren started to say something, but thought the better of it. El Charro had him by the balls. If Warren didn't do something about MaMaLu, Skye's life was on the line. He also knew that the only reason El Charro was willing to let him leave was because his father-in-law, Adriana's dad, had pulled some major strings to help him and Skye get out of the country, away from the cartel. "I understand," he replied. "I'll take care of it."

"The sooner, the better," said El Charro.

The meeting proceeded, but much of what was being said did not make sense to Esteban. He was glad when the men got up and shook hands.

After they left the room, Warren turned to

Victor. "The situation with MaMaLu. Look after it. Nothing . . . permanent. You understand?"

Victor gave a curt nod and followed Warren out. Esteban watched them leave, not sure what was going on, but he knew he had to tell MaMaLu. He had never seen Warren look so worn and dejected.

Esteban waited until the house was quiet before coming out of his hiding spot. It was dark by the time he made it back to the staff wing. As he approached, he saw Victor exit their room. Esteban ducked behind a tree as he walked by. Victor had not been back since MaMaLu had turned him down. Something was going on and Esteban did not like it. He waited for MaMaLu, but fell asleep before she got in.

She drew the covers over him and kissed his cheek. Her heart pulled when she realized he'd probably gone to sleep hungry. "*Mi chiquito. Mi* Estebandido."

MaMaLu set the alarm early. She was going to make him a big breakfast. Pan de yema, a soft sugarcoated bread made with lots of egg yolk, dipped in a bowl of thick, cinnamon-infused hot chocolate.

But Esteban never got his breakfast. He woke up to the harsh glare of flashlights in his face. It was the middle of the night, and the room was full of men in dark clothes.

"Esteban!" He heard MaMaLu yelling, but he was blinded.

"MaMaLu." He stumbled after her voice, but they were dragging her away.

Someone grabbed him by the scruff of his neck. Esteban struggled to free himself, but all he could do was watch as they put her in a car and drove away.

"You're coming with me." It was Victor.

"Where are they taking MaMaLu?" Esteban shrugged

out of his grasp and glared at him.

"If you want to see her again, you'll do as I say. *Entiendes*?"

Esteban nodded. He knew this had something to do with what had happened that afternoon, so he followed Victor into the other car.

"I'm taking you to your uncle, Fernando. You're to stay there until the situation with MaMaLu is resolved."

"What situation?" Esteban shivered in his nightclothes as they drove past dense, dark trees to Paza del Mar. He'd left his shoes behind.

Victor did not answer.

When they got to Fernando's, Victor instructed Esteban to wait outside. Esteban could hear the two men talking. Fernando staggered out. He smelled of piss and cheap liquor.

"Look at what Señor Sedgewick gave me to look after you." He had a stack of cash in his hands. "Come, my little jackpot. Come hug your *tío*."

Esteban walked past him. He hated everything about Fernando's place—the dankness, the cold cement floors, the memories of him and MaMaLu cowering in their room. Why had Warren sent him here?

"Where's MaMaLu?" he asked Victor.

"Your mother should have accepted my proposal, but she didn't think I was good enough for her. And now she's exactly where she deserves to be, with no one to protect her." His smile gave Esteban the chills.

"Tell me where she is!" Esteban shouted after him as he drove off.

"Shut your mouth." Fernando put his hands to his ears, nursing his perpetual hangover. He folded up the wad of cash Victor had given him and started heading out.

"Go to sleep. Your mother has been taken to Valdemoros and there's nothing you or I can do about it."

Valdemoros.

Esteban was horrified. Valdemoros was a women's prison, a few miles north of Paza del Mar. Esteban had no idea why they'd taken her there or how long it would be before she got out. He opened the door to the spare bedroom and sank into bed. The mattress was thin and the sheets were foul. He doubted if Fernando had washed them since he and MaMaLu had left for Casa Paloma. MaMaLu's new job had seemed like a blessing at the time, but now Esteban felt like it had been the start of a disaster neither of them had seen coming.

Fourteen

VALDEMOROS WAS AN ENDLESS CONCRETE wall, topped by rolls of razor wire and punctuated by sentry towers. In the center was a heavy metal gate that opened to let armored cars in and out of the facility. At the far end was an adjoining structure—a sad, diminutive visitors' entrance. It looked like a misplaced wheelbarrow trailing a giant gray train.

Esteban felt small and helpless as he stood in the shadow of the ominous wall. Correctional officers with sniper rifles manned the towers. At the main gate, armed guards patrolled the windowless barricade. MaMaLu was somewhere behind this impenetrable front and Esteban had to find a way to get her.

Esteban stood in a long line at the visitors' gate. The guard overlooked him several times when it was his turn.

"Excuse me," said Esteban, after he'd let yet another man through, "I'm here to see my mother."

But the guard pretended not to hear him. Esteban spent the whole day getting shuffled around, but he wouldn't give up. When the guards changed, his hopes soared, but the next one ignored him too.

"Here." A man who'd been waiting there almost as long as him gave him a paper cone filled with roasted peanuts. "They don't let you in unless you pay them."

Esteban looked at him blankly.

"Go home, boy." The man dusted off his pants and got up. "You're wasting your time."

In the evening, when the lines dwindled, Esteban tried again. He was sure that if he waited long enough, one of the guards would let him in, but the next one was just as mean and chased him out with a baton.

Esteban returned the next day. And the day after that. And the day after that. Finally, one of the guards acknowledged him.

"Name of inmate?"

"Maria Luisa Alvarez."

"Your name?"

"Esteban Samuel Alvarez."

"Did you bring me lunch?" asked the man.

"Lunch?"

The guard crossed his arms and narrowed his eyes. "I've seen you around. Haven't you learned yet? Who's going to pay for my lunch?"

Esteban suddenly understood how it worked. "How much is . . . your lunch?"

"Three hundred and fifty pesos, *amigo*. You can see your mother every day for a month."

"How much for just one day?"

"Same."

"Please. I don't have any money. Just let me see her. Tomorrow I'll come back with my uncle. I'll bring your lunch and—" said Esteban.

"No money, no *madre*." The guard shooed him away.

The next person in line replaced Esteban. He watched as she handed the guard something discreetly. Apparently, everyone knew the drill. Esteban thought of the big bundle of cash that Victor had handed Fernando.

When he got home, he found Fernando passed out in a pool of his own drool.

"*Tío* Fernando." He tried to rouse him, but he knew there was no point. Esteban patted him down. He found a few coins in his pocket, but Fernando had drunk his way through whatever money he'd had.

"No, no, no!" Esteban wanted to rip him open so he could grab three hundred and fifty pesos from his black, liquor-soaked liver. He went looking through the whole house, but found nothing, not even a can of beans he could sell for some cash.

Esteban had no choice but to turn to the one man who could help him: Warren Sedgewick.

Look after it, he'd told Victor, just as he'd done after Esteban had punched Gidiot.

Esteban was pretty sure Warren would have stepped in had he known about the punishment Victor had set for him, and he was pretty sure he'd step in now if he learned exactly how Victor had 'looked after' MaMaLu. Esteban believed that Skye's father was a fair man. He had tried to protect MaMaLu from El Charro, the man whose face Esteban had not seen. Warren had sent money, lots of money, to have Esteban cared for, not knowing that Fernando was a dirty, rotten alcoholic. Esteban was convinced that if Warren knew the truth, he would get MaMaLu out of Valdemoros.

The walk from Fernando's place, in Paza del Mar, to Casa Paloma was thirty minutes. Esteban sprinted the whole way, his feet getting cut on the small, jagged stones that littered the path through the jungle, but he was filled with hope. He ran through the dense foliage, ducking branches that swatted his face and arms, until the trees thinned out and he could see the gates of Casa Paloma.

He spotted Warren and Skye getting into their silver Peugeot. The driver pulled out of the circular driveway. They had just cleared the wrought iron gates when Esteban got there.

"Wait!" He ran after them on the dirt road that led out of Casa Paloma. The wheels were spinning clouds of dust in their wake. Esteban's lungs filled with dry, powdered earth.

"Skye," he shouted.

She turned around and looked at him through a haze of grime and grit.

"Stop. Skye!" He waved, coming to a standstill as a sharp pain gripped his side. He doubled over, trying to ease the runner's stitch.

Skye turned away and the car continued down the road.

"Skye," he sobbed, falling to his knees.

Beads of sweat dripped from his brow and mingled with the dusty, baked earth.

Esteban didn't understand why Skye had not asked her father to stop. He had not seen her since the night they took MaMaLu away. Didn't she wonder where he'd been? Didn't she miss him and MaMaLu?

Skye must have had a good reason, and when they

got back, she would tell him. Esteban decided to wait. The sooner he spoke to Warren about MaMaLu, the sooner he'd get to see her.

Esteban walked back to the gates. He saw Victor, locking them up with a chain and padlock. Victor. *He* was responsible for this. *He* had sent MaMaLu away. All of Esteban's rage and frustration boiled over. He forgot that he was a twelve-year-old boy up against a hired henchman. He forgot that even Blondie and Bruce Lee get the shit kicked out of them. He forgot everything except the fact that Victor Madera was the reason MaMaLu was in Valdemoros.

"Victor!" Esteban had the advantage of surprise, and he'd been practicing high kicks and punches for months. He went straight for Victor's torso.

"*Estás puto*—are you mad?" Victor staggered back and the chain clanged against the gate. "I thought I told you to stay at Fernando's. You should learn to listen!" He circled Esteban.

It wasn't much of a fight. Esteban closed his eyes as he felt the blows on his back and chest. When he fell to the ground, Victor kicked him in the stomach.

"Go home, you stupid little shit," he said.

But Esteban shook his head, cradling his tummy. "I'm not leaving until I see Señor Sedgewick."

"You think Señor Sedgewick gives a fuck about you? You think he's going to bring MaMaLu back?" Victor laughed. "You poor, naive *bastardo*. You are as expendable to these rich *gringos* as yesterday's newspaper."

"That's not true!" Esteban's face was caked with dirt. When he wiped the tears, they left brown streaks on his cheeks. "Skye is my friend."

"Really?" Victor shook his head in mock pity. "Tell

me, did your *friend* say goodbye? Did she tell you she was leaving and never coming back?"

"You're lying.You're a dirty, filthy liar!"

"Wait then. Wait for your *friend* and her father to come save you."

Esteban was too tired and too hurt to react when Victor walked away. He was bruised and battered on the outside, and simmering with shame and anger on the inside. He felt feeble and powerless and beaten down. He lay doubled up by the locked gates, under a merciless afternoon sun.

Hours passed, but Esteban waited. It was quiet. Too quiet. None of the help was around, and the gates were never chained down. Where was the guard? Where was the gardener? Esteban refused to believe they were all gone. He knew Skye would never leave without saying goodbye. He *knew*.

When the stars came out, Esteban limped to the entrance and looked through the gate. The outside lights had not come on and the path to the staff's quarters remained unlit. He climbed over the hedged fence in the back, and up the tree outside Skye's window. Esteban tried jiggling it open—it was still unlatched.

Esteban turned on the light and looked around. It felt weird being in Skye's room without her. It felt wrong. Her bed was made, but her closet looked like someone had been through it in a rush. All her favorite books and clothes were gone. Esteban felt something crunch under his feet. He looked down and saw that the floor was littered with paper—all the magical, mythical things he had fashioned out of the most colorful, special paper he could find. They were carelessly discarded around him. Some of them had been trampled into grotesque, malformed pieces.

Esteban picked up an origami scorpion. It had taken him a long time to get the folds just right. The body was flattened, but the stinger remained upright. He thought about what Victor had said. Maybe he was right. Maybe Warren didn't give a fuck about him or MaMaLu. Maybe Skye didn't care. Maybe he and MaMaLu were just like all of this paper—folded and molded to suit a purpose, and then stepped on, on the way out.

Esteban flung the scorpion away and winced from the blows Victor had inflicted on him. He looked out the window and saw the new moon reflected in the pond. He remembered when Skye had been curled up in bed and MaMaLu told them about the magic swan that hid in the gardens of Casa Paloma, a swan that came out once in a while, on the night of a new moon.

If you catch a glimpse of it, you will be blessed with the greatest treasure, she'd said.

Esteban hadn't believed her then, and he didn't believe her now. It was all made up—all the magic, all her stories, all the happy endings. They were all empty and meaningless and hollow. His father had never been a great fisherman. He had never loved him or MaMaLu. MaMaLu had lied. Skye had never been his friend.

You think Señor Sedgewick gives a fuck about you?

You think he's going to bring MaMaLu back?

You are as expendable to these rich gringos *as yesterday's newspaper.*

That was the cold, hard truth.

Esteban turned off the light and stood alone in the empty darkness. When he climbed out of Skye's window that night, he left something behind: his childhood, his innocence, his shining, naive ideals—all scattered on the floor like limp, trodden paper dreams.

Fifteen

ESTEBAN SAT ON THE CONCRETE stairs of *La Sombra*, one of the small cantinas in Paza del Mar. Its sloping tin roof protected him from the torrential downpour. He stared at the water, collecting in rivulets down the dirt street. It reflected yellow pools of light from kerosene lamps that hung on porches of the shops that were still open. A stereo was blasting Luis Miguel's "La Bikina", a tune about a beautiful, scarred woman with a pain so deep, it provokes rivers of tears.

"Hey, boy!" a man called from inside the restaurant.

Esteban turned around. "Me?"

"*Si*. You hungry?" he asked.

Esteban had noticed the man watching him. He assumed it was because his face was swollen and heavy. It was obvious he'd been in a fight.

"Juan Pablo," the man gestured to the waiter, "bring the boy *oreja de elefante* and something to drink. What's your name?"

"Esteban."

The man nodded and continued eating heartily, washing his food down with sips of *michelada*—beer with lemon and seasonings. He had a baby face, countered by eagle eyebrows, from which gray, unruly hair sprouted upwards. His hair was jet black, obviously dyed, and slicked back from his forehead. He must have been in his late forties, maybe a little older. A polished wooden walking cane rested on his table. It was glossy black, and the gold metal tip flashed like a shiny promise in the simple, run-down cantina.

Esteban sat across from him. His stomach growled at the sight of the man's dinner. Red enchiladas stuffed with cheese and topped with cream. The waiter brought him warm corn tortillas, a bowl of green jalapeños and *agua fresca*. Esteban forced himself to eat slowly, stretching it out until his dinner arrived—two large pieces of veal that look like elephant ears.

They ate in silence at the formica-topped table, listening to the rain and music, while murals of Pedro Infante and Maria Felix, stars from the golden age of Mexican cinema, watched them from a bullet-riddled wall. Casa Paloma had sheltered Esteban from the reality that lay beyond its iron gates, but now he was thrust into a different world. Not only did he have to look after himself, he also had to find a way to get MaMaLu out.

Cantina Man finished his enchiladas and opened up the newspaper. He scanned the headlines, and chuckled at something. "Hey, Juan Pablo." He pointed to an article when the waiter came to clear his plate. "*KABOOM*!" he said, his hands imitating an explosion. Both men laughed.

The rain had tapered to a fine drizzle by the time Esteban finished his dinner. It felt awkward to just get up and leave, and saying 'thank you' for Cantina Man's random act of kindness did not seem enough, so Esteban lingered. He was in no hurry to go home and deal with his uncle Fernando.

"Rough day?" asked the man.

Esteban didn't answer. The swelling over his eye had grown twice the size.

"Camila," the man called a short, round woman from the kitchen. She was wearing an apron streaked with red sauce and pico de gallo. "Bring the boy some ice."

"Thank you," said Esteban, when she handed him a small bundle of ice, wrapped in a dishtowel. He tried not to wince as he held it to his eye.

"Would you like to make some money, boy?" asked Cantina Man. He didn't have to wait for an answer. Esteban's face said it all. "Fifteen pesos," he continued. "Leave this newspaper in the urn by the statue of San Miguel Arcangel. You know where that is?"

Esteban nodded. He watched the man slip a clear plastic bag filled with white powder into the newspaper. He folded it twice before handing it to Esteban. "Meet me here tomorrow night and I'll pay you. *Tú entiendes*?"

"*Si*." Esteban knew he was doing something he shouldn't, but *fifteen pesos*. It was a long way from the three hundred and fifty pesos he needed to see MaMaLu, but it was a start.

He took the newspaper. He had nowhere to hide it. He was still in the clothes he'd worn to bed the night they came for MaMaLu—an apple green t-shirt sporting a cheeky monkey with neon yellow shades. 'Master of

Disaster', it said in a smiley curve underneath. The shorts were a matching green, in banana print.

The path to the village plaza was deserted. People were in their homes, watching their nightly TV *novelas*. The rain had turned the streets muddy and Esteban was thankful for the cool squelch of wet earth under his tired, worn feet.

The church of Archangel Michael anchored the village of Paza del Mar. Its whitewashed building was set in gardens of citrus, palms, and trickling fountains. A cemetery sat in the back, with tombstones that stood like sentinels in the dark. MaMaLu had brought him here every Sunday when they lived with Fernando. Esteban remembered flickering votives, wooden saints and the smell of old incense, but most of all, he remembered how tightly MaMaLu held his hand in hers as they sat in the pews, under high ceilings.

The gleaming white statue of Archangel Michael stood over the entrance. The locals said it spit on the heads of all sinners who entered the church. MaMaLu always took him through the side entrance.

Esteban looked for the urn that Cantina Man had told him about. It was about three-feet high, made of heavy marble and brimming with a profusion of ferns and flowers. He dropped the newspaper in the narrow gap between the pot that held the flowers and the urn. Then he turned around and went home.

THE NEXT NIGHT, WHEN ESTEBAN went back to *La Sombra* to collect his fifteen pesos, Cantina man gave him another package to deliver. Soon, Esteban was making regular drops. Sometimes it was to strangers who drove sedans with tinted windows; other times it was to beautiful women who invited him into loud, smoky establishments. Sometimes he made more money, sometimes less, but he never asked Cantina Man any questions and he always said 'thank you'.

Every night, Esteban counted his money.

Fifteen pesos.

Fifty pesos.

One hundred and thirty pesos.

Cantina Man didn't show up every night. Sometimes he was gone for weeks. Those nights, the waiter and the cook, Juan Pablo and Camila, would slip him a bowl of chicken in green sauce, or meatballs and bread, or whatever they had left over. Esteban repaid their kindness by washing dishes, cleaning tables, and sweeping the verandah at the end of the night. The other cantinas were always busier, even though Esteban thought Camila's cooking was far superior. When he watched her scurrying around the kitchen, wiping her hands on her stained apron, Esteban felt a sense of longing for his mother—so deep that he had to drop whatever he was doing and leave. He would stand in the dark alley between *La Sombra* and the fish shop beside it, taking deep breaths until it passed.

Every day, he went back to Valdemoros and sat in the shaded area across the street, where vendors sold fried churros, sweet empanadas, and strips of grilled beef stuffed into handmade tortillas. Esteban was careful with his money. He stuck to roasted peanuts and when the sun was hot, he allowed himself an ice cold bottle of Coca-Cola. He bought a pair of shoes, a few t-shirts and new shorts. He had a story prepared in case Fernando asked him where they'd come from, but his uncle never noticed, and Esteban was careful to hide his loot.

One afternoon as he sat outside the prison, Esteban thought he heard MaMaLu singing from beyond the cold, gray walls. Her voice piped over the blare of the boom box that played all day. "*Mexico Lindo y Querido*", she sang.

Even though it was a song of yearning, for home, and everything dear and familiar, it comforted Esteban. It had been a little over three weeks since he had last seen MaMaLu, but as long as he could hear her sing, he knew she was all right.

Esteban continued working for Cantina Man. He started learning the trade. The green, leafy bags sold for less than the clear crystals that looked like pieces of glass. He took on errands that became progressively more dangerous. There were times when he came face to face with the glinting edge of a knife, times when he had to run for his life. Cantina Man was not happy when he lost the product, and he docked Esteban's pay. At times, Esteban owed more than he earned, and he found himself tangled up in a web he could not get out of. Weeks turned to months, but the thought of seeing MaMaLu kept him going. Three hundred and fifty pesos took much longer to save up than he had bargained for, but one day Esteban had enough. *Almost.* He needed to make just one more drop.

When he got back that night, Esteban was ecstatic. Tomorrow he would get to see MaMaLu. His heart soared as he pried out the loose brick in the backyard that he'd been hiding his loot behind, but there was nothing there.

All his money was gone.

Esteban's fingers scraped rough, empty space.

"Esteban, come join me." Fernando swayed by the door, waving an empty bottle of tequila.

Esteban clenched his fists to keep from reacting. He

knew it was pointless to accuse Fernando of stealing his money; he knew it was pointless to confront him. His uncle remembered nothing, cared for nothing, except his next round of booze.

Esteban stuffed the money he'd made that night into his pocket. His eyes stung with tears he refused to shed. He was right back where he'd started. He wanted to hit something, kick someone, grab Fernando by the neck and choke him until his glazed eyes popped out. He would stomp on them and they would feel like soft, wet grapes.

Fernando weaved back inside and crashed on the sofa. The empty bottle of tequila rolled from his hands. Esteban walked past him and went to his room.

He had to find a way to earn more money. He would talk to Cantina Man, next time he was in town. Before he went to sleep, Esteban took the money out of his pocket and strapped it around his chest. If Fernando wanted his money, he would have to come and get it.

ESTEBAN TOOK ON MORE DUTIES for Cantina Man. He reported back on what he saw outside the prison—described the guards and prisoners that entered and left the facility, the times when armored cars made their rounds, and when the guards in the towers changed. He jotted down the officials who visited and the license plates of the cars they drove. Esteban didn't know it, but he was now part of the *halcones*—falcons—low level cartel members who functioned as the eyes and ears of the organization. All Esteban knew was that his logbook earned him more money, and more money meant he would get to see MaMaLu sooner. In the evenings, he continued doing whatever odd jobs Cantina Man had for him.

"Do you know what you're getting into, *chico*?" Juan Pablo, the waiter at *La Sombra*, asked Esteban one night.

They were sitting on the stairs. Juan Pablo was smoking Marlboro Reds. He and Camila had grown fond of Esteban. He was a good kid, wrapped up in bad business.

"Do you know why no one brings their family or girlfriends or kids to the cantina?" asked Juan Pablo. He let his apron fall to the side and Esteban saw a gun holstered in his waistband. "The man you work for owns *La Sombra*. He doesn't just pay me to serve food. He pays me to protect him. It's a place of business. Meetings, deals. You understand?"

Esteban nodded. Even though he had developed a bond with Juan Pablo and Camila, he had suspected as much. But he was almost there. He couldn't stop now.

"Everyone has a reason." Juan Pablo flicked his cigarette away. *A reason to get involved, to get their hands dirty.* "What's yours?"

"My mother. She's in jail, but she's innocent."

"Around here, everyone is guilty until proven innocent. You go to jail and wait for a trial. And if someone has greased a few palms to keep her in there—a jealous boyfriend, a business partner—it could take forever. You can't trust anyone, Esteban. Not the police or the judges or the guards. They all want a piece of the pie."

Don't get your hopes up, Juan Pablo was advising him.

Esteban pushed the hair away from his forehead. Hope was the only thing he had going, and if money was going to unlock the door to MaMaLu's cell, he was going to make lots of it.

THERE WAS ANOTHER MAN AT *La Sombra*, sitting at the table with Cantina Man. They were talking in low tones. Well, the man was talking. Cantina Man was listening. Esteban skirted around the front and walked into the kitchen. Something had boiled over on the stove, and the pot was now charred.

Esteban shut off the burner and walked over to the service window through which Camila passed the dishes to Juan Pablo. He helped himself to some corn chips as he waited for the visitor to leave. Cantina Man had a lot of meetings when he was in town—different people, different times.

Esteban popped his head through the window, hoping to catch Juan Pablo or Camila. He didn't see them, but someone had splattered ketchup all over the walls and tables. Esteban followed the trail and froze. Not ketchup. *Blood.*

Camila was lying on the floor, next to Juan Pablo. They had both been shot in the head. Juan Pablo's face was contorted. His eyes were still open. His gun was half way out, lying by his side.

The stranger Esteban had seen earlier had a gun pointed straight at Cantina Man. He was resting it on the table, so it looked like the two men were having dinner, but his finger was on the trigger. Cantina Man's knuckles were white as he clenched his walking stick.

Esteban knew he should back off, retrace his steps and run like hell. He knew he shouldn't crawl into the dining area, pick up Juan Pablo's gun, and wipe the blood off so it didn't slip from his fingers. He knew he shouldn't aim the gun at the back of the man's head and try to keep his hands from shaking as he took aim.

Esteban knew all of that, but the only thing he could see was the stranger putting a bullet in Juan Pablo and Camila. He saw the man turn the same gun to Cantina Man. He saw the bullet rip into Cantina Man, spewing blood and death over Esteban's only chance of seeing MaMaLu. Esteban saw *fifteen pesos* about to be splattered on the walls. He saw the prison guard asking him for lunch. He saw himself sitting in the shadow of the prison, day in and out, always short, always close, eating fucking peanuts like a fucking idiot.

He squeezed the trigger. The recoil sent him crashing into one of the tables.

Esteban wasn't sure if he'd gotten the man, who was still sitting in the chair. Then he toppled over sideways and hit the floor. A stream of blood sprang out from the back of his head.

Cantina Man and Esteban looked at each other.

Holy fuck.

Esteban let go of the gun like it had just burned his hand. His ears were ringing from the deep *boom* of the shot.

Cantina Man walked over to him and kissed him on both cheeks.

"I just wanted to see my mother." Esteban was shaking. He couldn't believe he had just killed a man. "I just wanted to see my mother."

Cantina Man picked up the gun and wiped it down. Then he put it back in Juan Pablo's hand. "I will take you to your mother," he said.

He made a couple of calls. A few minutes later, a dark car pulled up to the curb.

"Where is your mother, boy?" Cantina Man asked. He

ushered Esteban into the back seat.

"Valdemoros. But they won't let anyone in at this time."

A police car screeched to a halt outside the cantina. Two uniformed officers got out.

Cantina Man rolled down his window. "Look after it."

As the car pulled away, Esteban saw the police men line the back seat with garbage bags and throw three dead bodies in the car.

"Juan Pablo . . . Camila . . ." Esteban's voice no longer sounded like his. He felt like his body and soul had been snatched. His friends were dead and he had just killed a man.

Cantina Man didn't say anything. He tapped the glass partition between him and the driver with his cane. "Valdemoros. *Vámonos*!"

Valdemoros was even more imposing at night. Without the noise and activity of vendors and visitors, it was like a massive ghost ship stranded in the middle of nowhere. Spotlights were trained around the perimeter and someone from the tower beamed one straight at Cantina Man's car.

The driver got out and summoned one of the guards. "Concha!"

She walked over to the car and greeted Cantina Man.

"Escort this young man inside. He's here to see his mother," he said.

"*Si*, Señor. Please come with me." She banged her baton on the heavy, metal gate. It lifted with a loud thunderous rasp.

And just like that, Esteban was in. No waiting in line, no lunch money, no logging in.

"What's your mother's name?"

"Maria Luisa Alvarez." Esteban's heart was racing. He wished he had a comb. He wanted to look good for MaMaLu.

"Is my shirt clean?" he asked the guard.

Can you see any blood? Please don't let there be any blood. I don't want to shame my mother with the blood of the man I just killed.

"Maria Luisa Alvarez!" Concha shouted as they exited the short tunnel and stepped into an enormous outdoor compound. Various rooms surrounded the prison yard: dormitories, workshops and prison cells. Almost nobody was locked up in the cages. Women and little children, dressed in shabby street clothes, peeked out from the dormitories.

Concha conferred with a woman in dark military garb. She disappeared into an office and started rifling through the cabinets.

"You are looking for Maria Luisa Alvarez?" asked one of the prisoners.

"*Si,*" said Concha.

The prisoner took a long look at Esteban before calling them into her dorm.

The women had constructed their own little rooms in the giant space, using stick frames attached to blankets. Some had narrow bunk beds, some had cooking equipment and shelves for clothing, but they were all crammed on the rough cement floor like pieces of a jigsaw puzzle. Babies suckled on their mothers' bosoms while others slept on makeshift mattresses. The air was stale with the odor of confinement and hair oil and piss and sweat.

"Maria Luisa Alvarez." The lady walked over to her space and handed Esteban a rusted metal box. It was green, with a red circle in the middle that said 'Lucky

Strike', and underneath, in gold letters: 'Cigarettes'.

"No," said Estaban. "I'm looking for my mother."

"*Si.*" The prisoner pushed the box back into his hands. "*Tu madre.*"

Esteban opened the box. In it were the earrings MaMaLu had been wearing, a hair clip and a newspaper cutting. Esteban was about to shut it when he caught a glimpse of the headline. He spread out the crinkled paper and moved closer to the lantern so he could read.

'LOCAL NANNY ACCUSED OF STEALING FAMILY HEIRLOOM.'

Esteban scanned the words below. They were filled with heinous, horrible lies about how MaMaLu had stolen Skye's necklace and how it had been found in her quarters. In a statement issued to the police, when the necklace was returned to him, Warren Sedgewick had expressed his shock and disbelief:

"Maria Luisa Alvarez was a trusted employee and a friend of my wife's. This necklace belonged to Adriana and means a great deal to my daughter. I find it hard to believe that Skye's nanny would be capable of committing such a crime against our family."

It all fell into place for Esteban. The night he had seen Victor leaving their room, was the night Victor had planted the necklace. The cops who had swooped in to take MaMaLu away were all in on it. Esteban had been naive then, but now he understood how it worked.

Nothing . . . permanent, Warren had said to Victor.

Victor had framed MaMaLu for a crime she didn't commit, and Warren had made sure she stayed locked up with his fake statement. Esteban felt like an idiot, running to Casa Paloma, expecting Warren to help. Victor had followed orders, but it was Warren Sedgewick who'd issued them.

He was to blame for this. Him and the man they called El Charro. They had done this to protect themselves, because MaMaLu had seen them, she could connect them and all the other members of the cartel that had gathered at Casa Paloma that afternoon.

Look after it, Warren had said, because he didn't want to get his hands dirty; he never wanted to get his hands dirty. He'd left in a hurry, in case it caught up to him, in case MaMaLu talked, in case El Charro changed his mind about letting him leave the country.

The two of them had left MaMaLu to rot in jail.

"Where is she?" Esteban turned to the guard. "Where is my mother?"

"Concha." The guard who had been looking up files in the office stood at the entrance and held out a piece of paper.

Concha walked over to her and scanned it. "Sorry." She looked at Esteban. "Maria Luisa Alvarez is dead."

It was so ludicrous, Esteban laughed. "*What*? Are you mad? I heard her singing just the other day."

He started looking for her, flinging aside makeshift curtains and cardboard partitions. "MaMaLu!" He walked from dorm to dorm, leaving a trail of startled, wailing babies. "Sing, MaMaLu. Sing for your Estebandido, so I can find you."

Concha and the other guard pulled him into the courtyard. "Stop! Your mother contracted tuberculosis and died from complications related to it." They held up the paper for him. "We notified her next of kin, her brother Fernando, but no one came. She was buried with the other unclaimed prisoners. This is her prisoner and plot number."

Esteban wanted to shut their mouths. Every word they said made it worse. He wanted to shut his eyes and his ears. He wanted to go back, take Juan Pablo's gun, and point it to his own head.

"No."

"No."

"No."

He kept repeating.

He hated the way the women were staring at him from their dorms—some with pity, some with irritation at being disturbed, but most with blank, empty stares. They had seen it countless times. Prisoners had to buy their beds, their clothes, their privileges. If you couldn't pay for the doctor, no one came to see you. And here, cramped in tight spaces, they'd seen it all: AIDS, flu, measles, tuberculosis. It was a breeding ground for all kinds of bugs and diseases, which, if left untreated, turned fatal.

Concha picked up the box Esteban had dropped and gave it to him. The tiny, rusted tin was all that was left of his mother. MaMaLu didn't smoke, but it was probably the only thing she'd managed to scrounge up in this hell hole. He wondered how someone that took up so much space in his heart could be reduced to a scrap of red and green metal that smelled like tobacco.

"Mi madre está muerta," he said softly, as he weighed it in his palm.

"My mother is dead!" he shouted, announcing it to the whole prison. His voice bounced off the bleak, gray walls that surrounded the compound.

No one cared. No one had told him. No one had asked what kind of funeral she'd like. Did they know to put flowers in her hair? Did they know her favorite color? Esteban hoped they had buried her in an orange dress, the color of tangerines. MaMaLu was just like that—full of zest and gold and sunshine and bite.

He held up her earrings. She always wore the same pair: two doves joined at the beak to form a silver circle. Esteban wanted nothing more than to hear the jangle of the small turquoise stones that hung from the hoops as she chased after him. He needed that because he'd been bad. Really, really bad.

Get your broom, MaMaLu. I promise I won't run today. I'm sorry I didn't make it to you in time. I tried. I tried so hard. I did bad things. I killed a man. You have to come after me, MaMaLu. Come after me because only you can save me. Only you can make it better.

But MaMaLu's earrings hung limply in Esteban's hands. She was not coming to save him or chastise him or love him or sing to him.

Esteban waited for the tears. He didn't care if the guards manning the towers, or the women, or the children saw him. He wanted to release the sea of grief that was welling up in him, but the tears would not come. All Esteban felt was rage. He wanted to ram his fists into the tall, concrete walls, until big, gray boulders toppled over and buried everything. All of the helplessness and injustices and betrayal turned his heart into cold, hard stone. Esteban did not cry when it sank to the bottom of his soul like an abandoned anchor; he did not cry as he followed Concha through the tunnel, back to Cantina Man's car.

"Did you see your mother?" he asked.

"My mother is dead." Esteban's voice was as hard and corroded as the metallic cigarette box he was holding.

"I'm sorry." Cantina Man paused. "You have family?"

Esteban thought of the father who had abandoned

him. He thought of an empty bottle of tequila, rolling from his uncle's hand. He thought of the friend who'd left him in a cloud of dust. He thought of trampled paper animals, and three hundred and fifty pesos, and Juan Pablo, and Camila, and tangerine peels decaying in the dirt.

"I have no one," he said.

Cantina Man was quiet for a while. "You saved my life today. I will take care of you. From now on, you are not Esteban. You are Damian—the tamer, the slayer."

Dah-me-yahn. Esteban liked the way it sounded—like someone who didn't give a damn. All he cared about now was bringing Warren Sedgewick and El Charro to justice, the kind of justice they wouldn't be able to buy their way out of, the kind of justice MaMaLu had been denied.

Damian was going to make them pay for what they had done to his mother.

Cantina Man's driver gave Concha a whack of bills. The other guards watched, eager for a cut.

"Where to, Charro?" asked the driver, when he got back in the car.

Charro.

The name jump-started Damian's stone cold heart. He looked from the driver to Cantina Man and back again, as a sick, twisted realization hit him.

Cantina Man was El Fucking Charro.

Damian had saved the life of the man responsible for his mother's death—one of the two men he had just sworn to take vengeance against.

"Home, Hector," said El Charro. "We are taking Damian home."

Sixteen

'HOME' TURNED OUT TO BE the city of Caboras, a three-hour drive from Paza del Mar. Although El Charro had many bases, he lived behind gated walls on the misty hills surrounding Caboras, and even though Damian had saved his life, he wasn't about to invite the boy into his own home. El Charro didn't get to the top by being sentimental.

"Keep your mouth shut and stay low until I call for you," he said, when they were parked outside a pink three-storey building in a middle class neighborhood of the city. It looked innocuous enough, but it was one of the safe houses that the cartel ran in the city.

Damian understood. It wouldn't do to advertise the fact that a twelve-year-old had saved El Charro. Reputations had to be maintained, machismo kept intact, and Damian was happy to play along, to wait until the perfect opportunity presented itself.

Hector, the driver, let him into a second floor apartment. The smell of marijuana was heavy in the air. A dozen young men lounged on sofas, watching TV.

"Your new *compadre,* everyone." Hector introduced him to the group.

They seemed more interested in what they were watching. New recruits were on the lowest rung of the organization—disposable and barely worthy of acknowledgment.

Hector gave Damian a quick tour and settled him into a bedroom, where three others were already sleeping on mattresses, lined up in a row.

"Get some rest. Training starts tomorrow," he said, before leaving.

Damian lay in the dark and listened to the drone of the television. He slid MaMaLu's box under his pillow and caressed the worn edges. It wasn't rest that Damian craved. It was something much, much darker. Damian was going to train hard. He was going to learn everything El Charro could teach him, and then he was going to use that very knowledge to destroy him.

IT WASN'T LONG BEFORE EL Charro summoned Damian. News of the attempt on his life had sparked rumors and El Charro was itching to send a message to his enemies.

"You are going to accompany this boy to church," said El Charro, as they drove through the urban sprawl of concrete and glass that was Caboras.

Damian looked at the boy sitting between him and El

Charro. He looked about nine or ten and he was staring ahead vacantly. His hands were wrapped tightly around a canvas bag, like he was carrying a fragile baby.

"You know what to do." El Charro turned to him when they stopped outside a church. They had driven about four hours to get there.

The boy looked out the window, at the tall spires that framed the entrance and nodded.

"Damian, you wait for him by the door," said El Charro.

Damian got out and followed the boy up the wide, rounded steps to the church. It was only when he was at the entrance that he noticed the trail of blood dripping from the canvas bag the boy was holding. He stopped at the door, like he'd been instructed.

People were gathered inside for a funeral. There was a framed photograph of a middle-aged man in the front, propped up beside the coffin.

'In Loving Memory of Alfredo Ruben Zamora', it said.

His widow and children were sniffling in the front row. A priest was speaking to the congregation. They all paused when the boy walked in. He opened the canvas bag and sent something rolling down the aisle.

It was a few seconds before the screaming started, a few seconds before Damian realized that it was the severed head of the man they were holding the funeral for.

"For my parents," said the boy, before turning around.

Damian caught a glimpse of a bloody 'C' carved on the dead man's forehead.

"El Charro!" He heard someone say as he followed the boy out.

They got in the car, and the boy wiped his stained, red hands on his shirt. No one said a word on the way back.

"Damian," said El Charro, when they returned to the safe house. "Take him inside. He will be working for me."

"What's his name?" asked Damian, as the boy opened the door and let himself out.

"Rafael. He is Juan Pablo and Camila's son."

"I didn't know they had any children."

"They kept him away from the cantina."

For my parents, Rafael had said.

Damian nodded. "So the funeral was for . . ."

"Someone from Los Zetas, a rival cartel—the man who shot Rafael's parents, the man who tried to kill me."

The man I killed instead, thought Damian.

El Charro had dumped Alfredo Ruben Zamora's decapitated body outside his home, and had his head delivered during his funeral. In one move, El Charro had brought Rafael into the world of crime and violence, and ensured that Damian witnessed the funeral of the man he'd killed, recognized the consequences of his actions. There was no turning back for the two boys now. They were like flies trapped in El Charro's web.

"You see this?" El Charro uncapped the gold tip from his walking cane. On the bottom was a retractable blade in the shape of the letter 'C'. "This is how I like to send a message. Mess with me and your dead body shows up with my mark, the mark of El Charro—the horseman. I wasn't always *capo,* you know. I started off as a horse rancher. I branded animals then, and I brand animals now." He screwed the tip back on. "Tomorrow we attend another church, another funeral."

JUAN PABLO AND CAMILA WERE laid to rest like heroes, surrounded by flowers and candles and long lines of well-wishers who kissed Rafael on the cheeks after the ceremony. As far as they knew, Juan Pablo had saved El Charro's life and taken a bullet in the process. Camila had died by his side.

Damian and Rafael stood by their coffins when the last footsteps echoed out of the church.

"I know it was you," said Rafael. It was the first time Damian had heard him speak.

"What do you mean?"

"I saw the man shoot my parents. I was in the bathroom, but I was too scared to come out. I just stood there. I couldn't move. I couldn't do anything." Rafael looked at his shoes. He was wearing a coat even though it was hot inside, because he had not been able to get Alfredo Ruben Zamora's blood out of his shirt.

"Hey." Damian took his hand. It was cold and damp. "You did a good thing. You have nothing to be ashamed of. He would have shot you too."

"I want to be like you," said Rafael. "Will you teach me to be brave and shoot the bad guys?"

Damian thought of the man he'd killed, of the family he'd left bereaved. He should have shot El Charro instead. He wondered what he would have done if Juan Pablo had intervened, if Juan Pablo had not been his friend.

"It's all fucked up, Rafael. There are no good guys or bad guys. Everyone has a reason."

Juan Pablo had said that to him, on the steps of *La Sombra*. *Everyone has a reason.* Damian had no idea then that he would be standing by his coffin weeks later, repeating the same words to his son.

Seventeen

DAMIAN AND RAFAEL WERE YOUNG, but they weren't as young as some of the other kids the cartel used to serve its purposes—kids who smuggled heroin and cocaine across the border, who served as disposable diversions or inconspicuous messengers. Some of them did it willingly, seduced by the lure of money and power. Others were forced into it. Their parents had been killed or kidnapped, or they were destitute and desperate. They gave each other nicknames that gave them a sense of belonging, of being strong and invincible in a big, bad world: Slim Luis, Teflon Marco, Eddie the Lamb, Two Scars.

The first time they called Damian 'One Eye Damie', because he slept with one eye open, he gave them a look so chilling that they backed off. Damian was fierce, a lone wolf that no one dared to cross or disturb. There was no downtime for Damian. While the rest of them sang along to boastful lyrics over *oomph-oomph* narco music, Damian lined up pop cans and target-practiced with a slingshot. If the *comandante* made them do a dozen pull-ups at the training camp, Damian came home and did three dozen more.

The only one who wasn't afraid of Damian's dark, relentless intensity was Rafael. He trailed Damian around, content to watch, accepting the silences. He didn't ask Damian about the cigarette box that Damian held on to every night, or the newspaper clipping he pulled out to read when he thought no one was looking.

Every day, new recruits came. The girls and women were taken to the third storey, the rough, hardened men occupied the ground floor, and the second floor was assigned to boys and young males. Every day, some left and never made it back. The ones who had been personally recruited by El Charro had one thing in common. They had all been screwed over by someone: family, friends, their boss, their boyfriend, society or someone more powerful than them. They lacked opportunity. They were angry and uneducated, with no prospect of a job or a future. They were the ones who were most pissed off at everyone.

Regardless of how they got there, everyone had a role to play. Damian, Rafael, and some of the other boys were training to be *sicarios*—hitmen. Sicarios were the foot soldiers of the cartel, responsible for carrying out assassinations, kidnappings, theft, extortion, and defending the territory from rival groups and Mexican militia.

Caboras was the perfect ground for the temporary training camps that the cartel set up, in dust-whipped squatter's domains, scattered among the urban sprawl of concrete and metal. Here, young men and women practiced in live firing ranges and combat training courses, that were then abandoned or used intermittently. An elite few, who showed promise and had a steady hand, progressed to special facilities where they learned how to work with explosives. Damian fit the criteria perfectly. Years of folding paper into the sharpest creases, and creating intricate shapes and forms, made him a natural for making and diffusing bombs. He learned the difference between C-4 and TNT and gunpowder and fireworks; he learned about blast radius and circuit boards and timers and triggers.

Damian took some of the questions home with him. He was wrestling with the calculations when Rafael found him.

"I'll be right back," said Damian.

When he returned with the calculator, Rafael had filled in all the numbers. Damian double-checked.

"How the hell did you do that?" he asked. Every single one was correct.

"In my head."

Damian looked at him incredulously.

"I like math," Rafael replied. "It kept me busy when my parents were at the cantina."

"How about this one?" Damian pointed to another question.

Rafael smiled. He was happy there was something he could do to impress Damian. The two boys put their heads together and worked through the rest of the calculations.

THE RECRUITS STARTED GETTING REAL-LIFE

tasks to complete: follow an informer, steal a car, rob a store. Every time they succeeded, they were rewarded with money, drugs, alcohol, clothes and weapons. Those who got caught were carted to prison, became victims of vigilante justice, or ended up bleeding in the gutters. If they made it back, they were shamed.

Damian knew the real test would come when they were summoned to El Charro's ranch, in a desolate location near the mountains. That was where the men were separated from the boys, where El Charro either allowed you into his inner circle, or cut you off. While everyone carried on like there was no tomorrow, Damian prepared for that day. He had to get into that inner circle, destroy El Charro and then get out. On his days off, Damian disappeared. He bought a panga and a fishing rod, and spent hours on the water; he learned how to tie knots and how to read the sky and the water. Damian loved the solitude of the ocean. It was vast and endless and merciless—like the hole where his heart used to beat. Sometimes when he closed his eyes and lay back in his small canoe, he could hear the sound of MaMaLu's voice in the wind and the waves.

One day, when Damian returned from his trip, he found Rafael curled up in a corner. Damian felt his blood boil at the sight of his beaten and bruised body. Rafael was not like the other boys. The memory of his parents' death still terrorized him. It instilled in him a deep fear of firearms. He flinched every time he heard a gunshot, and he hated himself for it. The other boys bullied and ridiculed him, calling him a faggot and a coward.

"Who did this?" Damian asked Manuel, the little boy who sat with Rafael, trying to make him feel better.

"It doesn't matter." Rafael refused to name the boys who had beaten him up, but after that, wherever Damian went, he took Rafael with him. If someone wanted to get to Rafael, they had to go through Damian.

The *comandante* was not happy when he found out that Damian was taking Rafael on his assignments, and accompanying Rafael on his. He was Comandante 19. Eighteen *comandantes* had died before him. Twice he warned Damian. When Damian persisted, he pulled out his gun and confronted him. Damian walked up to Comandante 19's gun and butted his forehead against the barrel.

"Go ahead," he said. "Make my day."

Everyone stopped to witness the face-off. Everyone knew the *comandante* always won. If you don't listen, you don't live. They held their breath.

"Dirty Harry," said Comandante 19. "The fucker is quoting Dirty Harry." He started laughing and looked around. "Are you kidding me?" he said when no one responded. "My favorite *gringo* movie and this loser's the only one who's seen it?"

He waved them away and subjected Damian to extra drills until the sun came up. After that, everyone left Damian and Rafael alone. Damian suspected El Charro had something to do with it. He either had a soft spot for Damian, or he was grooming him for something bigger.

The call to El Charro's ranch came a year later. By then, only a handful of the original recruits remained. Comandante 19 put them all in a pick-up truck and drove them to the mountains at dawn. Damian knew it wasn't just a ranch—it was also an execution site where El Charro disposed of his enemies.

The boys were corralled into a sweltering, hot room with bare walls and a cement floor. The stench was nauseating. A dozen men and women were being held captive: members of rival gangs, informers, deserters, people who had stolen from the cartel or owed money and couldn't pay back. Some had been kidnapped and were being held for ransom. They all reeked of fear and blood and sweat.

"Who is going to be the next *sicario*?" El Charro greeted the recruits who had just got off the truck.

"You?" He put his gun under a boy's chin and forced it up.

"You?" He walked over to the next one. "Or are you going to end up in there today?" He pointed to the black garbage bags that had been placed by each recruit's feet. "Let's see, shall we?"

He put a shiny blade in the boy's hand and pointed to one of the prisoners. "Bring me his ear, Eduardo."

Eduardo walked up to the man, who was tied to a chair. His face was pock-marked with cigarette burns that were still healing over.

"What are you waiting for?" El Charro waved his gun.

"Which one do you want?" asked Eduardo. "The left ear or the right?"

El Charro's laughter mingled with the man's whimpers. "I like you, Eduardo." He surveyed the prisoner, tilting his head one way then another. "I'll take the left one."

Eduardo delivered. El Charro held up the man's ear while his screams filled the room. "And that's how it's done," he said, parading the mutilated ear before the rest of the boys. Eduardo took a seat beside Comandante 19.

One by one, El Charro tested the recruits. He gave them hammers to smash knees, acid to burn skin, buckets and rags for water torture. For those two hours, the small gray room in the isolated mountains turned into a hellish initiation ceremony. El Charro stole the souls of each and every one of those boys. He was the devil and he was forging them in fire and blood and brimstone.

When he got to the boy standing next to Rafael, he handed him a loaded gun.

"That one." He pointed to a woman who was curled up on the floor, terrorized by the wailing and screaming around her.

The boy pointed the gun, but couldn't bring himself to shoot. He tried again as she squirmed on the ground, her wrists tied behind her back.

"Charro—" said the boy.

Before he could say another word, El Charro shot him point blank in the chest. He tumbled sideways and fell on the woman. El Charro walked over to the body, removed the tip of his cane and stamped a blood red 'C' on him. Comandante 19 dragged his body away and stuffed it into a garbage bag.

"You." El Charro handed the gun to Rafael. It was still warm from the other boy's fingers. "Finish her off."

Rafael stepped forward.

"*Por favor,*" the woman pleaded.

Rafael raised the gun and took aim. Beads of sweat formed on his brow.

Damian clenched his fists. He knew Rafael was reliving the horror of Juan Pablo and Camila's deaths. He knew there was no protecting Rafael from this one.

"I can't." Rafael lowered the gun.

Damian was torn. A part of him wanted Rafael to shoot, to save his own life, and the other part was relieved. Rafael had stood up to the darkness. El Charro had not been able to corrupt him.

"Damian." El Charro took the gun from Rafael and gave it to him. "Shoot the boy." He waved his cane at

Rafael.

Damian went deathly still.

"Didn't you hear what I said? *Chingatelo*—fuck him over!"

Damian realized that he had gotten away with protecting Rafael all this time because El Charro had allowed it, because *this* was the test El Charro had set up for him—to kill Rafael, the only person he'd grown close to in the whole group. El Charro wanted to empty him of all emotions, all entanglements. He didn't want his *sicarios* to flinch or hesitate or question his orders. If Damian did this now, if he killed Rafael, he would prove himself to El Charro. He would get close enough to avenge MaMaLu. And *that* was the only thing that had kept Damian going so far.

Damian raised the gun. Tears were streaming down Rafael's face, but he held his ground. He knew Damian had no choice. If he didn't do as El Charro commanded, they would both lose their lives.

"Rafael." Damian stared down the barrel of the gun. "How many grams of cocaine can I get for a thousand pesos?"

Rafael looked at him, confused.

"Answer the question," said Damian.

Rafael quoted a number.

"And how many grams for a thousand U.S. dollars?"

Again, Rafael answered.

Damian repeated the question for euros, yens, rubles, rupees . . .

Each time, Rafael shot back with a figure.

"Is that right?" El Charro asked Comandante 19.

"I don't know. Let me check." Comandante 19 got out his phone and started punching numbers. His jaw dropped open. "He got them all right, Charro."

"Well, what do you know?" said El Charro. "The boy is no *sicario*, but he has a knack for numbers. We can use someone like him." El Charro lowered Damian's hand. "Well done, Damian. You managed to save your friend *and* impress me. *Sicarios*!" He turned to the boys who had made it, his arm still around Damian. "You too, my little whiz kid," he said to Rafael. "Congratulations! This is the beginning of a new chapter. Come. Let us celebrate."

Damian followed El Charro out, the horrific images of black garbage bags, and mangled body parts, and blood-splattered walls etched forever in his mind.

Yes. This is the beginning of a new chapter, El Charro. The beginning of your end, he thought. *Because I won't stop until I have destroyed both you and Warren Sedgewick.*

Eighteen

DESTROYING EL CHARRO TOOK TIME and careful deliberation. Damian knew he would only get one chance, so he had to make it count. Even if he managed to kill El Charro, the other members of the cartel would come after him, and Damian wasn't ready to call it quits without taking Warren Sedgewick down. Not only did Damian have to plan his attack, he also had to put together an escape plan.

Two things worked in Damian's favor. The first was that El Charro kept him clean. After Comandante 19 perished in a shoot-out, Damian slowly took over as the explosives expert, too valuable to waste on the streets. El Charro consulted him when he needed to obliterate rival safe houses, evidence, bodies—Damian had El Charro's complete trust. The second thing Damian was grateful for was that El Charro sent Rafael to a private school outside of Caboras. El Charro needed more than muscle to run his organization. He saw the value of investing in young professionals, early on in their careers. Damian knew that Rafael would have to work for El Charro, but he intended to finish the *capo* off long before it was time to collect.

Over the next few years, Damian saved his money—and there was a lot of it. By the time he was sixteen, he had moved into an apartment facing the ocean and traded in his panga for a secondhand yacht. When he saw the fishermen coming in, their boats heavy with the day's catch, Damian went down and bought fresh fish and crabs and shrimp. He loaned them money to repair their tired trawlers and fishing nets. In turn, they invited him on their voyages and shared their secrets of the sea with him. If they noticed the looks their daughters gave Damian when they took him home for dinner, they didn't say anything.

Damian didn't just work with explosives, he was a slow, burning fuse, waiting to detonate. The bad-ass vibe that surrounded him both thrilled and intimidated the girls. The fact that he was removed—unattainable and uninterested—only spurred their desire for him. But Damian steered clear of romantic liaisons, the heady flush of first love, the sweaty palms and stuttered words, the sweet, painful yearning for a lover's kiss. He remembered his first kiss, the night of the initiation ceremony, but not the lips or the face. El Charro had thrown a party in honor of the new *sicarios*. Food and booze and drugs and women. Damian had been introduced to the world of sex, and it suited him to keep his involvement limited to women who were paid to please him. Relationships were a weakness he did not allow himself.

Every year, Damian left a bouquet of Mexican

sunflowers on MaMaLu's grave. He picked the deepest orange blossoms with the brightest centers. MaMaLu was buried in Paza del Mar, in the cemetery behind the church of Archangel Michael—the same church where Damian had made his first drop for El Charro, the same church he had attended as a boy with MaMaLu. Her grave was surrounded by those of all the other dead, unclaimed prisoners from Valdemoros—a pile of rocks with a plain slab, engraved with her name and prisoner number. There was no date of death, because someone had forgotten to jot it down, and it broke Damian's heart that she had been robbed of that dignity. Damian did not get a new stone for MaMaLu. He needed that reminder. Every year, when he saw that incomplete slab, the fire in him blazed higher, and he needed it to burn eternally so he could take a chisel and hammer to the hearts of the two men who had put her there, and carve out retribution. Then, and only then, would he get MaMaLu a proper tombstone.

Once when Rafael came to visit Damian over the holidays, they drove to *La Sombra*, the cantina where Rafael's parents had worked. It was still El Charro's domain, one of the many bases he frequented. A new couple ran the place. They were younger than Juan Pablo and Camila. The woman's smudged apron strained against her pregnant belly. Damian and Rafael could not bring themselves to eat there, so they bought fish tacos from a street vendor.

"I would never have survived if it wasn't for you," said Rafael. He was thirteen, but tall for his age. "You saved my life."

They were sitting on the hood of the car, outside Casa Paloma.

"I saved *my* life, Rafael." He knew Rafael was thinking

about a small, blood-splattered room in the mountains. "If you were in my way, I'd have taken you out. Make no mistake about it."

Rafael took a swig of beer and laughed. "You like to think you're all *cojones*, no *corazón*. All balls, no heart. But I know better."

"You don't know shit." Damian walked up to the tall, wrought iron gates of the now-lifeless estate.

Casa Paloma was in disarray. Tall, thorny weeds had taken over the garden. All the windows were boarded up, and the lock that Victor had chained to the main gate was gritty with rust. Damian liked that. It felt just like his memories of the place—chained and dead and abandoned.

Keep Out.

This was the place where MaMaLu had fallen victim to the politics of wealth and power, to greedy men with a sense of entitlement that left them with no remorse for the lives they destroyed.

"One day I'm going to own this place," said Damian, when they got back in the car.

One day, he was going to bring down Warren with the same weapons he had used against MaMaLu: money and ruthlessness. One day, he was going to rob Warren of everything he held precious.

"Is that before or after you destroy El Charro?" asked Rafael, rolling his eyes. He wished Damian would give up his quest. El Charro was invincible and he didn't want his friend getting hurt.

Damian doubted if El Charro remembered the nanny who had come chasing after a little girl and chanced upon a meeting of black crows. No. El Charro was the scavenger of carrion. One dead body was no different from another. Damian was not going to waste his time trying to make him remember. El Charro didn't deserve explanations or justifications. He deserved fire and ashes, an incinerating descent to hell.

"First El Charro, then Warren Sedgewick." Damian started the engine. "Then I take the place where it all began."

As they drove away, Damian did not think of Skye. He never once thought of Skye. She was locked up in a room with windows that were boarded up with sheets of plywood. And Damian always, always stayed away from strawberries and gap-toothed girls with hair like spun gold.

THE RIVALRY BETWEEN THE SINALOA cartel and Los Zetas was escalating. Every day bodies were turning up in the ditches; blood was flowing in the gutters. El Charro called a meeting of his most trusted allies and advisers.

"Damian," he said, examining the 'C' he had just carved into the victim at his feet. "My blade needs replacing." He handed Damian his cane.

Every year, Damian took El Charro's cane to a blacksmith in Caboras, who fitted it with a new, razor-sharp, custom piece.

"We are meeting at the new warehouse in Paza del Mar tomorrow. 3 pm. Have it fixed by then," said El Charro. "Comandante 21, look after these bodies." He stepped over them, holding a handkerchief to his nose.

Damian followed El Charro out and watched him drive away in his air-conditioned sedan. He switched the sim card on his phone and made a call. "I have information for Emilio Zamora."

He didn't have to wait long. Emilio Zamora was the

younger brother of Alfredo Ruben Zamora, the man who had attempted to kill El Charro, the man Damian had shot in the cantina. Of course, Emilio, like everyone else, thought Juan Pablo was responsible for his brother's death. Ever since El Charro had sent Alfredo's severed head to his funeral, Emilio had been vying to get even.

"Tomorrow. The warehouse in Paza del Mar. 3 pm. El Charro and all of his right hand men."

"Who is this?" asked Emilio, but Damian hung up.

The perfect opportunity had finally presented itself.

DAMIAN GUARDED THE DOOR WHILE Comandante 21 accompanied El Charro inside the warehouse. One by one, men arrived in bodyguard-driven cars, and took a seat around the long table, with their muscle men standing a respectable distance behind them. The location had been disclosed last minute as an added security measure. For all intents and purposes, the warehouse functioned as a shipping facility for canned sardines, but Damian knew that the cardboard boxes and crates stacked around them were filled with shrink wrapped bales of marijuana, blocks of cocaine and methamphetamine, along with carefully sealed bags of brown powder heroin.

Every man in the room was connected to the cartel in one way or another. Some owned the farmers who grew local marijuana; others had contacts in Colombia, Peru or Bolivia. A few ran the hidden super labs that manufactured methamphetamine. They were all involved with the preparation, transportation and distribution of drugs, carrying them over the American border via cars, trucks, speedboats, drug tunnels and cross border mules. They had dirty cops and judges in their pockets, and stash houses in Los Angeles, El Paso, Houston, Tucson. From there, the drugs infiltrated other major cities, trickling down to hundreds of suburbs and communities beyond. Damian wondered which of them had been present the day MaMaLu had interrupted the meeting at Casa Paloma. He glanced at his watch. It was 2:45 pm.

"Damian! How's it going, man?" He felt a hard slap on his back.

Damian turned pale. "Rafael. What are you doing here?"

"I invited him. My mathemagician," said El Charro, patting the empty seat next to him. Rafael made him look good. El Charro slipped him notes during important meetings and Rafael came up with the numbers he needed for viable options.

"Listen, Rafael—" Damian pulled him back.

"Shut the door, Damian," said El Charro. "And bring me my cane. It's time we got started."

Damian unwrapped El Charro's cane from the plastic sheathing and handed it to him.

Outside, El Charro's men prowled the perimeter.

Inside, the king held court with his dark knights.

Damian glanced at his watch again. All the pieces of the puzzle were in place, except for one. Damian had to move quickly. He passed a note to Rafael under the table and got up. El Charro raised an eyebrow.

"Be right back," said Damian. He let himself out the back door. The two men stationed there recognized him. Damian stopped in the shade of a tall tree and pretended to take a piss. Behind him, a canopy of coconut palms covered the surrounding hills. A troop of howler monkeys let out loud, barking whoops as they swung from branch to branch across the treetops, startling one of the guards at the door.

"*Chupame la verga*," he said, when the other one laughed at him. Suck my dick.

They were still laughing when Emilio Zamora's men slashed their necks. Damian ducked behind the tree. The foliage concealed him.

The Zetas were vicious. And quiet. They had the advantage of surprise and they used it to methodically eliminate the guards outside. Machetes, knives, cords, chains, rocks, batons. No firearms. Emilio Zamora did not want to tip El Charro off, or bring him down in a blaze of gunfire. He wanted him alive so he could finish him off in the most painful way.

Of course, things didn't go as planned. El Charro's men started shooting when they realized what was happening, but they didn't stand a chance. Emilio Zamora did not trust anonymous tips received over the phone. He had his moles look into it, and then he brought a veritable army with him. It was paying off. They overwhelmed the guards outside and stormed into the warehouse, guns blazing.

Damian crawled to the back door, over the bodies of the dead guards. Going back inside was a fool's mission, but he had to get Rafael out. The only thing that kept him moving forward was his combat training, and the rush of adrenaline that jolted through his system. He ignored the zing of bullets, the splinters flying in the air, the steady stream of spent brass casings as they clanged on the floor. Half the lights were gone, bulbs shattered, and bodies lay around him—some lifeless, some screaming in agony. The warehouse was hazy with gunpowder and the grit of boxes spewing drugs into the air. It was hard to breathe, hard to see, but Damian kept crawling until he was under the table. Rafael was crouched at the other end. His hands were over his ears and he was rocking back and forth on his heels.

Damian had almost reached him when two men fell to the floor, toppling over the chairs. They rolled around, one trying to snatch the gun away from the other. Shoe-polish black hair glistened in the semi-darkness. El Charro was wrestling with Emilio Zamora.

"Damian!" El Charro spotted him under the table. They both saw the other gun, lying discarded by Damian's foot. "Give it to me." El Charro held out his hand.

Their eyes met for a fraction. Damian wanted to pick up the gun and pump El Charro's body full of lead, but he knew that would ruin his plan. At the same time, he couldn't let El Charro kill Emilio until he and Rafael were safely out of the building.

Damian kicked the gun out of El Charro's reach. "Maria Luisa Alavarez," he said. "Remember my mother's name when you meet your maker."

El Charro's face registered shock and disbelief, not because he had a clue what Damian was talking about, but because of the betrayal. It was momentary, because Emilio pulled El Charro up by the collar, and El Charro had more important things on the line. Like his life.

Damian continued making his way to Rafael. There was no turning back for him now. He had spoken his truth, let El Charro see the hate in his eyes. If El Charro survived, it would mean the end for Damian. But Damian needed him to survive just a little bit longer.

"Rafael." He shook him.

But Rafael was in shock, like he'd been when he'd peered through the bathroom door and witnessed his parents die. Gunfire was his biggest phobia.

"Rafael." Damian slapped him twice. It was enough to

rouse him out of his personal hell.

"I hid under the table. Like you said." Rafael still had Damian's note scrunched up in his fist.

"Good. Now listen to me," said Damian. "Keep your head down, keep crawling until you get to the door." He pointed to the exit in the back.

"What about you?"

"I'll be right behind you. Don't look back. Just keep going. When you make it to the door, run for the trees. You got that?"

Rafael flinched as a spray of bullets riddled the crates behind them.

"Rafael? You got that?"

Rafael nodded and started making his way under the table.

Damian spotted Comandante 21 lying on the floor. His eyes were open, but he was gone. Damian felt for the strap around his ankle. He removed the knife that Comandante 21 always carried with him. El Charro and Emilio Zamora were still struggling like giants in the arena. Crawling back under the table, Damian waited until their legs were inches from him. Then he reached out and slashed the back of Emilio Zamora legs, severing the tendons that held him up. Emilio Zamora fell to his knees.

"What did you do that for?" Rafael looked at Damian with his mouth open.

"I told you to keep going."

"But Emilio was just about to kill El—"

"Move, Rafael!"

Rafael didn't argue. The two boys made it out and dashed for the trees. Behind them, the carnage continued. When they got to the top of the hill, Damian turned around.

"I don't get it." Rafael was bent over, trying to catch his breath. "Why didn't you go after El Charro?"

"I needed him alive," said Damian.

"But—"

Just then, a fireball erupted in the warehouse, a thunderous explosion of heat and smoke. All they could hear through muffled ears was a highpitched *'eeeeee'*, as a second sun spewed glass and debris into the air. One side of the warehouse stood, quaking unsteadily, before collapsing in a cloud of dust and ash. Everything stopped—the wind in the trees, the birds, the animals. It was a strange silence, filled with the blaring of car alarms.

"What did you do?" asked Rafael, through the haze-filled heat.

"I rigged the place with explosives and placed the trigger in El Charro's cane. The moment he brought down the retractable blade . . . *KABOOM*."

"That's why you stopped Emilio from gaining the upper hand. You *wanted* El Charro to kill him. You knew El Charro wouldn't be able to resist marking him, just like he had marked his brother."

Damian kept staring at the warehouse. Nothing had survived—not the men, not the drugs, not the decoy cans of smoked sardines.

"Shit, Damian," said Rafael, as realization dawned on him. "We're free of El Charro and the cartel. They'll think we died in there, with everyone else. They'll think it was a fight to the death between El Charro and Emilio Zamora. 'C' for *cesado*. Finished. Dismissed. You fucking charbroiled El Charro and everyone else."

"We're not in the clear yet, Rafael. They'll find traces of explosives if they look closely."

"Yeah, but the Sinaloa cartel will point the finger at

Los Zetas and Los Zetas will turn around and blame them. Ingenious, Damian. Well worth the wait."

"One down, one to go," said Damian, dusting off his pants.

Rafael knew he was thinking about Warren Sedgewick. "Geez, Damian. You should allow yourself a breather. Even movies have intermissions."

"Really? And where would your ass be if I'd taken off for popcorn and candy?"

"True. That's twice you've saved my life," said Rafael. "So what now?"

"Now we lay low and wait for the dust to settle. Think of it as an intermission."

"For how long?"

"As long as it takes to put together the next plan, Rafael. As long as it takes."

Nineteen

"WE'VE COME A LONG WAY from Caboras," said Rafael, clinking his beer with Damian's.

Damian surveyed the tiki-torch lit patio overlooking Mission Bay, the exotic, tropical fish swimming in the ceiling-high aquarium and the pristine table setting before them.

"It's taken a long time to get here," he said.

"Eleven fucking years." Rafael scanned the menu. "What are you having?"

"A burger," replied Damian, without opening his menu. He fidgeted with his cuff links. "Was this really necessary?" he asked.

"You want to blend into fancy circles, you've got to look the part. How do you like the shoes? I had my guy custom make them."

"I get that they're standard issue for a hotshot financial advisor like you, but fuck it, Rafael, there's nothing like a pair of shoes broken in by hard labor and sweat."

"Screw hard labor and sweat. You deserve this. When are you going to start enjoying some of your hard-earned cash? If you don't start relaxing, Damian, your face is going to set into a permanent scowl and you'll scare the girls away. Permanently."

Damian waved his hand dismissively. At twenty-seven, he was completely oblivious to the polarized reactions of the women around him. When Damian walked into a room, he went for the shadows and dark corners. He never fit in and he never attempted to. But the very attention he sought to avoid always found him, because it was like dragging in a caged animal. The women flocked around him, afraid to touch him, afraid to talk to him, but at the same time, completely fascinated.

"The money means nothing," he said. "It's a means to an end."

"I know that, but take some credit for what you've achieved. After El Charro, we had nothing but the money you'd stashed away. And you managed to turn that around. From one boat to two, to five, to ten. From a small fishing company to a motherfucking shipping conglomerate. You put me through college while you worked your ass off. Everything I am, I owe to you. And now here you are. On the brink of toppling Warren Sedgewick over."

Damian thought back to those early years after El Charro's death. He had kept his ear to the ground about Warren. El Charro was a stranger who had sought to eliminate a threat, but Warren . . . Warren *knew* MaMaLu. She had looked after his daughter for nine years—*nine* fucking years—six of which she'd tried to fill the void his wife had left. She had loved Skye as dearly as she loved her own son, going so far as to put Damian second when it came to her time and affection. And how had Warren rewarded her? By betraying her to save his own skin. He was a coward who needed to atone for his sins, not by dying, but by *living*. Damian wanted him to feel pain his whole fucking life. He was going to strip Warren of his extravagant mansion in La Jolla, his fleet of chauffeur-driven cars, his line of immaculate, luxury resorts, scattered across the most idyllic spots in the world. One by one, Damian was going to take it all away—his fame, his fortune, his prestige—the very foundation his world was built on. And to get there, to battle Warren in his ivory tower, Damian had to amass his own weapons, build his own fortune, a fortune fueled by something far more powerful than anything Warren had in his arsenal: a rusty box of cigarettes and the memory of MaMaLu's incomplete tombstone.

Wherever Damian went, the *Lucky Strike* tin went with him. It was there when he scouted remote islands and atolls, looking for a place he and Rafael could lay low. It was there when the dust settled over the deaths of El Charro and Emilio Zamora, and everyone had forgotten two insignificant boys who had been there that day. It was there when they relocated to a fishing port, where Damian bought his first trawler, El Caballero, a name he took on as part of his new identity. It was there when he saw Rafael off to a prestigious boarding school, and again when he attended Rafael's graduation from college. It was there when Damian was big enough and wealthy enough to apply for a U.S. green card as an investor, and then years later, his citizenship. And it was there now, in his inner coat pocket, as he had dinner with Rafael, in Warren's

Polynesian themed flagship resort: The Sedgewick, San Diego.

When Warren had started out, he was still under the cartel's thumb. He had managed to get out of Mexico, but only because it suited their purposes. They needed ways to turn the dirty cash from drug sales and other illegal activities into clean, usable currency, and Warren was one of the cogs in their money-laundering machine. Damian understood his role well. Warren would buy a prime piece of U.S. real estate. He would build a five star resort, fill it with the finest linen, cutlery, china, the best furniture. From there, he would report his hotel at maximum occupancy, except it was never completely full. Every day, a security van would roll up and collect all the cash taken in from the rooms, nightclubs, casinos, bars and restaurants—dirty cash mixed in with legitimate income. Warren got a cut of the action. The rest made its way to offshore accounts that belonged to El Charro, who then dispersed it to his top men.

El Charro's death freed Warren from the clutches of the cartel. The direct link had been severed. That arm of the Sinaloa cartel no longer existed. Warren wrapped up his illegal dealings and continued to expand his chain of hotels with his own money. After a couple of years, he went public. Sedgewick Hotels became a hot commodity, traded on the stock exchange. Warren thought he was in the clear. He never, for one second, conceived of what was coming for him, *who* was coming for him.

When Warren walked into the restaurant that night, Rafael turned to Damian. "There he is, just like clockwork. Every Tuesday night, eight o'clock sharp."

Damian felt his hackles rise. He ignored the urge to turn around and bit into his burger. He had been buying

Sedgewick stock for years via shell companies that Rafael set up for him. Warren didn't know it, but Damian Caballero now held enough shares to control the future of Sedgwick Hotels and here, on the eve of a reckoning that had taken him over a decade to stage, Damian wanted to have one last look at the man responsible for destroying MaMaLu. Tomorrow, he would be a different man, a broken man.

"Everything is set?" he asked Rafael.

"Say the word and it's done."

Damian pushed his plate away. "I need a drink. I'm heading to the bar." From where he could watch Warren, and savor the last bittersweet dregs of the venom that had fueled him for so long.

Rafael nodded. He knew Damian well enough to understand when he needed time alone. "Take your time. I'll be right here."

Damian sat at the far end of the sleek, reflective counter, away from the crowd, where the lights were dim and the music was muted. He took a tall sip of beer before his eyes sought Warren out. He was sitting in a private booth. The wait staff obviously knew who he was and what he liked. They brought him a drink without asking, and some kind of appetizer on a long rectangular plate.

Damian had seen pictures of Warren, but nothing had prepared him for seeing him in the flesh fifteen years later—fifteen years after he had chased Warren's silver Peugeot down a dusty road. Warren looked smaller, shorter, not as all-pervading as he was in Damian's head. He was in his fifties now, but looked older, with a chunky mustache that was almost all silver. How could he sit there, eating and drinking, so pleasant and alive, when MaMaLu was cold bones and desiccated earth? How could *anyone* go on so indifferent, so unaffected, knowing they had destroyed worlds and dreams and lullabies? Warren was El Charro, except worse. Whereas El Charro had made no pretense about being a monster, Warren had built himself a facade of decency.

If Damian had left then, at that precise moment, he would have stuck to his original plan—to take over Warren's company, strip it, devalue it, dismantle it and rob him of the power and prestige he had traded his humanity in for. But just as he was finishing the last of his beer, Damian stopped mid-swig. A young lady slid into the booth with Warren. She didn't sit across from him; she sat next to him and engulfed him in the biggest, tightest hug. Damian couldn't see her face, but it was clear Warren had been expecting her. His whole face transformed. He *glowed* with something indefinable, something true but intangible, something Damian had only seen before in MaMaLu's eyes—when he picked flowers for her hair, when he made her a seashell necklace, when he was sick, when he was hurt, when he made her laugh and sometimes, when he made her cry. That look, that *look* which Damian would have given anything for, was the way Warren was looking at his dinner companion—with the whole Goddamned world in his eyes.

Damian sucked in his breath.

Look away, look away.

But he couldn't. And in that moment, Skye Sedgewick flipped her long, golden hair to the side and kissed her father on the cheek.

Fuck.

Damian felt like he had been punched in the gut. The memories he had locked up behind iron gates swelled against their chains.

"One more." Damian slammed his beer on the counter. The bartender jumped. When she poured him another, he grabbed it and gulped it down in one long guzzle, drowning out everything that threatened to break free—echoes of kites and cakes and trees with bright, yellow flowers.

When he looked at Skye again, fortified and controlled now, she was gushing over something her father had given her. She tore through the logo-emblazoned packaging and held out a bag.

"Hermes!" she squealed.

Gone was the endearing gap between her teeth, sealed and veneered, just like her heart. She was the girl who hadn't stopped when Damian had gone running after her car. She was the girl who hadn't bothered saying goodbye. She was the girl who had trampled on his heart and his paper animals, and on MaMaLu's love and songs and stories. She was, every inch, Warren's daughter—callous and uncaring and materialistic and fake. A fake friend, a fake confidante, a fake childhood memory. She was a counterfeit, wrapped up in genuine designer packaging. But most of all . . . most of all . . . she was *everything* to Warren. The way Warren looked at his daughter left Damian with no doubt about that. Nothing was more precious to Warren than his daughter—not his mansion, not his cars, not his company. If Damian wanted to make Warren suffer, *really* suffer, he had to take *her* away from him. Forever.

"A woman for a woman," said Damian when he returned to the table.

"A what?" asked Rafael.

"A woman for a woman. He kills my mother, I kill his daughter."

"What are you talking about?"

"See that over there?" Damian pointed to Warren's booth. "That's a father who adores his daughter. There is no greater pain in this world than losing a child, Rafael. And I'm going to make sure Warren feels it, for as long as he lives."

Rafael's eyes darted from Skye to Damian. "Violence? Do you really want to go there? We've spent our lives running from it."

"Not violence, Rafael. Justice. Skye Sedgewick for MaMaLu. *Una mujer por una mujer.*"

"I thought you were going after his company."

Damian pulled out the *Lucky Strike* box from his coat. "I changed my mind." He traced the worn, gold letters and thought of the newspaper article inside, of the lies, lies, lies Warren had spewed about his mother. "I'm going after Skye Sedgewick."

SKYE

. . . 3

Twenty

"AND *THAT'S* HOW ESTEBAN BECAME Damian," said Rafael. "When you prayed for him and MaMaLu, you threw him off. He couldn't bring himself to kill you, but he could make your father *think* you were dead. And now," Rafael raised the gun, "your time really *is* up, princess."

It was almost dark. I could hear the waves crashing on the beach, the squeaks and flutters of night insects stirring around us, the piercing cry of an island bird—like some kind of nature CD: *Sounds of the Jungle*.

Close your eyes. Relax. Don't fight it. Let Rafael shoot you in the head.

I was dead already. The truth doesn't always set you free. The truth can kill you, slice open your innards and turn everything inside out. Everything I believed, everything I thought was real had been turned upside down. My father wasn't the man I thought he was, Damian wasn't the man I thought he was, and MaMaLu wasn't living in a white-walled house with a backyard full of flowers.

"You're lying," I said. "MaMaLu isn't dead. Damian was taking me to see her."

"He was taking you to her grave, so you could see what your father did. It was important to him that you understood why he did what he did. He goes every year. This year he thought he was finally going to keep his promise and complete her tombstone. He was finally going to find his peace, but you . . . you turned out to be the chink in his armor. I knew he was cracking. The more time he spent with you, the harder he found it to distance himself. I could hear it in his voice. So fucking torn. I should have intercepted him sooner, but I'm here now, and it's time to end this."

Rafael's hands were unsteady as he took aim. I turned my face away. I wanted to go back to that late afternoon, to the dusty road, to Casa Paloma receding in the background. I wanted to part the haze, to make out my best friend's form, to stop the car and run to him.

Esteban. I wish the rains had come.

"Let her go," said Damian.

I opened my eyes and saw him, a dark, staggering form standing before us. He could barely stand, but he was holding his ground.

"We both know you won't shoot. You *can't,*" he said to Rafael.

"I will." Rafael kept his gun trained on me, clamping one hand over the other. "For you, I will. I'll get over my fucking fear of guns and shoot her brains out. It's either you or her, Damian. She called her father. Check the log on your phone. You know what that means, right? They're coming for you. It's only a matter of time."

"I *said* let her go." Damian drew a gun and pointed it at Rafael. He swayed unsteadily on his feet.

We were immobilized in a tense triangle: me on my knees between the two men, Rafael pointing a gun at me, Damian pointing a gun at him. Their bond was apparent to me now. The guns were props. They were working out something much deeper, each trying to keep the other from making a wrong move. Rafael was ready to eliminate anything that compromised Damian, and Damian knew that taking a life would haunt Rafael forever. When Damian looked at Rafael, he saw the one thing that he had done right. He saw a sliver of redemption. And Damian had shielded Rafael for far too long to let him get blood on his hands now.

But there was another factor at play. Me. Damian had swung me out of the way on the boat and taken the blow himself. I knew he was also doing this to protect *me.* I knew why I had instinctively turned to him when I thought I was surrounded by sharks. Some part of me had recognized that soul-deep part of him, the part that was still alive but buried under layers of hurt and rage.

"We both know you won't shoot me," Rafael said to Damian, his finger on the trigger, eyes on me.

"Try me," said Damian. "I told you before. You get in my way, I'll take you out."

Rafael didn't look the least bit convinced. "You're hurt, Damian. Delirious. You don't know what you're doing. As long as she's alive, you're in danger. They won't stop until they find her. We have to cut the trail off right here."

"*I* decide," growled Damian. "*I* decide what to do and

when to do it. This has nothing to do with you, so back the fuck off. Get on your boat, get off this island, and don't look back. My life, my fight, my rules."

Rafael didn't move. Damian didn't move. They both stood there, guns raised, too stubborn to admit that each was looking out for the other.

"I got the stuff you asked for, Rafael." It was Manuel, back from his trip. "Your face is all over the news, Damian. The mainland was crawling with cops and private security guys hired by Warren Sedgewick." He looked from Rafael to Damian, suddenly aware he'd tripped over a live wire. "Hey, man, what's going on?"

Rafael and Damian didn't respond. Manuel's news had just added fuel to the fire. They continued warring without words, locked in a duel that stretched out into a thin, taut silence. Then Rafael broke contact.

"This is bullshit, Damian, and you know it," he said. "If you're determined to go down, don't expect me to hang around and watch." He took the case from Manuel and shoved it into Damian's arms. "Medical supplies," he said. "But seeing as you don't give a fuck about your life, you probably won't use them." He was angry, so angry that he wouldn't look Damian in the eye. "You're not invincible, you know that? You're a bull-headed prick who can barely stand. You need to get back inside and stay put. At least until the heat is off. I'll look after the business end of things and get Manuel to plant your phone in Caboras. Let them go chasing for you there," he said. "And next time I see you, you better be damn sure your stubborn ass is still standing."

Damian stayed on his feet until Rafael and Manuel were out of sight. His legs didn't buckle until he heard the boat taking off. Then he dropped like a sack of potatoes. I ran to him, feeling the weight of all the things I now knew about him. I brushed the hair back from his brow. He was burning up—his breath was hot, his skin clammy. Not only had he lost a lot of blood, but it seemed like an infection had set in from his wound.

Yesterday, I would have given anything to be free of him.

Die, Dah-me-yahn, DIE!

Today I was rummaging through the supplies Manuel had brought. I needed antibiotics to fight the infection. I needed something to bring his fever down. I needed him to open his eyes, to look at me, to say something, anything.

Live, Dah-me-yahn, LIVE!

DAMIAN DANGLED BETWEEN LIFE AND death, slipping in and out of consciousness all night. His pulse was erratic, sometimes hard and fast, sometimes barely detectable. I hovered over him, monitoring his fever, wringing out a towel and laying it on his forehead, like I remembered MaMaLu doing when we were sick. When the cold compresses turned lukewarm, I changed the water. Again and again and again.

By morning, I wasn't running to the kitchen as often. Damian seemed to have made it through the worst of it. I stretched out beside him, emotionally and physically exhausted. I had managed to get him back to the villa and into bed, supporting his weight, dragging him step by excruciating step.

We were lying under gauzy, white netting. The house was rough, but charming. With no glass in the windows, it was open to the outside, letting the ocean air sweep through. The netting kept the mosquitoes and bugs away, but it also closed off the rest of the world. I could finally look at Damian—*really* look at him.

If you close your eyes and think about someone you love, what comes back is not a precise list of hair color, eye color, or the things that go on their driver's license. Rather, it's the bits and pieces that seep through your consciousness, the things about them that you never realized you were storing away. Like the shape of Damian's ears and the way his lids had a slight sheen. Everything else had changed—his Adam's apple, so pronounced, the stubble on his jaw, the way his mouth never seemed to relax—but I still knew his ear lobes, from all the times we lay next to each other on the grass. Every time the trees swayed in the wind, yellow flowers dropped on our faces.

I uncurled Damian's palm and traced the lines. It was a man's hand now, big and strong and rough. I felt a crushing tenderness for it. It was the same hand that had rocked me to sleep in the hammock, the same hand that had created paper worlds, the same hand that had showed me how to make a proper fist—not a girly fist, but a proper, Gidiot-busting fist.

I lay my cheek on Damian's palm and let myself imagine, just for a minute, that we were kids again.

"I missed you so much," I said to his crooked thumb. "I wrote to you and MaMaLu every day. I didn't know why you never replied. My heart broke in so many places. I never saw you running after the car, the day we left Casa Paloma. I never knew the hell you were going through. I'm sorry, Estebandido." I kissed the center of his palm. "So sorry." My tears trickled onto his hand.

When I woke up a few hours later, Damian's eyes were open, his hand was still pillowing my face.

"Is it true?" he asked. "What you said?"

Damian speaking softly. I had never heard him use that tone with me. His voice. God, his voice. I tried to reply, but he was looking at me in such a way that I couldn't find the words. He was looking at *me*. Skye. Not Warren Sedgewick's daughter. Not a means to an end. For the first time, Damian was seeing *me*.

I let him look at me, because I knew he needed that, just like I had needed it. I let him see the girl who had worshiped him, the girl who had smuggled strawberries in a stained dress for him, the girl who had wanted to impress him so badly, she'd asked him to let go of her bike before she was ready.

"Why are you looking after me? Why are you being *nice* to me?" he asked.

"Why did you push me out of the way on the boat? Why did you stand up to Rafael? " I reached out to touch his wound, but he flinched and held my hand away. His eyes fell on my bandaged finger and a look of such agony passed over his face that I wanted to wrap my arms around him. But right before my eyes, Damian snapped out of it. He went blank, expressionless, like a chalkboard wiped clean. I stared at his back as he turned away.

It was slowly starting to make sense. When the pain got too much, Damian shut down. He blocked everything out. It was a coping mechanism. I could only imagine the horrors he had witnessed through all those years with El Charro. He had learned to turn his emotions off. I remembered when he cut my finger off. He'd gone on to make potato salad, as if he mutilated people every day.

I watched him adjust his pillow. I knew that sleeping on that side had to hurt—his stitches were still raw. So I flipped over, and stared at the wall. A few minutes later, he shifted back around. I could feel him staring at my back. In a little while, I would get up and give him another dose of his pills, but for now I was content with not being invisible, with having this flickering acknowledgment even though I knew he would look away the moment I turned to face him. Still, there was a lingering undercurrent of fear. Except this time I wasn't afraid *of* Damian.

I was afraid *for* him.

ALL MY LIFE, PEOPLE HAD looked after me. My every whim had been catered to, every need fulfilled. I stood in the kitchen, staring at the shelves, realizing how ill prepared I was to care for someone. I could do coffee and toast, or a bowl of cereal, but now I was looking at condiments and jars of stuff that could no doubt be combined to make something nice, but I had no idea how.

I pulled out a can of tomato soup. Sick people did well on soup. And crackers. I grabbed a packet of those. I looked out of the window as the soup heated on the stove. The contrast of azure waters against the rough limestone wall looked like something out of a travel magazine. A tropical breeze swirled through the kitchen. It was painted soft and earthy, like marzipan and pumpkin butter. I couldn't imagine Damian choosing the color scheme. On the other hand, it was the perfect retreat from the cold, harsh world he lived in. Here, there was warmth and sunshine and light.

Damian eyed me warily when I entered the bedroom with his lunch tray. Clearly, he didn't enjoy being dependent on anyone, but I knew he was just using his gruffness to mask the vulnerability. He hated that he was weak and needed looking after. He hated the guilt that went with being looked after by *me*. But it was exactly what he needed. He needed to know that he was worth caring for, that I wasn't going to abandon him like he thought I'd done all those years ago, that in spite of everything that had happened, I was still standing by his side. I didn't know for how long though, because lord, just getting him to co-operate so I could prop him up to eat was a whole production.

I placed the tray on the bed and turned the spoon his way. He just stared at the tray. I knew he was thinking of all the times he had done the same for me on the boat, bringing me food, except under much different circumstances. I knew what it took for him to pick up that spoon. He held it over the bowl and put it down again. His throat spasmed as he fought whatever was tormenting him.

It dawned on me that no one had cared for Damian, not since MaMaLu, not when he was sick, and not when he was hurt. The world had denied him tenderness, and he didn't know what to do with it now, or how to react. He had singlehandedly brought down a drug lord, but a bowl of soup was breaking him down. He *wanted* me to hate him for what he'd done. An eye for an eye. That made sense to him. Not this, not kindness where he expected loathing. It was turning his whole world upside down.

I wanted to put my hand on his clenched fists and tell him it was okay, but I got up and left. I knew he would never eat while I watched. A few hours later, when I went back to his room, he was sleeping. He had taken his pills, but left the food untouched.

Rafael was right.

Damian was a bull-headed prick.

I OPENED MORE CANS OF soup. More trays went untouched. I was ready to hold him down and force feed him when I found a jar of roasted peanuts. When Damian opened his eyes that afternoon, I was sitting on a chair watching him.

"About time," I said, tossing a handful of peanuts into my mouth.

Crunch, crunch, crunch.

He looked from me to the cone of peanuts that I'd fashioned out of a magazine cover, but didn't say anything.

I continued munching. *Crunch, crunch, crunch.*

He had to be hungry. Starving. He was just too fucking proud to let me do anything for him.

"I thought you were allergic to peanuts," he said.

"You know very well I'm not."

For a fleeting second, the hint of a smile played on his lips.

There it was, a memory that had gotten past his defenses: me discovering chocolate peanut butter ice cream and hiding the container under my bed so I could share it with him. There was nothing left when he climbed through the window that evening. I had eaten the whole thing and was trying not to be sick.

I failed, and he helped me clean up the evidence.

"You knew," I said, realizing why he hadn't blinked when I told him I was allergic to peanuts. I thought of him moisturizing his feet. "You *asshole*."

He laughed, catching the peanut I threw at him.

Damian fucking Caballero *laughed*. And it was the most beautiful thing I'd ever seen. I pretended it didn't matter, like my breath hadn't caught, like my throat wasn't clenched, when I dumped the rest of the peanuts in his lap and walked away.

I needed to be alone so I could hug that moment, the moment his face had cracked into a smile. He needed to be alone so he could eat those peanuts without feeling like I had prepared anything special for him.

DAMIAN GOT BETTER. HE FINISHED his food. When we ran out of soup, I moved on to refried beans and cans of chili and peaches and pears. I hit the motherload when I opened the freezer and found TV dinners I could nuke in the microwave. I was going positively gourmet, adding a pinch of paprika to the mac and cheese, and a floret of thawed out broccoli (which Damian flicked out of the way, the ungrateful bastard).

Sometimes when he was sleeping, I turned on the radio. There was no TV, so I had to rely on crackly news broadcasts. They repeated my name and description, along with Damian's. He was considered armed and dangerous. I listened to a short plea from my father, addressed to Damian. He had a hotline and a reward set up for any leads. I had disappeared almost two weeks ago, and I could hear the strain in my father's voice. He was coming after Damian, guns blazing, not knowing the root of the story. He had no idea that Damian was Esteban, that he was paying for the repercussions of his own actions. I wavered between anger over what he'd done, the lies he'd told, and a deeper conviction, that there was more to the story. I *knew* my father, just as I *knew* Damian. I wanted to tell my father where I was, to put an end to his obvious distress, give him a chance to explain himself, but that meant exposing Damian, and I wasn't about to betray him, like he thought I'd betrayed him all those years ago.

I busied myself with nursing Damian back to health

and not thinking about anything else. One night, I opened up a can of tuna and decided it was time I *made* something. I looked in the fridge and found some lemons, an overripe tomato, and a lone onion rolling around in one of the drawers. I figured I could make ceviche. It was a summertime staple at my favorite restaurant. I had ordered it countless times, and let's face it—how hard can fish cured in lemon juice be? Granted, it was normally made with fresh, raw seafood, but I was all about innovation. I emptied the tuna into a bowl and juiced the lemons over it, being careful to keep my bandaged pinky out of the way.

Marinade. Done.

Next, tomato and onion. I tried to chop the tomato, but it was all squishy so I pulsed it in the blender with the onion, added a dash of hot sauce, and stirred the mixture into the fish.

Voila!

Feeling quite accomplished with my culinary venture, I arranged tortilla chips on the tray and placed the bowl in the center. I carried it to the bedroom and deposited it on Damian's lap.

"I made you something," I announced.

He eyed the lumpy concoction without touching it.

Dear God, he looked so rough and rugged with his almost-beard.

"Go ahead," I said. "It's ceviche."

"Ceviche?" He examined it.

"Yes. It's fish with—"

"I know what ceviche is." He was definitely wary. "You first."

"Fine." I shrugged, scooping up a mouthful with a tortilla chip. "*Mmmm*," I said. "It's really good."

Damian had a taste of it. We both chewed in silence. I swallowed. He spit out a lemon seed and swallowed. I went for another. He followed. Neither of us broke eye contact.

It was the most vile, putrid, goopy thing in the world. It tasted of bile and rotten tomatoes and Bart Simpson's butt.

I spit it out, but Damian kept going, bite after foul, rancid bite, until it was all gone. When he was done, he leaned back, holding his tummy like he was trying to keep it all down.

"Wha—?" I stared at him. "Why did you finish it?"

"Because you made it," he replied. "Don't make it again." He turned onto his side and went to sleep.

DAMIAN GOT OUT OF BED early the next morning. The threat of more of my cooking may have hastened his recovery. The first thing he did was to move the boat under a canopy of coconut trees. He covered the roof with palm fronds and secured them with a rope so no one could spot the boat from above.

Watching him work, lean and shirtless, I wondered how I had ever thought of him as ordinary. He was sculpted, but not overly muscular, with the kind of back and shoulders that came from hard work. His skin was the same color I remembered: warm sand with a dusting of bronze. He rarely combed his hair, but far from a tangled mess, it looked wind-worn and sexy, with the ends curled up from the humidity.

When Damian looked my way, I pretended I was engrossed in the seashell at my feet. I thought of our Sunday strolls on the beach, the two of us racing ahead of

MaMaLu, ready to pounce before the next wave pulled its treasures back into the ocean. We only picked shells that had been battered by the waves, smashed and worn so thin that they turned into iridescent slivers of light. Those were the ones MaMaLu loved best. We made necklaces for her. I sorted them by size and shape while he carefully made a hole through them. That was the hardest part—tapping a nail through their fragile forms without breaking them.

I collected a few shells before heading back inside, feeling like I was reclaiming little pieces of me. Here, on this remote island, with no beach chairs or loud music or attentive hostesses topping up my cocktail, I was getting back in touch with myself. I didn't care if my hair was frizzy, or what time dinner was being served, or my massage appointment, or the private cruise. There was a sense of freedom, a sense of simplicity that I didn't know I'd been missing.

That night, Damian cooked crabs on the beach over a small fire and a pot of water. We ate them with melted butter dribbling down our chins. Okay, so he was a much better cook than me, and he would make a hell of a contestant on Survivor, but all of that aside, I thought he was a motherfucking bad-ass because he had survived my ceviche.

He slashed open some green coconuts and we sipped the sweet, light water inside. Damian didn't look at me. Much. He kept his eyes on the water. Occasionally, he looked up at the sky. I wondered if he was scanning the area for boats or helicopters. I was pretty sure he'd tuned in to the news.

Once or twice when his eyes settled on me, he looked away quickly. I didn't know what he was thinking or how long we were supposed to lay low. There were so many things I wanted to ask him, so much I wanted to know, but sitting beside him, watching the fire as the waves rolled in, filled me up. I felt safe with Damian. I wanted to curl up and put my head on his lap, like I had done all those years ago at the start of our friendship.

But Damian was busy. He was making holes in the shells I had picked. He was so gentle, so careful with each piece that I couldn't take my eyes off him. His fingers felt each shell, before picking the right spot. Sometimes he caressed a shell, turning it over, giving it his full attention, before putting it aside. Those were the ones that would crack from the slightest dent, and Damian didn't want to damage any.

When he was done, Damian threaded a cord through the shells and tied the ends. He held it up before the fire. The necklace glowed in the golden light, frail and ethereal.

"Here." He gave it to me.

Damian had never made a seashell necklace for anyone except MaMaLu. Suddenly, I realized what he was doing. He was saying sorry. He was making up for the necklace he had thrown overboard, the necklace that had taken his mother away from him.

Have you ever held a life in your hand? He had dropped the locket in my hand and closed my fingers around it. *Here, feel it.*

I'd thought he was nuts, but my mother's necklace had cost his mother's life. And yet, here he was, giving me a memory of his mother to make up for taking away mine.

"She was my mother too," I said. "MaMaLu was the only mother I knew."

Huge, heavy sobs ripped through me. I reached for him, wrapping my arms around him, wanting to share this pain, this grief. Had anyone held him when she died?

Had anyone comforted him? He stiffened, but let me cry. I cried for him. I cried for MaMaLu. I cried for our mothers who were gone, and for all the years we'd lost in between.

When I was done, I realized that he was holding me just as tight as I was holding him. I felt like Damian was starting to thread his way through all the broken, battered, beautiful pieces of himself, back to me, back to *us*, and I held him tighter.

Twenty-One

SLEEPING NEXT TO DAMIAN WITHOUT touching him was torture, and not in a romantic or sexual way. I felt like a part of me that had been cast away had floated back, and I wanted to hold it, hug it, keep it from slipping away. I knew it would freak Damian out, so I suppressed the urge, although I may have accidentally, in my sleep, draped an occasional arm around him. For those few seconds, I allowed myself the luxury of re-acquaintance, the warmth of his skin, the realness of my long-lost best friend lying beside me. Then Damian would slowly pick up my hand and return it to my side. I had a feeling he knew it was a ruse. After all, I had stuck tenaciously to my side of the bed on the boat, my body as stiff and straight as a board, lest any part of me touch any part of him. And now I was all arms and legs. I knew he knew, and that made me smile, because he inched away, and I inched closer, until he was perched at the edge of the bed, and the only thing that kept him from falling was the mosquito netting tucked under the bed.

Whether I stuck to my side or invaded his, Damian was up at the crack of dawn. Not surprisingly, he looked after the cooking, although he left me chores without saying a word: a broom and a mop, standing square in the center of the kitchen, laundry detergent sitting on a stack of towels, a toilet brush dangling from the bathroom doorway. I fumbled through my tasks, but if Damian noticed that I mopped before I swept or that the towels were now a weird shade of pink, he didn't say anything.

He brought in all my shopping bags from the boat, and although my sequin skirt wasn't exactly toilet scrubbing gear, I caught him checking out my sparkly ass. I trailed him all day in that skirt, a cropped top, and the shell necklace he'd given me. I had pretty much been stuck to Damian's side the whole time he was recovering, so it was my first real look at the island. It was just a few square miles around, hemmed in by a white, sandy beach on one side, and lush, tropical forest on the other. The little house was nestled in between, under the shade of tall trees. The front faced mirror-calm waters, protected by a coral reef, and the back opened up to palm groves, papaya trees, and shrubs with thick, glossy leaves.

It was obvious that Damian knew the island like the back of his hand. He knew where to find small, red bananas with a texture so creamy that they tasted like thick, sweet custard, with a hint of raspberry. He knew where the sun hit, at what time, and where the coolest breezes came off the ocean.

"Do you come here often?" I asked, as he checked on

the generator. It seemed like the place was pretty self-sufficient. A generator, tanks to collect and process rain water, propane to heat up the water we used for cleaning and bathing.

"It was home for a while," he replied.

"You mean when you and Rafael were hiding, after the incident with El Charro?"

"How do you know about El Charro?"

"Rafael told me."

It didn't seem to bother him. He was who he was, with no pretense about his past or the things he had done.

"Does anyone know you're out here? I mean, whose property is this?" I asked.

"It's mine now," he said. "No one else had much use for it. It's too small for tourism, too much beach for farming, too remote for fishermen."

"But you don't live here?"

"No. I go where my work takes me."

"So . . ." I fiddled with the hem of my top. "We are okay here?"

Damian stilled at my words. "There is no '*we*', Skye. We grew up. We became different people. We live in different worlds. As soon as it's safe, I'm dropping you off at the mainland."

"You're just going to drop me off?" I stared at him incredulously. "What about MaMaLu? You said you were going to take me there. I need to see her, Damian. I need to see her grave. I never got to say goodbye."

"Neither did I," he spit out. "I was taking you there so you could see, so you could understand why I did what I did. But you already know the truth."

"So that's it? You unload me somewhere they can find me, like some unwanted cargo? And what am I supposed to do? Forget everything that happened? Forget that you abducted me, turned my life upside down, and then turned me loose? Just like that? Well, you know what? I *did* forget. I forgot about you until *you* came back into my life. You're a selfish fucking bastard, Damian. Pick me up when it suits you, drop me off when it suits you. I'm not some mindless, emotionless pawn you can move from here to there in this game you're playing with my father. I'm real and I'm here and I *care* about you."

And there it was, a flash of raw emotion on Damian's face, a hitching of his breath like he'd been punched in the gut. And just as quickly, it was gone.

"*Don't* care about me," he said. "I *am* a selfish fucking bastard. I've killed people, planned, plotted, and orchestrated the whole thing, and never felt an ounce of remorse. And I planned, plotted and orchestrated to kill *you*. So *don't* care about me, because I'm only going to disappoint you."

"Bullshit! You're just afraid to let me in, you're afraid to let *anyone* in."

We glared at each other, neither willing to back off.

Then Damian turned and disappeared into the trees.

Fine.

I stormed off to the beach.

I shimmied out of my skirt, tossed my top onto the sand and walked into the water. It was warm, and so clear that the sun's rays danced on my feet. I lay on my back and gave myself up to the ocean.

Take it. Take it all away, I thought. *I don't know what to do with any of it.*

I floated like a piece of driftwood, bobbing up and down on the waves. My finger still stung, but it was bearable. I opened my eyes as a seagull passed overhead, blocking the sun momentarily. I turned to the shore, following its path, and noticed Damian watching me from the verandah. I was wearing my underwear, but it was stuck to my body like second skin. He'd already seen me naked, but this was different. He hadn't looked at me then, the way he was looking at me now, with the kind of longing that made me feel like I was the Holy Grail to his quest, like I was the oasis and he was two burning feet in the desert sand. He looked away and went back to whittling whatever he was working on.

I came out of the water and picked up my clothes. Damian kept his gaze averted. When I stepped out of the shower, my black-and-blond hair freshly shampooed, he was waiting for me in the bedroom.

"Let me see your finger." He slipped off the wet, dirty bandage and inspected it. It was healing, although parts of it were still tender. "This will work better." He'd made me a wooden splint, padded on all sides, but not so bulky as to get in the way.

I sat on the bed and let him slip it on.

"How does that feel?" he asked, securing it with Band-Aids.

"Good." *Really, really good. Look at me like that again. With softness in your eyes.* "What about you?" I traced the stitches on his temple. One, two, three, four. Four crisscross latches.

"I'm fine," he said, but he let my fingers rest on his skin.

He was kneeling on the floor. His other hand hadn't moved from mine, even though the splint was now secured. Our eyes were level; there was nowhere to hide.

Whenever MaMaLu had sung about the Sierra Morena Mountains, I'd thought of Damian's eyes. I didn't know what those mountains looked like, but I always imagined they were just as dark, with ebony forests and caves of coal. Of course, I had no idea back then that the bandits I used to conjure up would be my own—my feelings, leaping from friendship to this falling, fluttering ambush that came at me from all sides.

Damian had thieving, stealing contraband eyes, and when they fell on my mouth, they robbed me of all breath and thought. I wondered if he was feeling the same undeniable pull, if his heart was racing as fast as mine, if past and present were making out like wild teenagers in the back seat of his mind.

A drop of water trickled from my hair to the shadow between my breasts. There was nothing separating me from Damian, except my towel. My heart was open—my lips, my skin, my eyes—all bare and naked. And in the end, that was my undoing, *his* undoing, because Damian could take my finger, but not my heart.

So, he let go of my hand and left the room.

Twenty-Two

I HAD FORGOTTEN THE TASTE of plump, juicy mangoes eaten right off the tree. The mangoes on the island were small, but remarkably sweet. I could fit three in the palm of my hand and when I peeled off the soft, thick skin, the juice dripped down my arms and turned into a sticky mess. I had to watch for ants as I ate them, especially if any got on my legs. Those suckers loved mango nectar and there were times when they went places I did not appreciate. It was a price I was willing to pay, for the pleasure of sitting in the shade of a mango tree, and sinking my teeth into the soft, orange flesh. The best was when I could fit a whole mango in my mouth and suck on it until all that remained was the dry, bearded pit.

The ripest, heaviest fruit fell off the tree on its own, so there was always some on the ground, but it was bruised or picked over by bugs and animals. Damian climbed the tree and shook the branches while I stood beneath, trying to catch them in a wicker basket.

"Ouch," I said for the fifth time when one bounced off my head. "Not yet! On five, okay?"

It was one of those things that we fell into so automatically that even Damian didn't notice. And it worked perfectly. I was still admiring our little haul when the sky broke loose. It wasn't a nice, gentle drizzle; it was like being splashed with a big wave at the end of a water ride. The tropical shower unleashed more mangoes on my head. I turned the wicker basket upside down over me to shield myself. All the mangoes we'd picked ricocheted off my head. I started running for cover, but the ground was quickly turning to mud and I had to dislodge one foot before pulling out the other. Damian jumped from the tree and was a few feet ahead of me, caught in the same predicament, except he was heavier so he sank lower with each step. We looked like two wet zombies, limbs stiff and awkward, making a run from the crypt.

Damian turned around when I started laughing. He took one look at me, with the upside basket perched on my head, ankle-deep in mud and guck, and started laughing too.

"This way." He grabbed my hand and steered me to a small wooden shack in the jungle.

The palapa-thatched roof protected us from the passing squall. I dropped to the ground, soaked to the bone, trying to catch my breath, but failing miserably because I couldn't stop laughing at Damian's muddy, hobbit feet.

"Dude, for someone who is so compulsive about moisturizing his feet, you need a pedicure. Bad," I said, sobering up when I realized he wasn't laughing anymore. "What?" I asked. He was looking at me with an intensity that was making me squirm.

"You still laugh the same," he said.

I froze and dropped my gaze to the wicker basket on my lap. I didn't want him to see how these brief, small bursts of familiarity made me want to throw my arms around him and tear down the walls that kept us from the easiness we'd once shared.

"Same laugh, except for that gap between your teeth," he continued, stretching out beside me.

"I'm still the same girl, Damian." I put my head down and we lay on the floor, wishing for the simplicity of childhood, the wholeness of hearts, the sweetness of pure, unadulterated life. Muddy puddles and chocolate faces and skinned knees and skipping rope; me hiding behind MaMaLu's skirts after painting his face ballerina pink as he slept under the tree.

"The day you visit MaMaLu's grave—is it the same every year?" I asked.

He nodded, staring at the dried up palm fronds that lined the roof. "I used to wait outside the prison. One day I heard her singing. It was the last time she sang for me. It was so clear I could hear it over all the noise and chaos, like she was right there, singing in my ear. I think that was her way of saying goodbye. I go every year on that day."

I wanted to reach for Damian's hand, clasp his fingers in mine. I wanted to tell him he'd been a good son and how much MaMaLu had loved him, but I couldn't get past the lump lodged in my throat.

We listened to the rain subside as the mud dried on our feet.

"What is this place?" I asked, looking around.

The shack was sparse, but with remnants of use: a lantern hung from one of the posts and there was a makeshift bench with tools and rusty screws and nails on it.

"It's kind of a workshop now. I set it up when Rafael and I first got here. It was just a grass shack then, but we got some wood and patched it up. Eventually, I built the house and outgrew this place."

"You built it yourself?"

"A little at a time. Lugging supplies over to this place was tough. It took a few years, but I like coming out here, working with my hands, having the time alone."

"How MacGyver of you."

"Mac who?"

"MacGyver. It was my father's favorite show, about a bomb technician who could pretty much fix anything with a paper clip and a Swiss army knife. I bet he could have shown you how to install glass in the windows too."

"What makes you think I didn't leave it out deliberately?"

"True. You never did like glass in the windows," I said, thinking of all the times I had to open mine so he could sneak in.

I knew he was recalling the same thing because he didn't move away when I touched the back of his fingers with mine. It was the closest I could get to holding hands with him.

"Remember the yellow flowers that fell from the trees?" I asked.

"Yes."

I smiled, because the rain had collected on the roof and was seeping through the leaves, falling on our faces with big, fat plops, but we stayed there, not wanting to move, pretending they were wet, sunny blossoms.

"Damian," I said, keeping my eyes closed, "I know I have to go back to that other world, the world you abducted me from. And I don't know what happens between now and then, but this right here—this rain, this shack, this island, this moment—I want it to go on forever."

Damian didn't reply, but he moved his fingers away. It was okay though. In fact, it was more than okay, because Damian Caballero was struggling with the one thing that scared the hell out of him. Me.

Twenty-Three

"READY?" ASKED DAMIAN.

"Are you sure it's safe?" I folded the list of supplies we needed and adjusted my sunglasses.

"It's a touristy town, busy streets, tons of people. I have a beard. Your hair is different. We don't look anything like our photos. No one will notice." Damian slipped on his baseball cap. SD.

So Damnfine

Rafael's plan had worked. Finding Damian's discarded phone in Caboras had thrown the search off, but they were running out of leads and the trail was turning cold. It wouldn't be long before they backtracked, but for now, we were okay.

"Don't forget this." Damian handed me the seashell necklace he'd made for me. "Nothing says tourist better than local handicraft."

I slipped it on and checked my reflection. I was wearing a black tank top and the pants I'd had on when Damian had abducted me. The runway look had been bleached out by the sun and heat and humidity. I didn't think twice about sitting my butt down on a mossy tree-trunk, or wearing them on grub-hunting trips in the jungle. Of course, I just held the pail while Damian unearthed the worms. It's one thing to get your hem muddy; but I wasn't about to touch those wiggly suckers.

Damian removed the camouflage roof of palm leaves he'd tied to the boat. It felt odd being back in the space I'd longed to escape from. I felt a sense of freedom now that I could not have imagined then. Being ripped out of my sparkling, tinsel world had been excruciatingly painful, but I didn't know if I could ever go back to being that person again. I was no longer mannequin-plastic, pretty and perfect; I was hacked up, inside and out. My hair was a mess, my nails were a mess, my heart was a mess. But my skin was alive and sun-kissed, and my face glowed from ocean breezes and salt spray.

I watched Damian steer and tried not to stare. The wind molded his shirt to his body, accentuating his shoulders and impeccable abs. He hadn't shaved since we'd been on the island, but his beard wasn't quite full. It made him look free-spirited and bohemian and uber masculine, like he belonged in the pages of a nautical magazine. His face had healed. His stitches were still there, but they were ready to come out, close to the hairline and hidden under his cap. He had a sharp nose, bronze skin stretched tight over his cheekbones, and black lashes that fringed deep, dark eyes. Damn. He had a fine, proud profile.

It was early afternoon when we anchored in a busy port. Cruise ships and yachts dotted the sparkling harbor. Golden beaches backed into sprawling resorts, shops, and restaurants. We cut through the clutter, dodging the hail of pink cabs, the souvenir stores crammed with tanned bodies, the sushi bars and pushy vendors. Crooked alleys opened up to the main square, where shops and banks faced teeming crowds from under deep, arched porticos.

I followed Damian as he zigzagged past the tall buildings, ignoring the supermarkets and chain stores, to the other side of the plaza. There, stretched out for blocks on either side of the street, was an outdoor market—stall after colorful stall filled with just about anything and everything: rows of watermelons and pineapples and oranges, jalapeños the size of small cucumbers, spices heaped in fragrant pyramids, pirated DVDs and CDs, piles of Gap and Hollister knock-offs, headbands with giant penises sticking out of them, and cactus paddles stacked in pillars at least six feet tall.

Damian was right. This dizzying cacophony of sight and sound and smell was the perfect place to disappear into the crowd. We bought eggs and white beans and tomatoes as big as cauliflowers. I sucked on chili-and-sugar coated tamarind balls that made my mouth buzz and my eyes water. We passed rows of seafood on ice: bass and octopus and angry-looking sharks called cazón. Damian picked up some clams with creamy, brown shells.

"Chocolate clams," he said. "For when you want *real* ceviche."

I made a face and waved another vendor away, wondering why no one was sticking slices of cheese and avocados under Damian's nose.

"You are the *worst* person to shop with," I said, as he

slapped my hand away from the locally crafted bags and shoes. I lingered a few seconds to admire the intricate patterns hand-carved into the leather, before dashing after Damian.

"I'm hungry," I said.

We were standing near the taco stands. I could smell fresh tortillas and wood smoke, roasted vegetables and grilled meat.

"We're almost done."

"But I'm hungry *now*."

"*You* are the worst person to shop with," he said.

I trailed him to a couple more stalls before staging a protest.

"For a seasoned shopper, you have a complete lack of focus and discipline." He pulled me off the curb. "Then again, you're used to air-conditioned malls and bubble tea breaks."

"I hate bubble tea," I said, as I followed him down a narrow cobblestoned pathway to a street cart.

"How about *Papas Locas*? Crazy potatoes?" he asked.

The vendor was roasting large potatoes in foil, mashing them with butter and fresh cheese, and serving them with an endless variety of condiments: grilled beef, pork, bacon, beans, onions, garlic, cilantro, salsa, and guacamole.

"Good?" asked Damian as I dug into the bulging spud.

"Heaven," I replied.

"Want some of this?" He held out his burrito: chargrilled beef with cumin, garlic and lime juice.

"No thanks." It looked delicious, but I wasn't about to admit I wanted his burrito.

I was still smiling at my silly private joke when a loud wedding procession entered the alley: a tipsy bride and groom, followed by a group of giggly children, followed by an entire mariachi band, followed by family and friends. Damian and I pressed into opposite sides of the path to let them through. The trumpets blared in our ears, slightly off-pitch, attacking us with tight bursts of vibrato. My potato quaked in despair and a few green onions slid off. My gaze met Damian's. Suddenly, we were kids again, and we were laughing as men with wide sombreros and twangy violins filed through between us.

He noticed them at the same time I did—the rows and rows of paper stuck to the walls on either side: pink and yellow flyers with our faces printed on them. I couldn't make out what they said, but I'm pretty sure the captions read 'Missing' for me and 'Wanted' for him. It was sobering, seeing ourselves up on display, as the entire wedding procession rambled past us, two at a time. Our eyes remained locked as we held our breaths. The street was so narrow, that two lovers standing on balconies across from each other could have leaned over for a kiss. There was nowhere to run.

We stayed glued to the walls until the last of the wedding party had shuffled through and the guitars had turned into a distant strum.

"Come on." Damian picked up the shopping bags at his feet.

We were making our way to the boat, through a maze of streets, when he stopped outside a walk-in medical clinic.

"I think you should get them to look at your finger," he said.

"It's fine." I waved the splint at him. "There's nothing they can do. Besides, don't you think it's a bit risky? If they've been watching the news they could put two and two together."

"Not if you go in alone. Maybe we should split up."

"And what? Make up a story about what happened?"

"Do what you have to, but get it checked out. Go. I'll wait for you out here."

"It's *fine*." I started walking away. "The last thing I need is for someone to go poking at it when it's finally healing over."

"Suit yourself." Damian wouldn't budge. "If you're not going in, I will. I need to get my stitches removed."

I wavered for a second. I just wanted to get back to the boat, but he was right. His stitches were ready to come out.

"Wait for me in the supermarket," said Damian. He motioned to the store across the street. "It shouldn't take too long."

"Okay." I started crossing the road, but he pulled me back.

"Here." He handed me some bills. "In case they have chocolate peanut butter ice cream."

"That's way too much for ice cream!" I laughed, but he was already walking into the clinic.

After the jostling crowds from earlier, the supermarket was cool and quiet. "Demons" by Imagine Dragons was playing over the loudspeaker. I wandered over to the freezer section. No chocolate peanut butter ice cream. I was checking out the frozen pancakes when the lyrics made me stop dead in my tracks.

Damian had been way too insistent—the clinic, my finger, his stitches. Any excuse for us to separate.

Maybe we should split up.

The fucker! He was letting me go.

As soon as it's safe, I'm dropping you off at the

mainland.

Don't forget this. He made sure I didn't leave the seashell necklace behind.

I ran back across the street, not caring that two cars narrowly missed me. The drivers honked and cursed at me, but all I could see was the door to the clinic. I flung it open and froze. There he was, seated on one of the plastic chairs, shopping bags at his feet, flipping through a magazine.

I backed out slowly, not wanting him to see how panicked I was, how the thought of being cut off from him again was so painful, I could barely breathe. I closed my eyes and breathed.

5, 4, 3, 2, 1 . . .

Again.

5, 4, 3, 2, 1 . . .

Then I went back into the supermarket. For a while, I wandered around, still feeling overwhelmed by the sense of emptiness that had gripped me. I was in love with Damian, completely, utterly, desolately. I had told myself that as long as I stayed with him, he had leverage, a bartering chip to negotiate his safety. Without me, he was an open target. But the truth was, I wanted to stay with him for *me*, because he had always, always been a part of me. I wanted to stay with him so I could put together all the dented, shattered parts of him, because I could never be whole where he was broken.

I found myself standing before the strawberries. Plump, flame-red strawberries with bright, green caps. I thought of the trampled cake Damian had never gotten to eat and decided I was going to buy all of them. I was going to feed him strawberries and he was going to fall in love with me.

Yes. I loved when I came up with a brilliant, foolproof plan.

I waited inside until the store started closing for the day. When the lights turned off, I headed to the clinic, carrying a shit load of strawberries. Damian wasn't there. No one was seated in the waiting room.

"Is anyone in with the doctor?" I asked the receptionist.

"No, but we're done for the day. Sorry, you'll have to come back tomorrow."

I stumbled back outside, lugging the strawberries behind me.

He'd left me. It had been his plan all along—drop me off at the clinic, have them call it in.

We think it's the same girl. She came in with a severed finger. That's what tipped us off. It's been all over the news, how her father received a piece of it. Gruesome stuff. No sign of the guy.

When that hadn't worked, he'd made up an excuse to go in himself. Maybe he did get his stitches removed. Maybe he came out, saw me waiting with two bags full of strawberries and decided that leaving me was the best thing he could do. For both of us. And yes, that made *sense.* I should find the nearest police station and contact my father. I could be back in La Jolla tomorrow, in my sweet room that was twice the size of Damian's island house, being fussed over and pampered and catered to. *That* made sense. Not this. Not me running down the streets that led to the harbor, hailing a cab in the mad hope that I could still catch him, clutching on to cartons of strawberries as they spilled all over the seats.

"Stop! Right here!" I threw some bills at the driver, recognizing the dock where we'd anchored, and got out before he came to a full stop.

I ran to the end of the pier just as Damian's boat was pulling out of the harbor.

"Damian!" I tiptoed at the very edge, as close to him as I could get, trying to catch his attention. "Damian!"

He turned around.

Yes.

There was no clearer way for me to show him that I had forgiven him, that what I felt went way beyond the hurt and pain I'd suffered. I understood the why. I understood *him*. It was his turn now, to let go, to take a chance, to let me stand up for him, to let me stand *with* him, come what may.

All you have to do is turn the boat around and come back, Damian.

He heard me, even though I didn't say a word. Our eyes met and I could see everything he felt. For a few, sky-blue, suspended moments, my heart and his were the same; they wanted the same thing. Then he turned back around and continued steering away.

I let go of the stupid strawberries. I let go of the stupid hope that had swelled up in my chest like a big, stupid balloon. I let go of my stupid pride and sat on the stupid pier and let myself stupid cry.

I had chased after Damian's boat, just as he had chased after my car all those years ago. But this was different. This was no dry, dusty road. This was clear day, clear sky. Nothing had obscured me from him. He had seen me, and he had heard me, and he had chosen to keep going. Because where there's hate, there can be no love, and Damian still hated my father.

"You have no right to punish me for it!" I chucked a strawberry after the boat. It was getting smaller and smaller by the minute. I was about to throw another one after him, but he didn't deserve any strawberries so I stuffed it into my mouth and wiped my tears.

"What's the matter, dear?" I felt a warm hand on my shoulder. It was an elderly lady wearing a sheer, fringed kimono over a tube top and long skirt. Her fingers sparkled with chunky cocktail rings.

"I missed my ride." I felt an instant kinship with the big, busty woman. She jingled and jangled from all the colorful necklaces and bracelets she was wearing.

"That one there?" She pointed at Damian's boat.

I nodded.

"It's not too late. We can still catch up. Ken and I were just getting ready to leave. Hop on, we'll give you a ride."

I followed her to a small sailboat on the pier.

"I'm Judy, by the way. And this is my husband, Ken." She gestured to a man with a large, kind face.

"Nice to meet you." I shook hands. If they thought it rude that I'd omitted my name, they didn't say anything. They seemed like nice people, and I didn't want to lie to them, but I wasn't taking any chances, in case they'd heard the news.

"Nothing like a lover's spat on the high seas," said Ken, after Judy explained the situation.

"I didn't say they were lovers. Please excuse my husband." Judy turned to me. Her blond hair was so bright it looked almost white. "All this sun is getting to him. We don't get much in Hamilton."

"Hamilton?" I asked, as we cast off. "Where is that?"

"In Canada. We run a little vintage store, but we sail a fair bit and sometimes we find all kinds of local knick-knacks to take back."

"She's wearing half of them." Ken winked at me. "If we sink somewhere off the Pacific Coast, it'll be from all of her shopping."

A fellow shopper. No wonder I'd felt an instant connection.

"Would you like some strawberries?" I asked. It was all I had to offer for their kindness.

"Oh no. We get plenty of those. Out here, it's all about guava and mangosteen and pineapple," said Ken. "And truth be told, it doesn't look like you have enough to go around."

Judy and I laughed. The wind had picked up and the sailboat was moving swiftly towards Damian.

"I'll signal him down," said Ken, when we caught up.

"Thank you," I replied. The boats were bobbing side by side. Ken started lowering the dinghy.

"No need," I said. I was almost afraid for Damian to see me. I didn't know what I'd do if he took off again. "I can take it from here." I jumped into the water.

"Well then. Don't let us keep you!" Ken shouted after me.

I climbed up the ladder to Damian's boat and stood on the deck in a big puddle, feeling a bit like a drowned rat.

"Don't forget these." Judy tossed the strawberries over. Two big bags full.

"Thanks!" I waved as Ken and Judy took off.

When I turned around, Damian was standing at the other end of the boat, looking like hell and fury, bundled up in a white cotton shirt.

"What do you think you're doing?"

"I'm going with you."

"I don't *want* you, Skye. I thought I made that clear. Are you so ridiculously spoiled, so used to getting what you want that you can't get that through your head?"

Oh God, this man. This fucking impossible man. I had

just left everything behind—my freedom, my cushy world, my *father*—for this man. I had tracked him down in the middle of ocean, jumped into the sea, climbed on board, all so I could love him. If he would *only* just let me love him.

But no. He was doing what he always did, shutting me out before I could shut him out, because that's what he expected from the world—hurt, betrayal, callousness. He wasn't even going to give us a chance.

"You're a fucking coward." I picked up a strawberry and flung it at him. It smacked him in the face, leaving a pink stain.

I chucked another one at him. And another and another and another, until he was covered in splotches—his face, his shirt, his arms, his neck.

"I hate you!"

I did. I hated that he could just stand there, unflinching, uncaring, unyielding, and watch me fall apart.

"You hear me?" I took a handful of strawberries and smashed them into his chest. "I *hate* you!"

When all the strawberries were gone, I started pounding him with my fists. I wanted to pulverize every single memory I had of him. I wanted him to hurt the way I was hurting. I wanted him to sob the way I was sobbing. I wante—

Damian grabbed my hands and pinned them behind my back. His lips found mine and he latched on with a hunger that left me breathless. He was an ocean of want and need. All the raging, submerged currents that he'd kept at bay unleashed themselves on me. I tried to keep afloat, clutching at him, but I didn't stand a chance. My hurt, my anger, my tears were tossed aside by something deeper, something vast and true and powerful and endless.

It was a kiss that had sneaked in through an open window, a kiss that lay folded in a paper giraffe, in the silences between *5, 4, 3, 2, 1,* in the pits of mini mangoes and here, now, at last, it was set free. And the *rightness* of it, the feeling of longing and belonging, made me want to hold on to it forever. I wanted Damian to keep kissing me, keep kissing, keep kissing, until every other kiss had been erased, until *this* was the only kiss.

My top was soaked, my pants were soaked, my hair was soaked, but Damian's mouth was like strawberry wildfire—hot and sweet, and completely out of control. All the intensity with which he'd pushed me away was pulling me right back, fusing my lips to his. It was almost painful when he let go.

"Don't cry, *güerita*." Damian's thumb swiped my cheek. "Hit me, slap me, punch me, but don't fucking cry."

"Don't fucking leave me then," I said. Was he really looking at me like that? Was he really breathing so hard? "And I'm not *güerita* anymore." I tugged at a strand of dark hair. "I'm not blondie anymore."

"Oh, but you are." Damian smiled.

I punched him because he'd seen me naked and I knew exactly what he was thinking. When he wrapped his arms around me, I hid my face in his chest and felt like I had come home.

WHEN WE GOT BACK TO the island, Damian made *real* ceviche while I showered and changed.

"Show off," I said. He really was a good cook. And a great kisser. I couldn't stop staring at his lips. Those lips had blown orange seeds through a straw at Gideon

Benedict St. John, but now there was an eroticism to them—every time he spoke, every time he took a bite. They were all I could see. And I wanted them on me.

"What happened to your face?" he asked.

"Your beard." I snapped out of it long enough to answer his question. The hot shower had turned my chin and upper lip red from where his beard had chafed my skin.

Damian grinned. Leaving his mark on me seemed to appease some Paleolithic, cave-dwelling part of him.

His grin did things to me too. I wished he would lean over and kiss me again.

He did lean over. To pick up my plate. And then he proceeded to wash the dishes while I put things away. I wished he'd hurry up so I could throw my arms around him again, but he was taking so darn long, scratching an imaginary speck, then washing the damn spot again, then *drying,* all the while keeping his eyes on the task.

He was avoiding me, and when I finally clued in to why, I wanted to kiss him even more. Damian wasn't doing the dishes. He was wrestling with something he'd never felt before. He was feeling *shy* and it was something completely foreign to him. He had never allowed himself to like a girl, never been on a date, never felt butterflies in his stomach.

I felt a stab of tenderness that was quickly overcome by the urge to jump him. I cleared my throat in an attempt to dislodge the treacherous minx that was quickly taking over.

"Why don't you go change? I'll finish here," I offered. He was still wearing his strawberry splattered shirt.

He jumped on it, like I had just thrown him a life raft. Anything to get away from me. I finished up the rest of the dishes and turned off the lights.

We bumped into each other in the hallway. He was coming out of the bathroom and I was going in. The first thing that struck me was his clean-shaven face. Bye, bye beard. The stitches were gone too. No baseball cap. It was like he was showing me his face for the first time—the ridges where the boy I once knew had hardened to a man, the places he'd stayed the same. The second thing I noticed was his skin, still warm and wet, bare except for the sweatpants that didn't look so ugly when they hugged his hip like that.

"I—"

"You—"

We stepped away from each other, aware of all the places our bodies had just touched.

I don't know who moved first, maybe him, maybe me, but we were zigzagging through the hallway, our lips locked, my back against the wall, then his, banging and colliding in the narrow space until we got to the bedroom.

Damian picked me up and carried me inside. His bare arms felt like heaven. We fumbled to get under the netting, neither of us wanting to stop kissing, but it was tucked under the mattress, sealing off the bed. When Damian knelt on the mattress, with me still in his arms, the whole thing ripped from the top.

"Problem solved," he said, tearing through the gauzy folds as he deposited me on the bed.

I would have laughed, but he slid his body on top of mine and I was lost. Limbs measured up against limbs, palm against palm, familiar yet so different. My t-shirt and panties came off, his sweatpants kicked to the foot of the bed. I lay on my side, shuddering when his finger dipped down my back, tracing the indentation of my spine. Hooking my ankle around his, I rubbed my toes against the sole of his foot.

It was discovery and wonder, a stirring of the senses, a medley of sighs. We were skin-to-skin, and then apart, touching and exploring until the distance became too much to bear. He was on his stomach and my lips were skimming across the broad expanse of his shoulders and back. I had barely tasted his skin when he growled and turned over. Damian was a take-charge lover. He knew what he wanted, when he wanted it, and how to make it happen. I was spooned into him, enraptured with the feel of his rough thumb on my nipple.

"Still crooked," I said, taking his thumb into my mouth.

The reaction was instantaneous, a rush of throbbing, inflamed blood to that very male, insistent part of him.

"Skye . . ." He moved away from me.

"What?" I wasn't done sucking his thumb.

He forgot what he was saying, and just lay back, watching me. "*That* is not helping," he groaned.

"How about this?" I moved on to the other thumb.

"Fuck you."

I giggled.

"Skye . . ." He tried again.

I moved on to the tip of his cock, teasing it with my tongue. His hips shot off the bed.

"Skye!" He yanked me away by my hair. "I don't have any condoms."

"I think I saw a mini sombrero in the living room." I went back to what I was doing. His head flopped back on the pillow and his fingers threaded through my hair.

"What do you mean *mini*?" he growled.

"I take that back," I mumbled, relishing the feel of

him expanding in my mouth. He started thrusting his cock through my lips, retreating, advancing, an inch at a time, until I couldn't contain him, all of him. The sounds coming from him were making my thighs clench as my need started overtaking me.

"My turn," he said, flipping me over.

It was oddly tentative, his lips on that most private part of me. And I realized that this was where it was different for Damian. He might have fucked a lot of women, but he'd never made love before, never thought about giving the same pleasure he received. And his baby steps—his hot breath, his tongue, his mouth—nudged me towards the sweetest release. When he slipped his fingers inside, first one, then another, I thought I was going to lose it.

"Damian." I grasped his shoulders. I wanted him inside. "Stop."

He paused, taking in my flushed face, the rise and fall of my chest, my taut nipples, begging for his touch.

"If you can't take, don't give," he said, sucking on my hot little button like I'd sucked on his thumb.

The fucking tease. His fingers continued their maddening dance, and just when I thought I was about to explode, his cock slid into me, full and hard. It was pure possession, unbridled and complete. The pleasure came, swift and explosive. I clung to him, unable to suppress the cry of delight as wave after wave of electric fire scorched through me. He held still, one hand cupping the back of my head, the other on the curve of my hip as I came in tight spasms around him.

"Again," he said, when I lay replete and breathless under him. "With me this time."

He started a relentless, masterful rhythm that carried

me to new crests of passion. As he fueled my desire, his own grew stronger, his body moving with mine in exquisite harmony. I rose to meet him, stroke for stroke, feeling a sense of completeness that I had never known.

Ban

Eban.

Esteban.

Damian.

I knew *all* of him now.

I opened my eyes at the peak and the intensity of the moment shot through both of us. I abandoned myself to the whirl of sensation, my heart bursting with all the raw, tender, fierce things exchanged in that one look.

"*Güerita.*" He surrendered with a long, shuddering moan.

I wrapped my arms around him. He kissed the top of my head and pulled me closer. He wasn't done touching me. His fingers moved up and down my back in long, languid strokes.

"You grew boobs," he said. "Really, really nice boobs."

"You grew hair." I traced the silky hair on his arms. "And a really, really big um . . ."

"A big what, Skye? Let me hear you say it."

"A really, really big personality."

"The thing about having a really, really big 'personality' is that it really, really needs a lot of attention. And just so you know, I'm always careful. This is the first time I've gone—"

"Sombrero-less?" I laughed. "I know you'd never do anything to put me at risk."

"How do you know that?"

"Because you love me." There. The words were out and I couldn't take them back. Let him deny what I'd seen in his eyes, what I knew was the truth.

Damian tensed, as if holding something in check. I held my breath, waiting for the mask to slip back on. My heart was going to break to the murmur of the ocean and the night wind rustling through palm trees. The lump in my throat grew to the size of a giant coconut.

"It's true," he said. "I've always loved you. Even when I hated you."

Oh God oh God oh God oh God.

"Loved? Past tense?" I was pushing it, but my heart took a perilous leap.

"Loved. Love. What does it matter?" He pulled me into the cradle of his arms. "Love don't die."

"Are you feeding me one of your movie lines, Damian?"

"It's a song." He laughed. "My tastes have expanded." His mouth covered my nipple, sending a warm shiver through me.

"Wait." I pulled his head back up. "There's something you should know."

"I know." His hands skimmed my waist possessively. "You love me, too."

"Was I *that* obvious?"

"Skye." He smiled. "You unleashed a fucking strawberry storm on me."

DAMIAN REATTACHED THE MOSQUITO NET over the bed and we stood back, surveying my handiwork.

"She can't cook, but she can sew," he said.

"Damn right, I can sew. I learned from the best."

"So stitching all those flowers onto MaMaLu's scarves paid off?"

"It's called embroidery, and yes. She taught me well."

"I don't know." Damian tugged at the patched up mesh. "I think we need to put it to the test."

"Are you suggesting an afternoon romp, because—"

I didn't get too far. Damian had me under the netting before I could protest. Not that I would. Or could. Because Damian in love was a thing of beauty—intoxicating, addictive, demanding, attentive, and always, always hungry.

Days passed like that, a whirling dance of sensation and passion and discovery. Nights too. I started taking the birth control pills that were still in the handbag that Damian had stashed away. I'd missed a couple of weeks, but it couldn't be helped.

Every morning, Damian went to pick mangoes for me, with strict instructions to *not* cook while he was gone. I made the bed, returning MaMaLu's *Lucky Strike* box back under his pillow. Sometimes I sat with it, thumbing through the contents, trying to catch a whiff of her, but all I smelled was stale tobacco.

When Damian returned, we would sit on the verandah and have breakfast. We sat on the same chair, with me on his lap, although there were three others that were just as comfortable. I played with his hair. He let me, even though we both knew he hated it. He put sand in my belly button. I let him, even though I hated it. But that's what made it special, allowing each other those small, personal liberties that only come with true intimacy.

We had picnics on the beach. Damian roasted peanuts in the sand and sprinkled them with salt water. We ate them warm, with red bananas and ice cream beans—foot long pods packed with lima bean-sized seeds that were covered with a juicy white pulp. They tasted like wet cotton candy, but when left exposed to the air for a while, they took on a distinct vanilla flavor.

We snorkeled over the reef tops, mesmerized by an underwater ballet, as schools of vivid fish darted in and out of living corals and anemones. Soft gorgonian fans and giant sponges glowed over the sun-dappled ocean floor. Blue tangs and angelfish and spotted eagle rays glided past us. Where the seabed was covered in grass, we swam with turtles, with flippers that spread like wings.

Afterward, we lay on the beach, letting the sun warm our skin. Damian decided to shield me from harmful UV rays. With his body. I thought sex on the beach was a great idea. Until the wind started blowing sand in our faces and in-between our bodies. Sex on the beach was too gritty for my taste.

"Such a princess." Damian laughed when I broke our kiss to spit out a grain of sand.

We rinsed off in the water and swam to the boat.

"Here," I said, leading him to the bed where I'd spent so many nights hating him.

"No. Not here." Damian didn't want to be reminded of that time.

"Yes. Right here. Because you need to get over it. I've forgiven you, but you still haven't forgiven yourself."

"Skye—"

I shut him up with a kiss, because everything he needed to know was in the way my lips moved against his, the way my tongue melded with his, lingering and savoring the way he felt, the way he tasted. I felt him melt, slowly, undeniably, because it didn't matter where we were—here, on the boat, where he'd kidnapped me, or on the beach, or on the moon—because there is no space too dark or too vast or too irredeemable that can't be filled with love.

Damian worshiped me on that bed. For every cut and bruise he'd inflicted, there was the salve of his kisses; for every restraint was a chain of caresses. He was surprisingly, touchingly restrained although his desire throbbed, hard and palpable between us. The more Damian gave, the more his passion soared, until we were lost in a sea of sensations: the thrill of his hands on my thighs, the way our hip bones grazed against each other, the slide of skin against palm.

He buried his throat in my face and whispered sweet confessions in my hair: how he felt, when he felt, what he felt. My legs clung to him, my fingers tracing the tendons of his back, wanting to hold him closer, and closer still. My hand trailed down to the space between our bellies and I guided him to me.

"Take me. Take me now," I whispered.

I exalted in his possession, writhing as our bodies found a tempo that bound us together. We were pressed against each other, flesh-to-flesh, so close that I could feel Damian's heart pounding through his chest. He was rotating his pelvis clockwise then counterclockwise, then quick, shallow thrusts. I pulled on a fistful of his hair and kissed him, open mouthed, wild with need. He bucked, grabbed my ass with both hands, and drove deep into me. My thoughts fragmented; I gasped in sweet agony as fiery sensations ripped through me. Damian clutched my body, a tormented groan escaping him as he gave in to his release.

I snuggled up to him, my head fitting perfectly in the hollow between his neck and shoulder. "You think we'll have any more issues with this room now?"

"Skye?"

"What?"

"I can't think right now."

THERE WAS A SALTWATER POOL on the beach, carved into a rocky ledge. Two channels flushed the pool with passing waves, allowing fish to pass through. Damian built a stone wall that allowed the fish in at high tide, but trapped them when the water receded. The fish weren't as big as when he went fishing, and they had a gazillion bones, but neither one of us cared because it allowed us to spend more time together.

"So tell me about the guy you were seeing in San Diego." He was massaging my feet with a mix of sand and coconut oil—his homemade spa treatment for me.

"Nick?"

"Whoever you were out to dinner with that night."

"Were you spying on me?"

"I was."

"Creep," I said. "Nick's a nice guy. I dated him for four months, but we never took it to the next level. We were never 'boyfriend and girlfriend'." I should have felt more remorse for not thinking about Nick, but whatever I felt for him had paled in comparison to this.

"And what are we?" asked Damian, recapping the jar of coconut oil and helping me up.

We walked into the water, and I let the waves wash away the sand, leaving my feet silky smooth.

"Not bad," I said. "You might be on to something with this island exfoliation treatment of yours."

"You didn't answer my question."

I put my newly pampered feet on his and framed his face. "We are a question that hasn't been answered yet, a hiding place that hasn't been found yet, a battle that hasn't been fought yet."

I looped my arms around his waist and we walked the beach like that, with Damian carrying me on his feet. We stopped to watch three iguanas sunning themselves on a rock.

"Blondie, Bruce Lee, and Dirty Harry," said Damian. "Bruce Lee is the little one. Blondie is the one missing part of his tail, and Dirty Harry is the mean looking one."

"You named an iguana after me?"

"Not you, *güerita*. The other Blondie: Clint Eastwood, in *The Good, The Bad and The Ugly*."

"Ah. All your heroes, lined up in the sun."

"Until the bad guys come."

I hopped off his feet and we turned back. "You think my father is a bad guy," I said. "Let me talk to him, Damian. We can fix this. He doesn't know you're Esteban. He hasn't made the connection. He'll call off the search. He'll understand. What he did was terrible, but I know he would never maliciously set out to hurt you or MaMaLu. Everyone has a reason. You said it yourself."

"After everything he's done, you're still defending him to me?" He looked at me disbelievingly.

"After everything *you've* done, I would still defend *you* to him. Give him a chance. He's a decent man, Damian."

"We're never going to see eye to eye on that. You have your loyalties. I have mine." Damian looked down at the waves rushing past our feet. "You know what we are, Skye?"

I watched the foam gather around our legs as the waves receded, feeling the warmth seep out of me as Damian took his hand away.

"We are sand that hasn't been washed away yet," he

said.

A cold knot formed in my stomach. The two men that I loved the most, with all my heart, were out to destroy each other. I had a feeling that by the time it was all said and done, only one would be left standing.

Twenty-Four

FOR THE FIRST TIME SINCE our strawberry fight, Damian and I spent the night together but apart. The hopelessness of our situation, the consequences of what I had done when I'd followed him back were starting to weigh on me. I had gone with my heart, with the hope that I would be able to mend things between him and my father. I had bought into the crazy conviction that love conquers all. My love for Damian certainly felt big enough and wide enough, and yet it lay crammed into the few inches that separated us, wrestling with his need for retribution.

Lovengeance.

I traced the letters on my pillow.

It kept us from speaking to each other for much of the next day. It's not that we were sulking or punishing each other. I understood exactly how he felt, and he knew all the things that were going through my mind. We just didn't know what to do or say to make the other feel better, so we said nothing.

I spent the morning feeding Blondie and Bruce Lee hibiscus flowers. Dirty Harry held out until I offered him a banana. Apparently, he had a sweet tooth. There was no sign of Damian. There were no mangoes in the morning. I had a feeling he was hiding out in the shack, but in the afternoon, I found a note from him, propped up on the counter.

"A truce. A date. Pick you up at sunset."

It was folded in the shape of a giraffe, the last thing he had made for me all those years ago, on my birthday. I sat with it for a while because it was one of those moments you know you're going to cherish the rest of your life. And there aren't enough of those. You go through life, turning pages and turning pages, black and white words, running into each other, and then bam! Three rainbow sentences and a paper animal, and you're rummaging through your clothes and washing your hair and changing your outfit again and again, because you've gone giddy and silly and sappy. Because that's what those moments do.

"Wow. What a mess."

I spun around and saw Damian climbing in through the bedroom window. He must have changed and showered on the boat because damn, he looked good. He was wearing a blue button-down shirt, black jacket, and jeans. Golden light framed his face as he surveyed the trail of clothes and bags scattered all over the room.

"For you, *güerita*." He held out something wrapped in a banana leaf.

I took it from him, aware of the way his eyes were

eating me up. I had found a figure-hugging cream dress with long sleeves and a plunging back. It complemented my newly tanned skin and offset the blond roots that were starting to show through my dark hair.

"What's this?" I asked, unwrapping his gift. Seeing him standing before me, I was suddenly aware of not having held him all day.

"Just returning something."

"My shoes!" I exclaimed. Gold Louboutins with spiked heels, the ones I had been wearing when he abducted me.

He knelt before me and held out his hand. I gave him one shoe, and then the other, relishing his touch as he slipped them on.

"So what's the occasion?" I asked.

"I just want to make up for the fact that you missed your birthday this year," he said. "Also, I just want to make up."

"You *drugged* me on my birthday. I don't even remember what happened that day."

"I know. I'm so sorry. And I can't stand it when we're not talking."

I was such an ass, but I couldn't hold a thing against him when he was kissing my neck like that, leaving behind the sweetest, softest string of apologies.

"I'm sorry, too. About yester—"

"Let's not." He shushed me. *Let's not apologize for the things we can't help feeling, the loyalties that are tearing us apart. My mother. Your father. The whole world waiting to see how this will unfold.* "Just you and me tonight, okay?"

I nodded and followed him out to the verandah, where he'd set up the table. With one chair.

We ate in silence, no longer taking anything for

granted: the way his neck tilted to make room for my nose, how I finished one mouthful to his three, how he ate the parts with the most bones and left the rest of the fish for me, how I smothered everything in gravy and he liked it plain. It was an evening we didn't want to end. The sand glistened with the warmth of the sunset and the water lapped up in soft, golden waves.

"Dessert?" he asked when we were done.

"Don't tell me you baked a cake."

"I have something better in mind." He led me to the beach, smiling because I refused to take off my newly reclaimed heels.

I followed him to a pile of hot rocks in the sand. The fire had been doused, but the rocks sizzled when Damian sprinkled water on them.

"Ready?" he asked.

"Ready." I smiled.

He uncovered a basket full of black, wrinkly bananas.

"Please tell me you're not going to make me eat rotten bananas."

"Hey, I ate your ceviche. Besides, these are not bananas. It's plantain, and it's the sweetest at this stage, when the skin has turned all black." He peeled one, cut it in half lengthwise, and threw it on the stone. When it started to caramelize, Damian poured tequila over it. I squealed as it ignited in a glorious blue-tinged flambé.

"Want some now?" He pried the plantain off the rock and put it on a plate.

I looked at the wrinkly peel and back at the plate. Damian shrugged and popped a piece into his mouth. He lay back, elbows out, fingers interlaced under his head, looking at me. I took a tentative bite. It was warm and sweet and gooey, and so, so good.

"Better than cake?" he asked.

"What's cake?" I smiled and stretched out next to him.

We alternated between dessert and trying to guess where the next star would appear, as the blue velvet of night unfolded over us.

"Tomorrow," said Damian.

"What about tomorrow?"

"Tomorrow's the day I visit MaMaLu."

"You think it's safe?" My arms tightened around him.

"They're looking for Damian, not Esteban. Esteban disappeared a long time ago, and there's nothing to connect him to me, nothing to trace MaMaLu back to me. I don't think they'll be staking out the gravesite of a woman no one remembers."

"*I* remember," I said. "*You* remember."

He laced his fingers through mine and we listened to the song of the waves. "Why does it feel like we are the only two people in the world right now?"

"Because right now, we are." I slipped my arms inside his jacket and around his back.

"Do you know what I remember?" he asked. "I remember thinking that MaMaLu's lullaby was about a beautiful little piece of sky, something that dispelled all the darkness. Then we came to Casa Paloma, and I felt like it was about you. *Cielito lindo.*"

"And I always thought she was singing about you. I imagined mountains, dark and black, just like your eyes." I kissed Damian's eyes and his eyelashes, his straight brows, the row of scars from his stitches.

"I'm going with you tomorrow," I said, sliding the jacket off his shoulders.

"I know." He flung it aside.

MaMaLu bound us together. The fact that Damian

was willing to share her with me, in death as he had when she was alive, made me love him all the more.

"No wind today." I unbuttoned his shirt and trailed my hand down his hard, smooth belly, to the trail of male hair that disappeared under his pants. "No sand." I ran my tongue over it.

"Let me see." He rolled me over and returned the favor, his lips taking full advantage of my exposed back. "*Mmmm*. You're right. Not a grain. Just smooth, silky skin."

I squirmed as his fingers slid under my dress, raising it higher, until it was wrapped around my waist.

"God. This ass." He pulled my panties down and kneaded the flesh. "No sand here either," he mumbled, leaving teeth marks on my skin."

I kept my shoes on. And the necklace of seashells. Damian let me ride him. I think he liked the sight of me like that, in the moonlight. He kept his hands on my hips, trying to control the rhythm, and I kept slapping them away. We went back and forth for a while until the games dissolved, until passion overtook and we began moving as one.

The roughened pad of Damian's thumb found my clit and he flicked it, on, off, on, off, like a switch that allowed me sharp, spiky peaks of pleasure, and then took it away. Each time I moaned, his mouth fell open, as if we were connected by some invisible thread. Damian was focused on my face, my body, like he was recording every moment, every movement. His strokes pushed me closer and closer to the edge. I rocked against the hard length of him, driving him just as crazy, reaching, reaching, reaching, until we exploded in spirals of liquid fire. I collapsed over him, heated and flushed, my heart hammering in my chest as he wrapped his arms around me.

We were both quiet in the aftermath, at a loss because it was at once beautiful and scary—beautiful because when we were together, we were whole and complete, and scary because we knew there was no turning back. We were too far gone to take any of it back.

I PUT AWAY THE PILE of clothes that lay scattered in the bedroom and slipped into one of Damian's shirts. I had to fold back the sleeves, but it was soft and warm, and fell just short of my knees. Twenty-one days ago, I'd abhorred putting on his t-shirt, yet here I was, burying my nose in the fabric because I couldn't get enough of his smell.

I walked into the living room and found Damian sitting on the couch, with his gun dismantled on the coffee table.

"What are you doing?"

"Cleaning my gun."

I watched silently as he reassembled it. The familiarity with which he held it, the precision of his movements, reminded me of the path down which he'd come. He was getting ready for tomorrow, in case we ran into trouble in Paza del Mar, in the cemetery where MaMaLu was buried. I knew Damian would not hesitate to use that gun if anything or anyone threatened to take me away from him.

"Damian, how long are we going to hide?"

He reloaded the gun and looked at me. "You want to go back?"

"You know that's not what I mean. I could spend my whole life here, with you. I'm just tired of the uncertainty, of not knowing what happens next. I'm scared for you and what would happen if they find us. I think we should talk to someone, someone who can intervene with the authorities and help us figure out a way to resolve the situation."

"You're saying we should talk to your father, turn ourselves in? Correction. *I* should turn myself in so you can intervene on my behalf? Ask him to go easy, because we both know he'd do anything for you?"

"It's not like that—"

"It's *exactly* like that, Skye. I've been ready to face the consequences all along, from the time I shoved you into the trunk of your car. I knew what I was getting into, but I had nothing to lose. Now I do. I have you, and I won't let anyone take that away. As long as that's what you want. But if you think you can have both me *and* your father in your life, you're wrong. Either you're with him, or you're with me."

"You're not being fair, Damian."

"Fair? You want to talk about *fair*? I pushed you away, Skye. Time and time again, but you wouldn't stop. You kept tearing down my defenses until I couldn't fight you anymore. I'm in love with you, Skye. Bare, stripped down, completely vulnerable, in love. And this whole situation kills me because I know it's tearing you up. But I can't help the way I feel about your father. I hated him then and I hate him now. Mark my words, Skye, I'm going to make him pay."

My head throbbed; my heart throbbed. The vendetta between Damian and my father stood like a fang-baring monster, ripping to shreds everything good and true and precious between us. It was eating us up with dead, dark futility.

"You want to make someone pay for what happened to MaMaLu? Here." I took the gun he was holding and pointed it to myself. "It was me. *I* ran into the room that afternoon. *I'm* the reason MaMaLu was there. *I* set the whole thing in motion. So shoot *me*, Damian."

The gun was flush against my chest, rising and falling with every breath.

"You had it right all along," I said. "It should have ended on the boat the night you abducted me. So let's put a stop to this thirst for revenge. Once and for all. Shoot me, Damian. And when you're done, shoot yourself too. Because I came looking for *you,* because I knew you were hiding in that hutch."

Our hands stayed on the gun, our eyes locked. I could feel Damian's thoughts, the force of his ragged emotions. I wanted to wrap my arms around him, to pull him out of the turmoil, but this was a web only he could untangle himself from. By going along with this, by doing nothing, I was essentially saying 'yes' to the darkness that had tormented him for years, a darkness that would only disappear when *he* let it go.

I lowered the gun and placed it back on the coffee table, next to the paper giraffe note that I'd tried to fold up again.

"It's either this or that." I pointed to one and then the other. "You can either choose love or you can choose hate, because where one lives, the other will die."

Damian kept his eyes on the two objects, equally torn in both directions.

"Tomorrow morning, whatever you leave on the table will tell me, whether we part ways in Paza del Mar or not. Whatever you choose, Damian, know that I will always, *always* love you."

He looked at me, with eyes that punched me right in the gut. "I told you I would only disappoint you."

I cradled his face between my hands. "You told me

'love don't die'."

I left him there, on the flamingo couch that was still stained with his blood, knowing there would be no sleep that night, not for him and not for me. And I knew with resounding finality that there was nothing *fair* about life.

Twenty-Five

I OPENED MY EYES AND reached for Damian. Morning had come, but he was gone. Today was the day we were going to visit MaMaLu's grave, and sitting on the coffee table was an answer to the question I'd left Damian with. I sank back under the sheets, not sure if I really wanted to know.

Two brilliant yellow butterflies flitted through hazy sunbeams. Sometimes birds went in and out of the open windows, sometimes geckos and the kind of bugs that would have had me screaming bloody murder at one time. Damian had changed me, and I had changed him. We were like the shells we had once picked for MaMaLu—all the hard parts worn so thin that we could see right through each other. And no matter what happened today, no matter what lay waiting for me on that coffee table, we would always be like those iridescent slivers of light, pieces of a time and space removed from everyone and everything else.

I walked into the kitchen and poured myself some coffee. It felt too quiet, padding around by myself, avoiding the one thing that was screaming for my attention. I turned on the CD player. "Roads" by Portishead. Bleak, vulnerable, desolate, beautiful. It sent an icy chill running down my spine. Or maybe that was just the apprehension of walking into the living room. I scanned the walls, the fan on the ceiling, the indent on the couch where Damian had been sitting, until my eyes ran out of excuses, until I couldn't avoid looking at what he'd left behind for me.

5, 4, 3, 2, 1 . . .

My gaze fell on the coffee table. I was doomed to cry either way, whether I found the gun or the paper giraffe. But Damian had spared me the dark, shattered tears. There, lying on the glass was his folded note, propped up on four spindly legs. His gun was sitting on the shelf, like a piece of retired memorabilia, along with dog-eared books and mismatched souvenirs.

I put my coffee down and picked up the giraffe. It was so much bigger than the space it took up, so much heavier than it weighed. I knew what it must have taken Damian to lock up his demons, but he had done it. For me.

A distant *whoomp-whoomp-whoomp* mixed in with the music. I figured the song was transitioning into the next track, but the noise grew louder. It was coming from behind me now, close enough that I could recognize it. The whirring, sonic boom of helicopter blades.

Fuck.

I ran outside, barefoot in a t-shirt, knowing Damian had gone to get mangoes for me, like he did every morning. One helicopter was already on the ground, while a second was landing on the beach in a flurry of sand and grit. Armed men in camouflaged gear were everywhere, running towards the jungle.

"Miss? Miss Sedgewick?" One of the men pulled me back. "Are you all right?"

I tore free of him and ran towards the mangoes that were scattered in the shadows of the trees. They were covered in blood.

"Where is he?" I grabbed the man who was yelling something about getting me to safety. "Is he hurt? Take me to him!"

But he wouldn't listen. He started dragging me back to one of the choppers. The sickening *bratatat* of machine guns came from the jungle. Another helicopter swept over us, scanning the ground below. A crackly voice issued rapid commands over the man's radio device. The air was thick with the hunt for Damian—all these men tracking him down—but all I could see was the trail of blood that led from the mangoes.

Damian had been coming back to me when they'd ambushed him. I closed my eyes and lived the horror of it: a bullet ripping through him, mangoes rolling to the ground, his blood staining their spotted yellow-green skins; Damian picking himself up, stumbling into the trees for cover, while I poured myself a cup of coffee.

A cup of fucking coffee.

I knew exactly where to go. I knew where Damian was—holed up in the wooden shack, as they closed in on him, with nothing to protect himself, because I'd made him give up his gun.

Oh God. What I have done?

I broke free and ran into the trees, not caring about

the bullets that were zinging past me and ricocheting off the trees in flying splinters of wood and bark.

"Hold your fire! Hold your fire!" someone screamed as I stormed into the shack. I knew they wouldn't shoot as long as I was with Damian, as long as there was any chance I'd get caught in the crossfire.

I stood by the door, panting, as my eyes adjusted to the room.

He was propped up in the corner, like a trapped animal, gripping his thigh, his sweatpants soaked with blood.

"Get out of here, Skye." He might have been hurt, but his voice was steely—calm and controlled.

"Let me have that." I took a strip of fabric from him. It was torn off his shirt, the one that was stained with faded strawberry splotches.

"It's just a flesh wound," he said, as I wrapped it around his leg, my fingers shaking as I tied it into a tight knot. "You need to leave. Now."

"Skye!" We both turned at the sound of my father's voice.

He looked like he hadn't slept in days. My father took great pride in his appearance, but today he looked like hell. There was no sharp crease in his pants; his shirt hung wrinkled and limp around his shoulders.

"I found you." He stared at me like he couldn't believe it, like I was an apparition that would disappear if he blinked. "Are you all right?"

I went to him, knowing he had moved heaven and earth to get here, not sleeping, not eating, not resting. "Dad."

He gave me three gray-whiskered kisses, then three more, then three more, before engulfing me in his hug. "I didn't know if I was ever going to see you again."

We stayed like that for a while until his eyes settled on Damian. I felt his arms tighten around me. "You." He spat out. "You're going to pay for every second you've made her suffer."

"Dad, no." I shifted so we were facing away from Damian. "Listen to me. I need to expla—" I stopped mid-sentence, noticing the man who stood behind my dad for the first time. He looked oddly familiar, with a dark, menacing air that reminded me of what was waiting outside.

"Señor Sedgewick," he said. "My men are ready to escort you and Skye back to the chopper. Don't worry. He's not going anywhere." He pointed his gun at Damian.

Damian's gaze swung from the man to my father, and back again. He was on the floor, with his injured leg stretched out before him, but his fists were clenched, his jaw clamped tight.

"Good," said my father, pulling me towards the door. "You know what to do, Victor."

Suddenly, I understood the look in Damian's eyes, the reason why the man had seemed so familiar. My father had hired Victor Madera, his ex-bodyguard, to track us down, and there, in the shack, after so many years, the two men were together again—the men who had taken MaMaLu away from Damian. And now they were taking me away too. Damian had put away his vengeance, but I could feel it rising now, like a crimson tide ready to crash around us.

"No. Stop!" I wrenched my hand away from my father and stood between the men and Damian. "No one touches him."

"Skye?" My father looked bewildered. "What are you

doing? Get away from him."

"Back off," I said to Victor, who had stepped forward, his gun aimed at Damian.

"It's okay." Victor inched forward. His hair was gray at the temples, but he was still in good shape. "You're suffering from post-traumatic stress disorder. It happens. Just step away from him and listen to your father."

"Skye, honey." My father beckoned. "You're safe now. He has no hold over you. Come. Take my hand. I promise it's going to be all right."

"I *am* all right! Can't you see? I'm *fine*. I just need you to listen to me. Please, just listen."

"Okay, okay. You're fine." My father's eyes settled on the splint around my finger. He exchanged a look with Victor. "Let's talk about this outside."

"No! Right here. Right now. I'm not leaving him." I could see the torment in my father's eyes, the incomprehension, but I knew he'd understand once I told him the truth about who Damian was, about why he'd done this. He *had* to.

"Remember Esteb—" I didn't get any further.

Victor yanked me towards him, grasping me by the waist. "Take her," he said to my father. "Go!"

That split second of taking his eyes off Damian cost him. Damian struck with lightning precision, tackling Victor's ankles. Victor fell back on the workbench. Rusty pliers and hammers and nails cluttered to the floor as it tipped over. The two men wrestled on the ground, each trying to reach for the gun that lay a few inches from their grasp.

"Don't!" I stopped my father from grabbing the gun, clenching on to his arm.

"What's wrong with you? Snap out of it, Skye!"

Damian and Victor were still struggling. Victor on top, then Damian, then Victor again. Damian kicked the gun out of the way. Then Victor was up and he was kicking Damian. He drove his thick, heavy boots into Damian's ribs, his stomach, the wound on his leg. Again and again.

History was repeating itself. I knew Damian was back outside the gates of Casa Paloma, broken and battered, as Victor pummeled him. I knew the rage, the hurt, the sense of injustice that was flooding through his veins. But Damian wasn't twelve years old anymore, and Victor was past his prime. Most of all, Damian had years and years of bottled-up wrath, clamoring to be set free.

Damian's fingers closed around the hacksaw that was lying on the ground, and all of his fury exploded in a single move, a gash so deep that when it was done, the teeth of the saw remained lodged deep in Victor's bone.

Victor staggered back, watching the blood spurt from his arm like he was in some kind of horrific trance. Damian had cleaved the flesh right under his elbow. The rest of his arm hung from the joint, dead and limp. Blood pooled at Victor's feet, splattering on his rough, tan boots. Then Victor fell to his knees, swaying for a few beats, before his face hit the floor.

What happened next was over in a few seconds, but it unfolded before my eyes in excruciatingly slow, clear detail, like I was stuck in some parallel universe, unable to save the two men that I loved. They both lunged for the gun, but Damian got to it first.

"No!" I shielded my father from him.

"We can still get out of here, Skye." Damian limped as he took a step towards me. "We walk out. I take you as hostage. No one will shoot."

"You step out of this shack and you die," said my

father.

"Stop it." I whirled around, from one to the other. "Both of you. Just stop it!"

"Skye." Damian held his hand out, the other still pointing the gun at my dad.

"Don't listen to him. Come to me, Skye." My father held his hand out.

I stood between them and felt the whole shack tilting like a see-saw, with me at the pivot point, three kisses on one side, a paper giraffe on the other. Damian's life was on the line; my father's life was on the line. One of them was going down, and it was up to me to decide who.

"I love him, Dad," I said.

"You *think* you love him, but he's a monster. Take my hand, Skye, and let the men look after it."

Damian's whole face changed with those three words.

Look after it, and MaMaLu had been taken away from him.

Look after it, and they would take me away, too.

No. This time Warren Sedgewick was not going to have his way. This time *Damian* was going to look after it. I could see it in the way his whole body tensed, the way it had before he chopped my finger off, the way it had when he thought I was going to jump off the boat.

Damian was blind to everything except the raw pain in his heart. The wound I had tried to heal with love was ripped open. Vengeance oozed from it, infecting everything sweet and kind and soft, obliterating the tender shoots that were starting to bud through. There was no more Skye, just darkness and dust and a plague of bitter, black memories.

Damian squeezed the trigger.

I moved at the same time.

You can either choose love or you can choose hate, because where one lives, the other will die.

“Skye!” I heard both men calling as the bullet ripped through me.

The room stopped tilting. Everything went still. No more fighting. No more tug of war. I held my breath.

Sweet, sweet silence.

Then I exhaled and lurched forward, as the blood spread like a red blot across my t-shirt.

DAMIAN

Twenty-Six

IT WAS A HIGH PROFILE case. People go missing every day, but a kidnapped heiress who beats the odds and gets shot during a rescue mission has everyone buzzing. Damian could have told his side of the story. Reporters were hungry for it, but he was tight lipped through the proceedings. He had done what he had done and nothing was going to change it. It was almost a relief when the judge handed down his sentence, and the media got their pound of flesh.

On his first day in prison, Damian knew that he could walk in like a lamb or he could take the bull by the horns. Whatever he chose would set the tone for the rest of his incarceration. He kept his head down for most of the day, watching and learning. Survival was the name of the game, and his time in Caboras had served him well.

Most prisoners segregated themselves according to racial allegiance. There was power in numbers. If you were in a gang, you were protected. People thought twice about getting in your face, so you picked a camp and stuck with it. Damian made out three distinct groups in the yard: BMW. Black, Mexican, and White. There was always someone who didn't fit, and some of them splintered into smaller factions. There were those who ran with God, mostly Christians and Muslims, those who were homosexuals and transgenders, and those who stood out as loners: lifers, career criminals, and roughened, toughened old men. No matter what group they belonged to, they were all men who had committed major felonies—murder, robbery, kidnapping, treason. There was another section, separate and removed, for prisoners who couldn't be put in with the general population: the Sensitive Needs Yard. This was where they fenced off high notoriety inmates (ex-cops, celebrities, serial killers), sex offenders (rapists and pedophiles), and men with mental health issues.

The Robert Dailey Correctional Facility, east of San Diego, was not a place that housed white-collar criminals or those who committed minor misdemeanors. It was a desolate prison outpost, ringed by curtains of wire and thickets of dusty wildflowers, a stone's throw from the *colonias* and *maquilidoras* of Tijuana. It was the place Damian had been sent to, to serve out his sentence.

When the bell for supper rang at 4 pm, Damian shuffled out in a single line with the other inmates in his housing unit. The chow hall was a cavernous rectangular room with a dozen stainless steel tables, each of which sat eight people. On both sides of the hall were armed guards, monitoring the prisoners from behind glass cubicles. A row of six convict kitchen workers moved trays along, assembly style, behind a cafeteria-like glass barrier. That day, they were serving chicken fried steak with mashed potatoes, gravy, a thin slice of cornbread, and Jell-O.

Damian got his tray, filled his state-issued plastic mug with cold water, and joined the gay prisoners. Monique, the six-foot-four burly, black inmate, raised a razor thin eyebrow when Damian took the seat across from him. For a moment, Damian wavered, wondering if Monique was his best option to establish a reputation. Monique was a lifer and the shot caller for the group, an ex-boxer with biceps as thick and corded as tree trunks. The correctional officers required a representative from every group. If there was trouble between different affiliations, the guards locked everyone down and got the shot callers together to resolve the situation. This allowed the prisoners to police themselves, and the system ran better for everyone. In return, the shot callers won favors or 'juice cards' from the guards. Monique obviously held a lot of those, from his purple lipstick to his black nail polish, to the Mardi Gras beads around his neck. He was the biggest, most powerful, most flamboyant character in the room. So, when Damian reached across the table, speared Monique's chicken patty and ripped off a big bite, everything came to a faltering halt. The kitchen staff stopped mid-ladle, gravy dripping from their spoons. Chatter ceased. All eyes focused on Monique and Damian.

Monique blinked. Had this piece of fresh meat, this newcomer, just swiped the food off his plate? Only a fool would disrespect another prisoner so blatantly, and this fool had chosen to tangle with *him*?

Damian needed a reaction. Fast. Before the guards got involved. He picked up his mug and splashed icy, cold water in Monique's face. Monique let the water drip off his nose and down his chin. He wiped his face without breaking eye contact with Damian. And then all hell broke loose.

If you're going to get in a prison fight, be the first to strike, thought Damian, as he slammed his elbow into Monique's throat, getting him in the voice box. It took the bigger guy a second to recover. By then, they were surrounded by a circle of convicts, keeping the guards at bay.

Monique lunged across the table, toppling Damian off his chair. The two men crashed to the floor, grappling with each other. Damian took heavy blows to his chin, his jaw, his chest. Each hit felt like he was being pounded by a hammer. Monique powered over him, stomping on his instep to keep him pinned down, so he couldn't fight his way back on top. He grabbed Damian's neck, clamping down on his windpipe, choking him with an iron grip, before bashing his head against the floor. All the air in Damian's lungs left him in a sharp *whoosh*. Damian felt like his face was going to explode, like all the blood had collected in his head and Monique was tightening the wrench, cutting it off from the rest of his body. Monique was dodging his punches, punches that were quickly losing force as Damian's vision started to fade. The inmates looking down on them turned blurry, one blue uniform melding into another. The noise, the chaos, the chants turned distant. Skye's face floated before him, haunting and frozen, the moment before he'd pulled the trigger, her eyes stricken, the silent 'no' she'd mouthed.

What do you do, Damian? He heard her voice in his head.

I fight back and I fight hard.

Damian's eyes shot open. He grabbed hold of the beads

around Monique's neck and pulled. When Monique's face was close enough, Damian head-butted his nose. Monique let go of Damian and clutched his nose. Blood spewed over his blue chambray shirt. Damian punched Monique in the jaw and got on top of him. By the time the guards got through, Monique's face was raw and purple from smeared lipstick and Damian's blows.

As they dragged Damian and Monique away, the sea of prisoners parted. Both men were unsteady on their feet, bloodied and battered, but one thing was clear: Damian Caballero was not a man anyone wanted to mess with.

DAMIAN WAS THROWN INTO ISOLATION for instigating a fight. Isolation was the prison's purest punishment. 'The Hole', or Solitary Confinement Unit was nine feet long and seven feet wide, with walls and ceilings of heavy gauge sheet metal. The floor was cold concrete. There was nothing in the cell except a metal bedframe with a thin mattress, crammed up against a toilet and a sink. Damian's only point of contact with the outside world was the feeding slot. They took away his uniform and gave him a thin t-shirt and boxer shorts. At night, they turned up the air conditioning so he couldn't sleep.

For ninety minutes a day, Damian was allowed into an exercise pen where he stretched and lunged and squatted, making the most of the extra space. For the remaining twenty-two and a half hours, Damian was left in total silence and darkness. For the first time since he pleaded guilty to the charges brought against him, Damian was alone. The isolation was supposed to break him, but he welcomed it. He had gone far too long without being held accountable for all the men whose blood was still on his hands:

Alfredo Ruben Zamora, the man who had tried to take down El Charro in the cantina.

El Charro.

Countless members of the Sinaloa cartel and Los Zetas, in the warehouse explosion.

But it was what he had done to Skye that weighed most heavily on Damian's mind. He couldn't stop thinking about the last time he had seen her, and even though it hurt like hell, he recalled every last detail.

WHEN DAMIAN WALKED INTO THE courtroom, Skye was the first person he saw. His eyes automatically went to her because that's how it was. When they were in the same space, she commanded all of his attention.

She looked different—not the girl who belonged in an ivory tower and not the girl who belonged in his island bed. She didn't look like Warren's Skye, or Damian's Skye, or a torn up, in-between Skye. This Skye belonged to herself. Whatever she'd been through since the island had changed her. Damian felt the retraction, like she had closed herself off, not just to him, but to everything around her. She was sitting in the same room, but in her own zone, breathing her own air.

The bullet had grazed her shoulder and although it had exited without permanent damage, her arm was still in a sling from the injury. Damian could not look at her without thinking of her blood trickling through his fingers the moment he'd caught her. Blood that he had spilled. Warren's men had apprehended him. They had carried Skye and Victor, who had passed out from blood loss, to the helicopter. Warren had flown to the hospital with them, while Damian was taken—handcuffed and guarded—to the police station. Rafael had kept him updated on Skye's status and recovery, but he had not seen her since his arrest.

She was blond again. Her sleek, chin length hair was tucked behind one ear. From Damian's angle, it accentuated her full, pink lips and made him yearn for things he'd lost the rights to when he'd pulled the trigger.

Skye was wedged between her father and Nick Turner, the guy she'd had dinner with on the night Damian had abducted her. Damian hated him for sitting so close to her, for being able *to sit so close to her, his shoulder touching hers. He hated him more for that one single privilege than all the charges Nick had brought against him, because Nick was also the lawyer who was prosecuting Damian.*

Although Damian had dual citizenship—Mexican and American—he was tried in San Diego because he had kidnapped Skye on U.S. soil. Except it never got to a trial. Damian pled guilty. He had maimed Victor, kidnapped Skye, held her captive, cut off her finger and finally, shot her. Damian's lawyer and Nick worked out a plea bargain, with Nick pushing for the harshest sentence.

Nick despised Damian for taking away the girl he had come to adore, and for the things he believed he had done to her. Although Skye refused to see Nick outside of legal proceedings, Nick was convinced it was because of the trauma she had suffered, and that with time, she would give him another chance. He did not believe her when she told him she had fallen in love with Damian. So what if Damian was this Esteban kid she had once known? Skye was not in her right mind and it was up to him and Warren to put Damian behind bars forever.

They trumped the kidnapping charge to aggravated kidnapping, given that Damian had caused Skye bodily harm. They wanted to tack on aggravated rape, but Skye insisted that the sex had been consensual, and refused to let them turn it into something ugly.

Of course, Damian knew none of this as he watched Skye between the two men. He saw them as a unit, a trio of joined forces.

Whatever you choose, Damian, know that I will always, always love you, *she had said to him.*

He wanted to believe that. He wanted to believe that so much, but how could he, knowing that she was withholding the one thing that would have earned him some lenience? The fact that he had let her go. He had set her free, dropped her off and she had come back to him. That was something only the two of them knew. Yes, he had made the wrong choice. He had given in to the darkness when he should have stood by her, but he needed to know that she still cared. He would happily spend the rest of his life locked up in a cage for all the things he had done, but he needed that one fleeting moment of light, so he could go knowing that it had been real for her.

As Damian stood before the judge, ready to receive his sentence, his eyes fell on Skye. One look, one glance from those haunting gray eyes, and he'd be redeemed.

Say something, I'm giving up on you.

But she kept her head bowed. She had not looked at him the entire time, and she did not look at him then. Skye knew that if she did, if she looked up from her lap, she wouldn't be able to keep anything from him, and she had held it together for too long to let everything fall apart now. The sooner this case got wrapped up, the better for them all.

She had told her father and Nick that Damian had let her go, that she was the one who had gone back, but they were convinced she had suffered some kind of psychological breakdown. They were prepared to call in a psychiatrist to discredit anything favorable she had to say about Damian, and testify that she was suffering from Stockholm syndrome and Post Traumatic Stress Disorder.

"I can't understand why you're defending him, Skye." Her father had paced the hospital room where she was recovering from the bullet wound. "Look at what he's done to you. He shot you, Skye. He was going to shoot me, *but he ended up shooting* you. *Is this the kind of guy you want walking free? Someone who is so blinded by revenge that he can't see straight?"*

"You were blind too, Dad, so blind that you couldn't see what you did to MaMaL—"

"You want to know what I did to MaMaLu?" Warren's eyes flashed with indignation. "I saved *MaMaLu. That's right. I* saved *her. El Charro and his men would have killed her. Prison was the safest place for her. Out of sight, out of mind. I paid Victor a small fortune to make sure Esteban was looked after and that MaMaLu got everything she needed in Valdemoros. I don't know if any of that money made it to her. I suspect Victor used that money to start up his private security business, but that's irrelevant now. As soon as we were settled in our new home, I was going to send for MaMaLu and Esteban, get them new identities, and sponsor them over. I owed it to her. A new life, a fresh start. But it didn't work out that way. She died before I could get them out. I went looking for Esteban, but his uncle was gone and he had disappeared. There was no trace of him. No one knew*

where he went or what happened to him. I closed that chapter of our lives with a heavy heart, Skye. I burned the letters you wrote. It broke my heart, but I wanted to protect you. You were so young, I was sure you'd forget. I thought it would be easier if you assumed they'd moved on." Warren sighed and sank down onto the chair. "If there's one thing I regret, apart from not leaving Mexico while your mother was alive, it's MaMaLu. And if Damian wants to come after me for that, fine. But I'm not letting him get away with this." He gestured to Skye's bed and all the machines beeping around them.

Skye closed her eyes. So many misunderstandings, so much time wasted, each man standing stubbornly in his corner.

"Damian needs to know what happened, Dad, what your intentions were."

"He never gave me the chance to explain, did he? He just made his assumptions. Judge, jury and vigilante justice. He kidnapped you, hurt you, and he permanently injured a man. Victor will never have use of that arm. The doctors have reattached it, but the nerves are severed. That's irreversible."

"It was self-defense!" said Skye. She was sick of the endless tug of war. "Victor was under contract with you. He knew what he was getting into. The risks go hand in hand with his job. Damian didn't have a weapon. He was hurt. It was Victor who threatened him with a gun."

"Why?" Her father looked exhausted. "Why do you have to fight me at every turn? Let me handle this, Skye. One day you'll look back and you'll see. You're not yourself right now. You don't know—"

"Enough!" Skye cut her father off. "Enough."

That was when the old Skye switched off and a new

Skye took her place.

"I'm done," she said. "I'm done with you. And I'm done with Damian. I won't let either of you use me to get to each other."

Nick urged her to turn down the plea bargain that Damian's lawyer offered, but Skye knew that if the case went to trial, they would paint Damian as a monster and have her testimony negated. Everything they had shared would be sullied and violated. And so, she came to an agreement with Nick and her father. They wouldn't subject Skye to a psychiatrist if she didn't force their hand, if she kept her mouth shut about Damian letting her go.

And so she sat there, in the court room, staring into her lap, even as her face burned where Damian's eyes skimmed over her. Her love had not been enough. He had retired one gun, only to pick up another. When push came to shove, her love had not been enough.

The judge sentenced Damian to eight years, because he had shown remorse by pleading guilty, and had spared the court the time and expense of a lengthy trial.

Nick and Warren didn't look too happy, but it was a time frame they had anticipated and come to terms with.

Rafael gave Damian a curt nod as they handcuffed him.

Damian turned to look at Skye one last time before they led him out, still hungry, still desperate for one glance. What he felt, he couldn't put into words—sadness, loss, a feeling of having disappointed her, and of being let down himself.

Skye kept her eyes trained on her lap.

DAMIAN HAD LOVED TWO WOMEN in his life. He had been unable to save one and he'd made things impossible for the other one. In the darkness, when the weight of his isolation sat on his chest like a stony gargoyle, MaMaLu came to him. He felt her presence settle around him. When he closed his eyes, he could hear her singing. He was a little boy again, sitting in church with her, his hand clasped firmly in hers, as angels and saints looked down on them.

Damian realized that MaMaLu had not been alone, that even in her last days in Valdemoros, he had been with her, just as she was with him now. Because when we love, we carry it on the inside, and we can turn on its light even in our darkest moments. The deeper we love, the brighter it shines. And even though MaMaLu was long gone, she was still there with him, in his darkest, loneliest moments.

It's true, he thought.

Love don't die.

It gave Damian reason to hold on to his sanity, because without focusing on something, a man can go crazy in solitary confinement. Damian tore off a button from his boxers, turned around in a circle, and flung it in the air. Then he got on his hands and knees and searched for it in the darkness. When he found it, he repeated the process again and again until he was exhausted. After a while, he used his game to figure out the time between meals, and day from night. Sometimes he ran on the spot, sometimes he balanced on his head. He kept busy and he kept fit, and when they opened up the door to let him back into his cell, he surprised everyone with his resilience.

Monique had served no more than a few days in the hole, because Monique was important. He played a key role in keeping the peace. The first day Damian was back in the chow hall, a nervous energy surrounded the whole place. The guards were extra vigilant and the prisoners fidgeted as Damian took the same seat across from Monique. The menu was spaghetti with meatballs, a side of peas, and the ubiquitous Jell-O. Damian forked a meatball from Monique's tray and put it into his mouth. Monique stopped chewing. His nose had healed, but it was now slightly crooked. The tension between the two men was palpable. Then Monique reached across and picked a forkful of Damian's peas. He held the fork between them, the peas hovering in a slippery stack of machismo, before shoveling them in his mouth. They stared at each other, taking their time, chomping down each other's food. Damian swallowed and turned his attention back to his tray. Monique continued eating silently from his. Everyone returned to what they were doing.

"Nice scarf," mumbled Damian.

Monique was wearing a bright floral scarf around his head and sporting a pair of dainty pearl earrings.

"Bitch please," replied Monique without lifting his eyes from his spaghetti. "You ain't ever getting a piece of this action."

Twenty-Seven

"DAMIAN, YOU HAVE A VISITOR." A correctional officer stopped by the Release and Receiving area where Damian and Monique were painting a mural.

"Praise the lord." Monique raised his palms to the ceiling. "Take this useless piece of shit away. He's been messing with my field of corn."

"It's corn," said Damian, putting his brush away. "Not some phallic representation of corn."

He followed the guard through heavy steel doors with plexiglass windows. Each door buzzed a warning, opened with a puff of compressed air, and slid shut behind them with a definitive *fffphut*.

Damian walked into the visiting room and looked for Rafael. In the year that he had been there, Rafael had been his only visitor. Damian monitored his business from behind bars, and Rafael followed through with his directives. Sometimes they sat out in the adjoining patio, which had patches of green grass, and caught up on their lives. Damian was going nowhere, but Rafael's visits gave him glimpses of the outside world.

"They told me no strapless or halter tops. And nothing more than two inches above the knee." Rafael was always ribbing Damian about his unlikely friendship with Monique.

Damian wondered what wisecracks Rafael would make that day, but there was no sign of his friend. Half of the little seating areas in the room were occupied by visiting kids and families. He glanced at the guard manning the podium.

"Outside," said the guard.

Damian stepped onto the patio and froze. Sitting on one of the bolted-down benches was Skye, more beautiful, more real, more *everything* than he remembered. She had her back to him and he felt a pang of pure agony because her hair was almost at her waist now, because he had missed a whole ticker tape of moments—what it looked like when it reached her shoulders, when it grazed past her breasts, when it curled into the hollow of her back. The sparse, soft down of hair on her arms was almost silver-white where the sun fell on it. It gave her an aura of brightness that lit up every dark, dusty corner of his heart.

He would have stood there indefinitely, paralyzed by the sight of Skye, but one of the guards prodded him along. Damian stood behind her for a moment, trying to find the words, when she turned around, sensing his presence.

Skye had been expecting something different. A small booth, a glass barrier, a phone through which they would communicate.

Distance.

She had been expecting distance.

She had replayed the scene in her mind, over and over. Fluorescent bulbs overhead, a closet-like space, surveillance cameras monitoring their interaction. She would sit down. He would be brought in. That's what she had envisioned, that's what she had prepared herself for. But there was no glass between them, nothing to confine the raw emotions crackling between them, nothing to contain the pull Damian still had on her.

"Sit!" one of the guards called out, breaking their bittersweet scrutiny of each other.

Damian slid onto the bench across from her. A small, rectangular table separated them.

"I—"

"You—"

They stopped at the same time.

"You first," said Damian, thinking of another time they had interrupted each other, and the mad kisses that had followed in a dark hallway.

"They told me I was on your approved list when I asked to visit," said Skye.

"I didn't think you'd come."

They stopped talking because they were too busy looking. Skye had braced herself for the worst, but Damian was a survivor. He had survived El Charro and Caboras, and he was surviving prison. If anything, his chest was broader and his shirt hinted at muscles that had grown bigger and stronger. But his face was leaner and his eyes were different. They had shifted yet again. Still black, yes, but with the darkness of loss, of possibilities embraced and then turned to ash.

"How . . ." She swallowed, trying to hold up under the intensity of his gaze. "How have you been?"

"You look good," he said, as if he hadn't heard her, as if the sight of her was overwhelming all of his senses. *You look so, so good.*

He wasn't talking about the fact that she'd put on some weight, or that her breasts were rounder under the long-sleeved blouse, or that her cheeks had filled in from the last time he had seen her in court. He meant that she looked good to *him*, no matter where, no matter when.

"How's your shoulder?" he asked.

"Fine." *It's not my shoulder that hurts. It's my heart.* "How's your leg?"

Damian didn't give a damn about the old wound on his thigh, a reminder of their last day on the island when Victor's men had cornered him in the shack. He leaned across the table, as close to her as he knew the guards would let him. "What's wrong, Skye? Is there something you're not telling me?"

She looked startled, although he couldn't imagine why. They had always been able to read each other.

"Why did you do it?" she asked. "After everything we went through, you still had to go after my father's company?"

Damian sighed. He didn't want to talk about all the things that had torn them apart, not when he was seeing her after so long, but he told her what she wanted to know. "Because even after he put me away, he wasn't done. Your father sent someone in here to rough me up, with a warning to stay away from you. He said that if I ever tried to contact you, I wouldn't have to worry about serving out the rest of my sentence because he'd put me in a box long before then."

"When? When did he do this?"

"A few months after I got here." Damian could feel the pieces of the puzzle moving around in her head. He wished he could get inside her mind and rearrange every single piece so they weren't wasting this time, this precious time discussing Warren Fucking Sedgewick.

"So you sold your Sedgewick Hotels stock short and sent his shares plummeting. You must have lost a lot of money. Why shoot yourself in the leg? Why not just take over?"

"I don't react well to threats, Skye. And that company was built on dirty money. Cartel money. I would have given anything to see the look on Warren's face when it all came tumbling down."

"Well, that's never going to happen now. He's gone, Damian. My father died a few days ago. You got your revenge. It took a while for everything to crumble, for him to lose everything, piece by piece. The stress was too much for him. Foreclosures and debt collectors. Everywhere he turned. He had a stroke last year, and then another one a few months later. He didn't survive the third one. So congratulations. You finally did it. You avenged MaMaLu."

"Good." Damian sat back and folded his arms. He should have felt a small measure of victory, of justice, but it did nothing to fill the Skye-less hole that was gnawing away pieces of his soul. "I can't say he didn't deserve it."

"Don't, Damian. It's time to let it go. My father meant to get you and MaMaLu out of there. He was going to get you new lives, new identities. He came looking for you after MaMaLu died, but you were nowhere to be found. He couldn't undo what he did, but he never meant you or MaMaLu any harm."

A sick, slow heaviness curdled in Damian's veins, the

initial burst of happiness at seeing Skye dissipating like cool ether. She wasn't here for him. She was here for her father.

"So that's it?" he asked. "That's why you showed up? A year later? To berate me for something *he* started? I walked away, Skye. For you. But he couldn't leave it alone, could he? He just had to try to strong-arm me into keeping my distance. As if I could ever bring myself to contact you. You deserve better. I knew that. He knew that, but he had to prove that he still held the cards."

"That's not why he did it!"

"Then why, Skye? Why? I lost MaMaLu. I lost you. I lost eight years of my life. Why the fuck couldn't he just leave me alone?"

"Because!"

"Because what?" Damian slammed his palms down on the table. "I hated that fucking bastard and I'm glad he's gone. What did you expect, Skye? Did you expect an apology? You want me to say *I'm sorry*?"

"Stop it, Damian." Skye could see the guard making his way towards them. "I thought it would be different. I thought *you* would be different. But you're still filled with so much rage."

"And you're still defending him." Damian got up and let the guard cuff him. His outburst was going to cost him. He wished Skye had never come. He wished he'd never known her or Warren Sedgewick. He wished he could stop the pain that was shooting through him. "I guess blood will always be thicker than water."

Skye's face changed at his parting remark. She looked both heart-broken and enraged. The last thing Damian saw as they led him away was her back, shoulders hunched over the table.

That was the only time Skye came to see Damian in prison. He didn't see her again for the rest of his incarceration, not once over the next seven years.

Twenty-Eight

DAMIAN STOOD AT THE ENTRANCE of Casa Paloma, by the tall wrought iron gates that had once barred his way. The first thing he'd done when he got out of prison was to put in an offer, and he stood now as master, where his mother had been the help. The few prospective buyers with the means to afford the property had turned away from the daunting task of restoring it. Years of neglect had left it in disarray. Vine-smothered walls and balconies obscured Casa Paloma's graceful lines. Overgrown trees encroached like dark shadows around the edges. The garden had transformed into a jaundiced mess of dry, tangled weeds, trash bags, and empty beer bottles.

Damian removed the chains and pushed the gates open. They squeaked from worn, rusty joints. The main house stood before him, its boarded-up windows staring at him with pale, blank eyes. Damian walked past it, ignoring the flurry of grasshoppers that clamored out of his way, to the small, modest building in the back that had once housed the staff. It was a single row of dormitory style rooms with a communal bathroom and kitchen. He stood outside the third door, overcome with nostalgia and a strange, tight knot in his throat. MaMaLu's broom was still leaning against the wall, mummified in layers of dust and cobwebs. Damian shuffled his feet at the entrance.

"It's me, MaMaLu," he said, trying to get the words past his clenched throat. "Your Estebandido is home."

The door remained shut. There was no one to let him in, no one to stare him down for being a bad boy. Damian leaned his forehead against the door and traced the frame. Flakes of peeling paint fell on his shoes. He let his hand rest on the knob for a minute before walking in.

The room was much smaller than he remembered. A single shaft of sunlight lit up the dark, musty space. There was no lingering scent of the jasmine hair oil that MaMaLu used. The fabric partition between their beds lay crumbled on the ground, from the night they'd taken MaMaLu away. There were no *tostadas* waiting for him, no glass of *horchata*, but what broke Damian that quiet morning was her bed. MaMaLu's bed was never unmade, but now it sat there, sheets pulled back, pillow askew, covered in dust. They had dragged her out, and it had stayed behind, empty and forgotten, unmade for the last twenty-three years.

Damian was moved to action. He took the bed sheets outside and shook the dust out of them. He pounded the pillow, turned the case upside down and shook it some more. He made the bed up, stretched the sheets out tight so not a single crease marked the surface. He turned down the top sheet and tucked the ends in. He returned MaMaLu's pillow, stood back, repositioned it, and stood back again. A speck of dust settled on the covers, and Damian, determined to have nothing mar MaMaLu's bed, started the whole process over again.

He was still fussing over the sheets when the bottled up sensation that had been building in his throat erupted. Damian had not cried for MaMaLu, not in Valdemoros when they'd told him she was dead, not when he placed sunflowers on her grave every year, and not when he opened her little *Lucky Strike* tin. His grief had been curtailed by rage. But now the rage was done. He had avenged her, made El Charro pay, made Warren Sedgewick pay. They were gone, and with them, his burning need for vengeance. Damian had nothing to hold on to, nothing to keep the storm of tears at bay. All the deep, dark emotions that had tormented him lay hollow and spent, like a pile of powdery skeletons. Hate was an illusion, rage was an illusion, vengeance was an illusion. They were all empty husks that he had watered and nurtured, and in the end, they bore no fruit.

Damian crawled into MaMaLu's bed and rolled up into a ball. He was a boy when he'd left and he had returned a man. He had been alone then and he was alone now. The only difference, the only cruel, bitter difference, was that he had lost his one chance at redemption. He had been so busy holding on to hate, that he had let go of love.

Damian thought of the last time he had seen Skye.

You're still filled with so much rage, she'd said.

He finally understood what she'd been trying to tell him.

Twenty-Nine

THE TASK OF RESTORING CASA Paloma was colossal, but Damian had both the time and the resources. For eight years, he had run his company from prison. His direction was necessary, but his presence was optional. Damian had achieved what he had set out to do, but it had brought him no comfort. He found solace in gutting and painting and patching the main house. He ripped the vines off the facade, cleaned out the pumps so the fountains worked again, and hired a team of landscapers to restore the grounds. He had the roof replaced with terracotta tiles and gave the exterior stucco a fresh coat of white paint.

Slowly, the house started looking alive again. Flowers bloomed in the garden. Butterflies and hummingbirds returned. The place had been ransacked over the years, but a lot of the original furniture remained, along with the chandeliers. Skye's mother, Adriana, had had a flair for drama. Damian wasn't sure if he wanted to keep the velvet curtains in the dining room. He sat at the table where Warren had once convened with El Charro and his men, and considered the heavy crimson fabric. It added a touch of old world opulence, but it also blocked out much of the light.

A soft thud interrupted his thoughts. The renovation crew was gone for the day, but old houses made all kinds of noises. Damian ignored it and got up to examine the curtains.

There it was again. Another little thud. Damian spun around. It was coming from the antique hutch he used to hide in, the same hutch from where he'd spied Skye and MaMaLu interrupting Warren's meeting. Damian stood before it and heard a distinct thump. Whatever was in there, possibly a bird or stray cat, had seen him. On the other hand, it could be something not quite as harmless, like a snake. Damian got on all fours and opened the door slowly.

She was a bony little thing with brown skin and a long, messy braid. Her knees were folded up to her chin and she peered at him with huge, cocoa eyes. She was wearing a white shirt with a school crest, and a navy skirt. Her socks were askew, one pulled up to her knees, the other at her ankle.

"It's okay," said Damian, as she eyed him warily. "You don't need to hide." He held out his hand, but she refused to take it.

The last thing he'd expected to find was a little girl hiding in the hutch. Perhaps her father was one of the workers he'd hired, and she'd come looking for him.

Perhaps she walked by on her way to school and curiosity had drawn her into Casa Paloma—years of walking by an abandoned house that was suddenly ablaze with activity. The renovation crew had been in and out in muddy pick-up trucks, drilling, clanging, banging, hammering. Wheelbarrows of broken tiles and old flooring were lined up by the gates, but flowers spilled from the hedges and what was once dull and dead was now lush and green. Damian was surprised no one else had ventured in. The little girl was his first visitor, and she was obviously scared for getting caught.

"I'm not going to hurt you." He sat back on his heels and waited while she assessed him. He must have passed her threat level detection scan because she crawled out of the hutch and stood before him, fidgeting with her skirt.

Damian remembered all too well the feeling of knowing you were in trouble, but not knowing how you were going to be dealt with. In many ways, it was worse than the punishment itself.

"What's your name?" he asked.

She stared at him for a moment, before dropping her gaze to her shoes. They were scuffed up and looked like they had been put to good use.

"Do you live around here?" He leaned closer, trying to meet her gaze.

"Get away from me!" She swung her leg back and kicked him hard, right in the balls.

There was moment of poignant eye contact between the two.

Dude, how could you? Damian looked at the girl in disbelief before he crumpled to the floor, his hands cupped between his legs in testicle-protection mode.

OhGodnofugwtuf. That.shit.fucking.hurt.

He doubled over, trying to catch his breath.

Pain radiated out of Damian's testicles, igniting his midsection in hellfire before settling in his kidneys. Every muscle from his knees to his chest felt like it was cramping all at once. Damian's head started spinning. He felt violently nauseous, but he suppressed the desire to hurl because the slightest movement amplified the pain After a few sharp, agonizing breaths, the pain gave way to a dull throbbing that radiated out with each heartbeat.

Damian opened his eyes. The girl was gone. His nuts were destroyed. Obliterated. He was pretty sure of it. He lay on the floor, taking stock of the rest of his body.

Legs? Yup, still there.

Arms? Present. And functional.

Torso? All systems go.

Junk?

Come in, junk? Alive, captain. Not happy, but alive.

Damian took a deep breath and stared at the empty space in the hutch. He had survived eight years in prison, but one kick from a little girl had sent him into a fit of convulsions and existential crisis. He remained curled up like a baby and started laughing. For the first time since Skye and the island, Damian laughed long and hard, holding his throbbing balls as they protested with twinges of indignation.

Thirty

THERE WAS ONE ROOM THAT remained untouched in Casa Paloma. Damian had ignored it for as long as he could, and although the door to Skye's room remained shut, it called him every time he walked by. When Damian finally walked in, he awakened childhood ghosts that laughed and sang and jumped up and down on the bed. They scattered faded paper animals in his path and filled his head with whispers of distant memories. Damian was defenseless against them now. He had no barrier to keep them at bay, no chains of anger or hatred to tie them down with. He heard them, saw them, felt them all.

This was where Skye had chucked up chocolate peanut butter ice cream. Well, whatever hadn't landed on his shoes.

Here, he'd watched her scrutinize her reflection and ask him to make her a cardboard tooth.

Here, they'd held hands in a circle—him and MaMaLu and Skye—before Skye said her bedtime prayer.

As Damian swept the room and cleared the cobwebs, the memories became sharper, clearer, more painful, but at the same time sweeter, like little shards of glass candy that dissolved into pockets of nostalgic flavor, to be sampled and tasted and savored, again and again.

Damian rolled up the dusty bed covers and pried the plywood off the window. The sun streamed in, lighting up the walls and corners and bookshelves. The tree outside Skye's bedroom had grown taller; the branch he'd used to climb in was now scraping the roof. Damian tilted his head back, following it, and saw a pair of brown legs dangling through the leaves. It was the nut-busting girl, with her scuffed-up, nut-busting shoes. She was leaning against the trunk, reading a book, unaware of being observed.

Damian instinctively cupped his balls.

What the fuck was she doing back here?

He ducked back inside and considered boarding the window up again. His balls still ached, but he had to hand it to her. She wasn't one to tangle with. He laughed and started sorting through the shelves, thumbing over the books that MaMaLu had once read to him and Skye. The best stories were the ones that weren't there, the ones she'd made up. They hung suspended around him. Damian took a deep breath, wanting to inhale them, to fill up his lungs with MaMaLu's voice and her words. He stretched his arms out, rotating three hundred and sixty degrees, taking it all in and . . . stopped short.

A pair of dark eyes was watching him.

The girl was sitting on one of the lower branches now,

level with the window. She was wearing a school uniform again. Her book was tucked in the waistband of her skirt and she looked like she'd been ready to scoot down the tree when she'd seen him.

It wasn't Damian's finest moment, chest puffed up, spinning around in a dusty room like a would-be ballerina. He put his hands down and met the girl's stare. Perhaps if he gave her the old western, squinty-eyed glare, she'd resume her descent.

She didn't. She squinted back at him, smug in the knowledge that the branch wasn't going to support him, so he couldn't get to her even if he tried.

A few seconds into the stare down, Damian felt the corners of his mouth lifting. He managed to transform it into a snarl and turned away, busying himself with the task of cleaning up the room. He kept the girl in his periphery. He wasn't about to drop his guard in case she decided to go all ninja on him again.

He was almost done when he found a pile of colorful papers, the kind he'd once used for origami. Skye had gotten them for him, and he had an instant flashback of the delight on her face whenever he made her something.

It seemed like another lifetime, but Damian's fingers yearned for the feel of that paper. He picked up a green sheet, yellowed and faded now, but still the brightest thing in that room, and folded it into a swan. It was the last story he remembered MaMaLu telling him and Skye, before all of their lives had changed. Damian felt like he was picking up where he'd left off, except MaMaLu wasn't there anymore, and Skye wasn't there anymore. No one was. Except a little girl who was watching him like he afforded her more entertainment than the book she was now pretending to read.

Damian offered her the swan, but she ignored him, keeping her eyes on the book. So, he placed it on the windowsill, picked up two bags filled with garbage and went downstairs to dump them. When he came back up, she was gone. And so was the paper swan.

Thirty-One

DAMIAN WAS PAINTING THE KITCHEN when he spotted the girl again. She seemed to stop by at the same time every day, after school. She was kneeling by the pond, feeding the fish that he had just reintroduced into the water. A half peeled orange lay on her lap. She nipped each segment with her teeth and turned it inside out, picking out some of the flesh for the fish and eating the rest.

To Damian, it was one of those perfect snapshots of childhood, the way her world was condensed into an orange and a fish pond, surrounded by sunshine and grass. She was completely immersed in that moment, free of past and future, in it for the sheer enjoyment of the here and now—the things that *can* be grasped and lived and experienced. It was a lesson Damian needed to learn. He had let the past overshadow his life. He didn't know what the future held, but he had *now*. And now was a beautiful, cloudless day. Damian pictured the ocean before him, calm and endless. Although his boat was docked nearby, he hadn't been on the water since prison. He'd been so caught up with restoring Casa Paloma that he hadn't taken the time to enjoy his freedom, and more importantly, he hadn't felt like it. But as he watched the little girl finish her orange and rinse her hands in the pond before leaving, Damian yearned for the wind and the sea again.

He put away the paint, locked the house and spent the afternoon getting reacquainted with old friends: his boat, a blue, blue sky and a sparkling ocean.

DAMIAN MADE MORE PAPER SWANS for the little girl. He left them lying about where he knew she'd find them: tacked to the gate, sitting on the porch, hanging on a string from the tree by Skye's window. She never talked to him, but she always took the swans, and she always left before it got dark.

Damian stopped by one of the outdoor markets that had sprung up between Casa Paloma and Paza del Mar. He picked up fresh fruits and vegetables and meat. He was almost done when he spotted cans of tuna stacked on a shelf.

I made you something, Skye had said.

Her ceviche had turned out to be the foulest thing he'd ever tasted, but those four words, those four words had blown his tightly guarded world apart. No one had loved him or fought for him, or made him feel the way Skye had. The way she still did.

Most days, Damian kept busy enough to ward off

thoughts of Skye. Nights were different. At night, he had no defense. He lay in bed with a hunger so wide and so vast that he felt himself get swallowed up in it. Nothing, not even the *Lucky Strike* box under his pillow, could keep him from falling into the soul-sucking hole in the center of his heart.

As he drove home from the market, Damian wondered where Skye was, if she had found someone who deserved her more than he did, someone who brought her more happiness than pain. He had deliberately kept himself from any information about her. If he knew where she lived, where she worked, where she shopped, he couldn't have stopped himself from looking her up, and he wasn't sure what he'd do if he saw her again, even if it was just from across the street. Living without her was agony, but the thought of seeing her with someone else, no matter how happy and fulfilled, was unbearable.

Damian dropped four bags of groceries in the kitchen and went back to the car for the rest. As he reached the main door, the little girl walked past him, dragging the rest inside.

"Can't you make anything else?" She plopped herself up on one of the stools and placed a paper swan on the counter.

"You don't like swans?" He had left that one tucked under a stone by the pond, a few days ago, with its neck peeking out.

"Why do you only make swans?"

"Because my mama told me about a magic swan that hides on the grounds here. I haven't found one, but you remind me of it."

"Me?"

"Yes. You make me laugh. That's some powerful

magic. And I think you're going to grow up into a beautiful swan."

"Are you calling me an ugly duckling?" She hopped off the stool and confronted him.

"No. I'm just . . ." Damian cupped his groin and jumped back instinctively. He didn't like the way this little girl had him hopping around like a bunny rabbit.

"You know what you are? You're a big bully. You kick me, you spy on me, you walk in and out of here without my permission, and now you're trying to intimidate me."

They glared at each other, her hands on her hips, and him guarding his balls.

"What does 'intimidate' mean?" she asked.

"To frighten, terrify, or push someone around."

Her scowl softened. She seemed to like the idea. "You're funny," she said, her face breaking into a grin.

"And you have dimples." Damian faked disgust.

She stood quietly and watched him put things away.

"This place looks pretty now," she said. "It was always sad."

"You like it?"

"It's nice." She regarded him for a moment. "What's your name?"

"*Bandidos* don't have names."

"You're no *bandido.*" She giggled. "*Bandidos* make a mess. You made it nice."

"Thank you. And you're welcome to come by any time, as long as your parents are all right with it."

"I can take care of myself."

"That may be so, but I'm sure your mother would like to know where you are. Is she home, waiting for you?"

"My mama's in Valdemoros."

Damian felt a sinking feeling in the pit of his stomach.

The word itself conjured up gray, concrete-laden memories. He wanted to ask about her father, but growing up without one, he tended to be more sensitive. "You have other family?"

She shrugged.

"Who looks after you?" asked Damian.

"My mama, of course." She seemed surprised by the question.

Damian knew kids were allowed in Valdemoros with their mothers, up to a certain age. He hadn't realized that they let them out for school.

"When does your mama get out?"

"Soon."

She seemed to be taking it all in stride, but it explained why she stopped by Casa Paloma. It was a brief respite before she headed back to the grimness of Valdemoros.

"I have to go now," she said, reclaiming the swan on the counter and tucking it into her pocket.

Damian watched her collect the green canvas school bag she'd left by the door.

"You didn't tell me your name," he said.

"Sierra. My name is Sierra." She turned around, walking in reverse towards the gates.

DAMIAN HAD JUST GOTTEN OFF the phone with Rafael when he saw Sierra again. He damn near dropped the glass panel he was installing in the cabinets.

"What the hell happened to you?"

"Lice," she replied.

Her long, dark locks had been reduced to a buzz cut and she looked like she had shrunk overnight. It was probably because her big, doe eyes swallowed all of her face now, but Damian felt a tugging of his heart strings. Valdemoros was no place for a kid. Lice was the least of the horrors that she faced. If he had been younger when they took MaMaLu to prison, he could have been this kid. He could have been Sierra.

"Hey, you want to do something fun today?"

She dropped her bag on the floor and took up the stool that was quickly becoming her spot. "What?"

"Have you ever been on a boat?"

Sierra's eyes lit up.

It was the beginning of many adventures, both on the water, and off. Damian taught Sierra how to bait a fishing hook, how to steer, how to read the sky. She tried to trick him into doing her math until he started answering every question wrong, earning him permanent banishment from homework duty. He tried to show her how to make paper swans, but it needed focus and discipline, and how could she when there were banisters to slide down, and ladybugs to catch, and ice cream to eat before she headed back? Her swans were sloppy and messy and fell over on their faces, beak down.

Damian and Sierra fought and argued and laughed for the two hours she was there after school. A week went by, and then two, and then three. Slowly, Damian started healing. His nights were still filled with a deep sense of longing for Skye, but he had something to look forward to on the days Sierra came around. When Rafael came to visit, he picked up on the subtle change.

"Damn. This place looks fantastic." He walked around, from room to room. "But you." He slapped Damian on the back. "You look better."

Damian had lost the pallor that came with years of confinement. He had kept fit in prison, but now he had the sturdiness of a man with roots. Casa Paloma was home, and Damian was not just restoring the structure, he was re-learning happiness, re-wiring himself, re-seeing the world through Sierra.

"So, am I going to meet this little girl?" asked Rafael, putting away the business documents that needed Damian's attention.

"Not today. It's *Dia de Los Muertos.*"

Day of the Dead was a Mexican festival that was celebrated over two days: *Dia de los Angelitos,* dedicated to souls of children who had passed away, and *Dia de Los Muertos,* celebrated the following day, to honor the spirits of deceased adults. Day of the Dead was a remembrance of loved ones that had passed on, and a celebration of the continuity of life. It was an important day for Damian because he had finally got a new tombstone for MaMaLu, a completed one that was fit to honor her memory. It had taken him weeks to have it custom made and he had received a call that morning, that it was now installed.

"You all set?" asked Rafael.

"I am," said Damian.

They drove to Paza del Mar, noting the new developments that were now lining either side of the road—modest little homes, interspersed with lavish mansions, hotels, shops, and restaurants. The area had gone through two distinct phases: before El Charro and after El Charro. What had once been a small fishing village that had served as an outpost for the drug lord's dealings had bloomed after his death. Crime rates dropped and tourists began to trickle in, opening up jobs and commerce. The presence of foreigners deterred the cartel from trying to re-establish its hold over Paza del Mar. A tourist caught in the crossfire was bad news. It inevitably attracted international attention, and the *capos* preferred to stay out of the limelight. The shadow of fear slowly lifted off the sleepy little village. It transformed into a charming, laid back getaway, its residents never knowing of the two boys who had made it happen, the two boys who as men now, were parked outside *Camila's*.

Rafael had bought and renamed *La Sombra*, the cantina his parents had worked in, and turned it into a favorite spot for the locals. He stopped by whenever he was in town, checking in with the management, approving the menu and sorting out what needed to be looked after. It was twice the size now, painted white, blue and a cool yellow, with high ceilings and a verdant wrap-around patio. The cuisine was fresh and flavorful. On weekends it pulsed with live music. Accordions and guitars accompanied icy cold *cervezas,* while the kitchen served steaming tacos stuffed with steak, cheese and jalapeños, and skewers of dunkable scallops with pumpkin seed sauce.

Camila's was closed on the Day of the Dead, but Rafael laid a bucket of *cempasuchil*—wild marigolds—in the spot his parents had died. Damian recalled MaMaLu explaining the celebration to him. She believed it was a time when the deceased were given back to their families and friends, when the living and dead were joined, if only for a brief time. Marigolds were supposed to guide the spirits to their loved ones, with their vibrant color and scent. Damian and Rafael stood in silence, in the empty restaurant where Juan Pablo and Camila had once danced to crackly tunes on the radio, each honoring their memories of the couple.

When they stepped outside, they followed the streams of people making their way to the cemetery. The streets were lined with decorative paper skulls, colorful lanterns, and plastic skeletons that danced in the wind. Fishermen held vigil in their rowboats, with torches that reflected in the water.

The statue of Archangel Michael gleamed in the late afternoon, guarding the entrance to the church. Behind it, in the cemetery, families sat on picnic blankets next to gravesites, eating the favorite food of their loved ones: mounds of fruits, peanuts, plates of turkey mole, stacks of tortillas and Day of the Dead breads called *pan de muerto*. Others were still clearing out tombs and setting up *ofrendas,* decorative altars adorned with candles, incense, marigolds, sugar skulls, and bright red cockscomb flowers. Toys, water, hot cocoa, and candies were spread out for the *angelitos*, while shots of mezcal, tequila, and cigarettes were offered to the adult spirits. Everywhere, people were eating, drinking, playing cards or reminiscing.

Damian stood at the foot of MaMaLu's grave. The new tombstone was simple, not too big or ornate, exactly as she would have wanted it. A sense of peace settled over him as he read the inscription. He had made sure her prisoner number was removed. She was not a thief, and shouldn't be remembered as such. Damian was never able to determine the exact day she passed away, but her date of death was now filled in. He had chosen the day he had last heard her singing, in the shade of the trees across from Valdemoros.

"Who brought the candles and flowers?" asked Rafael.

MaMaLu's grave was decorated with colorful paper garlands and pillars of candles flickering in glass jars. In the center was a papier mâché skull on a bed of bright marigolds.

"Hey, Bandido!" Damian felt someone tugging his sleeve.

"Sierra!" He grinned and scooped her up.

She was wearing jeans, a black hoodie, and sneakers with neon green laces.

"Please put me down," she said, rather solemnly, as if he had just embarrassed the crap out of her.

"Of course." Damian obliged.

"Finally, a girl you actually listen to," said Rafael.

"Who are you?" Sierra squinted up at him.

Damian introduced them, before turning to Sierra. "What are you doing here?"

"I'm here with my mama." She pointed to someone in the crowd.

"I thought your mama was in prison. Is she out now?"

Sierra scratched her head.

"You said she was in Valdemoros."

"She *works* there, silly."

"So you don't live there . . . with her?"

"Live in Valdemoros?" Sierra laughed.

"But your hair. The lice. I thought you got it from the prison."

"That's coz I go there with her sometimes. And sometimes I forget what she tells me. I let one of the girls there braid my hair, and I did hers, and we shared the same comb."

Damian had not realized just how much his misplaced assumptions about Sierra had affected him, until he felt the weight lift off his shoulders. The little nut-busting girl had managed to worm her way into his heart.

"I still have some graves to decorate." She lifted up the two buckets she was holding. "My grandma's and grandpa's. Want to help?"

"You two go ahead," said Rafael. "I'll wait here."

Damian let Sierra drag him through the crowd, to

another grave on the far side of the cemetery. The plots were bigger and marked with tall slabs of marble and smooth granite. Definitely not the prison lot.

"Here," said Sierra. She started wiping the dust off the marker and gave him the buckets. "You do the flowers and other stuff."

"Yes, boss," said Damian, smiling as he arranged marigolds on the grave.

He reached into the other bucket and pulled out some candles. And a papier mâché skull much like the one he'd seen on MaMaLu's grave.

"They must sell a lot of these," he said, holding it up.

"I made that," said Sierra, stepping back from the tombstone.

In Loving Memory of Adriana Nina Sedgewick, it read.

Damian dropped the skull he was holding. "Adriana . . . Sedgewick." His head was spinning so hard, he could barely speak.

"She's my mama's mother. My dad's mother is buried on the other side. I made her a paper skull too. And this is my grandpa." Sierra moved to the adjacent grave. It was newer and didn't need as much cleaning.

Damian didn't see anything beyond the name carved in stone:

Warren Henderson Sedgewick.

"I didn't know them, but my mama says Grandpa Warren loved Grandma Adriana very much," Sierra chattered on, oblivious to the fact that her words were coming at Damian like rogue asteroids, knocking him out of orbit, sending him dizzy and disoriented into total, boundless chaos.

"When he died," she continued, "he wanted to be

buried next to her. My mama and grandpa lived in San Diego. That's in the States. But when she came to bury grandpa, my mama stayed. She says it's because she grew up here, but I think it's also because three of my grandparents are buried here. I don't know my other grandfather. I don't know my father either. His name is Damian. He's the one in prison. *Real* prison. Not working there, like my ma—"

"Sierra! I've been looking all over for you. I told you to meet me by—" Skye skidded to a halt. She was holding candles, one in each hand. They snuffed out with her sharp exhalation.

They stood paralyzed, Damian kneeling on a bed of marigolds, and Skye between her parents' tombstones, holding on to them, as their daughter introduced them.

"This is my new friend, Mama. I visit him after school sometimes . . ." she said, but neither Damian nor Skye were listening.

All around them, families were gathered in little units around lost loved ones, and there they were, lost to each other, but brought together by MaMaLu, and Warren, and Adriana. For a moment, it felt like the dead really had joined the living, like they were all gathered in that one spot, at that one time, and all of their flaws and choices and mistakes didn't make them any less perfect. It didn't matter why Warren did what he did, why Damian did what he did, why Skye kept Sierra from Damian.

In the grand scheme of things, we do the best we can, all of us, and we make up our stories as we go along; we write them and direct them and project them into the world. And sometimes we get other people's stories, and sometimes we don't, but always there is a story behind a story behind a story, linked in a chain that we can only see a small part of, because it's there when we're born and it continues after we're gone. And who can comprehend all of it in one lifetime?

Skye and Damian could barely handle that one moment. It was loaded with too much—too many thoughts and emotions, revelations and separations. Too many years. Too much space. Everything expanded, straining at the seams, and then contracted, losing shape, losing form, until the moment hung between them, like a wobbly bubble ready to burst at the slightest shift.

"Where do you want the rest of these?" Nick Turner caught up to Skye and dropped the bags he was holding.

Damian felt himself snap back to reality. He had lost so much, and then gained so much—Sierra, Skye, within his reach, within his grasp—only to lose it all again. Skye might have had his baby, but she had gone back to Nick. And why not? She had dated him at one point. He was familiar and successful and stable. Her father had obviously approved. He was the lawyer who'd handled the case so he knew exactly what she'd been through. Had he accompanied her for Warren's funeral? Been the shoulder she cried on, when Damian had shunned her in prison? How old had Sierra been then? A few months? Had they been together all along? Is that why Skye worked in the prison? As Nick's partner, helping him with his cases? Had Nick stepped in and claimed Sierra?

Each question tore deeper and deeper at Damian's insides. Damian had grown up without a father and it killed him to think that his daughter was growing up without hers, too. Sierra obviously knew more about him than he did about her. What had Skye told her about him, apart from the fact that he was in prison? Had she ever asked to see him? Wondered why she never heard from him? What would she say if she knew the truth now? Would she be ashamed? Horrified? Would she shrink back from him?

It took Nick a few seconds to realize who Skye was staring at and why she was standing so still. When his eyes fell on Damian, he looked from Skye to Sierra and back at Damian again. His discomfort was clear. He didn't know how to handle the situation any more than Skye or Damian. Sierra was arranging paper garlands on Warren's grave, oblivious to the tension around her.

Damian saw the snuffed out candles in Skye's hands, the bags of decorations by Nick's feet, the stunned looks on their faces. He was the outsider, the wild card who had upset the balance of their perfect evening. He had been let out of prison a few months early but he wished he were still behind bars, so he could lock out the pain. Not knowing had been hell, but this, this was a completely different level of torment.

Damian got up, crushed marigolds sticking to his jeans, and turned into the swell of people surrounding them. He was thankful for the nameless, faceless sea of bodies around him. He imagined this was what it felt like to be dead among the living.

"Get me out of here," he said, when he found Rafael. "Get me far, far away."

SKYE ...5

Thirty-Two

I SKIMMED THE SURFACE BETWEEN sleep and wake, half submerged in wild, crazy dreams, where Sierra, Damian, and I were green iguanas, sunning ourselves on a deserted island. I was the one with the tail chopped off, but it didn't matter because it was warm and beautiful. We were eating ice cream beans, and Sierra kept chewing on the seeds instead of discarding them.

Crunch, crunch, crunch.

"Don't," I mumbled, the sound of my voice nudging me awake.

It had been like that ever since I'd seen Damian at the cemetery two weeks ago—restless nights spent tossing and turning until the sheets ended up in a contorted pile at my feet. Seeing Damian again had set off tiny explosions that left me quaking in their wake. Learning he had bought

Casa Paloma, and that Sierra had been spending time with him had come as a bigger aftershock. Being a single mom had always been a challenge, but now I felt both foolish and neglectful for thinking Sierra was going straight home after school, as instructed. On the outside it looked like I had it together, but on the inside I was a complete mess.

Crunch, crunch, crunch.

There it was again. That damn sound. Exactly like—

I bolted upright and turned on the bedside lamp.

Damian was sitting on a chair by the foot of my bed, watching me. He didn't move when the light came on; he just continued tossing peanuts into his mouth. It was impossible to ignore how he owned the space, how he molded it to suit his presence, a palpitation-inducing silhouette from my past, all dressed in black. He might as well have been sitting there all along, all eight years that he was away, because he was there in my head, insinuated in the cracks of my heart. I saw him every day in Sierra's face, in the strong, white crescents of her nails, in the ends of her hair, that curled up when she twisted her finger around them. I smelled him on her breath, heard him in her bedtime voice, battled him in the stubbornness of her spirit, and felt him in the warmth of her hugs. But pieces of him were nothing compared to the man himself—whole, real and commanding, a thousand suns fused into one, scorching me with his gaze, with whatever emotions were broiling beneath his coal dark eyes.

I clutched the covers to my chest, as if the fabric would keep me from incinerating. I'd always known this day would come, this confrontation, and I'd dreaded it. If there was one thing I knew, it was that you never, *ever* lock horns with Damian. He had not forgiven my father for taking his mother away. What would he do to me, for keeping his daughter from him?

"Why didn't you tell me?" He put away the paper cone of peanuts he was holding with such calm and precision that goosebumps raced across my skin. For the first time, I noticed the folder on his lap. He opened it, scanned the top sheet, and threw it at me. It fluttered through the air and landed beside me.

Damian didn't give me the chance to pick it up. He flung another sheet at me, and then another and then another, until they were floating like feathers around me. I grabbed one of them and skimmed over the contents. From the private investigator's logo on the top, it looked like a report on me: my address, financial records, marital status. I picked up another one. It was a copy of Sierra's birth certificate. The next one outlined my job, my schedule, my work in Valdemoros. Where I'd been, what I'd done, where I'd lived, my credit card statements, magazine subscriptions—everything and anything pertaining to the last eight years was laid out before me in letter-sized black and white pages.

Damian emptied the entire folder on me. When it was done, and the last sheet flitted to the bed, the fear I'd felt about his reaction was replaced by something else, a sense of outrage that he could presume to stuff everything I'd been through since the island, into one shiny, glossy folder and throw it all in my face.

"You want to know why I didn't tell you about Sierra?" I asked. "Because this is what you do, Damian." I scrunched up the papers in my fists. "You research, you plan, you plot your way to vengeance. I had a photo of Sierra when I came to see you in prison. I wanted you to know we had a daughter. My father was gone. I thought there was no one left to fight, but I was wrong. I was wrong, Damian, because you were still fighting. You're always fighting! You put my father in the grave, but I came anyway, to give you a daughter. But there was no room for us because you were still the same. Still wrestling with your demons. And if you think you know everything there is to know about me from this report, I have news for you. You don't have a clue, Damian."

I DIDN'T REALIZE I WAS pregnant until I went for a follow-up appointment for my shoulder, and the doctor asked me the date of my last period. I had thought it was stress-related, or perhaps my cycle was off because I had missed a few weeks of my birth control pills, but the blood test confirmed it. It had been a bittersweet revelation, given that the baby's father and grandfather, Damian and Warren, were embroiled in a ceaseless battle that was being played out in the courts.

Everywhere I went, photographers flashed their cameras in my face. How would they twist the story if they knew I was having Damian's child? If they knew I was in love with my kidnapper? What would my father say? He was convinced I was going through some kind of mental and emotional breakdown. Would he try to coerce me into having an abortion? Failing that, could he have a psychiatrist declare me incompetent? Force me to give up the baby? How would Damian react to the news? He was going to prison. For how long, I didn't know, but I knew that it would only make it harder.

I kept the pregnancy to myself, and as difficult as it was, the thought of a new life emerging out of all the chaos was like a beacon of light that got me through the darkness. I sat through long sessions with Nick and my father, hugging my little secret, while they discussed the charges and legal strategies. I wanted the case wrapped up before I started showing so I went through the motions. Yes to this, no to this, yes to this. I sat through Damian's sentence hearing, four months pregnant, knowing that I had a piece of him, and no matter how wrong or warped or crazy everyone else would think it was, it felt right.

When my father realized I was pregnant, he could not hide his disappointment. He was convinced Damian had used me to get back at him, that getting me pregnant had been a part of his plan, his ultimate revenge against my father. How deluded we become when we start believing that everything in the world is about us. How hard we work to make things fit into our made-up theories. How blindly we follow our worked-up emotions, the good, the bad and the ugly. My father would believe what he wanted. Damian would believe what he wanted. I could either let myself be ripped in half between them, or accept that I would never be able to change their way of looking at things.

At times, I questioned my own sanity. Was I wrong? Had I been naive and trusting? Had Damian played me all along? He couldn't bring himself to kill me, so had he done the next best thing? Drive a wedge between my father and the one person that meant the most to him? Me. Had he really planned to send me back, carrying his child, so my father would have to live with it the rest of his life?

Used, *my father said.*

I thought of what Damian and I had shared, the way he looked at me, the way he touched me, and I thought no. *An absolute, soul-rooted, emphatic* no. *I couldn't think of anything more beautiful, more life affirming than Damian's lips on mine—his body, my body, melded into one. And now I had a part of him, a part of MaMaLu, to look after, and that's exactly what I did. Damian had hurt me, my father had hurt me, but I loved them both. No doubt, they felt I had let them down too, but I didn't want to stay lodged between them, not when I had a new life to think about.*

When someone started undercutting Sedgewick stock by selling significant shares at a lower cost and devaluing the company, I suspected Damian was behind it. Investors panicked and started offloading their stock, alarmed by plummeting figures. It didn't take long for my father to trace it back to Damian, but Rafael had done such a good job of covering up the paper trail that there was no substantial evidence against Damian.

At the time, I didn't know that Damian was reacting to something my father had done. My father had accepted that I was going to have Damian's child, but he was never going to accept Damian in my life, child or no child, so he'd sent him a message in prison, a message that had provoked Damian into replying with one of his own. Theirs was a feud that put one man behind bars and another in his grave.

Sierra was a few months old when my father passed away.

"She has your mother's eyes," he said to me one morning. He'd been uneasy around Sierra for the first few weeks, but that day he bent over her crib and looked at her for the first time. "Yes. Adriana's big, brown eyes."

After a while, he picked her up and gave her three kisses when he thought I wasn't looking. Our relationship had been strained, but he doted on Sierra. Eventually it proved impossible for him to hold a grudge against me for having her. She was the one thing that made him smile when everything else was collapsing around him. I was thankful that he died in his room, with his dignity intact, before we lost the mansion.

With his death, I was truly an orphan. I felt like a three-pronged hole in the wall, with empty spaces where my mother, my father, and MaMaLu had been. People plug in to you, and when they're gone, you stop working for a while. You have to reconfigure yourself, rework your wiring, so you can get out of bed in the morning. Not only had I lost my father, but I had also lost the roof over my head, at a time when I needed it the most—when I had a little one to take care of. My father's assets were long gone, picked over one by one to pay his debts. I collected all my designer clothes and shoes and bags, and dropped them off at a consignment store. Beautiful things are always hard to part with, but between the sales from that, and my jewelry and watches, I had enough for Sierra and I to get by until I figured things out. But first, I had to bury my father.

Nick came through in ways I never imagined he would. Things had changed after he found out I was pregnant. A child wasn't something he had factored in, least of all one that wasn't his. He backed off and stopped pursuing me, but when my father had a stroke, he showed up at the hospital. He tried not to stare at my round, pregnant belly and swollen ankles. He helped me wrap up my father's estate after his death and flew with me and Sierra to Paza del Mar for the funeral.

I broke down as I stood at my parents' graves, clutching Sierra. The soil around my father's site was still fresh, unlike my mother's and MaMaLu's. I hadn't realized the prison lot was in the same cemetery, and seeing MaMaLu's name carved in stone made her death that much more final. I wanted Damian there so I could draw from his strength, so I could lean on him, as he held our daughter at his mother's tomb. We had never made it that day, the day they'd stormed the island and captured him.

How do we end up like this? How do we make a mess of something so beautiful and true?

I felt lost and unanchored, like a ship in the storm. No mother, no father, no MaMaLu, and no Damian. But I had Sierra, and I held on to her tiny body like it was my lifeline.

I VISITED VALDEMOROS BEFORE WE returned to San Diego. I wanted to see the place that had taken MaMaLu, and pay homage to the woman who'd filled my mother's shoes. I took enough "lunch" to earn me an escorted tour.

Behind the ominous barbed wire and bleak, gray walls, hard-faced guards mauled through my bag before letting me in. My footsteps echoed in the dark tunnel that led to the main compound as I followed Daniela, the officer who was showing me around. The central area was all concrete, but it was nothing like the highly regimented place I'd been expecting. It was hard to tell the prisoners from their visitors because they wore no uniforms. Small kiosks were set up around the inner perimeter, selling food and other staples. Mothers carried babies on their hips in the exercise yard. Children weaved through the corridors, chasing each other. There was a makeshift nursery with colorful walls, a maze of swings and slides, and a jungle gym. Tough-looking women eyed me with curiosity, suspicion, or both, and then went back to bouncing toddlers on their knees or weaving or sewing.

Daniela told me that over half of the women had yet to see a judge. "In the meantime, the prison encourages entrepreneurship. Some of the inmates make money running the kiosks. Others sew soccer balls and clothes. They make jewelry, hammocks, picture frames." Daniela pointed to groups of women sitting in circles, working on different projects.

"What happens to these items?" I picked up a hand-stitched leather bag and examined it. It was similar to the one I'd admired in the market, the day Damian and I had gone shopping.

"Sometimes their families will pick them up and sell them in local shops. The more talented prisoners take orders for their goods from outside merchants."

"How much does something like this go for?" I asked, holding up the bag. The leather was robust but soft. It had mitered gusset corners and rouleaux handles.

Daniela quoted a paltry figure.

I put the bag down and looked around, watching as one of the women unrolled a huge cowhide. She cut it following the outline of a rough stencil and started dyeing the exposed edges with a small brush. Another was burnishing the pieces, rubbing them with a soft cotton cloth to enhance the shine. It was an assembly line process, each of the women working on a task and moving it along to the next phase. The finished product was tossed into a pile with the others, under the shade.

As I sorted through the different styles, an idea started forming in my head. I had a degree in fine arts and a flair for designing bags, shoes, and clothes. I knew people who would pay big bucks for the kind of products these women were handcrafting. If I could connect the two, I would be helping these women and perhaps providing them with the tools to stay out of trouble when they got out. Most of the inmates were in prison because they lacked the resources to support themselves, and had turned to crime.

"Who provides the raw materials for these?"

Daniela shrugged. "Sometimes the prisoners pool their money, buy the raw materials themselves, and share in the profit. But it's a risk. No one trusts anyone when it comes to money. Sometimes a merchant will sponsor them and pay them a small portion of the sales when the goods are sold."

"And the women are willing to wait until then?"

Daniela laughed. "They have nothing better to do."

That night, I put Sierra to bed and toyed with the possibility of earning a living while helping the prisoners in Valdemoros. I kept seeing their busy hands cutting and stitching and gluing and sanding. With a little finesse and direction, I was sure they could produce high quality custom products with local flair.

The next morning, I started looking for a place to stay. The money I had would stretch a lot further in Paza del Mar than in San Diego. But that wasn't the only reason I wanted to stay. My roots were here. I felt it when I walked barefoot on the beach with Sierra. The wind played in my hair, laced with salt and seaweed. My feet sank into the sand and I felt soft waves thawing me out.

Home. Come home. Come home, *they said.*

Nick tried to talk me out of it, but when he saw my mind was made up, he got on the plane and wished me and Sierra well. There was a moment of panic as I watched the plane take off. Everything familiar was in San Diego. I knew where to go, what to do, how to speak, what to expect. Damian was there. In prison, but there.

I felt an ache deep in my soul, a longing to turn back the time so we were the only two people on a little speck of land surrounded by a big, big ocean. In that moment, as the planes lifted off the runway, one after the other, I was overwhelmed by my loneliness. Then I felt my mother and my father and MaMaLu settle around me. An intangible sense of safety and security, of comfort and belonging, came over me, and I knew I was exactly where I was meant to be.

HOME WAS A SMALL, LOW-RISE condo with a balcony that faced an open-air market. It was in the newer neighborhood, between Paza del Mar and Casa Paloma. The bus that took me to Valdemoros stopped across the street. The beach and Sierra's school were within walking distance. The location made up for the ceaseless traffic and noise from the market during the day. At night, when everyone was gone, you could hear the sound of the ocean. Sometimes I closed my eyes and pretended I was lying under gauzy, mosquito netting in a little villa nestled among the trees.

But today, all pretenses were stripped away. Papers lay strewn around me. There was no escaping the reality before me, the reality that was Damian—in my room, in my chair. It was pointless to ask how he'd gotten in. He had picked up more than a few tricks in Caboras, and no doubt, in prison too. What alarmed me was not that he had broken into my place, or that he'd hired a private investigator to look into the last eight years of my life. What alarmed me was that Sierra was sleeping in the next room and I had no idea what Damian's intentions were, now that he had found out about her.

"You should have told me." He got up and walked over to the bed. The air shifted around him, like a force field of barely contained energy.

"What do you want?" I shrank back against the headboard. Being alone in a room with Damian, with all of his attention focused on you was heady and dangerous. "Nick—"

"Nick is in San Diego. Happily married. He was here to help you set up a charity for the women in Valdemoros. Or should I show you *his* folder?"

Shit. So much for trying to get the man to leave. I had seen the way Damian had looked at Nick. His jealousy had burned like a red-hot spear, ready to gouge the other man's eyes out, before he'd retracted it and left.

"You've done well for yourself, all things considered." Damian sat on the edge of my bed and regarded me, his eyes falling on the strap that had slipped off my shoulder. "The princess who lives among the peasants."

"I did what I had to. No thanks to you."

"I didn't know." He slid the strap back into place and let his fingers linger on the small scar that the bullet had left.

It took every bit of control not to close my eyes. Eight years. Eight long, lonely years. I'd gone out on a number of dates. I'd *wanted* to fall for someone else, but nothing came close to what Damian's touch did to me. Once you've been loved by a man like Damian, once you've been branded and molded in the fires of that possession, you will never be moved by tepid, impostor kisses.

"I assumed that your father had set up some kind of fund for you, something separate from his finances."

"He did. But I used it to pay for his medical expenses towards the end." I couldn't stop scrutinizing his face. The jaw was more solid. Everything was more set—his brows, his nose, his mouth—like they'd finally found their place. If he leaned any closer, I'd feel his breath on my neck.

"You and Sierra had nothing?" He let go of the strap and tilted my chin, forcing me to meet his midnight black orbs. They glittered with something raw and fierce.

"We managed." I pushed his hand away.

"You should have told me."

"Why?" My temper flared. "So you could swoop in and make things right? You can never make things right, Damian. You can never take back what you did. Maybe I took a page from your book. Maybe I wanted to punish you for destroying my father. Did you ever think of that? Vengeance begets venge—"

He cut off my tirade mid-sentence, one arm around the small of my back, crushing me up against him. He ravaged my mouth, forcing my lips open, thrusting his tongue inside. This was no soft, dreamy kiss. It was a blistering, roaring flame that crackled and fizzed through my veins. The kind of kiss that welds hungry souls together. It was Damian, wild and erratic, like a summer storm. His fingers twisted in my hair, yanking my head back, holding it immobile. There was no escaping him, no denying him. He didn't let up until my body went limp in his arms, until the resistance ebbed out of me.

"You lie," he said, breaking the kiss. "That's not vengeance I taste on your tongue. It's fear. You're afraid of me, Skye."

"Do you blame me?" I spit out. "You shot me. You

were going to kill my father. I couldn't stop you. You're ruled by things I can't compete with. Your rage trumps love, and hope, and faith. If you've come back hoping to pick up where we left off, I'm sorry to disappoint you. I've worked too hard to build a life for Sierra and myself. I won't let anything jeopardize that. I won't pin our future on a man who couldn't let go of the past. I don't need you, Damian. I don't need anyone."

"Liar." His eyes raked my face. "Let's try that again. This time without the lies." His mouth hovered over mine, but I refused to close the distance. He laughed. One swift, forward tug and his lips were on me again, gentler this time, but I could sense his restraint. He was like a beautiful Arabian stallion, pure power and drive, reining himself in. The way his fingers trembled as he stroked my arm slowly, up and down, betrayed him. The way his entire body throbbed with a need so deep and palpable, told me he hadn't been with a woman in eons.

My unbridled reaction took me by surprise. Even in remembrance, I had felt the intensity of his kisses, relived them, given in to the wild rush of pleasure that swept through me at the mere thought of him. It was a well-worn track that I had gone over, again and again, the feel of his tongue on that most intimate, hidden part of me, the way his muscles bunched as he moved over me, the pleasure he took in watching me come, the way his movements intensified when he was close.

And now here he was, igniting every switch in that network of erotic memories. Every single one led back to him. He was my pleasure center. Everything throbbed outwards from him.

"Damian," I moaned as he pushed my nightgown aside and caressed my breast with tantalizing possessiveness.

He made a tortured sound as his mouth closed over a taut, dusky nipple. My body arched, driving him insane. He pulled my legs around his hips, letting me feel the full, inflamed length of him, hot and heavy through all the layers between us. We couldn't get close enough, fast enough. My hands were tearing down his zipper, his lips were on the hollow of my throat. We were hot skin and muffled breath, void of reason and logic and consequence. He pushed my hands away, too impatient with my fumbling, and started undoing his pants, his eyes pinned on me the whole time. I knew that he was about to fuck my brains out.

"Mama?"

We jumped apart so quick, I barely had time to blink.

Sierra was standing in the doorway, rubbing sleep-drenched eyes. I couldn't be sure what she'd seen, but she was staring at Damian like she'd seen a ghost.

He was holding a pillow over his lap, trying to catch his breath. Another second and Sierra would have caught us in a compromising situation. I fixed my gown and called her in.

"Everything all right, sweetie?"

"I thought you went away," she addressed Damian.

"I was out of town, but now I'm back. And I'm not going anywhere."

It was the first time they'd spoken since Damian had found out she was his daughter. Every word he said resonated with a deeper meaning.

"Did you miss me?" He smiled.

"Why were you kissing my mama?"

"You . . . saw that. Right. Well . . ." He cast a furtive glance my way.

I'd never seen Damian flustered, but that's exactly

what he was, and although I was tempted to let him flounder a little longer, I interceded.

"This is your father, Sierra." I had planned to break it to her gently after Damian showed up at the cemetery, but then he'd disappeared. Now that she'd caught him in my bed, I didn't want to drag it out any longer than I had to. "I didn't know he was out until I saw him on The Day of the Dead," I continued. "He didn't know you were his daughter until then either. I'm so sorry, Sierra. I wanted to tell you, but I wanted your father and me to do it together, properly. I'm sorry you had to find out like this."

Damian and Sierra regarded each other, him gauging her reaction and her considering him in a new light. My heart pounded in my ears as the silence stretched out. I had thought about this moment forever, thought about the two of them face to face for the first time, father and daughter, and no matter what scenario played out in my head, it was never perfect.

"You really are a *bandido*," Sierra said to Damian.

"I really am." He nodded. "That's why I was in prison."

"Can I ask him now?" She looked at me. I nodded because I couldn't speak, because my throat was clamped tight. I had told her the truth about her father, everything except for why he was in prison. That was for him to tell her. She deserved a clean slate with her father, and he deserved a chance to explain it to her in his own words. Maybe it was a cop out on my part, maybe it had been unfair to keep her in the dark, but that was as far as I was willing to go. She got into scuffles at school because the kids taunted her about the father she didn't know, but she learned to stand her ground early on and if push came to shove, Sierra kicked ass. She was free-willed and strong, but she was just a little girl. My heart ached as she stood before her father, her hair just starting to grow out from the buzz cut.

"What did you do?" she asked.

Damian stared at his hands for a moment. "Bad things," he said. "I hurt your mother. See this?" He picked up my pinky finger and held it up. "I did that. I was angry because someone hurt my mother. I thought getting even would make me feel better. For a while it did, but then it just hurt more."

"Mama said it was an accident." Sierra's gaze was locked on our hands. Damian was still holding on to mine, like he needed me to get through this.

"In a way it was. I was going to do something much worse." He tried to keep his voice steady, but I could feel his agony, his torment, at having to explain things to Sierra, unprepared and unrehearsed. There were no lawyers or judges now, just a father and daughter getting to know each other. When all the chips had fallen, it came down to real people and real moments, to repercussions that stretched far beyond the courts. Damian had served his time, but this was the stuff that really mattered.

"I wasn't always a good person, Sierra," he said. "I don't know if I can ever be the kind of father you'd be proud of, but I hope you'll let me try. Because you make me want to stop being a *bandido*, and maybe someday . . . maybe someday I'll be the hero that you and your mama deserve."

Sierra's eyes moved from Damian to me. I knew she was trying to process everything she'd learned. She walked over to the bed and traced my stubbed pinky. For a second all three of us focused on the point where our hands touched—Damian's large, rough palm cradling ours. Something in me started cracking open, like a long-frozen surface bearing too much weight.

"Come on," I said to Sierra. "Let me tuck you back in."

She stopped at the door and looked back at Damian. "If she kissed you, it means she likes you."

"Sierra!" I tugged her into her bedroom.

"I bet it hurt real bad," she said as I slipped into bed with her. I needed to collect my thoughts before I faced Damian again.

"What?"

"This." She entwined her perfect little finger with my damaged one and threw her leg over mine. Sierra was a sprawler. She slept claiming all the space she could.

"Sing to me," she said, snuggling closer.

I didn't know what was going through her head. Was she relieved to finally meet her father? Was she disturbed by what he'd done? Whatever her reaction, sleep didn't elude her for too long. Children have the remarkable ability to digest, adapt, and take things in stride. Her arms slackened around me and her breath turned long and peaceful as I sang MaMaLu's lullaby.

I breathed in her scent and closed my eyes, stroking her hair. She was my calm in the middle of chaos, a little piece of innocence untouched by the turbulence of the past. I didn't know how Damian's presence was going to affect our lives, but I knew things were going to change. I'd had her to myself for seven years and all I wanted to do was hold on to that moment for as long as I could, her cheek next to mine, the weight of her leg securing me from leaving.

A floorboard creaked in the room. I opened my eyes and froze. Damian was standing by the door. The expression on his face was so painfully intense, so filled with longing, that the words to the lullaby I was singing left me. It wasn't the raw carnality with which he'd assaulted me earlier. It was much deeper, as if all of his happiness was contained in that one scene before him: Sierra sleeping beside me, while he stood at the threshold, cut off from it all.

A lifetime ago, it had been me, him and MaMaLu, curled up like this.

I didn't have any words, and neither did he. He tried to say something, but his throat clenched, so he turned on his heel and left. A moment later, I heard the soft click of the door as he let himself out.

Thirty-Three

THE GATES TO CASA PALOMA were open. It looked vastly different from the last time I'd seen it, but I had no time to admire the changes. I marched up to the front door, surprised to find it was also unlocked.

Damian was in the study room, poring over some papers, when I barged in.

"What's the meaning of this?" I waved my bank statement at him.

"Good morning to you too," he said, without looking up.

Seeing him in the space I had always associated with my father was strange. Of course, my father had not been around much back then, and when he was, I knew better than to disturb him in the study. Damian did not seem the least bit perturbed by the intrusion. He let me fume for a few seconds before turning his attention to me.

"It's for Sierra," he said.

I almost wished he'd go back to his papers because he was looking at me like he'd been up all night, thinking about me, about what had almost happened the night before.

"And you didn't think to check with me before making a deposit?"

He obviously had all kinds of information on me, including my bank account number. I'd blinked twice when I'd seen my balance, but the teller had assured me it was no mistake. Someone had transferred a small fortune into my account. Guilt money. Damian had seen where I lived. He knew how much I made, how much I paid the women in Valdemoros, and what I struggled with to make ends meet. It infuriated me that he didn't think I was making enough. Sierra and I weren't living in the lap of luxury, but how dare he make me feel like I wasn't giving her the kind of life she deserved?

"She's my daughter, Skye. The daughter you kept from me. I have a lot of years to make up for. You can expect a deposit every month, so get used to it."

"I've been taking care of Sierra without your help all this time. If you think you can use her to get to me, you—"

"I don't need to use Sierra. I get to you just fine."

We both knew he was talking about my fevered response to his kisses.

"Last night changes nothing," I said.

"Last night changes everything."

Our eyes clashed, gray on black.

"Fine," I said. "Make your deposits. See if I touch a single penny."

Damian got up and walked around to my side of the

desk.

"It's very simple. You want the deposits to stop. I want you and Sierra," he said. "Marry me, Skye."

"Marry you?" I blinked. It was the last thing I'd been expecting. Proposals were supposed to be epic—grand moments that swept you off your feet, not negotiated like some business transaction. "You're out of your mind."

"Am I?" He swept one arm around the small of my back and pulled me in. "Tell me you haven't missed me. Tell me you haven't stayed up nights thinking of how good we are together. Because right at this moment, all I want to do is push you up against the wall and take you so hard that I can't tell where I end and where you begin. I *ache* where you're supposed to be, Skye, and I'm not going to stop until you're mine. So we can draw this out or we can quit wasting more time. Either way, we're going to end up right here. Me about to fuck you."

"Is that what this is about? You want to fuck? Let's do it, Damian. Let's do it right here on my father's desk. You'd like that, wouldn't you? Nailing his daughter on his desk. You've taken everything else—his company, his home, his life—so why not his daughter? He's gone, Damian, but you're still trying to prove a point."

"This is not about that," Damian growled. "You and I have *never* been about that, so let it go." He clamped down on my wrists as if trying to make me drop it.

"Really? Let it go? You couldn't let it go with MaMaLu, but you expect me to just move on when it comes to my father?"

"I did let it go." He spoke slowly, each word punctuated with razor sharp control. "I let you go. Back to your father. I left you in that supermarket, but *you* tracked *me* down. That's something that you conveniently omitted from your statement. I knew they were working on you, and you let them coerce you. You picked a side, Skye, and it sure as hell wasn't mine."

"I was *protecting* you."

"You couldn't even look at me in court."

"Because I was pregnant! Because you can read me like a book."

His hold softened on my wrists and he tugged me towards him. "Precisely. So I know you still want me. I can tell by the way your breathing changes. The curve of your spine changes. Everything in you is screaming for me, Skye. So why are we fighting?"

"Just because we have mind-blowing sex doesn't mean I want to spend the rest of my life with you."

"Need I remind you? You said you would always, always love me."

"I do. I always will. But it's not enough."

"Mind-blowing sex and love? That's enough for a damn good start in my book." He bent his head and said it in my ear, sending icy shivers down my skin. "And I'm not even throwing in the fact that we have a daughter. Say yes, Skye. Tell me you'll marry me."

"I don't trust you, Damian. That's the problem. There was a time when I would have followed you to the ends of the earth. I fought for you, but you know what you fought for? Vengeance. Retribution. Revenge. Even when you were in prison, you couldn't let it go. You didn't just bring down my father's company, Damian. You ruined the lives of all the people who worked there, who depended on it for their livelihood. They were real people with real lives—kids, dreams, mortgages. Some of them were just weeks from retiring. Some depended on the health benefits. Do you ever think about that? Does it ever keep you up at night? Or are you still caught up with your own needs and your own pain? Open your eyes, Damian. There's a bigger world out there and it's not all about you. I've finally got my life together and you waltz in, expecting me to rearrange it because it suits you? Well, guess what? It's not going to happen. You want to see Sierra? Fine. I won't stand in your way. But stop trying to strong-arm your way into my life. That's a right you have to earn."

For a second, Damian stared at me. The raw desire in his eyes gave way to something else. Respect. He stepped back and allowed me my space.

I was almost out the door when I heard him speak.

"It's not over, you know. It never has been," he said. "Whether you say yes or no, you will always be my forever."

IF ANYTHING GIVES AMATEUR CRAFTSMANSHIP away, it's wonky stitches. Hand stitching is what made my brand stand out from mass-produced goods, so it was a skill I held regular workshops on. Anyone could attend, including the prisoners that I didn't employ. I hoped that learning a new trade would help them when they got out. A lot of the lifers took the workshops too. It broke up the daily drudgery of prison life, and many of them ended up joining the production team afterwards. They used the money to buy small comforts that made their lives more bearable. Some of them were brute, hardened women, prone to fits of rage. I'd been plagued by second thoughts when I first started, and I'd had my fair share of panic attacks. There were times when I'd wanted to drop everything and run back to San Diego.

Now the guards welcomed me and the women were

protective of me. I was showing them how to saddle stitch when I looked up and lost my train of thought. Damian was standing in the center of the compound, scanning the walls. He was the one constant, rooted thing in the middle of all the commotion. People were milling all around, but they gave him wide berth, clearing a small circle around him. His eyes were open, but he was lost to everyone and everything. I sensed it was the first time he had visited Valdemoros since the night he'd found out that MaMaLu was dead. Had he stood in the same spot then? Had my Esteban died there?

I wondered when my heart would stop aching for him, when my body would stop reacting to him, when my soul would stop humming around him. Why do we fall for people who are no good for us? Why, when we've been there, done that, and we know better? I was about to turn away when he shifted and stared straight at me. He could always freeze me with a single look, but he did something different then. He smiled. One minute, his face was frozen in the past, and the next he looked like he had found a ray of sunshine.

Damn. When Damian threw one of his rare smiles your way, it took a few moments to catch your breath.

I fumbled with my words, trying to recall what I'd been saying. It didn't help that he made his way over, stood at the far end, and watched me interact with the women for the rest of the workshop.

"What are you doing here?" I asked when it was over.

"Opening my eyes. Seeing the bigger world around me." He started picking up the scraps of rawhide that littered the floor, scraps that I saved for smaller projects like key chains and coin purses.

"I'll give you a ride home," he said, when I had

bundled up all the material.

"I can manage." I juggled four bulky bags, two on each hip, as we stepped outside.

He didn't push it when I joined the line at the bus station. It often took two or three buses before I caught one that wasn't brimming with passengers, leaning dangerously off the sides.

"Sierra stopped by after school today." He stood next to me, on the side closest to the road, shielding me from the dust that stirred up as cars went by.

"Good." I didn't want any misgivings between Damian and me to affect her. "How was she?"

"Cocky. She said she was glad she kicked me in the balls the first time she saw me. I deserved it because her mama only has nine nails to paint instead of ten."

"She kicked you in the balls?" My lips twitched at the thought.

"Damn near took out my junk. Today, she threatened me some more. Said she'd make it hurt worse if I did anything to hurt you again."

"Typical father-daughter conversation, then?"

"She talked. I listened. Then I made her something to eat and dropped her home."

I thought about the last time Damian had cooked for me. Plantains on hot stones, under an inky sky. When we'd been the only two people in the world.

"My bus is here."

He took one look at it and grimaced. I knew he wanted to haul me over his shoulder and throw me in his car. He gave me a curt nod instead and watched me board. Then he followed the bus all the way to my stop before driving on to Casa Paloma.

DAMIAN CAME TO VALDEMOROS AGAIN the next day. He didn't talk or hang around the booth where I worked, but he showed up when I was ready to leave and joined the line at the bus stop with me.

"What are you doing?" I didn't know what he was playing at, but it made me uncomfortable.

"Catching a ride."

Ugh. He was impossible.

"I got Sierra started on her homework," he said. "She has a math test tomorrow."

I felt a pang of jealousy. The two of them bonding. Every day after school. I had to work around the prison schedule, which meant I got home late. When Sierra first started school, I had a babysitter pick her up and cover the gap. It didn't last long. Sierra was her own person—stubborn and fiercely independent. Just like her father. I could relate to MaMaLu's exasperation now.

Estebandido! she used to shout.

When our bus arrived, Damian glowered at a young man, until he got up and offered me his seat. I settled the bags on my lap as I squeezed in between a mother doing her toddler's hair, and a man holding a glossy red rooster. We'd made six totes in stylish dark-red leather with camel-colored straps that I still had to stamp with my standard logo: *WAM!,* in memory of Warren, Adriana and MaMaLu. The lady beside me left the comb sticking out of her daughter's hair to run her hands appreciatively over the hand crafted bags. Damian swayed over me, holding on to the overhead bars through the bumpy ride to Paza del Mar. Most of the passengers got off at the main square. As we left the storefronts and cafes and art vendors behind, Damian took the seat across from me.

"What?" I asked.

"Nothing," he replied. "Just sitting here thinking how far you've come, and I'm overwhelmed with how much I love you."

He stared out the window and my entire world flipped over as the bus rattled on. I looked down at myself and saw a dull, plain version of the person I'd been. I hadn't had a pedicure in years. My toes were sticking out of a pair of low-heeled sandals that hadn't made the cut when I'd first designed them. The straps were too bulky, but the soles were soft and durable, so I'd decided to keep them. My thick, waist-long hair was tied back in a careless braid, and I wore a breezy tiered skirt with a crop top. I was a far cry from the fashionista he'd abducted. I wished I could see myself through his eyes. Then again, Damian never looked at me with his eyes. He looked at me with his soul.

I didn't say anything when he got off the bus with me. He took the bags from my hands and carried them up the stairs to my condo.

"You want to . . . come in?" I asked when he turned to leave. I didn't want him to go even though a part of me was chanting: *don't let him in, don't let him in, don't let him in.*

"When you mean it, *güerita*." He was gone before I could say anything.

"Was that Bandido?" asked Sierra when I opened the door.

"Yes. And you need to stop calling him that."

"Bandido," she repeated.

"Ban-*Dad*-o." She mulled over the word as she bent over her books.

"Dad." She stopped what she was doing and stared off

into the distance. Then she picked up her pen and nodded.

"Dad," she said softly, tasting the word in her mouth again.

For the second time that day, my entire world flipped over.

Was I wrong to shut Damian out? Was I keeping us from being one big, happy family? I didn't have the answers. He had spent eight years paying for his actions, but loving him had shattered me. I would never be able to piece myself together a second time if I let him break me again.

Thirty-Four

DINNER AT CASA PALOMA HAD always been served in the courtyard. I didn't remember when my mother had been there, but the traditions she'd set carried on long after she was gone. My mother had always preferred dining under an open sky. I remembered the last time my father and I had dined there, surrounded by fragrant trees and soft, twinkling lights.

It was odd returning as a guest now, seeing my childhood home after all these years. The last time I had come to see Damian, I hadn't stopped to admire its beauty—the tall ceilings that had echoed with our laughter, the kitchen where MaMaLu had made us sweet potato flautas. The renovations had given the mansion a new life, but its bones were still the same. I breathed in the nostalgia of another time as I walked through the house.

No amount of paint or sanding could strip away the smell of Casa Paloma. It was in my soul.

"Damian?" I popped my head into the dining room. The table was now a sleek affair in dark wood, but the hutch that Damian used to hide in was still there.

"Sierra?" I followed the sound of her laughter outside, and found them sprawled out under a tree—father and daughter, looking up at the clouds.

"That one looks like a bunny tail," said Damian.

"Where's the bunny?" Sierra squinted. "Oh. There. It got sucked up by that dementor. See the ear sticking out?"

"For such a cute kid, you're one morbid—"

"Mama!" Sierra caught sight of me first. "Come sit."

It was late afternoon on a Saturday, my day off. Damian had offered to babysit Sierra so I could look after the shipments for that week. Most of my merchandise was going to exclusive boutiques in the States, but after a small piece in a fashion magazine, I was getting inquiries from all over. I sighed as I stretched out beside Sierra. I'd accepted Damian's invitation to have dinner at Casa Paloma, but I was exhausted and still not caught up on all the orders. I looked up at the glossy, green leaves swaying over me. The yellow blooms were still a few months away, but the breeze was warm and the grass tickled my skin.

I must have dozed off because the next thing I knew, Damian was standing over me.

"Dinner's ready," he said, holding out his hand.

His silhouette was outlined against the evening sky. The same silhouette I'd glimpsed through a wooden crate on the boat, where he'd held me captive. I was still terrified of him, but in a different way. He made me miss things that I had bolted down, and every time I was around him, they rattled in their crates, threatening to break free.

I'm doing this for Sierra, I reminded myself, as I took his hand. *She deserves parents who can be civil around each other.*

I followed Damian inside and froze.

"Skye." Rafael tipped his head.

The man who had been ready to kill me at one time. Then again, I could say the same for Damian.

"My apologies for intruding. I thought I'd surprise Damian. I didn't realize you and Sierra would be here," he said.

"I told Rafael he was welcome to stay for dinner." Damian didn't ask. His house, his rules. The three people he cared for were all under one roof.

Suck it up and make nice.

It didn't take me long to warm up to Rafael. I understood it had never been personal. He had simply been looking out for his friend.

We ate a simple meal in the courtyard: seashell pasta with ground beef and *cotija,* a crumbly cheese that Sierra loved. I smiled when she reached for seconds. My culinary skills hadn't improved much. She never complained, but she obviously preferred Damian's cooking.

"I actually stopped by to give you this." Rafael handed Damian a metallic envelope with embossed initials.

"You're getting married?" said Damian as he read the card inside. "Holy hell!"

They followed through with hearty thumps on the back.

"You're all invited," said Rafael, looking at Sierra and me. "The ceremony is at the church of San Miguel Arcangel, and the reception is at *Camila's.*" He was about to elaborate when his phone rang. "Sorry." He excused himself. "I have to take this." From the smile on his face, it was obviously his bride-to-be.

"So, when do I get to meet her?" asked Damian, when Rafael returned.

"She gets in tomorrow. We're staying at a hotel in Paza del Mar. I came in early to give you a heads up."

"You finally bit the bullet?"

"I sure did." Rafael put his phone down and picked up his glass. "To old friends," he said.

"To old friends." We raised a toast.

My heart and your heart are old, old friends, Damian's eyes said to me.

I was glad when he got up and the moment passed. Sierra roped Rafael into playing a video game with her, while Damian and I cleaned up.

"I don't know if that's a suitable game for her to play with Rafael," said Damian.

"She seems to be handling it fine."

"It's not her I'm worried about."

Our eyes met as Rafael winced on the couch. Sierra was taking maximum advantage of his reaction to the sound of gunfire.

"Spawn of Satan," said Rafael.

Sierra giggled.

Damian's lips twitched, and I had to look away to keep from laughing.

WE FOUND SIERRA IN MY old bedroom after Rafael left. She was curled up on the bed, hugging a pillow in her sleep. Damian sat at the foot of the bed, looking at her.

"I've never seen her sleep, up close."

It was a simple observation, made more to himself than me, but it gripped my heart. He had missed out on all the moments I took for granted.

"She's half MaMaLu, half Adriana," he said.

Sierra had none of my coloring—not the blond hair or the gray eyes. When we walked down the street, her darker hand in mind, people assumed I was her nanny. She had my mother's aristocratic presence and MaMaLu's earthiness; her eyes were Adriana, her smile was MaMaLu.

"Let's not wake her," I said. "It's probably best if she sleeps over." I didn't want to deny Damian the simple pleasure of watching over his daughter as she slept.

"If I close my eyes, it's as if nothing's changed," he said, his voice so low I could barely make out the words. "There's a little girl in this room and she's stolen my heart. For the second time."

I was glad he kept his eyes on Sierra. It was overwhelming being back in my room with him, but having him remind me of all the ways he'd adored me when we were children was almost too much to bear.

Damian peeled off Sierra's socks, careful not to wake her. He kissed her soles gently before pulling the covers over her.

"Thank you," he said. "For letting her stay."

I nodded because I couldn't speak, because it hurt like hell to leave her there. I couldn't remember spending a single night away from her.

"Why don't you stay?"

The man could read me so well. Too well. But there was no way I was accepting his invitation. It would be the equivalent of stepping into the lion's cave.

"You can sleep with her. It's her first night here. She might wake up disoriented."

I wavered. I was dead tired. I wanted nothing more than to crawl into bed, and he had a point. Sierra wasn't used to waking up in a different place.

Damian didn't wait for an answer. "There's a spare toothbrush and extra towels in the bathroom. Do you need anything else?"

Yes. I need things to be right again so I can be with you, so we don't have to say good night.

"Good night, Damian"

"Good night, Skye." He shut the door behind him.

I let out my breath and crashed beside Sierra.

The room wasn't as girly anymore. The pink and cream decor had been replaced with bright, bold pops of color against a soft, neutral backdrop. One wall was covered in chalkboard paint and had a grid of tic-tac-toe games. Damian's *X*'s and Sierra's *O*'s. The built-in shelves were still the same, but Damian had given them a fresh coat of paint. My eyes lingered on the paper swans that were lined up on them, a comical progression of Sierra's clumsy attempts, and I realized just how close Damian and Sierra had grown in a short space of time. The room looked like something that Sierra had helped put together. It was brimming with her personality.

I got up and was about to step out of my pants when I looked out the window. Damian was walking down the path that led to the staff wing. He disappeared behind the trees. After a while, a light came on in one of the rooms. MaMaLu's room. I wondered what he was doing there as I brushed my teeth. When I came back, it was still on. I debated for a moment before putting my shoes on. I wanted to see MaMaLu's room. She had never let me accompany her there, insisting it wasn't proper for me to hang around her quarters. Well, tonight was my chance to finally see it.

The door was open when I got there. "Damian?" I

peered inside. He wasn't there, so I let myself in.

The room was small and sparsely furnished. A bare bulb was screwed in to the ceiling. The bed was made up, but the pillow was propped and Damian's clothes were flung on it. I reached for the *Lucky Strike* tin that was sitting at the edge of a worn dresser. He had held on to it, his last physical link to MaMaLu.

I knew now why she had not wanted me to visit. I could not imagine the two of them living in this small, tight space while rooms and rooms lay empty in Casa Paloma. I had not understood the distinctions then, but Damian had. He had experienced the other side of wealth and power. It was the reason he wasn't allowed to attend my birthday parties, the reason why I had private lessons while he hid in the hutch. I would have hated living in the shadow of our big mansion, watching the food other people got to eat, the shiny cars they drove, the parties with music and bright lights. I would have hated my mother being taken away from me, to look after someone else, but Damian had looked past all of that. He had grown to love me. He had never complained or compared, only accepted, and he had gone on accepting until everything was ripped away from him.

Standing in the room he had shared with MaMaLu, I felt like I was wearing his skin. I could see them being torn apart in the middle of the night, the last time he had seen her. *Had* he seen her? Or had it been too dark? At what point had his faith in the world been broken, the one that every child is born with? Stifling a sob, I turned to leave, the same moment that Damian stepped inside.

He was wiping his face with a towel, and stopped short when he saw me.

"What's wrong?" he asked.

I shook my head. I should have listened to MaMaLu. I should never have come.

"Skye."

The way he said it damn near broke me. Damian might be all steel on the outside, but his emotions ran deep. He never did anything halfway. When he hated, he hated with every cell in his body, and when he loved . . . God, when he loved, he said your name like that—like a sigh from his soul, wrapped around his tongue.

"What are you doing here?" I asked.

"I sleep here."

"You sleep . . . *here*?" I looked around. It explained the clothes on the bed and why he was wearing nothing but a pair of boxers. The warmth emanating from his skin was like a heater in the small space.

"Why would you sleep . . . ?" I stopped. It suddenly hit me why Damian would forego the luxury of Casa Paloma for the staff wing. He didn't think he belonged there. He didn't think he was good enough. He might have bought it and restored it, but he would rather be here, where he had last felt loved, where the guilt of what he had done didn't eat him up. Casa Paloma was mine. Damian had been trying to restore all the things he thought he had taken away from me.

Whether you say yes or no, you will always be my forever.

My eyes welled up. I stared at my feet, trying to stem the rush of emotions that clamored to my throat, words that got clogged because there were so many of them, all fighting to get out.

"Come." I held out my hand. "Home." The only two words that managed to escape. I couldn't fight it anymore. Loving Damian might destroy me, but not loving him was killing me.

I didn't wait for an answer. I took his hand, turned off the light, and led him to the mansion.

"Wait," he said at the door. "I don't—"

"I love you, Damian. Always you. Only you. This is where you belong. With me and Sierra."

"But you said—"

"I know. I said a lot of things. To you, to myself. Then I remembered what you said. 'Love don't die.' It's true, Damian. I have never stopped loving you, from the time I was a little girl up in that room. When I follow my heart, it always leads me back to you."

For a moment, Damian just looked at me. He had what he'd always wanted, but he faced an unexpected hurdle, a final battle. With himself. Was he worthy of redemption? Of love? Of forgiveness? That was something only he could decide for himself.

He leaned his forehead against mine and closed his eyes. "I am so tired, *güerita*. Tired of pretending I can go on without you when all the while it's breaking my heart. Tell me this is it. Tell me this is forever. You, me, and Sierra."

I told him what he wanted to hear with a kiss, a whisper soft promise against his lips. All of the muscles in his body relaxed as if he'd finally let go of some heavy burden.

"I want to remember this," he said, pulling me into his arms. "If I die tonight, I want to die remembering what it was like to hold the whole world in my hands."

We climbed up the stairs to the master bedroom. When Damian shut the door, my legs started to quake. I never knew what to expect with him. He played my body like a maestro, at times to the rhythm of a harsh, primal beat, at times like a finely tuned rhapsody.

"Take off your pants and get in bed," he said.

I did as he told me, jittery with nerves and anticipation. I hadn't been with anyone in eight years. My body had changed after Sierra. I shimmied out of my bra, but kept my top on.

The bed shifted when he slipped in beside me. One arm slid around my shoulder, cradling me to his chest. His skin was warm and smooth under my cheek. God, I'd missed the way he felt, his scent, his touch, the steady beat of his heart.

"Sleep." He kissed the top of my forehead, stroking my hair like it was made of the finest gold.

I must have registered surprise because he chuckled. I had been expecting a fiery reunion.

"Just this," he said. "This feels so, so good."

The last time we'd been together, when Sierra interrupted us, he had been like a raging bull coming out of the pen, and although I could feel his undeniable arousal, I could also feel something else. Damian was content. For the first time, no one was closing in on us, no one was tearing us apart. We had found our way back to each other. We were finally free to *be*. It was a feeling Damian wanted to savor, something that surpassed lust and desire and carnal pleasure. It was a sense of belonging that blurs the lines between two people, when you find your ankle wrapped around someone else's, or your fingers intertwined, and it's so natural, so automatic, that you have no conscious thought of it happening. When I think of God, I think of all these magical, inexplicable things, multiplied by infinity.

"Was it hard? Sierra's birth?" Damian was still stroking my hair.

"Yes." I wasn't going to lie. "But it had more to do with my heart than my body."

We lay quietly for a while, knowing we would do it all over again, for the little miracle that slept in the next room.

"You named her after the mountains in MaMaLu's lullaby."

"I did." I smiled. "Did she tell you her middle name?"

He shook his head.

"Mariana."

"For MaMaLu and Adriana." Damian shifted so we were lying side to side on the bed. "Her feet are just like yours."

"They're not."

"I saw them when I tucked her in tonight. The big toe doesn't want anything to do with the rest of them. There's a huge space in-between."

"My feet aren't like that."

"Oh no?" Damian flung the covers aside and knelt by my foot. "See this?" He held out my big toe. "I can fit my entire nose between this and the next toe." He proceeded to try to prove his point.

I started laughing because it tickled, but then I caught a glimpse of something and my breath hitched. Esteban was back.

"What?" asked Damian, sliding next to me.

"Nothing." I pushed the hair away from his forehead and kissed him on the nose. "I love you."

"I love you too, *güerita*." He held my pinky finger to his chest, next to his heart. "And now I'm going to kiss you until you feel it in the tip of your anti-social toe."

And he did. His tongue parted my mouth, one hand gripped the back of my neck, the other pulling me so close that every inch of my body came in hot, electric contact with every inch of his. My back arched as he pulled my leg over his, bending my knee around his hip, and grinding himself into me. A throaty moan escaped me as we fell into a frantic rhythm, his hands on my ass, squeezing and releasing.

"It's been so long, Skye, I'm not going to last." His voice was muffled by my neck, his face tangled in my hair.

"I don't think I will either." I was spiraling out of control, so ready for his possession that I couldn't focus on anything else.

"Not yet." He pulled away when I reached for his boxers. "I want to taste you. Do you know how many times I've thought of this?"

I expected him to go down on me, but he rolled us over so I was on top. "Straddle my face, Skye. That's it. God, yes."

All my inhibitions went out the window when Damian pushed my panties aside. His tongue parted my folds, all the way up to my clit. He licked. My thighs clenched. His lips closed around the tight, little button and he sucked, in short, sweet bursts. When it got too intense, he switched to licking, alternating between the two.

"Damian." I was close. So close. My fingers curled around his hair.

"Let me look at you." He tugged my panties down and I shimmied out of them. One long finger slid inside. "So fucking wet."

I threw my head back as his thumb circled my clit.

"Ride my face, Skye. Come for me. I want your juices all over me."

"No." It came out breathless. "You and me together." I slid my hand under his boxers and squeezed. My touch inflamed him. His cock surged for more.

"You shouldn't have done that," he growled, tossing me on my back. "Because now, I have to do this." He filled me in one hard, powerful thrust. My body protested, but I was so lubed up, so hungry for him, that the pain gave way to a hot, aching fullness.

"There's been no one here." He knew. He fucking knew. He picked up the tempo, carrying me with him. "I've missed this. I've missed you. So fucking much." His breath was hot and labored.

It started at the base of my spine, electric tendrils reaching out from my pelvis, building, building, to a white-hot explosion that buzzed through me in waves of sharp ecstasy. I clutched Damian as it rolled through me and felt him stiffen as it hit him. Our bodies were momentarily fused, the same current flowing through both of us. I held on as Damian convulsed into me.

We came down slowly. First our hearts, then our breath.

"I don't want to let go." Damian stayed inside me, sated but loathe to withdraw.

"Then don't." I wrapped my legs around him. "And the answer is yes."

"What's the question?"

"You asked if I would marry you. The answer is yes."

"That was when you had a choice. Try getting away from me now."

"How am I supposed to do that when your dick is still inside of me?"

"Get used to it. I'm moving in. Next time, I might even stop long enough to remove your top."

I laughed, but it faded quickly. "What is it?"

He knew every single detail of my face, but he was

looking at me as if it was all new. His hand brushed my hair to the side, exposing my neck. "Just making sure this is real." He dropped a soft kiss before withdrawing and tucking me in the crook of his arm. "You think there's such a thing as too much happiness?" he asked. "Because right now, I feel like I can't contain it and the universe is going to step in to restore the balance."

"The universe *is* stepping in. To right all the wrongs, Damian. Not the other way round."

His chest rose and fell with a long exhale. When the world has always taken from you, when it's constantly tilted and shifted under your feet, it's hard to attach permanence to the things it gives.

He held on to me like I was the most precious thing in the world. I felt like every cell was saturated with joy, full and swollen. I felt like ice cream and seashells and towering red-soled heels.

I might have fixed the gap between my teeth, MaMaLu, but my true love didn't need a space to slip his heart in. I'd had it all along.

I hugged him close and smiled, the happiest I'd ever been.

"Where do you think you're going?" asked Damian, when I swung my legs over the bed a few minutes later.

"I want to check on Sierra." I searched for my panties and put them back on.

"Hurry back. I miss you."

I laughed and opened the door. The hallway was dark, but I knew the house like the back of my hand. A nightlight was on in Sierra's room. She had kicked back the covers and her arm was hanging over the edge. I pulled the comforter over her and nudged her towards the center of the bed. She didn't move. I tucked her arm back in and was about to leave when I spotted something on the bedside table. I picked it up and frowned.

A syringe.

I was pretty sure it hadn't been there before. Whatever was inside had been used, but why would Damian leave a syringe lying around? Especially with Sierra—

"Don't move." A figure came out of the shadows.

I felt something cold pressing against my temple. A gun. I knew it was a gun because once upon a time, Damian had held one to the back of my head. I had the same sinking feeling now as I did then, except this time it was much, much deeper.

"Call him." The intruder pulled me towards the door.

"Who?"

"Stop playing games, Skye. Call Esteban or Damian or whatever the fuck he's calling himself these days."

I knew that voice.

"Victor!" I swung around to face him, but he hit me with the gun. A stinging whack across cheek.

"Do as I say or she dies." He pointed to Sierra.

"Damian," I called, but my voice quivered.

Oh God. The syringe. What had he done to Sierra?

"Louder." Victor prodded.

"Damian."

He stepped out from the bedroom, pulling a t-shirt over his head. "Skye?" His voice was so warm and relaxed, I bit my lip to control the anguish. He had no idea what he was walking into.

You think there's such a thing as too much happiness?

Victor swung me away from the door. We were standing in the center of the room, his gun aimed at me, when Damian walked in. For a split second, he froze, and then something kicked in—maybe it was his training at Caboras or maybe it was his take-charge personality. Either way, Damian assessed the situation and did the opposite of panic; he went lethally calm.

"Whatever you want, Victor. Let them go and it's yours."

"I want my arm back, motherfucker. You think you can give me that? Because if you can reattach every nerve you severed, you go right ahead. Do you know what it's like to walk around with a paralyzed arm in my business? I lost everything. I—"

"Cut the drama, Victor. I get it. It was your dominant arm. You can't shoot. Or use a can opener. Or stroke your dick right. You took a hit on the job, a job of *your* choosing, and now you're holding me accountable for it. What do you want?"

It took Victor a moment to regroup. He had been expecting fear, submission, compliance.

"I want you to pay for it," he said. "I've been waiting for you to get out of prison. Of course, I wasn't expecting this cozy reunion." He tilted his head towards me and Sierra. "A ready-made family, Damian. The bastard son has a bastard daughter."

Damian's fists clenched. "If you do anything to hurt her—"

"Don't worry. I haven't harmed a hair on her head. Just given her a little tranquilizer. Babysitting screaming kids in these situations is really not my thing."

"You *drugged* my daughter?" There was a nerve ticking on Damian's forehead. One I'd never seen before.

Victor laughed. "You drugged Warren's daughter, didn't you? Don't like it when the tables are turned?" He yanked me closer.

"Your problem is with me, not them."

"Your problem was with Warren, but it didn't stop you from kidnapping Skye. Casualties get caught in the crossfire." Victor shrugged. "You know that."

Victor was worming his way under Damian's skin, making him relive the horror of shooting me.

"You and I are more alike than you think," he said. "Mercenaries at heart. You didn't really think you could start over, did you? I thought it was a brilliant move, manipulating Skye to get to Warren, but I'm starting to think you fancy yourself in love with her now. I'll save you the trouble. Women like her don't love men like us. I loved your mother, but she shunned me. She said she wanted a better role model for you. I hated her, and I hated you. Warren set me up with a nice sum to keep her comfortable in Valdemoros. I left her to rot in there. I should have finished you off too. You came back to bite me, but I still have the final say."

"You don't have to do this," said Damian. "Take everything. I can set you up for the rest of your life. You won't ever need for anything."

It sounded a lot like what I'd said to him on the boat, bargaining for my freedom. A cold knot formed in my stomach. Nothing could have deterred Damian then. His thirst for vengeance had set off a domino effect that was staring back at us now.

"You think this is about money?" Victor laughed. "I got a hefty settlement out of Warren. Part of our contract. And I have a nice disability check coming in every month. This isn't about money, it's about—"

"Revenge." Damian said the word like it had filled his mouth with poison. "Trust me. I understand it all too well. It won't bring you anything, Victor. It's an empty promise. Walk away and—"

"Enough chit chat!" Victor barked. "Which one goes first? Her?" He pointed the gun at me. "Or her?" I started trembling when he trained it on Sierra. The stakes were too high. Damian couldn't risk attacking him, not when he had us both at his mercy.

"Take me." Damian put his hands up and got down on his knees. "Right here, right now. Pump as many bullets into me as you like. You don't really want them."

Icy fear tightened around my heart. He meant every word. Damian was willing to lay down his life for Sierra and me. He *wanted* to do it. He was blaming himself for bringing this down on us. If he'd stayed away, Sierra and I wouldn't be here.

Maybe someday I'll be the hero that you and your mama deserve.

"Witnesses are messy, Damian. You're all dead anyway," said Victor. "Choose. Or I'll choose for you."

My heart started pounding erratically as fearful images flashed through my mind.

"What do you do, Skye?" Damian's voice pulled me out of the downward spiral.

I fight back and I fight hard.

I raised the syringe I was holding and plunged it into Victor's thigh. He screamed and let go of me. Damian moved at the same time, knocking him off his feet. Victor pulled the syringe out of his flesh, and got up, still holding the gun. Damian stood like a shield between him and me. I knew what he was planning to do.

"Don't," I said.

He did it anyway—threw himself straight at Victor. The gun went off, but Damian deflected Victor's hand so it zinged to the ceiling. The two men crashed through the doorway and fell on the railing that opened to the foyer below. It was dark, but I could make out their forms, grappling for control. Victor still had the gun, but with one arm paralyzed, he was no match for Damian. He lost his grip and it fell below. Damian punched him. Hard. Twice in the gut. Victor doubled over. When he straightened, he was holding another gun.

"I always carry a spare." He smirked, but the pain in his gut made him flinch when he tried to move. "I think we've wasted enough time, don't you? Kneel. Both of you!"

He was standing at the top of the stairs, facing the room.

"Her first, then you, then the kid," he said to Damian.

He had it worked out so that any which way, Damian had something to lose. As long as he kept his gun trained on me, he knew Damian wouldn't try anything. Once he shot me, he'd still have Sierra as leverage.

Damian and I held hands as we knelt. I don't know when I started crying, but tears were spilling down my cheeks. It had started here, and this is where it was going to end. All three of us in one night.

"Please don't hurt her," I begged Victor. "She's just a little girl."

"She's lucky. She'll go in her sleep," he replied.

Damian's fingers squeezed around mine, so tight that I thought my bones would crack. It was the only way he could hold himself back from ripping Victor's throat. If he went for him, he risked losing me, but if he waited, he risked losing Sierra.

"On five, Damian," I whispered.

His eyes widened a fraction.

5 . . .

We were going to do this together. No matter what happened to the two of us, we were going to make sure

Sierra remained unharmed.

4 . . .

Victor aimed the gun at my head.

3 . . .

I love you, Estebandido. Always you. Only you.

2 . . .

I love you, güerita. *Don't be afraid. Love don't die.*

The gun went off before we moved. My eyes squeezed shut at the deafening bang. I waited for the pain that was sure to follow.

It never came.

Fuck!!!!!!!!!!

He'd shot Damian.

My soul felt an agony so deep, the bullet might as well have ripped through it. Damian's hand was still in mine, so warm, so real. The pain was so raw that I gasped, forgetting, for a moment, the simple act of how to breathe. A part of me wanted to die right then.

Shoot me. Shoot me now.

But the other part, the part that was a mother, refused to surrender.

Sierra.

I thought of her helpless little form. It was pure torture. I always tucked her in at night, always put her to sleep. I'd skipped that tonight, and now I would never know the sweetness of her breath, the weight of her leg keeping me from leaving, the way she bounced on my bed in the morning.

Wake up, wake up, wake up.

I had lost Damian and now I was going to die, knowing my daughter would be next. How can anyone feel so much pain and still be alive?

Dear Lord, bless my soul. And watch over Sierra.

I couldn't go on. I heaved through the torment that was clawing at my insides, and squeezed Damian's hand, anticipating the next bullet.

He squeezed back.

My eyes flew open.

Damian was still kneeling beside me, unharmed. Victor was standing in front of us, eyes vacant, staring straight ahead. His collar was splattered with blood. He stood there for a beat before falling backwards. His body toppled down the stairs. Rafael stood at the foot of the stairs, holding the gun that Victor had dropped earlier.

"I came back for my phone," he said.

Damian and I stared at each other, and then at him. He'd shot Victor in the back of the head.

"You took him down in one shot," said Damian, his eyes on the gun that was still smoking in Rafael's hand.

"I saw a man shoot my mother and father. I wasn't about to stand by and witness someone do the same to you and Skye."

Damian let out his breath and wrapped me up in his arms. "You picked a hell of a good day to come through," he said to Rafael. Our bodies were so tense, it took a few seconds for relief to settle in.

"The wedding would have been crap without a best man."

We tried to laugh, but none of us could. Victor's contorted body lay in a pool of blood at the base of the staircase. My knees wobbled when Damian helped me up.

"I thought he killed you." I clutched his shirt and sobbed.

"I saw myself in him. The way I'd been." He held me so fiercely I could barely breathe. "You were my saving grace, Skye."

We clung to each other, acknowledging the glorious miracle of being alive.

"Let's go check on Sierra," I said.

"Call the police," Damian said to Rafael. "And an ambulance. I want to make sure Sierra's all right. Victor sedated her."

"I'm on it," he replied. "Go look after your girls."

"I will. And Rafael?" Damian turned to him. "Are you all right?"

Rafael nodded and dropped the gun. "I'm just glad I got here when I did."

"I owe you one. Big time."

"You saved my life twice, Damian. I simply returned the favor. Two for two. Accounts balanced."

"There were three of us. Don't tell me this screwed up your brain cells, Mr. Mathemagician."

Rafael attempted a smile, but we were all too shaken up. "Tell Sierra I want a rematch when she's ready."

"Game on, Rambo. But I have a feeling she's still going to kick your butt."

Thirty-Five

DAMIAN AND SIERRA WERE TOSSING peanuts into each other's mouths.

Crunch. Crunch Crunch.

Crunch. Crunch. Crunch.

"Oh my God. Would you two stop that? It's driving me insane! We're never going to get this place ready." I swept up the stray peanuts rolling on the floor.

We were at Damian's island retreat, getting it ready so Rafael and his fiancée could honeymoon there.

"You know you don't have to lift a finger." Damian took the broom from me and set it aside. "I can have a crew come in and fix up the place in no time."

"The man saved our lives, Damian. It's the least I can do."

"Clean is clean whether you do it yourself or hire

someone to look after it."

"You used to insist I do the chores around here."

"That's when I thought you were a self-entitled princess."

"And now?" I linked my arms around his neck.

"Now I want you fully focused on other tasks." Lifting one hand, he slipped his fingers under my shoulder strap and kissed the small, puckered scar.

I nudged him gently and motioned to our rapt audience. Sierra was watching us as if we were her favorite movie.

"Sierra—"

"I know, I know." She cut Damian off. "*Go read a book*. Do you know how many books I've read this week? You guys are *always* kissing." She made a face, but I caught her grin before she left.

"This bedroom is way too crowded for the three of us." Damian went back to nuzzling my neck. "I'm thinking we could use an extension. Maybe a second storey."

"Or you could sleep in the shack." I trailed my nails down his back.

"Keep doing that and I'll carry you off there right now." One large hand tightened around my midriff.

"Not now," I said, extracting myself from his grip. "When she's napping."

"She never naps," Damian growled.

"Unless she's tired."

"Right." He grinned and grabbed my hand. "Let's go tire her out."

DAMIAN CAME OUT OF THE ocean, skin glistening in the sun, and walked towards me. I wished there was a longer stretch of beach between us because I could watch him forever. He was molded bronze in motion, hair wet and wild from his swim, sand sticking to his feet. He plunked down on the towel beside me and leaned over to kiss me. Salty drops on warm lips.

"She's a bundle of energy," he said.

I put my head on his chest and we watched Sierra jump the waves.

"I can't see," I said, after a while.

"I can't help it," he replied. His erection was blocking my view.

I laughed and handed him a bottle of sunblock. "Another twenty minutes and she'll be all worn out."

"Flip." Damian straddled my back and started working the lotion in. "I have a wedding gift for you. I was going to surprise you with it, but I need your input. I bought some property in Paza del Mar. The site of the old warehouse."

"The one you blew up? Where El Charro and his men died?"

"That's the one. I want to build something good there, something worthwhile."

"What did you have in mind?"

"How would you like to expand the work you do in Valdemoros? A permanent facility where you can employ some of the women you work with, when they get out. They can help you fulfill your orders and you can focus on training and education. You can still hold your workshops in Valdemoros, but you'd have a bigger base. There's nothing to stop you from going international. I already have a shipping network in place. You can put some of the profits towards the charity you had Nick set up and use the rest to your discretion. Fair wages, women's shelters, clinics, education programs—" He stopped rubbing lotion on my back and froze. "Skye?"

"I wish MaMaLu had those options back then," I said, as I wiped the tears. "I wish you did, too."

"Hey." He rolled on to his back and stretched out beside me. "Sometimes everything gets dismantled so something better can be pieced together."

I nodded, and traced his jaw. He was the perfect example. "Let's do it," I said. "Let's build something that Sierra can be proud of."

She came bounding out of the ocean, spraying us with seawater and enthusiasm. "Look!" She held up a seashell. "This one?"

I had been showing her how to pick the right ones for a necklace. She'd seen the one Damian had made for me and wanted one for herself.

"This one's perfect." I opened up the picnic basket and added it to the collection she was raking up. "When you have enough, Dad will make you a necklace."

Damian and Sierra exchanged a strange look.

"What's that about?" I asked.

"I'm hungry!" she said. "I want the ceviche."

Damian had packed it for us in three separate containers.

"This one for me. This one for Dad. This one for you." She handed them out, looking at Damian for confirmation.

He winked.

She smiled.

"Hey, all I get is a clam?" I asked, staring into mine. "What's going on?" My eyes slid from her to Damian.

"Open it!" Sierra was so excited, Damian had to hold her down.

I pried the creamy, brown shell open. The inside was filled with sand. Lodged in the center was a ring with three sparkling alexandrites.

"You like it? You like it?" Sierra was prancing around me.

"It's beautiful." I smiled at Damian.

My mother's necklace lay somewhere at the bottom of the ocean, where he'd thrown it. I'd never get it back, but I had something of my own now.

"Thank you." I leaned over and kissed him.

He deepened the kiss, burying his hands in my hair. "Sierra—"

"But I didn't bring any books!"

"You said twenty minutes." Damian groaned into my ear.

"Maybe twenty more?" I laughed. "Where are you going?"

"For a swim," he answered. "In the cold, deep end of the ocean."

I watched him take off, slicing through the water with fluid, graceful strokes.

Sierra and I finished lunch and stretched out in the sun. Blondie, Bruce Lee, and Dirty Harry watched us from their rock. I didn't know how long green iguanas lived, but I was glad Sierra had the chance to make friends with them. Damian had given her the task of naming the island, and she had spent the morning conferring with them. The verdict was still out.

By the time Damian returned, Sierra had fallen asleep. He adjusted the umbrella so she was in the shade, and tiptoed around her, to my side. His wet skin gave me goosebumps that had nothing to do with the temperature.

"Put it on," he said.

I raised an eyebrow. "I was betting you'd tell me to take it off."

"I like the way you think, but I was talking about the ring." He gave me a wicked smile as he slipped it over my finger. "I want to see what it looks like on you."

I held my hand out, against the endless blue horizon. Rainbow glints reflected off our faces. It wasn't just a ring. It was an open window and paper animals, a boy clutching fifteen pesos and a girl writing strawberry letters. It was the story of two people who had come full circle, and it was wrapped in gold around my finger.

What are we? Damian had asked on this very beach.

There on our little piece of paradise, with Sierra sleeping beside us, I finally figured it out.

We are sand and rock and water and sky, anchors on ships and sails in the wind. We are a journey to a destination that shifts every time we dream or fall or leap or weep. We are stars with flaws that still sparkle and shine. We will always strive, always want, always have more questions than answers, but there are moments like these, full of magic and contentment, when souls get a glimpse of the divine and quite simply, lose their breath.

EPILOGUE

A NEW MOON PERCHED IN the dusky sky, a slender arc of the softest silver. The small group of guests who had shared our special day—Nick, Rafael, their wives, some of the women I worked with, and a handful of Damian's associates—were all gone, but the gardens of Casa Paloma were still twinkling with lights. Damian, Sierra, and I were sitting by the pond.

"Who's Monique?" I asked, holding up a card personalized with a deep-purple lip print.

"Let me see that." Damian put aside his cake. Pink frosting, topped with fresh strawberries. It was an unusual choice for a wedding, a replica of the birthday cake he'd never got around to having. He'd laughed when they'd wheeled it in. The cake topper was a giant white tooth, a private joke harking back to when he'd knocked Gideon Benedict St. John's tooth out.

He looked the card over and grinned. "Monique was someone who made my time in prison so much more pleasant."

I crossed my arms and waited for an explanation.

"Don't scowl. It's not very bride-like," he said.

"Don't bring up exes on our wedding day. It's not very groom-like."

"I can think of a few very groom-like things I'd like to do to you."

"Don't even." I pushed him away. I didn't feel the least bit threatened by this Monique, but it was fun playing it up. Rafael had not been able to convince Damian to wear a tux, but he looked so damn fine in a crisp, white shirt and tailored jacket.

"Fine. I'll take you to see Monique one day, but don't say I didn't warn you." He tossed the card aside and grabbed my waist. "I have something for you and Sierra."

He reached inside his jacket for MaMaLu's *Lucky Strike* tin and opened it. "She would have wanted you to have these." He handed me her earrings.

I held them up: two doves joined at the beak to form a circle, with turquoise stones hanging from them. I had a flashback of cool, blue stones brushing against my skin as MaMaLu kissed me goodnight.

"Hey." Damian wrapped his arms around me. He knew it had been an emotional day for me. I'd missed my father's three kisses, missed him walking me down the aisle. Sierra had filled in. She'd picked out her own dress: Kermit-the-frog-green, accessorized with a new pair of sneakers. Her one wedding day concession had been a floral hairband that matched the color of her orange shoelaces. Apart from a headache, she had come around from the sedative Victor had administered with no idea of the disaster we had escaped. When I thought about how close we'd come to losing it all, I hugged Damian tighter.

"You think she'll like it?" he asked, holding up MaMaLu's hair clip.

It was shaped like a fan, made from abalone shells and alpaca metal—pretty without being too girly.

Sierra examined it before handing it to me. She turned around and motioned to her hair, voicing her silent approval. I gathered two sections of her hair from the sides and secured the clip in center.

"What's this?" she asked, unfolding the newspaper article that Damian had saved all these years:

'LOCAL NANNY ACCUSED OF STEALING FAMILY HEIRLOOM.'

"This is a little piece of paper that caused a whole lot of trouble," said Damian.

"Look." I caught a yellow flower as the night breeze rustled through the trees. In the moonlight, it looked almost ivory, like my dress. Damian tucked it behind my ear.

"Have I told you how beautiful you look today?"

I had planned on designing my own wedding gown, but then Damian had found the Louboutins I'd left behind on the island, and once I'd strapped them on, I felt a full-fledged celebration coming on. The *WAM!* facility was up and running, and I splurged on a strapless Vera Wang design.

"Hey! I did it!" Sierra was sitting at the edge of the pond, pointing to something in the water. Floating away from her was a perfect paper swan.

"Nice." Damian crouched next to her, but then his smile faded. "Is that . . . what did you use to make it?"

"The piece of paper in that old tin."

Damian swung his hand out and pulled the swan out of the water.

"What's the matter?" asked Sierra.

Damian had carried that newspaper article with him for so long, his first instinct was to preserve it. He looked at me as he held it, and we both thought of the story MaMaLu had told us, about a magic swan that graced the grounds of Casa Paloma, a swan that could bless you with the rarest of treasures.

I caught my breath as Damian placed the swan back in the water and realization hit me.

You don't always get the treasure by holding on. Sometimes the magic happens when you let go.

And Damian was letting go of all the things that had fueled him for so long—the rage, the injustices, the horrors he had witnessed in Caboras, the guilt he felt over his actions. Sierra had folded them up and set them free. We watched in silence as the swan disappeared into the shadow side of the pond, and all that remained was an empty *Lucky Strike* tin.

"What do you want to do with this?" I asked.

"Exactly what should be done with a smelly old tin of tobacco." He filled it with rocks and flung it into the water. It sank to the bottom of the pond with a reverberating gurgle.

"Race you two back to the house!" said Sierra.

"Hey, not fair!" I kicked off my shoes and gathered my gown around me.

"On five!" said Damian.

5, 4, 3, 2, 1 . . .

The End

Acknowledgements

FIRST AND FOREMOST, I'D LIKE to thank you—yes, *you*, for picking up and reading The Paper Swan. There are so many amazing books out there, I consider it a privilege to be let into your world. I hope this book was worthy of your time and attention.

I am grateful to every single person who has read or recommended my books, shared something of mine, contacted or encouraged me. I cannot thank you enough for all the love and kindness you have shown.

So many wonderful people have supported me through the writing of this novel.

Hang Le—for understanding my vision and devoting your incredible talent into designing this phenomenal cover. You have mad skills, woman!

Lea Burn, editor extraordinaire, en dash/em dash

specialist, and overall perfectionist—thank you for pouring your heart and soul into this novel.

Christine Borgford of *Perfectly Publishable*—for making my work look so pretty, with your seamless formatting, design, and astounding creativity.

Christine Estevez of *Shh Mom's Reading*—my multi-talented, go-to person for proof-reading, handling all the promos, lighting fires to get me moving, supporting me from start to finish, and putting up with all my nincompoopery. You get the award for being the sweetest person ever.

My incredible team of beta readers: Chelsea Peden McCrory, G.G., Jackie Bagley White, Lisa Chamberlin, Luisa Hansen, Tasha B, Trisha Rai. Thank you for your invaluable feedback. I couldn't have done it without you!

Soulla Georgiou, your friendship has carried me through all the ups and downs. *Thank you* is not enough for your daily missives, support and encouragement. This book is as much yours as it is mine. You are all kinds of EPIC.

Christine Brae, I am so blessed to have met you. You have been with me from the start, and you continue to blow me away with your grace, generosity and kindness. I can't wait for That Darn Book!

Claire Contreras—my role model and hero. You inspire me with your words, your attitude, and all round amazeballness. Also, you make me invent new words.

Bloggers: the hardest working, most passionate group of book lovers. For every author who has reached an extra reader because of something you loved, reviewed, recommended or shared, I thank you! You continue to overwhelm me with your passion, generosity and professionalism.

My brilliant author friends—Mia Asher, KA Linde, K Larsen, BL Berry, Willow Aster, Colleen Hoover, Corinne Michaels, Cat-Porter Porter, NJ Frost, Tarryn Fisher, SL Jennings, Kennedy Ryan, Ava Bell, Amy Harmon, Gail McHugh, Gretchen de la O, Mara White, Tillie Cole, AL Jackson, Monica Murphy, EK Blair, Lindy Zart, Lori Otto—each of you has touched me in some way, and all of you have gone out of your way to make me feel welcome.

I am forever grateful to the little band of Leylaholics on Facebook. You deserve all the stars!

And finally, thanks to my family. Without you, none of this would be possible or mean anything. It might also have wrapped up sooner if you hadn't kept popping in, asking, "Are you done yet? How about now? NOW?" I love you! Thank you for allowing me the gift of time to write this book.

About the Author

Leylah Attar is *a New York Times, USA Today and Wall Street Journal* bestselling author. She writes stories about love—shaken, stirred and served with a twist. Sometimes she disappears into the black hole of the internet, but can usually be enticed out with chocolate.

Connect with her at:
www.leylahattar.com

For exclusives and information on new releases, sign up for Leylah Attar's mailing list:
www.leylahattar.com/subscribe

Other titles by Leylah Attar:

53 Letters For My Lover
From His Lips: a 53 Letters Short Story

CPSIA information can be obtained at www.ICGtesting.com
Printed in the USA
LVOW08s1632201215

467301LV00007B/831/P